Breaking Cover

Breaking Cover

Stella Rimington

B L O O M S B U R Y
LONDON · OXFORD · NEW YORK · NEW DELHI · SYDNEY

Bloomsbury Publishing
An imprint of Bloomsbury Publishing Plc

50 Bedford Square
London
WC1B 3DP
UK

1385 Broadway
New York
NY 10018
USA

www.bloomsbury.com

BLOOMSBURY and the Diana logo are trademarks of Bloomsbury Publishing Plc

First published in Great Britain 2016

British Library Cataloguing-in-Publication Data
A catalogue record for this book is available from the British Library.

ISBN: HB: 978-1-4088-5970-4
      TPB: 978-1-4088-5971-1
     EPUB: 978-1-4088-5972-8

2 4 6 8 10 9 7 5 3 1

Typeset by Integra Software Services Pvt. Ltd.
Printed and bound in Great Britain by CPI Group (UK) Ltd, Croydon CR0 4YY

MIX
Paper from
responsible sources
FSC® C020471

To find out more about our authors and books visit www.bloomsbury.com.
Here you will find extracts, author interviews, details of forthcoming events
and the option to sign up for our newsletters.

'WHAT DID YOU MAKE of that?' asked Jasminder Kapoor as she and her friend Emma Wickes extricated themselves from the crowd leaving the Almeida. The theatre, an elegant Victorian building converted from a semi-derelict factory, was in a narrow Islington side street where the audience could hang around chatting and arguing about the performance they had just seen. The Almeida specialised in sharp-edged productions of new and well-known plays and there was usually much to discuss. As ever the audience was a mix of well-heeled, middle-aged local residents who lived in the once run-down and now very valuable Georgian and Victorian houses nearby and young professionals who occupied the trendy flats newly built around the Angel, the centre of this now prosperous North London borough.

'I couldn't take my eyes off that great big crack in the back of the set,' replied Emma. 'It was so huge by the end, I thought the whole thing was going to fall down.'

'It was supposed to symbolise the cracking up of his personality,' said Jasminder, who took her theatre seriously.

'I'm sure you're right, but it almost had *me* cracking up. Still, it wasn't the weirdest thing we've seen here. Do you remember the one where they all sat round a big wooden box drinking champagne, while we knew, and they didn't, that there was the body of a murdered man inside?'

'It went on to the West End and was a great hit.'

'Can't think why,' said Emma.

Walking side by side now, the two young women made an interesting contrast – Jasminder tall, slim and elegant, her long glossy black hair framing her face with its striking dark eyes and smooth light brown skin; Emma much shorter and chubbier, cheerful-looking with blue eyes and cropped light brown hair. They had been friends since meeting at Durham University where they had both studied law. They had kept in touch, though their careers had gone in different directions. Emma worked in the legal department of a big software company while Jasminder had stayed in the academic world. They both lived in Islington now, not far from each other, and were regulars at the Almeida.

As they turned into Upper Street, the wind, which had swung round to the north, was sharp in their faces. Emma shivered. 'Let's go for a drink,' she suggested as they reached the brightly lit doors of a pub.

'I think I'd better go home,' replied Jasminder. 'I've got an early start tomorrow and some papers to read.' She pointed at the briefcase she was clutching in one hand.

'You work too hard,' said Emma, hugging her and kissing her cheek. 'You care too much.'

'Probably,' replied Jasminder. 'That's just how I am.'

'There's a great film at the Screen on the Green. Maybe we can go this weekend if you're free. I'll give you a ring,' called Emma as she walked on.

Jasminder turned into Barnsbury Street, reflecting that she didn't have any other plans for the weekend, except doing the washing and cleaning her flat, and – she sighed – writing another lecture.

Though Upper Street had been busy with cars and buses and people going in and out of the pubs and restaurants, there were very few people around in the side streets. Lights were glowing in the windows of the terraced houses but the basement areas were dark. Wheelie bins lined the pavement waiting for the collection in the morning. The lid of one was open and something, a cat perhaps or a fox, had dragged out its contents, littering the ground with what looked like bits of a chicken carcass. Jasminder glanced at the mess, wrinkling her nose in disgust, and hurried on, conscious now of the weight of her handbag on her shoulder and the briefcase in her hand. She was looking forward to a bath and a warm bed and wondering if she could put off opening the briefcase until morning. Perhaps if she got up very early…

She passed the church on the opposite side of the road and walked along by the railings of the square's gardens, where the children's playground was, though the bushes and the lime trees overhanging the road obscured it. She could just see the tops of the climbing frame and the slide through the leafless branches. The empty street suddenly seemed slightly spooky, and she was thinking of crossing to the better-lit side when she saw a man coming towards her. His face was in shadow but she could see he was wearing dark trousers and a leather jacket. Jasminder moved to the inner side of the pavement to let him go past, but the man moved with her, blocking her way.

'Excuse me,' she started to say, when she became aware of someone else at her side. Alarmed, she turned just as something metal flashed only a few inches away from her face. Almost instantaneously she felt the strap of her bag, tight over her shoulder, give way.

The man ahead was suddenly on her, grabbing her arm and twisting it round until Jasminder faced the entrance to the gardens. He pulled hard and pressed her tight against him, then forced her forward, his legs controlling hers so she could only move when he did, like a marionette. The other man, holding the knife, went ahead and kicked open the gate to the gardens. He was holding her bag in his other hand – and her briefcase, which she must have dropped in fright.

If they were mugging her, why hadn't they run off when they'd got her bag? Why was this man pushing her into the gardens?

As if reading her thoughts, he tightened his grip, lifting her arm behind her back until Jasminder bent forward with a scream of pain. He reached around her with his other hand and cupped it over her breast, squeezing and kneading. As he pushed her towards the open gate he pressed his hardening groin against her. She could hear him panting and felt him breathing against her neck. A wave of panic struck her as she realised that once inside the gardens no one else would see her. These two could do whatever they liked to her and no one would know.

She drew in a breath to scream, but the man moved his hand from her breast and clamped it over her mouth. He was wearing gloves that smelled of camphor; Jasminder retched as she struggled for air. Then someone called out sharply, 'Get off her! Leave her alone!'

It was a man's voice coming from further down the street. But it did not deter her attackers. They pushed her through the gate, towards the nearest patch of shrubbery. The voice called again, 'Let her go!' And she heard the sound of running feet, and this time the man with gloves reacted. Pushing her so hard that she fell into the bushes, he and the man with her bags moved quickly towards the gate. Scrabbling to her feet, Jasminder lifted her head in time to see a male figure running towards them. He slowed down as he approached her assailants, and she could see that he was tall and well built and wore a dark overcoat.

The man with the gloves had taken charge of Jasminder's bag and briefcase now, while the other man moved to confront the new arrival, waving the knife menacingly. The newcomer came on and when the knife swung towards his face, he lashed out with a fierce sideways kick. The knife flew into the air. The newcomer kicked again, this time catching the other man in the groin – he crumpled in pain, and fell to his knees.

The man with gloves on dropped Jasminder's bags and ran at the newcomer, who stood stock still then suddenly threw a short straight punch that hit the gloved man flush in his Adam's apple. He went down, clutching his throat and making a horrible choking sound. For a moment Jasminder wondered if her rescuer had killed him. But he rolled over and, staggering to his feet, ran off into the darkness of the gardens.

His friend was also on his feet by now, looking dazed. He took a tentative step towards the tall newcomer, but seemed to realise that he no longer had a knife and that his accomplice had gone. A second later, he too was running away.

Jasminder looked up at the tall man who had saved her. She was breathing in short gasps and swaying slightly. He came over to her and reached out one hand to take her arm. 'Did they hurt you?'

'No, I'm fine. Just a bit shaken. They were trying to force me over there.' She gestured with her head to the dark shadows under the nearby trees. 'They were going to…'

'Best not think about it,' said the man. 'Come on, let's get your things.'

They collected her briefcase, which the man carried while Jasminder clutched her handbag, its cut strap dangling uselessly, in both arms.

'Thank you,' she said. It sounded feeble. 'You were very brave. It was amazing how you fought them off,' she added.

'Not at all,' he said. 'Anyone would have done the same.'

I'm not sure about that, thought Jasminder, but what she said was, 'We should call the police.'

'We can if you want, but frankly I'm not sure there's much they could do.' He pointed into the dark interior of the gardens. 'Those two will be long gone by now. And I'm not certain I'd be able to give a good description of either of them. Could you?'

'No. I didn't really see their faces. It all happened so fast. If you hadn't come along—'

'But I did. Tell me, where were you going when you were so rudely interrupted?' He was smiling, which Jasminder found immensely reassuring. She felt safe now.

'I was going home. I live just in the next street. Down there.' She pointed towards the far end of the gardens.

'I'll walk you home then. In the circumstances it seems wise.'

As they walked, the man introduced himself. His name was Laurenz Hansen, he said, and he was Norwegian. Jasminder recognised the faintest hint of an accent in his voice, though otherwise his English was flawless. Laurenz explained that he had lived in England on and off for several years, and was hoping to settle permanently in the

UK. Beyond that he said very little, and after Jasminder had told him her name they walked on in silence – for which she was grateful. Just then she had no wish to make small talk.

They arrived at her street, one of several in this part of Islington that were still lined with small Georgian houses. Number seven, where Jasminder had a flat on the ground floor, looked well cared for, its door painted a fashionable greyish-green. They stopped on the pavement by the front steps.

'Is your husband at home?' he asked solicitously.

'I'm not married. I live alone.'

'Is there anyone to come round and look after you? A friend? Or a relative?'

'It's all right. I'll be fine once I'm in my own flat.' She hoped this was true; she still felt very shaken by what had happened. She'd barely had time to be scared while she was being attacked – it had all happened so fast. With the immediate danger over, she was starting to feel fearful, aware of what a narrow escape she'd had. The men hadn't just wanted to rob her; they'd been about to… Jasminder shook her head, determined not to scare herself further.

'I'd be happy to stay with you,' said the man called Laurenz. 'But you don't know me, we've only just met.' He gave her a friendly smile. 'Still, it would probably be better if you were with someone.'

She nodded shakily. 'I have a friend who lives not far away. We've been to the theatre together tonight; I was just on my way home. If I need any company I'll ring her. But are you sure we shouldn't tell the police?'

Laurenz seemed to consider this. 'We could, and obviously if you insist I'll be glad to. But you do have your bag and briefcase back – so in that sense the mugging was

7

entirely unsuccessful. And I don't think you were badly hurt. Just a few bruises perhaps, and shock of course.' He hesitated. 'The thing is, I wasn't actually meant to be here tonight. In this neighbourhood, I mean. I can't really explain – and I'm not sure it would make much sense to you if I did – but to be perfectly honest, involving the police would make things a little tricky for me. Nothing illegal,' he reassured her. 'Just… tricky.'

'All right,' she said. 'I suppose there wouldn't be anything much they could do anyway and it would probably take a long time.'

He nodded. 'You're right. They wouldn't have any chance of catching the muggers now and it would just involve a lot of questions when you'd probably like to go to bed. So if you're sure you are OK, I'll say goodnight, though I'll wait here until you're safe inside your house.'

'I don't know how to thank you. You have been so kind, and it was amazing how you dealt with those men. Are you a black belt or something? '

'No, I just keep fit. I was pleased to help. Perhaps we can have coffee some time – in happier circumstances. I'll give you a ring.'

She gave him her mobile number, which he wrote down on the back of a scrap of paper he produced from his pocket. 'Or ring me at work,' she said. 'I teach part-time at King's College.'

'I'll do that.' He held out his hand and she shook it.

A minute later she waved to him from her living-room window and he waved back. She watched his tall back as he walked away. She drew the curtains and sat down; her legs seemed to have given way suddenly and she was trembling. She wondered if she should ring Emma, but it was eleven-thirty and her friend would probably be in bed. As she sat, Jasminder was going over the attack in her mind; she could remember every detail, feel the man's hot breath on her neck and his hands on her body.

After half an hour of sitting in her chair she got up and turned on a bath, pouring in a generous dose of bath oil; she needed to get rid of all traces of her attacker. As she lay back in the comforting warmth of the scented water she found herself thinking about this man Laurenz. She wondered if he was married. He was very attractive but rather mysterious. She wondered why he'd said he wasn't actually meant to be in the neighbourhood. Maybe if he rang her she would find out. She hoped he would. Sometimes good things happen from bad ones, she mused – at least that was what her mother had often said. Maybe that would be the case this time.

2

LIZ CARLYLE WAS WALKING slowly along the Embankment towards her office in Thames House, the headquarters of MI5. The sun, glancing through the branches of the trees lining the busy road, had some warmth in it for the first time that year and she felt a small thrill of pleasure at the sight of the river sparkling in the sun. Since Martin Seurat had died she had found it difficult to rouse herself to take much interest in anything, but suddenly and quite unexpectedly she found she was actually looking forward to getting to work and dealing with whatever the day might bring. Her oval face was still very pale, the skin around the grey-green eyes looking bruised from lack of sleep, and her fine brown hair was dragged carelessly back into a pony tail, but she was standing up straight again, as though the burden of grief that had settled on her shoulders since the tragic events in Paris the year before was shifting slightly. Her pace quickened almost automatically and she lifted her head and looked towards the long white building crouching on the other side of the road. She had been conscious for some minutes of the sound of shouting voices and now she could see that it was coming from a crowd of people, gathered at the small roundabout where Lambeth Bridge joined Milbank and Thames House began. The traffic was backed up along the bridge and along Millbank.

As she drew nearer she could read some of the placards carried by the demonstrators: 'Get out of my Facebook', '#stopwatchingus'. One displayed a large photograph of Edward Snowden and another read 'Democracy is watching you'. Liz stopped at the edge of the crowd and spoke to a policeman standing beside his motorbike. 'I need to get in there,' she said, pointing towards Thames House. 'I work there.'

'Can I see your pass, miss?' Then: 'Staff member to come through,' he said into his radio. 'Just wait a minute, miss. My colleague will escort you in. They don't seem violent. Quite polite, in fact, as mobs go.'

Liz waited, listening to the chanting – *'What do we want? No snooping. When do we want it? Now!'* – until a large uniformed officer arrived and said, 'Follow me, miss.'

He headed straight into the crowd with Liz close behind him. 'Move away, please. Step back now. Clear a space.' They moved forward slowly into the crowd, which parted obligingly to let them through. Liz followed closely behind her brawny protector until they reached the bottom of the steps leading up to the front entrance of Thames House where a couple more policemen were facing the protesters, to deter them from getting any closer to the building. Her guardian turned to let her go ahead of him and, standing with his back firmly to the crowd, feet apart, hands on hips, said, 'In you go, miss.'

'Thanks very much,' said Liz, and she started to run up the steps when suddenly a man rushed forward. He was wearing sunglasses and a cycle helmet with a pair of outsize pink cardboard ears attached. He was shouting *'Stop snooping!'* and holding his placard with both hands in front of him, like a weapon. He hit the policeman on the side of the head with it, knocking him off balance, and rushed up the steps obviously intent on hitting Liz as well. He'd almost reached her when he was brought down in a flying rugby tackle by another policeman. As they both rolled down to the bottom of the steps, Liz ran forward and escaped inside.

'Phew,' she said to the security guard who was holding the door open for her, 'that was a close one.'

Upstairs on the fourth floor she looked out of her window and saw that the police had now moved in on the crowd and were dispersing them. Some who resisted were being arrested. There was no sign of her assailant with the big ears.

Liz was lucky to have a window of her own to look out of. As in so many organisations – from publishers to law firms – most of the staff of MI5 now worked on open-plan floors. The pressure on space in the building, as staff numbers had increased to meet the increased security threats, meant that the days of offices for small teams, or even individuals, were over. Only Directors had their own office nowadays and rumour had it that even they might have to give up the privilege soon. However the Director General and his team, known as 'The Private Office', were still ensconced in their suite, which included a dining room and waiting room. The DG's own office, lined as it was with panelling listed as of architectural significance, could not be altered.

Through some anomaly, two small rooms on Liz's floor had remained untouched, and for the time being she had one of them. Though there was barely enough space in it for her desk and two chairs, she was not planning to complain. In fact she was keeping her head down and hoping the building administrators had forgotten about her.

From her desk she had a panoramic view, across the Thames to Lambeth Palace and upstream to Vauxhall and the MI6 building, Vauxhall Cross. Downstream, thanks to the twists and turns of the river, she could see, on a clear day, the tower blocks of Canary Wharf and, nearer, the pointing glass finger of The Shard. Liz was no fan of skyscrapers, but there was no denying their dramatic effect on the London skyline, particularly after dark. Today it was the nearer view that was capturing her attention, as she looked down on the heads of the crowd and the tops of their placards all intermingling with policemen's helmets and TV cameras, like some weird modern ballet.

It wasn't just the view that made Liz happy to have her own private space. Recovering as she was from a personal tragedy, she still felt more need for quiet and her own company than she had ever done before, so that she could think over everything that had happened. The Service's psychiatrist, to whom she had been sent by the Personnel Branch, had advised her not to spend too much time alone, but she chose to ignore the advice and deal with things in her own way.

There was a faint knock on the door, and as it opened a familiar voice said, 'Good morning, Elizabeth. What on earth have you and your colleagues been doing to cause all this fuss? It's like a war zone out there.'

'You wait, Geoffrey. It'll be your turn tomorrow. Don't assume you're immune just because they think you're all James Bonds.'

The man who now walked into the tiny office was in his early fifties, tall, with dark hair going grey over the ears, a long face and a thin, straight nose. He was distinguished-looking, and would have been handsome had there not been a distancing arrogance in his expression and a hint of the sardonic in his dark eyes. He was wearing a well-cut navy blue suit with polished black brogues and an Old Wykehamist tie – Liz knew about this because she had once offended him by complimenting him on the attractive colour combination. Shocked, he had told her it was his old school tie.

'How did you get in?' she enquired. 'I almost got knocked out by a madman with enormous ears.'

'Oh, I came in through the garage,' he replied airily. 'I got a warning that you were under siege.'

'I wish someone had warned me. I thought I was going to be a stretcher case. Come in and have the chair or shall we go down for some coffee?'

Geoffrey Fane shook his head. 'I had a cup just before I left Vauxhall Cross.'

Liz and he had worked together on various investigations over the years. It had been a successful partnership on the whole; Liz found him sharp, experienced, decisive – and as trustworthy as a snake. What Fane thought of Liz he never said but close observers of the two suspected that on his side there was an interest that was more than purely professional.

Fane ignored her invitation to sit down, and stood looking out of the window. '*Change and decay in all around I see,*' he intoned, staring downstream towards the scaffolding and cranes marking sites where new buildings were being erected.

'*O Thou who changest not, abide with me!*' responded Liz.

He turned round, and said with a wolfish smile, 'If I thought you were serious I might take you up on that.

I didn't know you were a student of *Hymns Ancient and Modern*.'

'We sang hymns at school too, you know. Even if it was only a girls' day school.'

Fane hummed to himself, and glanced back out of the window. 'If they do move you out into the open-plan, I'm not sure you'll miss this view. Look at it,' he said scathingly, pointing across the water towards the towers of Canary Wharf. 'The depredations of the money men have extended well beyond the City.'

There had always been a lugubrious side to Fane, but this seemed excessive, even for him. 'Why so gloomy today, Geoffrey? What's happened?'

'Nothing yet. But our new Grand Mufti seems determined to rock the boat a bit.'

'What's he doing?' Liz didn't know much about the new Chief of MI6 across the river, but from the few bits and pieces she'd picked up he sounded like a good thing. His name was Treadwell and he was ex-Foreign Office, where he had dealt with intelligence in various posts; he'd also done a stint in MI6 in his thirties. So he was coming to the post familiar with the Service and, from Fane's remark, must have ideas about how it should change.

'Do you know what he's proposing to do?' Fane demanded.

'Tell me. The smoke signals have not yet crossed the river.'

'He's worried about this sort of thing.' Fane waved in the direction of the rapidly thinning crowd. 'He thinks we need to create a better understanding among the public of what we really do and what we don't do. According to him, there's an unholy combination of civil libertarians and

James Bond obsessives that's obscuring our valuable contribution to the nation's wellbeing.'

'Mmm,' said Liz noncommittally. 'What's he going to do about it?'

'He wants to create a "Corporate Communications Director". A ridiculous idea! Our job isn't to "communicate" – we don't tell secrets; we keep them.'

Actually, it wasn't a bad idea, thought Liz, though she felt it politic to keep this to herself. As Liz saw it, there was a necessary amount of secrecy about the intelligence services and their operations and people – but there was also *un*necessary secrecy, which could be positively harmful to effectiveness in the modern world. But Fane was of the old school – thinking that it was safer to keep quiet about everything, in case you unwittingly gave something important away. He also found change abhorrent, and Liz sometimes thought that he viewed the mere passage of time as a cause for lament – if you listened to him, it had been downhill all the way for British intelligence since the end of the Cold War.

'I'm sorry you're upset,' she said mildly.

'It gets worse,' said Fane. He shook his head, and at last sat down. 'Do you know, they've actually appointed some head-hunters to find this Communications person.' He seemed to spit out the last two words. 'You know what that means, don't you?'

'Tell me.'

'It means they're going to look *outside*. It's not even necessarily going to be one of us – an insider, I mean. They're intending to *advertise* the post.' Fane's outrage seemed entirely genuine. 'It's bad enough to create this position, but then to advertise it and possibly appoint someone who's never set foot in Vauxhall Cross...' He paused, to allow the idiocy of it to sink in. Liz contented herself with a raised eyebrow. Fane went on, 'I tell you, I can see nothing but disaster looming.'

'I suppose you'll just have to ignore it,' said Liz, wishing they could get down to business. They met occasionally to exchange information. It was rarely a long meeting, but it could be helpful – sometimes crucially so. 'Maybe it won't turn out to be such a bad idea. Perhaps he won't find a suitable outsider and he'll appoint an insider after all.'

But Fane wasn't mollified. 'How *can* I ignore it? Treadwell's put me on the selection board. I told him to his face that the whole thing was ridiculous. He just smiled and said in that case my contribution would be especially useful.'

Liz tried not to laugh. This man Treadwell, the new C as he was by tradition called, after the first head of MI6, Captain Cumming, sounded rather interesting. Not that she would have dreamed of saying so to Fane.

3

A N HOUR LATER, WITH a still-fuming Fane gone, Peggy Kinsolving came into Liz's office. If Liz had been asked to name her most valuable member of staff, Peggy would have topped the list. She was in her early thirties now, having joined MI5 after first spending two years in MI6. Seconded to MI5 to assist Liz on a tricky case, she had found the work more suited to her skills, and her career prospects better, on the defensive side of the intelligence business. A former librarian, Peggy combined a researcher's precision and love of detail with a growing aptitude in the field. She had become a brilliant interviewer, transforming her undergraduate interest in drama into a professional asset as an intelligence officer.

There was something different about her this morning, and it took Liz a moment to twig. 'Where are your glasses?' she said suddenly as Peggy sat down.

'I've got contacts. What do you think?'

'You look great,' said Liz, a little taken aback by the transformation. The Peggy she'd first come to know had been an uncertain bookish girl with rather wispy hair. In those days Peggy had worn horn-rimmed spectacles, which never seemed quite to fit her face. Over the years

Liz had come to recognise that during an investigation the sight of Peggy pushing her glasses firmly into place meant that she was on to something, and it had always lifted Liz's heart. But as Peggy had become more confident her appearance had subtly changed. Now she often wore her hair up, held in place by some sort of clasp, and instead of dun-coloured jumpers and skirts, she went for blues and lilacs. The contact lenses seemed to complete a transformation that had been slowly taking place for years, and for the first time Liz saw that the eyes that had been hidden behind the spectacles were a rather remarkable blue.

'What does Tim think?' asked Liz.

'Oh, Tim!' said Peggy, sighing. 'He hasn't even noticed. If there's a typo in the edition of Donne he's reading, you can be sure he'll catch it. But if I walked through the flat in biker's leathers he'd just ask me when supper would be ready.'

Liz laughed, though she sensed that something in Peggy's attitude had changed. Previously she had treated her partner Tim's academic absent-mindedness as a joke and had laughed fondly at his eccentricities. But now she sounded irritated.

'Give him time,' Liz said soothingly, but Peggy just shrugged.

'How is he otherwise?' Liz persevered.

'Oh, he's all right,' said Peggy, sounding resigned. 'But he's got seriously into civil liberties. He thinks it's today's big issue.'

'Maybe it is,' said Liz, who was essentially well disposed towards Tim. She found his attachment to vegetarianism and Ayurvedic medicine difficult to take and thought him rather wet in a donnish way – he was a lecturer in English at King's College, London – but she knew he adored Peggy, and Liz thought he was good for her.

'Possibly, but being Tim, he's gone for it hook, line and sinker. He thinks Edward Snowden is a hero. Says Orwell didn't imagine the half of it – soon we won't be able to breathe without the state monitoring our exhalation rate.'

'Oh, dear. That must be a bit difficult to live with. But I'm sure he'll mellow a bit when he thinks about it. Can't you reason with him? He must know that you're no advocate of massive state surveillance. He's lived with you long enough. You're in a pretty good position to explain the balance between freedom and protection. He knows how hard we work and what we are trying to do. Tell him that if we had even a third of the power of surveillance that he's imagining, our job of keeping people safe would be a lot easier.'

'I've tried. But so far he's not listening. He wants me to go to a lecture with him tonight at the university. It's on civil liberties, naturally. It used to be poetry readings he dragged me off to, or lectures on diphthongs in medieval literature. But now it's Snowden he's obsessed with instead of the Metaphysical Poets. When the *Guardian* published all those revelations, Tim didn't read anything else for days.' She shook her head wearily. Then she asked, 'Have you heard of Jasminder Kapoor?'

'Sounds familiar.' Liz racked her brains for a moment. 'I know – she's the civil liberties woman; I heard her the other morning, on the *Today* programme. She edits some magazine, doesn't she?'

'That's right. It's a monthly called *Democratic Affairs*. Tim brings it home. He gets it at the College. She lectures in the Law department there but I don't think he's ever met her.'

Liz nodded; she'd occasionally leafed through copies of it in bookshops. 'There's some pretty wild stuff in it, isn't there?'

'Well, Jasminder Kapoor's own stuff is pretty balanced, I think. But some of the others who write for it seem a bit off the wall.'

'I remember thinking she sounded rather sensible when I heard her on the radio.' Jasminder had been on the programme with an American politician, talking about the remaining prisoners in Guantanamo. The American, a conservative Republican, had grown heated, suggesting that his interlocutor was either a naïve dupe or on the side of al Qaeda. Kapoor had made her points very calmly in the face of his blustering, suggesting that his caricature of an argument did as much damage to democracy as its extremist opponents.

'I agree. She's the person giving the lecture tonight.'

'Actually, that could be quite interesting,' said Liz.

'I hope so. It's called "Security and Democracy: Where's the Conflict?" I think Tim will be very disappointed that she's not more radical in her views.'

They turned to business. Liz chaired an inter-agency working party on the activities of foreign intelligence agencies. Counter-espionage had been something of a poor relation to counter-terrorism for a few years, but now the focus was back on it, following an increase in cyber-attacks from various countries and renewed aggression from Russia. Resources had been moved on to the subject in MI6 and GCHQ and Liz had been put in charge both of MI5's work and coordinating it with the other agencies. She had asked Peggy to move with her.

'You remember we decided we needed to brief the CIA on our meetings,' Liz said. 'I've been thinking about the best way of doing that. I'm not sure we want to invite them to come or to send them the minutes. There might be some sensitive UK cases we wouldn't necessarily want to share with them. It might be better if we set up a regular briefing meeting with Grosvenor. We'd probably get more feedback from them that way too – and learn what they're doing.'

The CIA Station in London was known as 'Grosvenor' from its location, along with most of the rest of the US Embassy, in Grosvenor Square, though soon it would move to the Embassy's new quarters in Wandsworth.

'There's a new Head of Station now, isn't there?'

'There is,' said Liz. 'Andy Bokus has gone. The new man used to be here as his deputy a few years ago. You probably remember him. It's Miles Brookhaven – you know, the guy who was attacked in Syria and then did a rather good job in Sana'a. I think you should go over and meet him. Then you could be the contact point with the working group.'

'Me?' Peggy looked surprised. 'Wouldn't he expect you to do it?'

'No. Why would he? I should think he'd be pleased to see you. After all, we are offering him a regular briefing.' And, of course, hoping to get something in return, Liz thought, but didn't say.

Something else she didn't say was that Miles Brookhaven was someone she'd rather not encounter just then. Their paths had crossed when he was at Grosvenor previously. Liz had nothing against him – the problem back then was that he had made it pretty clear that he was keen on her. Too keen, as far as Liz was concerned. It was one thing to be friendly with her CIA counterpart, quite another to be the recipient of flowers, phone calls, and unsolicited invitations to dinner. That was several years ago and he had probably grown up. For all she knew he might be married now. He'd obviously had quite a tough time professionally during the intervening years and the Agency must think highly of him – Head of the London Station was a big, important job. Still, it would do Peggy good to represent the Service with the Americans and it would enable Liz to put off meeting Miles again for a bit longer.

'Ring the Embassy and make an appointment,' she said to Peggy. 'Let me know if there's any problem. And I hope you enjoy the lecture tonight.'

4

IT WAS JUST GETTING dark when Liz left Thames House to go home. The streetlights were coming on and the starlings in the trees along Millbank were chattering and arguing as they settled down for the night. The tiny leaves just emerging were outlined against the luminous blue sky. London was on the cusp of spring. Soon it would be light when she left work and then light when she got home.

She had always loved this time of year but today it made her sad. She couldn't help thinking what Paris would be looking like this evening and imagining how the linden trees in the square outside Martin's flat would be bursting into leaf. Diners would be arriving to sit at the tables in the local bistro where she and Martin had dined so often. She wondered who was living in his flat now and whether they had changed things much.

As she emerged onto the now dark streets at Kentish Town station she was wondering if she should sell her flat and move nearer to Thames House. She remembered how thrilled she had been when she'd moved from the dark basement flat, which had been her first property purchase, to the much more airy and spacious accommodation on the ground floor. She had loved buying bits of furniture and ornaments for her new place and she and Martin had spent many a happy weekend in the junk shops of Camden Market and Islington.

She thought that prices in Pimlico would probably be broadly on a par with those in Kentish Town, and she would be able to walk to work. But she knew, as she opened the door and her heart sank, that any thought of moving wasn't about walking to work; it was because of the memories that seemed to haunt the flat.

Martin Seurat had been dead four months. Liz knew this was early days in the normal schedule of grief, but it still felt like yesterday – and the idea that time would heal this wound seemed absurd. If it was two years before life felt at all normal again – as everyone seemed to say – how was she ever going to get through the next twenty months?

She had just started to make herself some supper, doing her best to ignore the ghost-like memories, when the phone rang. She answered it on the fourth ring, hoping it was social – her mother, a friend – and not work. It was neither but a marketing company telling her she could get a grant for cavity-wall insulation. As she put the phone down she saw the red light glowing on her answering machine. When had that happened?

She played back the message. A low male voice said, 'Good evening, Liz. It's Richard Pearson... Chief Constable Pearson, if you remember.' He gave a slightly embarrassed laugh. 'It's been a while since we last met, but I've thought about you often and wondered how you were getting on. And I – er, I mean to say, I'm coming to London next month for a Chief Constables' meeting, and I wondered if perhaps we could meet up. Lunch? Or coffee? Or a drink in the evening? Whatever suits you. Let me know when you can. It would be lovely to see you again.' And he gave his number and rang off.

Her initial reaction was to ignore this – and delete the message. Since Martin's death she hadn't thought about seeing anyone else – not even for coffee or a drink. It seemed a betrayal somehow. No one measured up to Martin right now in Liz's mind.

Yet there was something rather endearing about this message – Pearson's hesitancy for one thing, not a trait he had shown in Manchester where he had seemed effortlessly in charge of the operation they'd worked on together. He'd been unflappable, brave even when the whole thing ended violently; in fact he had probably saved her life. Pearson was an attractive man – that she remembered – and she'd liked him, not least because of his obvious sympathy for her after things had gone so wrong in Paris and she'd lost Martin. Maybe she should have a drink with him, if only to be polite.

She listened to the message again and then picked up the phone.

5

T HE LECTURE WAS SURPRISINGLY good. Over half the seats in the large auditorium were filled, which was a tribute to the speaker, since the title of Jasminder Kapoor's lecture was never going to grab anyone by the lapels, though it was true that she had a growing reputation among those people concerned about the issues she was going to address. *Guardian* readers all, thought Peggy sardonically as she sat down next to Tim, a *Guardian* reader himself. She was there as a duty, to support him, but was pleasantly surprised within minutes of the start of the lecture to find her attention held by what Kapoor had to say.

There was nothing revolutionary about her remarks, nothing that Peggy, on reflection, hadn't thought herself. What was impressive was the calm, persuasive way in which Kapoor went to the heart of her subject: without prejudice as lawyers would say, dissecting the points before arriving at a conclusion. Whether one agreed with it or not, one could only admire her dispassionate thoughtfulness.

There were many questions after the talk, and not everyone present seemed to appreciate Kapoor's ability to look at both sides of a question. A few were actively hostile, implying that she was colluding in the massive programmes of government surveillance, which – they didn't have to say it, it seemed to be assumed – were operating unchecked in the UK and USA. As the Q&A finally seemed to peter out, Tim suddenly shot up his hand.

'Is there any credible evidence that surveillance by governments of the kind you seemed to be justifying tonight… I'm thinking especially about the indiscriminate interception of internet communications… has done one jot to prevent terrorist attacks?'

Peggy suppressed a strong desire to give her boyfriend a good kick. How many evenings had she sat tensely at home, waiting for the results of another investigation, unable to tell him any detail about her work? If only you knew, she thought angrily.

Jasminder Kapoor nodded politely as Tim went on. 'More generally, is there actually any evidence that surveillance protects us more than invades us?'

Jasminder thought for a moment. 'I'd have thought so. Though obviously I'm not in a position to quote chapter and verse as I don't have access to the information.' She looked at him from the rostrum, slightly impatiently. 'Look, I'm not here tonight as an apologist for state intrusions. And the last thing I want to see is carte blanche given to the authorities simply because they say it has to be that way in order to protect us. But at the same time, there is a danger – let's be clear about that. Al Qaeda, Islamic State, Boko Haram – these are extremist groups intent on indiscriminate slaughter, and there are individuals and small groups who follow them and want to achieve some sort of heroic status by violence. Many of them are experts at using all the new forms of communication, particularly to recruit young people to join them. It seems to me that giving the state proportionate powers to keep tabs on these people, provided the use of those powers is supervised and controlled by law, is appropriate. To think otherwise is, in my view, naïve at best, dangerous at worst.'

Tim was shaking his head. 'You haven't answered my question. Is there any *evidence* that surveillance does any good? Or do we have to take it on faith?' he added scornfully.

Jasminder looked at him coolly. 'If you're asking if we should take it for granted that government agencies are working on our behalf and not against us, then my answer is a qualified yes. Governments and their agencies need oversight, they need accountability; I'm completely committed to ensuring we have both of them. But they also need our recognition that they are working to protect us.'

This sounded deeply felt, if not designed to win the applause of her audience. Peggy found it annoying that Tim was still cynically shaking his head, and was relieved when the chairperson stepped forward and called an end to the Q&A.

After the talk there were drinks in a common room for the audience, but Tim seemed reluctant to go. 'Oh, let's,' said Peggy, thinking that otherwise the evening was going to end with an argument over leftover macaroni cheese back in their flat. A dismal prospect.

'Why?'

'I'd like to meet the speaker. I thought she was very impressive.'

Tim groaned. 'If we must,' he said grudgingly.

At first they just talked to some of Tim's colleagues and drank the warm white wine. The consensus seemed to be that the lecturer had been brave to tackle the subject but had not been altogether convincing. There was a blonde woman who joined them after a bit; she was expensively dressed in a smart coat and polished leather boots, and didn't look to Peggy like an academic. A journalist maybe. Whoever she was, she was very interested in the subject, and she and Tim were soon deep in conversation about the talk while Peggy kept one eye on Jasminder Kapoor – she was surrounded by an argumentative group of dissenters, and seemed to be having rather a rough time. At last, her critics let up for a moment, and seeing this, Peggy went over to introduce herself.

Face to face, the Jasminder who had appeared so confident on the rostrum seemed a little shy. Peggy's opening remark that she must be exhausted made her smile and from then on the conversation took off. She was clearly delighted to talk about something other than civil liberties and, when Peggy admired her embroidered jacket, told her about her mother in India who had sent it. Peggy had noticed from her seat in the second row the nasty bruise on Jasminder's cheek, even though she had clearly tried to disguise it with makeup. 'What happened?' she asked.

Jasminder laughed. 'I'm sure I should say it's nothing, but actually it was rather awful. I got it the other night. Two men tried to mug me when I was walking home from the theatre. Fortunately someone came past and chased them off. They ran away and dropped my bag and briefcase – but I got this and some other bruises that you can't see.' And she touched the purplish mark on her face gently.

'How terrible,' said Peggy. She could see that for all her lightness of tone, Jasminder had been through a shocking experience. 'Did the police catch them?'

'They didn't get the chance. The man who chased them off said they'd be long gone; he thought calling the police would be a waste of time.'

This seemed wrong to Peggy, but then she hadn't been the one attacked. 'Well, he sounds pretty heroic. Did they do him any harm? Did they have weapons?'

'One of them had a knife. But this man just kicked it out of his hand. It was like something out of a film. Quite thrilling if I hadn't been so scared.'

Peggy laughed. 'Well, you didn't seem very scared by the attackers tonight. I'm sorry about Tim; he was the one who asked the last question. He's a colleague of yours at King's – he's in the English department. I thought you saw him off excellently. We live together but I don't share his views.'

They kept chatting easily for a few minutes, and when Jasminder asked Peggy what she did for a living, Peggy barely hesitated. 'I'm at the Ministry of Defence. I work in HR.'

The other woman looked at her thoughtfully, as if she had heard this white lie before. She either decided to believe it, or else to *pretend* to believe it, for she moved on and started talking about how much she disliked winter in London. Then after a few minutes she announced she had to go to dinner with her hosts, as well as some other colleagues. 'But I'd love to talk to you some more some time. Would you like to meet for lunch?'

'I'd like that very much,' said Peggy. They exchanged numbers and went their separate ways. Peggy rejoined Tim, who was grumbling with a colleague about their teaching loads. 'So you met the great apologist, I see,' he said sourly.

'I like her,' said Peggy firmly, and after that to her relief Tim left the subject alone.

6

I T HAD BEEN TEN days since she had been attacked, the bruises had gone and Jasminder had decided she was over it. She wasn't going to think about it any more, and above all she wasn't going to let it alter her life one bit. She had walked by herself down Barnsbury Street and alongside the gardens of the square twice now, though admittedly not at eleven o'clock at night. She'd gone back to work the following day, though she had felt very shaky. She'd taken her tutorials at the college and gone on in the afternoons to the charity where she advised clients on cases involving civil liberties or immigration (often both at the same time). She'd even managed to give her public lecture a few days after the incident, where she'd handled some difficult questions from members of the audience, some of whom had clearly come expecting to hear something rather different from what she'd said.

That was the problem. People liked a Manichean view of the world, a black-and-white perspective on even the most complex questions, to reinforce whatever prejudices they held. Jasminder prided herself on not being like that. She knew that she had acquired a reputation as a radical civil libertarian, but though there was an element of truth to this, she felt it didn't do her justice. Her position was more subtle. Above all she knew that there was nothing to be gained by exaggerating the flaws she wanted to fix or by impugning the motives of people merely because they took a different point of view.

She hadn't heard from her rescuer, Laurenz Hansen, and had decided that probably she never would. She had parked him in a mental pending tray but was beginning to think of moving him to 'Out'. Nothing to be done about that, she told herself – *there are other fish in the sea.* But in fact her life was fish-less at the moment, since the end of a three-year relationship she'd had with a young barrister from one of the civil liberties chambers. He had been kind and was a good lawyer, but his political sympathies, superficially akin to hers, had not extended to his plans for their relationship. He'd have had Jasminder in a pinny, tending an Edwardian semi in a London suburb, taking their 2.4 children to school and watching the afternoon film on TV until he came home, ready for supper. It had never crossed her mind that anyone with such an antediluvian vision of a relationship was a serious prospect.

Since him, her weekends were spent working, seeing plays or films with her friend Emma, or occasionally going to dinner as the 'single woman' with friends who tried to set her up with men who were 'available' – which seemed to mean, in most cases, divorced.

She was at the charity's office in Camden Town reading a deposition from a Somali client. The young woman had come to the UK eighteen months before, and was now facing deportation – something made more likely by her husband's pending trial for terrorist offences. Yet Jasminder was convinced the woman was innocent of any illegal activities herself, and was busy listing arguments for her release from detention when her mobile phone rang.

Impatiently she took it out of her bag and hit the answer button. 'Is that Jasminder?' a voice asked. It sounded slightly foreign.

'Yes. Who is it?' Her mind was still on the brief she was composing.

'You can call me the White Knight if you like.'

'What?' If this was a cold call from a marketing company it wasn't an appealing one.

'Sorry, it's Laurenz Hansen. Do you remember me? The week before last. I hope you haven't been having nightmares.'

'Oh, hello. I hadn't heard from you and…'

'I've been out of town or I would have rung sooner. How are you?'

'I'm fine, thanks. Busy, but fine.' She wondered what he wanted.

'I hope I'm not calling you at a bad time…'

'No, no.'

'I thought it might be nice to meet up. Maybe go somewhere for a drink?'

She looked a little guiltily at the brief she had been working on. Actually, there was no reason why she couldn't finish it later this evening. So she said, 'That would be nice. When were you thinking of?'

'Could you manage tonight? Or perhaps another evening this week?'

'Tonight would be fine. I'm working in Camden Town. Where are you?'

They met in a wine bar across the road from Camden Market. It turned out that they both liked to wander round the stalls there on Saturday mornings. Jasminder was wearing an ivory cameo brooch which she'd picked up at one of the second-hand jewellery stalls; he said he'd found a first edition of *The Thirty-Nine Steps* for a fiver.

Then he said, 'I hope you don't mind but I Googled you. I saw you were giving a talk at the university. I would have liked to come but I was away on business.'

'Do you travel a lot?' she asked, realising she didn't even know what he did.

'More than I'd like. Though soon I should have permanent residency in the UK, and then I hope I can do something that won't have me on an aeroplane twice a week.'

'What takes you away so often?'

'Don't tell anyone,' he said with mock seriousness. He leaned forward conspiratorially. 'I'm a banker,' he whispered.

Jasminder laughed. 'Don't worry – your secret's safe with me. Do you think it's that bad?'

'Well,' he said with a shrug, 'I work for a private bank. We manage the money of wealthy clients, not the man in the street, so I don't think anyone can blame the banking crisis on us. My job is keeping rich people rich – though most of them would say I'm supposed to make them even richer. I don't think it does a lot of harm, but I wouldn't say it was a noble calling.'

'Did you always want to be a banker?'

Laurenz looked slightly startled. 'Good heavens, no. I'm not sure anyone does. I wish I'd studied law. I envy you.'

'The law has plenty of drawbacks too.'

'Yes, I'm sure it does for lots of people. But what you do is truly important.'

The waiter came with the bottle of Beaujolais they'd ordered and filled their glasses. When he left, Jasminder said, 'I don't know about that. It's not as if we can always see the effect of what we do. At least you know whether your clients are happy or not.'

'But I'm not saving them from prison – or, worse, from what an asylum seeker gets if they're sent back to the country they're fleeing from.'

'What brought you to the UK to begin with?'

Laurenz shrugged. 'Work. The bank is based in Bermuda and that's where I used to be. But we have a number of British clients and a London office to look after them. When a job came up here I was happy to volunteer, partly because my wife wanted to be in London.'

So, he was married. At least he was honest enough to tell her from the start. 'Is she British, your wife?' asked Jasminder, hoping she sounded interested.

He shook his head. 'Oh, no. She's Norwegian, like me. She's back in Oslo now. She found out she didn't like it here as much as she thought she would.'

'That must be difficult. Do you get to see each other very often?'

'No.' He didn't seem unhappy about this. 'We're only communicating these days through lawyers. Another three months and we won't have to communicate at all. I may be penniless after that, but it's a price worth paying. This is not what anyone would call an amicable separation.'

She hardly knew this man, but felt rather relieved to hear he was getting divorced. Fortunately, he didn't seem to want to talk about it – unlike more than one of the dinner-party table mates she'd been partnered with, who seemed eager to talk about little else, usually with a mix of self-pity and bitter recrimination. But Laurenz carefully steered their talk away from his absent wife, and soon Jasminder found herself describing the particularly difficult case of the Somali woman whose husband had terrorist connections. Laurenz seemed both pleasingly knowledgeable about the issues and interested in the case. Their talk moved on to internet privacy and surveillance by government agencies – flatteringly, he had read an account of her talk at King's online. For a banker, he seemed very progressive in his thinking, and more sceptical than Jasminder herself about the corrupting influences intelligence services were prone to.

It was serious conversation, lightened by a second glass of wine, and she found herself hoping they'd move on to dinner when Laurenz announced he had to leave soon: he was catching the night train to Edinburgh, for a meeting the next morning.

'I'll be back the day after tomorrow,' he said. He paused, and Jasminder looked at him; he was very attractive, she decided, and it wasn't just the wine speaking. He had high Nordic cheekbones, but dark hair and dark blue eyes – not at all the stereotypical Scandinavian.

'I imagine you're busy at the weekend,' he was saying.

'Well, not this weekend actually,' she said, as if all the others were jammed full.

His face brightened. 'Would you like to have dinner on Saturday then? There's a nice new place in Primrose Hill.'

You bet I would, thought Jasminder, and said coolly, 'That would be lovely. Could it be late-ish, say eight-thirty? I've got to see a client first.'

7

L IZ COULD TELL THAT Catherine Palmer was slightly nervous, but she couldn't understand why. The Head of MI6's HR department was the first woman to hold that post, and in Liz's limited contact with her previously she had seemed very able and pretty sure of herself. She had rung to ask if she could 'pick Liz's brains', though she didn't say what about. It seemed an odd request but there had been no reason to refuse.

They sat in the café in the atrium on the ground floor of Thames House where a decent cup of coffee could be obtained. Catherine Palmer was an attractive woman, about Liz's age, with rather striking wavy red hair cut very short, like a boy's. She had a sprinkling of freckles across her nose and cheeks and very pale blue eyes. In spite of her gamine appearance she had a firm business-like manner and Liz could easily understand how she had reached her present position.

They made small talk at first – about how overcrowded Thames House was getting and how the open-plan arrangements were working out. 'The new C is all in favour of it. But we're having some trouble with the old guard.'

Liz knew who one of the 'old guard' would be and suppressed a smile at the thought of her patrician counterpart Geoffrey Fane losing his eyrie high up at Vauxhall Cross, with its antique furniture and fine Persian rugs.

'The reason I wanted to talk to you,' said Catherine at last, seeming to summon up the courage to get to the point, 'was because C asked me to.'

'Really?' Liz was surprised, since she had yet to meet Treadwell.

'Yes. You see, he has decided that our service needs a Communications Director. We do have a small press team as you know, responsible for contact with the media, but this would be a more prominent position, and involve a more proactive role.'

Catherine hesitated before she continued. 'In the past, this would have been a post filled by a member of the service, but C feels strongly that we should cast the net more widely. Not all of his directors agree, as I'm sure you can imagine.' Liz nodded, remembering how vociferous Fane had been on the topic. 'They feel only an experienced case officer could properly represent the Service. I was at the meeting where this was discussed, and C agreed that initially we should take soundings in the intelligence community. That's where you come in,' she added, almost apologetically.

'I do?' asked Liz, slightly perplexed.

Catherine nodded. 'Yes, your name came up at the meeting.'

'Well, I'm flattered that you think I can help, but—'

Catherine interrupted, shaking her head. 'I should have been clearer. It's not your advice we want, though I'm sure it would be excellent. Rather, it was thought that conceivably you might think about applying for the post yourself.'

Liz was taken aback. 'Me? Did C suggest that?'

'No. It was one of the senior officers. But several others seconded the idea.'

Fane again, thought Liz. She thought for a moment about the proposition. It was certainly flattering to be approached, and a small part of her was actually intrigued by the idea. What a mission, after all: to represent to the world a service that traditionally prided itself on its secrecy – too much so, in Liz's view. And it would be a significant promotion.

But then she thought of all she would surrender by taking such a job – MI5, to begin with, where her greatest loyalties lay; her colleagues, especially Peggy; and most of all the job itself, which, whatever its frustrations, was immensely stimulating, always challenging, and always important. Swapping it for lunches with sympathetic journalists (or, worse still, *un*sympathetic journalists) would be an uneven exchange she was sure she would regret.

'I'm very flattered by the suggestion – I really am. And I would like to think about it, and maybe talk more to you about exactly what it would involve. But I have to say that my first reaction is that it's just not something I would want to do. It's so different from the way I see my career going and I think it might be difficult ever to return to operational work from such a high-profile role.'

Catherine nodded regretfully. 'I understand; I did think it was a long shot. Think about it, and if there's any chance you might be interested, give me a ring and I'll arrange for you to meet C and some others for a chat. We're planning on asking some head-hunters to do a search so we'll be producing a detailed job spec and profile very shortly. I'll send you a copy just in case.' She seemed weighed down by the prospect of trying to fill the post; Liz sensed the meeting with C and senior MI6 officers had been a contentious one. Old hands like Geoffrey Fane were experts at digging their heels in. Catherine went on, 'I'd be really grateful if you have any ideas for people who might be interested and suitable.'

Liz thought for a moment. 'In the intelligence community?'

'Or outside. C would not be against an outsider, provided they had the right skills and profile. Frankly, I think when he agreed to look first inside the intelligence community, he didn't think it likely anyone suitable would emerge. And he's already made it clear he doesn't want an MI6 insider.'

Interesting, thought Liz. Her respect for this man Treadwell was growing. He was lulling old recidivists like Fane into thinking he was backing down by compromising, all the while confident that they'd be forced in the end to revert to his original idea of going outside. Fane – for Liz was certain it would have been he who'd first raised her name – was going to be furious. And not just with C – Liz expected she'd bear the brunt of his displeasure for turning down this 'golden opportunity' to cross the river and work with him.

But something else was stirring in her. She remembered how Peggy had reported back on the talk she'd been to at King's, given by Jasminder Kapoor. Peggy's account of it had been positively glowing, and she'd been equally laudatory of Kapoor's ability to handle tough questions.

And, slightly to Liz's surprise, from Peggy's account it seemed clear that Jasminder wasn't a firebrand, but that rarer bird – a dispassionate observer of the Janus-like problem of keeping the country's citizens safe without destroying the rights that gave them something to be safe for. In Liz's view, MI6 and the intelligence world in general could only benefit from having someone represent their views publicly; she liked the sound of this chap Treadwell, moreover, who seemed keen to sweep a new broom through the dusty corridors of Vauxhall Cross. And, to be honest, there was something that appealed to Liz's mischievous side in the idea of Geoffrey Fane sitting on a selection board interviewing a highly intelligent and personable female civil rights lawyer for a post he didn't approve of. That would set the cat among his pigeons; he'd set plenty among Liz's in his time.

So she said cheerfully, 'Actually, I do have one thought. Why don't we have another cup of coffee and I'll tell you about it.'

8

As the hands of the clock in the small tutorial room moved towards noon Jasminder said, 'That's it for today. I'd like you each to do an outline brief for the defence of this case, making the points we've been discussing as convincingly as you can. Put it in my pigeon hole by Friday evening, please.'

She watched as the students gathered their papers together, scraped their chairs back and filed out of the room. When they'd left she sighed. She knew that one of them would make most of the relevant points, a couple more would include some of them, and the remaining three would produce something that showed they had understood very little of what she'd been saying. But the most dispiriting part was that even the brightest didn't seem to have been taught how to write; how to marshal an argument; how to make points effectively. She shouldn't have to waste her time teaching undergraduates how to write English; the schools should have done that before they ever reached university.

She got up to collect her things. She had a couple of clients to see at the charity in an hour and a half and was intending to grab some lunch in the restaurant before she left the college. As she was putting on her coat, the phone rang.

A woman's voice said, 'Oh, hello. This is Rosamund Butler from Egerton Smith, the executive search company. We do a lot of our work for Government departments and agencies. May I take a moment of your time to explain one of the searches we have been commissioned to do? I wanted to ask your advice, and to ask particularly if you had any suggestions as to who might be interested in applying for the position.'

Jasminder sat down. She had had dealings with head-hunters before and she recognised the approach. This woman was going to try and persuade her to apply for the job.

'Before you go any further,' she said, 'I am not interested in applying for anything in Government service. And if I were, I don't think I'd be successful. I assume you know something about me, and if so you'll know that my views are not the same as those of the Government on lots of things. I'm a civil liberties lawyer and I spend a lot of my time helping people work their way through Government regulations.'

'The reason I am approaching you is that this post is directly about civil liberties,' Rosamund broke in. 'I saw a report of your lecture a few weeks ago and I've read the text online. It was the views you expressed on the balance between our rights to a private life and freedom of expression, and the Government's need for information to protect us at a time of high security threat, that made me think you might be the ideal person for this job. It is a post in a Government agency directly concerned with the security of the country. They are looking to appoint a Director of Communications. They don't want a cheerleader for their work. They need someone who understands the arguments of their critics, and who can, in a sense, represent one side to the other and so help bring the two sides nearer together. From what you said the other week it is clear that you do.'

Jasminder didn't reply. Unusually for her, she didn't know what to say. Surely this could only be one of the intelligence agencies and the thought that they might be trying to head-hunt her took her breath away. But it also intrigued her. While she was still thinking what to say, Rosamund broke the silence. 'Look, why don't you come over to my office when you have a moment? I can show you the detailed job description, and I'll get someone who knows about the job from the inside to come and join us. The only thing I would say is there is a certain confidentiality attached to the search at this stage, so I would be grateful if you wouldn't talk about it.'

By this time Jasminder was far too intrigued to say no, and a meeting was fixed up for the following week at which Rosamund and this mysterious 'someone' would explain more.

During the next few days Jasminder said nothing to anyone about the approach from the head-hunter, though she was very tempted to ring her friend Emma and ask her opinion. She thought about the job a lot. In fact she couldn't get it out of her head. Twice she decided not to go to the meeting and twice she changed her mind, curiosity overcoming her doubts.

On the agreed day, at the agreed time, she rang the bell on the door of an anonymous Georgian house in a street off Berkeley Square. A smartly dressed young woman showed her into a small room, more like a drawing room than a waiting room, furnished with draped curtains, a couple of soft grey-upholstered armchairs, and a low table holding copies of *Country Life* and *The World of Interiors* plus a stack of glossy company reports.

Jasminder sat down on the edge of one of the chairs, putting her bulging bag, full of students' essays, on the floor beside her, feeling very out of place. She wished she hadn't come; she was sure she was not going to like Rosamund Butler, who had sounded so smooth on the phone.

She had just started to flick through one of the magazines when the door opened and a short, middle-aged woman, wearing a grey flannel skirt and a jumper, with her glasses dangling from a chain round her neck, came in. Jasminder stood up as the woman walked across the room and, shaking her warmly by the hand, introduced herself as Rosamund.

'I am so pleased to meet you,' she said. 'Let's go into my office. I have someone there for you to meet. You can leave your bag here.'

Jasminder, who had been expecting a cool, elegant woman in a sharp suit and Louboutins, started to feel much better. The other person turned out to be a red-haired woman just a few years older than Jasminder herself, who was introduced as 'Catherine'. From her, Jasminder learned that the post was Communications Director in one of the intelligence agencies. It was a new post and something of an experiment. The person appointed would be working closely with the senior management, and the Head of the Service himself was taking a keen interest. They were looking for someone who would be an intermediary with the media and other external contacts. It was important, Catherine said, that whoever was appointed should understand the current freedom of information and data access issues, not to bang the drum for the agencies but to listen and explain and act as a sort of conduit between the Service and its critics. The post was for a year in the first instance and if it were a success it would be made permanent. If Jasminder were appointed they could help her negotiate a sabbatical from King's.

Three-quarters of an hour later, when she walked out into Berkeley Square carrying a folder containing a description of the post (which actually told her not much more than Catherine had said), and several long and daunting-looking forms, Jasminder was exhilarated. How very much more interesting this would be than reading her students' confused and garbled scripts. It would be a risk to her reputation, of course, because a lot of people would think that she had sold out and gone over to the other side. But if what the two women had told her were true, she could have a big influence on a very important national issue. She would be in a better position than anyone else to see all sides of the freedom versus security debate. She hadn't expected to be interested at all, and here she was getting excited about a job she hadn't even been offered. She told herself she needed to slow down and think things over.

9

IN REORGANISING THE INTERNAL space in Thames House to provide large open-plan floors, a few small corners had been partitioned off as meeting rooms. It was in one of these featureless, windowless rooms that the Counter-Espionage Group was to assemble for its meeting. Peggy, who was the group's secretary, had given Liz an agenda headed 'Counter-Espionage Assessment Committee (CEAC)'. There were four items on the agenda:

1. Review of terms of reference and membership
2. Report by GCHQ
3. Review of current cases
4. AOB and date of next meeting

'Do we really need to be this formal?' enquired Liz, agenda in hand.

'Yes,' replied Peggy firmly. 'I think we do. There was a bit of moaning and people saying "not another committee" when I rang round to invite them. I think if we don't make it formal we'll get poor attendance.'

Peggy's forecast seemed to be borne out when Liz arrived at the meeting room dead on eleven o'clock to find there was no one there except her colleague, who had set the table with pens and paper, water and coffee in a thermos jug.

'Where is everyone?' Liz asked irritably. She hated hanging around waiting for people.

'Charlie Simmons's train from Cheltenham was delayed but he should be here in about ten minutes; DI Ferguson from Special Branch said he was coming, as did Rona Benson from the Home Office, and we'll have the pleasure of the company of your second-favourite Six officer.'

'Bruno Mackay?' When Peggy nodded, Liz demanded, 'What's he doing here? Last I heard, he was in Libya.'

'I gather he covered himself with glory and had some sort of nervous collapse, so he's on light duties for a change.'

'Hmm.' Liz said nothing else but she knew (and she knew that Peggy knew) that she too was on 'light duties'. No one had ever actually said so, but it was obvious to her that the decision to post her away from counter-terrorism into counter-espionage had been taken because the powers that be thought she needed a period of comparative calm after Martin's death. Untypically, she had not complained. Counter-espionage was fascinating and important even if cases proceeded at a less hectic pace than in counter-terrorism. That suited her for now, but not for too long.

There was a loud guffaw and the door opened to admit a man in a belted raincoat, and a young woman.

'What's the joke?' asked Liz.

'I was just telling our colleague from the Home Office something she didn't know about one of her Ministers. It's amazing what you can learn from the Protection boys.'

Liz raised her eyebrows. She was not impressed by DI Ferguson's indiscretion, but at least Rona Benson looked embarrassed.

Hot on their heels came Bruno Mackay of MI6. Liz and Bruno were about the same age and had worked together before, though not recently. When she'd first met him, she'd joked with her friends that he fancied himself as T. E. Lawrence – tanned face, bright blue eyes, skin taut and lined from gazing into the sun. Bruno had been in Afghanistan, where he had been running an agent against the Taliban, and was very pleased with himself – his manner towards Liz and her colleagues was one of ineffable superiority. Since then he had been Head of the MI6 Station in Paris and after that he'd been in Libya. The grapevine reported that something very unpleasant had happened to him there but no one was saying what it was.

So Liz had been half expecting Bruno to look different from the young man she'd first met, but she was still surprised by how changed he was. His face was no longer tanned but a yellowy-white, and the blue eyes seemed to have sunk into his face. He was still an elegant figure, in a beautifully cut dark blue tweed jacket worn with striped shirt and flannels, but he had lost a lot of weight and his clothes now hung on him limply.

He greeted Liz with a handshake. Instead of the teasing personal remark he would once have made, he said, 'Good morning, Liz. It's good to see you again. I was very sorry to hear about Martin.'

'Thank you,' she replied, rather taken aback. 'I'm sorry to hear you've had a rough time.' He just nodded and sat down at the table.

A few moments later Charlie Simmons arrived, looking like a student who had slept in his clothes, his spiky hair standing straight up, khaki anorak undone and hanging half off his shoulders. Had Liz not known what a vital role he had played in the Paris operation, she would have found it difficult to take him seriously.

'Sorry to be late,' he said, dropping his backpack on the floor beside a chair and sitting down. 'Those trains get more and more unreliable.'

Liz rattled through the first item on Peggy's agenda and then asked Charlie to explain why he had asked for the meeting to be brought forward.

'Well,' he said, sitting up in his chair, rather more focused, 'you will all remember that after the murder of Alexander Litvinenko in 2011, police and other investigations showed without much doubt that a special operations team of at least two or three Russians had brought the polonium into the country and then administered it. We've assumed it was an FSB assassination, either formally or informally approved. After that was uncovered, I and a couple of colleagues looked back at our data to see whether anything might have given us a clue that a special op was going to be carried out. We thought it likely that relevant *Rezidentura* in countries might have been alerted in case anything went wrong and the special ops team needed assistance of some kind.

'When we looked, we saw some traffic in the run-up to the murder that we couldn't read, but that was unusual – because it was sent to just a few Stations. Including London of course. There was a lot more unusual activity from London during the period when Litvinenko was dying in hospital and the investigation was getting under way. We think the traffic was being sent out of St Petersburg, not the main communications centre in Moscow. That may mean that the operation was organised by a special unit outside the mainstream.

'After that,' Charlie went on, 'we decided to continue to monitor, looking for any similar pattern, in case we were seeing the start of some concerted plan to eliminate critics in the West. And the reason I asked for a meeting of this committee is that in the last few weeks, beginning about a month ago, we've seen something similar. It's traffic out of St Petersburg to London but it has also gone to Riga, Oslo and, rather unexpectedly, New York.'

By now everyone round the table was looking interested. Eventually it was agreed that, despite the vagueness of the intelligence, resource should be committed to trying to prevent attacks on Russians or ex-Russians living in the UK, whether they were oligarchs or political defectors (or both). It was also agreed that all UK police forces should be alerted at senior level; that Bruno would alert MI6 Stations, particularly in the Baltic and Scandinavian states, to keep their ears to the ground; and that MI5 would ensure that all domestic sources were similarly alerted. Rona Benson would discreetly report upwards in White-hall, trying to ensure that no overreaction took place in the Home Office.

Following a quick review of current investigations, the meeting broke up, the participants leaving considerably more animated than when they had arrived. But as Liz watched them go she felt uneasy. She had a strong sense of a threat and it seemed fairly clear where it was coming from, but its precise nature and what could be done about it were not at all clear. This was very different from her recent experience in counter-terrorism where at the first sign of a threat all the cogs fell into place and started working to defeat it. With this threat she could only wait for further developments – and that worried her.

10

I T WAS RAINING WHEN Peggy Kinsolving got out of
the cab in Grosvenor Square. She put up her umbrella
and peered out from under it at the American Embassy at
the west end of the square. As always, armed police stood
guarding the entrance, where despite the rain a queue of
visa applicants snaked back along the pavement. Concrete
crash barriers extended out into the square, and a lane on
one of the streets had been closed off with cones. Above
the 1960s edifice of pre-stressed concrete, the enormous
gold figure of the American eagle spread its wings, as if
struggling to fly off. Soon it would get its wish, since the
Embassy was moving south of the Thames, to a building
safely located without immediate neighbours.

Peggy showed her credentials to the guard in the small
shelter outside, put her bag and her wet umbrella under
the X-ray machine and went through the entrance, shaking the remaining water off the umbrella. The receptionist
on the desk put a call through and Peggy took a seat in the
large waiting area. She hoped this meeting wasn't going to
take too long.

Peggy had had a sleepless night, thanks to Tim's coming
to bed at two. He had been working long hours lately,

though to her chagrin it was not on the article he was meant to be writing for *Essays and Criticism*. Instead he was always at his computer, surfing the net for articles about internet surveillance and the intrusions of governments on the private lives of their citizens. When Peggy had tactfully suggested this wasn't the best way to be spending his time, he had bridled. 'This is important,' he'd insisted angrily, and Peggy bit her lip and said no more. At some point she was going to have to have a proper conversation with him about it. He had students to teach, and his own academic work to pursue – he had a book to write in which Oxford University Press had expressed strong interest. Yet Peggy knew that however gently she pointed this out, he would react badly.

She couldn't understand where this new fascination with half-baked conspiracy theories had come from. In his own subject Tim was indefatigable in his pursuit of source material and a rigorous judge of authenticity. Now he was spending hours in murky chat rooms, exchanging 'views'. Usually the mildest of men, recently he had become terribly opinionated, and very aggressive in argument – and arguments were what most of their conversations were these days. She felt she was watching him change in front of her eyes, and she didn't like it one bit. What had happened to the gentle scholar she had fallen in love with?

A tall woman in a bright blue suit came out to collect her. She led Peggy up to the fourth floor, through a series of combination-locked doors, into what seemed to be a waiting room furnished with sofas and low tables, off which led four or five heavy wooden doors, all closed.

'This looks different from the last time I was here,' remarked Peggy.

'Yes,' replied her escort, in a Southern accent. 'We've had a security upgrade. But nothing's very secure in this old place.'

Hmm, thought Peggy. Not much faith in our counter-terrorism measures then, but she said, 'I expect you're looking forward to the new building.'

The blue-suited woman raised her eyebrows. 'I'll be home by the time that's finished.' Then, opening one of the doors, she said, 'Miss Kinsolving is here for you, sir,' and turning back to Peggy, waved her into the room.

Miles Brookhaven stood up from behind a large steel-and-glass desk as Peggy walked in. He seemed taller and thinner than she remembered him, and no longer wore the heavy horn-rimmed spectacles he'd sported as a younger man. He looks as though he needs feeding up, she thought, and remembered that he had been badly wounded in Syria a year or so before, knifed by an unknown assailant in a Damascus market. Liz had told her that he had almost bled to death and had been lucky to pull through. Since then he had been commended for his work in Yemen, where he'd recruited a source whose information had helped prevent a terrorist attack on Britain. This post as Head of the CIA Station in London was his reward. It was said that he was the youngest ever to hold it. But his responsibilities didn't seem to be weighing on him; he looked cheerful and friendly as he energetically pumped her hand, then ushered her to a seat on the sofa, while he sat down in an easy chair.

'It's really good to see you again, Peggy. We have met before... do you remember?' he said with a wide grin.

'Yes. Of course I do,' she said, finding her own formality starting to melt in the face of such friendliness.

'And you're still working for the redoubtable Miss Carlyle?'

55

'I am,' she said with a half-smile.

'And surviving?'

'Loving it,' she replied. She wasn't used to being teased in this building. Miles's predecessor, Andy Bokus, was a much grumpier character, but she remembered now that Miles was something of an Anglophile, having spent a year at Westminster School when he was a boy.

'I was rather hoping ...' and he hesitated '... that Liz might come with you today.'

Peggy knew this meant he'd been hoping Liz would come alone. It was well known that he had made a pass at her years ago when he was here as a much more junior officer. But Peggy didn't take offence; according to protocol, meetings with the CIA Head of Station would normally be conducted by someone more senior than she was. 'Liz sends her apologies. There's a meeting at Cheltenham she couldn't get out of.' Peggy had prepared this excuse in advance.

Brookhaven seemed to accept it. He nodded. 'And how is she?' There was concern in his voice, which his cheerfulness could not disguise.

'She's fine,' said Peggy, knowing the subtext here was the death of Martin Seurat.

'Good,' said Brookhaven briskly. 'So what can I do for you?'

Relieved to turn to business at last, Peggy said, 'I expect you've heard that Liz has moved back into counter-espionage and I've moved with her. Liz is concerned that with all the focus on terrorism, we may have got rather out of touch with you on espionage. She wants to set up a channel for a regular exchange of views. I've come over really to start the ball rolling with that and also to brief you on some things we have become aware of recently.'

Peggy talked for a few minutes about the increasing number of cyber-attacks on British companies, and also mentioned two recent cases where a couple of employees of defence firms had been subjected to old-fashioned sexual compromise. 'It all seems very Cold War,' she said, 'and the intelligence component at the Russian Embassy here is as high as it's ever been.'

'From what I hear, it's the same all over Western Europe.'

'Yes,' Peggy went on, 'but there's one added problem that is perhaps unique to us: the possibility of physical attacks on the anti-Putin oligarchs who are living in Britain. The Government is most anxious that there shouldn't be another Litvinenko.'

Brookhaven was listening closely, occasionally making a note on a yellow legal pad he'd taken from his desk. 'Have you seen anything to indicate something like that might be in the air?' he asked.

'We have – though just the vaguest hint. It's possible we might have misread it,' replied Peggy, and told him what Charlie Simmons had revealed at the Counter-Espionage Assessment Committee meeting. 'Charlie thinks it might mean that some kind of special unit is on the move. What bothers us is the similarity between these new messages and some traffic that was picked up before the Litvinenko murder.'

'They've always kept a close eye on the oligarchs here, haven't they? It may be that, given the raised tension between Russia and Europe, they want to prevent anything remotely resembling a movement in exile from growing up.'

'Well, if it involves killing people with radioactive poison, we need to stop it.'

Brookhaven considered this for a minute. He was an attractive man, thought Peggy; he appeared rather English in his well-cut dark suit, and though he was thin he looked athletic, confident, but with a certain vulnerability she rather liked. He said, 'Do you know, what you've said doesn't surprise me at all.'

'Oh?'

'About ten days ago a new source came to us in…' He paused. 'Let's just say the Middle East for now. He said he had important information about FSB activity in the West. At first, we thought he must mean America – you remember the Illegals the FBI flushed out a few years ago?'

'Of course.' It had been the stuff of Hollywood – over half a dozen Russians who had been living as Americans in the United States, some for many years, undetected.

'In fact, it turned out he was talking about the UK – and France. I was about to arrange a meeting with you all at Thames House but you beat me to it.'

Peggy said nothing, wanting to believe him. Everyone knew the Americans were forthcoming when it suited their interests, silent when it didn't. Peggy was not alone in thinking the Special Relationship was only special on one side of the Atlantic.

Brookhaven went on, 'I'm due to go meet this source later this month. When I get back, why don't I come over to Thames House and brief you and Liz?'

'Terrific,' said Peggy. She couldn't resist adding, 'I'll make sure she's not in Cheltenham that day.'

11

'HI, JASMINDER, ANY CHANCE of dinner tonight? I was thinking we could meet at La Sambuca?'

She was surprised to hear Laurenz Hansen on the phone. She'd enjoyed their second meeting, a few weeks ago, for dinner in Primrose Hill, though she had been a bit taken aback when afterwards he had seen her into a taxi outside the restaurant with only a chaste peck on the cheek for goodbye and no mention of a future meeting. He'd said rather vaguely that he'd ring her, but she had more or less decided that nothing was going to come of the relationship.

It wasn't surprising he was reluctant to get involved. From the sound of it, his divorce was enough to put anyone off relationships. He and his wife had separated almost two years before and it was only now the divorce was coming through – and that after months of such acrimony that they were only communicating through lawyers.

Jasminder usually found the details of other people's divorces too tedious to bother with, but she had asked Laurenz why his had become so unpleasant. 'Money,' he'd replied. 'I made some successful investments when I was working in Bermuda and I'd previously worked in Venezuela for a couple of years and have holdings there as well.

I declared everything to the court months ago but she doesn't believe me. She's hired private detectives to try and find the fortune I'm meant to have hidden away.'

In spite of herself Jasminder had found his candour attractive and she thought that perhaps the divorce proceedings explained some things about him that had puzzled her. If he had private investigators on his tail it was not surprising he hadn't wanted to call the police after her mugging the other week. And maybe the fact that he'd given her his office number rather than a mobile or a home number had the same explanation.

Now here he was on the phone again, just when Jasminder had more or less given up on him. She hesitated, tempted by his invitation – and the restaurant he was proposing was conveniently close to her flat. But this would be her second night out this week – she'd had dinner with her friend Emma in Covent Garden two evenings before – and there were student essays to mark and a long brief to review for an urgent political asylum case. It wasn't as if she had a lot of time on her hands.

Laurenz Hansen seemed to pick up that she was wavering. 'I'll tell you what,' he said. 'Why don't we scratch the restaurant idea? Let me come over and cook while you get on with your work. We can talk over supper. You do have to eat, you know.'

And eventually she accepted, telling herself that he was right; she could do her work and still make time to see him. She couldn't remember a moment, not even in early childhood, when she hadn't felt she had too much to do, and too little time to do it. From primary-school days she had always been busy and hard-working, and it had paid off. She'd won a full fees-paid scholarship to Leicester Girls' High School and had gone on to

Durham. There she'd got a first, then a distinction in her supplementary year at law college in London. She'd had her choice between four firms of solicitors who were vying for her services. All this before she'd turned twenty-three.

Looking back now, she supposed this urgency must have come from her parents, who like so many immigrants to the UK were desperately eager for their children to succeed. Her father had been a successful pharmacist in Kampala, until Idi Amin had suddenly decided that Uganda didn't need its Asian community any more and had thrown them all out. Arriving in England with hardly any possessions, her father had discovered that his professional qualifications didn't transfer to the UK. Settling in Leicester, where so many Indian arrivals were living, he had managed with the help of a cousin to buy a tiny corner shop, selling cigarettes and newspapers and, at first, not much else.

Virtually as soon as Jasminder could count, she worked in the shop with her elder brothers, stacking shelves and sweeping the floor, and throughout her school years she had taken money from customers with one hand while doing her homework with the other. By the time her father had died a few years ago, the tiny shop had become a small chain of grocery stores in the city, which her brothers now ran very successfully.

Unlike her brothers, though, there had never been any question of Jasminder joining the business. She had been a bright girl and the apple of her father's eye – unable to resume his own profession, he had been determined that his youngest child would break through the barriers he had found in Great Britain. The day she'd received the acceptance letter from Durham, her father had spent the afternoon announcing the news proudly to every customer who'd come into the shop.

She'd felt guilty from time to time for disappointing her parents. Her father hadn't been able to understand why she had chosen to become an academic lawyer and work for civil liberties charities rather than making a lot of money in a City firm. Her mother had been mystified by her failure to get married and provide them with more grandchildren. Jasminder herself wasn't sure about having children. She liked kids, and was a loving aunt to her brothers' offspring, especially little Ali, a doe-eyed girl who had just turned seven and was both clever and full of energy. But she was also well aware that being a mother and having a high-powered career was difficult; too often both roles could suffer.

Yet Jasminder knew her parents' disappointment was minor compared to their pride in her. Even now, years after her mother had moved to India following her husband's death, she still kept a close watch on her daughter's career from a distance. When Jasminder had recently made her debut on *Question Time*, her mother had alerted half the Kapoor clan in the Punjab to watch her famous daughter on the BBC.

As she put away the vacuum cleaner, Jasminder reflected that she hadn't actually saved herself any time by agreeing to Laurenz cooking dinner at her flat, rather than going out with him to a restaurant. As soon as she'd got home she'd realised that the place was even more of a bombsite than usual. It had taken her over an hour to make it presentable and she hoped he wouldn't notice the stacks of papers she had hidden behind the sofa, or open the door to the hall cupboard where she had stuffed two bags of recycling that she had forgotten to put out for collection.

But her anxiety about the state of her place dissolved as soon as Laurenz arrived, with a large carrier bag in one hand and a bunch of early daffodils in the other. After she'd found a vase, he calmly ordered her to go and get on with her work, and by the time he summoned her to the kitchen, she'd marked six essays. He'd made mushroom omelettes with a green salad, and there was a lemon tart and a bowl of berries for dessert, and as she sat down at the table he poured her a glass of Sancerre from the fridge. The conversation flowed easily as they ate and she was glad he kept off the subject of his divorce.

After dinner they moved into the living room for coffee. It seemed natural to sit together on the sofa in front of the fire. He asked her about her lecture, which he had already said he was sorry to have missed, and she told him about the hostile response it had drawn from some of the King's College audience. She said, 'I'm getting used to being shouted down now – by both sides. People see things in such black-and-white terms. They either think the Government is intent on spying on every single thing we do – reading all our emails, monitoring our Facebook pages and every Twitter message – or else they think that no one should be allowed to wear a headscarf or a beard, that nothing is being done to protect us and we need vigilantes on every street corner.

'I'm exaggerating, of course, but that's how it some-times seems. Most of those I meet come from the first camp and it is very difficult to persuade them that there is a sensible middle ground.' She stopped and took a sip of her coffee, suddenly feeling self-conscious. Here she was, sitting next to a handsome man in a romantic situation, and she had to bang on about civil liberties. She said, with a weak smile, 'Sorry about the monologue. I suppose the point I'm trying to make is that I'm not the firebrand people think I am.'

'That's okay. And I don't think you should care too much about what people think. As long as *you* know what you are, that's all that really matters. I'm an expert on misperceptions.' He suddenly imitated with comic precision the voice of a dinner-party companion: '*Private banking sounds absolutely fascinating, Mr Hansen.*'

Jasminder laughed. For a moment, she wondered if she should tell Laurenz about the head-hunter's recent approach. Rosamund Butler had originally asked her not to talk to anyone about it, but in their face-to-face she had said Jasminder could mention it to her parents or her partner if she wanted to. Since her father was dead, her mother was in India and she didn't have a partner, she wondered if she was allowed a surrogate instead. But she told herself it couldn't be Laurenz, since she hardly knew him...

He put his coffee cup down on the table and moved closer to her. 'I hope you won't mind, Jasminder,' he said, as his arm slid along the back of the sofa behind her shoulders, 'but I've been wanting to kiss you for the last two hours, so you'd better say no right now if you don't want me to.'

In the morning, while Laurenz was out getting croissants from the bakery across the road and Jasminder was making coffee, she decided to tell him about the head-hunter's approach. He'd said that he must be off straight after breakfast, which was in some ways a relief (she was thinking of work again) though part of her would have liked him to stay for a while. She felt an ease with him she had never experienced so early on with other boyfriends, yet he retained a slight air of detachment that made him, even in their new-found intimacy, a little mysterious. She sensed there was a lot to Laurenz that she would want to get to know.

So she told him about the strange phone call she'd had, and the subsequent meeting with Rosamund Butler. 'She gave me all these forms to fill in if I decide to apply. I'm not sure what to do.'

'Do you know which agency it is?'

'No. There are only three of them to choose from, though: GCHQ, MI5 and MI6.'

'Are you sure there are only three?' he asked teasingly.

'If there's another one, it's so secret they couldn't be looking for a Communications Director.'

They both laughed. Laurenz put his knife down on his plate, and looked thoughtful. 'You should be flattered, you know.'

'Why's that?'

'Whoever it is, they must think a lot of you to make an approach like that. After all, you haven't exactly been a public supporter of the intelligence services.'

'I know. My first reaction was that they must have confused me with someone else.'

'I doubt it. I have to say, it makes me think a lot more of them to know they're willing to consider you for this post.'

'Yes, but should *I* seriously consider it? I'm not so sure it's a good idea.'

'Why not?' He was eating again, his eyes focused on his plate.

'Well, you know – if I stay true to my beliefs, it could be a disaster. If I don't – well, I could become a laughing stock. People will say I've sold out, that I'll be doing the work of the very devil I'm always complaining about.'

Laurenz looked up at her thoughtfully. 'I don't know, Jasminder. Life's not that simple. Sometimes you have to compromise your principles a bit in order to achieve the goals you're being principled about. Then again, sometimes you have to stand firm. I can't advise you. I don't know which way this would go. But in my opinion, it's worth taking it further. After all, if they do offer you the job, you can always say no.'

12

B Y THE TIME PEGGY got home from work, she was starving. After tossing and turning the night before, she'd skipped breakfast in a rush. Then she'd had a quick lunch with her new friend Jasminder Kapoor, but it had only been a salad and a very small one at that, and because the conversation had been so interesting, Peggy had barely picked at it.

With food on her mind and thinking about what was in the fridge, she opened the door to the flat she shared with Tim in Muswell Hill. She found him in their little kitchen, already preparing supper. Her heart sank. Lately Tim had taken to cooking elaborate vegetarian meals, which were doubtless healthy but left Peggy yearning for the simple joys of a grilled pork chop or a nice bit of steak.

Tonight was no exception. As she lifted the lid of the casserole, her nose was assailed by the strong aroma of stewing cabbage; inspecting the dish, she could also see carrots, onions and a sludgy mass she guessed was aubergine.

'Put the lid back,' Tim said from the sink. 'You're letting all the steam escape.'

'Smells delicious,' she lied.

'I found the recipe online,' he said proudly, and Peggy thought, Of course you did.

While Tim finished preparing his vegetarian master-piece, Peggy suddenly remembered she had a guest coming in an hour. To her surprise, Jasminder had rather shyly explained that she'd been approached about a Government post and had decided to apply, but had confessed baffle-ment about how to deal with the endless paperwork required in the application process. Peggy could well imag-ine the daunting pile of forms and explanatory leaflets, so she'd been happy to volunteer to help steer Jasminder through the process – inviting her to bring the forms to the flat this evening.

She couldn't do much about the smell of cabbage but she could tidy up a bit so she scooted around the sitting room, stacking the magazines and plumping up the cush-ions on the sofa. She had just finished when Tim called her in to the kitchen for supper.

They sat at the small table where they ate all their meals. Peggy looked without enthusiasm at the vegetable stew in the soup bowl in front of her. There was half a baguette to go with it, though she knew it was the one she had bought two days ago and it should really be turned into breadcrumbs. She wanted to open a bottle of wine, but lately Tim had gone teetotal and it seemed a waste just for her.

'So how was your day?' she asked as they started to eat.

'The usual,' he said sourly. 'I taught the Metaphysicals while the students all looked at their iPhones. I'd say it went right over their heads, since all their heads were down.' He laughed hollowly.

Peggy tried to smile. 'Some of them must be interested. I mean, they didn't come to King's just to text their mates.'

'You'd be surprised.' He fiddled with a chunk of dry baguette. 'Not that I can blame them.'

'What do you mean?'

'In this day and age the Metaphysical Poets seem pretty irrelevant to most people. That's supposing they've heard of them in the first place.'

'I don't know about that—'

'Of course you do. I'm starting to realise how inconsequential it all is.'

'What is?'

'I teach people about poems they would never read by choice, written by people they've never heard of. That's what's inconsequential.'

'Don't be silly.' She'd never heard him be quite so dismissive about his own line of work before. 'Of course they've heard of them and they're reading them by choice, or they wouldn't be in your class to begin with.'

'They just want a degree – a piece of paper that will get them a job.'

'I can't believe none of your students is interested. You've just had a bad day. And you've got your own work to be getting on with.' She had put her spoon down now.

He shook his head, making it clear she didn't understand. 'I could write the world's greatest monograph on John Donne and it wouldn't change one thing anywhere. Not one thing.'

'Why does it have to *change* anything? Why can't you be satisfied with writing something new and original that people will enjoy, and maybe learn from?'

He looked at her scornfully then turned back to his stew. Gloom descended on the table. Then she remembered her visitor.

'I've got someone coming over.'

'What, now?' he asked, looking alarmed.

'In a little while. Don't worry – you haven't got to entertain them. You can stay in your study.'

'Who is it?' he asked accusingly.

She didn't look at him. 'Jasminder Kapoor. The woman who gave the lecture I went to a few weeks ago.'

'What, here? You must be joking. She's coming to socialise with us?'

'It isn't socialising. She wants some help from me. She's decided to apply for a job with the Civil Service – they approached her, believe it or not – and she's finding the forms a bit of a nightmare. I offered to help her fill them in.'

'Why on earth did you do that?'

'Because she asked me if I would. How could I say no? Besides, she's very nice, Tim. You'd like her if you gave her half a chance. She's not what you think.'

Ignoring this, he asked, 'Does she know who you work for?'

'No – I just said I was a civil servant at the MOD. But I think she may have guessed. No flies on her.'

'And that doesn't bother her?' he demanded.

'It doesn't seem to,' said Peggy, trying to stay calm. She didn't like rows, especially with Tim. They never used to have them. She'd always thought he was proud of what she did for a living. He knew she couldn't talk about the details of it, but previously he'd seemed entirely supportive. She couldn't help asking, 'Does it bother *you*?' She found her voice wobbling slightly.

He didn't answer, but only shook his head wearily. Then he said, 'If Kapoor's applying for a Government job she's an even greater phony than I thought. Some radical,' he added sarcastically. He gave Peggy an angry look. 'Don't expect me to play host to her.'

'I don't,' Peggy protested. 'I told you – you can stay in your study. You don't even have to say hello.'

'Don't worry, I won't.' He seemed unaccountably furious. 'In fact, you can have the place to yourselves.'

He stood up suddenly and left the room. Peggy sat at the table, stunned, wondering what she had done to trigger this reaction. Was it really so awful to be helping Jasminder? Turning, she saw through the open door that Tim had his coat on. Without saying goodbye, he left the flat.

Peggy sighed, and looked at her watch. Jasminder would be here any minute. She'd better make coffee. As she stood up to clear the table, she realised her hands were shaking. And she noticed that Tim hadn't finished his stew.

13

SINCE THE MUGGING JASMINDER had felt uneasy walking by herself in the evenings. It was still only early spring and by the time she emerged from Bounds Green tube station it was dark. As she started to walk to the address Peggy had given her, she felt the by-now familiar tingling sensation in her spine. Outside the station the streets were well lit, with plenty of cars and vans passing in the road. A few people had got off the train with her and, as usual since the mugging, she was alert for anyone following her. She had already looked up the route to Peggy's flat before she left the charity offices in Camden Town; she didn't want to be seen consulting her phone – it invited approaches from strangers. She hadn't always been this nervous. Before the assault she used to travel around by herself anywhere and at any time with never a second thought. It angered her to think that those men had changed her – made her frightened.

As far as she could remember she had never been to Muswell Hill, though it wasn't that far from where she lived. It had the reputation of being respectably middle-class with streets of large Edwardian villas that no one but well-off professionals could afford to buy nowadays. But

Peggy seemed to live on the very edges of it, where it merged into an area of small shops and run-down houses. As she walked Jasminder mused that this must be one of the districts estate agents described as 'ripe for gentrification'. The rain had stopped now and the sky was clear, though as usual the yellow halogen haze of London meant the stars were only just discernible.

She was relieved when at last she saw the name of Peggy's street and turned along it. It was very quiet, with no one else in sight. Then ahead of her she heard a door bang and someone came out of one of the gardens. Her stomach contracted with momentary fear, but as the person passed through the arc of a street lamp she relaxed. It was a young man, thin and gangly, with curly red hair, wearing a student's duffel coat and trainers. He looked vaguely familiar, and not remotely threatening – geeky but nice. As he neared her on the pavement she smiled politely at him, but to her astonishment he glared back at her as he passed.

She found Peggy's house; it was the same one as the young man had just emerged from. Pushing the buzzer for the top flat, Jasminder wondered who he could have been. From Peggy's fulsome description at lunch, her boyfriend Tim was a gentle soul, the kind of academic so absorbed in his researches that he usually didn't know what day of the week it was. Not the kind of man who stared at strangers with hostility.

Peggy buzzed her in and Jasminder walked two flights up a narrow staircase to the top floor. The flat turned out to be roomy and comfortable, with a large sitting room, and a kitchen off to one side.

'What a nice flat,' said Jasminder as Peggy put mugs on a tray.

'Tim found it,' she said. 'We've been here about a year. It's a good neighbourhood and very quiet – at least it is down this street, away from the main road.'

'Is Tim here?'

'You've just missed him actually. He's had to go out.'

So the sourpuss she'd passed had been Tim. How strange. Maybe he was annoyed to have a visitor on a weeknight. Jasminder said, 'I hope I'm not disrupting your evening.'

'Not at all,' said Peggy. 'Let's have some coffee – or would you rather have a glass of wine, or some herb tea? We always have a huge assortment of weird teas. Tim doesn't approve of caffeine in any form. Thinks it destroys the brain cells.'

'He may be right, but I can't do without it – so coffee for me, please,' said Jasminder. 'Though when you've seen this form, you may think we also need some alcoholic support.'

Peggy grinned. She knew the form. She'd filled in one herself not very many years ago when she joined MI6, before transferring to MI5 to work with Liz.

'Don't worry. I'm sure we can crack it, between us. And there's a bottle of wine waiting over there in case we need help.'

They sat in the kitchen until the coffee was ready, then Jasminder took a large brown envelope from her bag and spread the contents on the dining-room table.

'I feel a bit pathetic asking for your help,' she admitted. 'It's not as if I'm seventeen and applying to university. I have filled out plenty of forms before. But it's just these seem so different – and they want to know so much. One of the problems is that I don't really know if I actually want the job, and whether I want to tell them all this stuff about myself.'

'Well, let's have a look at it. I'm sure when we break it down it won't seem so bad. Let's start with this part,' Peggy said briskly, pulling out the personal particulars page. 'Were you born in the UK?' Jasminder nodded. 'Parents born here? No? Well, you'll need to explain when and why they came here.'

After Jasminder had told her all about Uganda and Idi Amin, Peggy began to realise that this wasn't going to be as straightforward as she'd thought. 'Let's just explain it in a few words in that box there, and if they want any more they can ask you about it when they come to interview you for the vetting.'

'They want to know all about my relatives next,' said Jasminder. 'My brothers will slaughter me if some man in a pinstripe suit comes to the shop to quiz them about their political views.'

'I don't suppose they will.' Peggy wasn't at all sure if they would or not. 'I expect they'll just look them up in some database somewhere. And provided they're not terrorists or organised criminals, I don't suppose they'll take it any further. What's next?'

It was a question about close personal relationships. Was she married? No. Was she in a relationship? Jasminder hesitated. 'I'm not sure what to put here,' she said, flushing slightly. 'I would have said no, but you remember I told you that I was mugged and how a man drove the muggers off?' Peggy nodded. 'Well, I've seen him occasionally since then and the other night, well, he stayed over.'

'Is he going to go on staying?' asked Peggy. 'Because it seems to be asking about co-habitation and if you've only seen him two or three times, and he's only stayed once, I don't think it counts. Not unless he's moving in.'

'Oh, no. I don't see that happening. He's married and waiting for his divorce to be finalised and he has to be pretty careful. Apparently she's after his money.'

'Well, I don't think he qualifies for the form then. If they ask, when they come to interview you, you could explain it but I don't think he's relevant. Not as things are.'

'That's good. I don't know all his details anyway and I'd be very embarrassed to ask him. It's enough to put any man off if he thinks he's going to be written down on a form.'

'That's true,' said Peggy. 'I had to notify the MOD about Tim when we took this flat together and he wasn't thrilled about it.'

The next few questions caused Jasminder no problem until they came to bank details. 'What do they want to know about my bank account for and whether I have a mortgage and loans and all this stuff? I don't want to tell them. It's not their business.'

'I think they are trying to protect you,' said Peggy. 'They want to make sure you are not liable to be blackmailed. I suppose they also want to make sure you're not receiving funds from a mysterious foreign source.'

'You mean they want to be sure I'm not a spy?'

'Well, yes. I suppose so,' said Peggy, looking wide-eyed. 'That may well be it.'

Jasminder shook her head. 'How ridiculous,' she said, as she filled in the details. 'As if I'd tell them if I were.'

By the time the forms were finished it was past eleven o'clock and a bottle of Cabernet Sauvignon was almost empty. The final problem had been who Jasminder should choose for her three referees. There was no problem about work and university but who to put for her personal life?

'Could I put you?' she asked Peggy.

'No, I don't think so. I'd have to say that I had only known you a few weeks and I'm sure they wouldn't think that was long enough. Don't you have any friends from school or university?'

'Well, there's Emma whom I still see quite often. We were at Durham together. She's a lawyer but she's quite anti-establishment and if she knew I was applying for a job with the secret state she'd think I'd gone off my head. She might refuse to answer any questions.'

'Why don't you ask her? Tell her you're infiltrating the secret state to make it change its ways and become more accountable.'

'Maybe that's what I think I *am* doing. Otherwise why on earth am I applying for this job?' asked Jasminder, almost to herself, as she tucked the now closely written pages back into the envelope and put it into her bag.

'Look, it's far too late for you to go back on the tube. Why don't you stay? We've got a spare room – it's only a box room but the bed's OK. I don't know where Tim's gone. I would have expected him back by now.'

'I won't stay, thanks. I've got an early start tomorrow. Do you have a local minicab firm we could call?'

And ten minutes later, with a hug and a kiss and many thanks, Jasminder left the flat. As the front door closed downstairs, Peggy yawned. It had been a long day. She put the kettle on and made herself a mug of camomile tea, leaving a mug and the packet of tea bags out for when Tim came home.

But as she discovered several hours later when she woke up briefly and reached out in bed, he did not come back that night.

77

14

S PRING WAS NOW MORE than just a hint. The tour
boats were out on the Thames as Liz walked along the
Embankment. Outside the Houses of Parliament a
gardener was giving the grass its first cut of the year. A
crispness still lingered in the air, but it was clear that winter
had lost the battle.

Liz crossed Parliament Square, then walked along the
edge of St James's Park until she came to the Duke of
York's Steps leading up to Carlton House Terrace. After
climbing them, she turned left on Pall Mall, past the row
of mausoleum-like edifices that housed some of London's
oldest clubs – the Traveller's, the Reform, the RAC, the
Oxford and Cambridge. This was not Liz's territory; she
felt out of place in an area that seemed to be filled with
men who looked like Geoffrey Fane. Though most of these
clubs admitted women now, they were not Liz's kind of
women and to her the place still seemed overwhelmingly
male.

She turned up St James's Street, another masculine
bastion of clubs, bespoke shoe- and hat-makers, and old-
fashioned wine merchants. But the restaurant for which
she was heading, where she had arranged to meet Chief

Constable Pearson, was refreshingly unstuffy, with an enormous front window through which passers-by could see bright modern furniture and walls decorated with abstract murals. As she walked in, it occurred to her that she really knew very little of the man with whom she was about to lunch.

They'd worked together on a terrorism case in Manchester in the immediate aftermath of Martin Seurat's murder, but looking back she realised that the shock of his sudden death had put her on autopilot and her memories of the whole affair were vague. Pearson had been in charge during the operation, and had shown Liz a mix of compassion and tact she had only properly been aware of in retrospect.

He was already sitting at the table. As Liz approached he stood up to greet her with a warm handshake. He was tall – a couple of inches over six foot – and lean, with fair hair worn a little longer than Liz remembered. She had also forgotten how good-looking he was, with regular features and startling green eyes. He was wearing a lightweight grey check suit with a blue silk tie decorated with small hippos. He looked, thought Liz, extremely un-policeman-like.

Pearson said, 'I'm glad you could make time for lunch.'

'It's good to see you. What brings you down to London?'

'It was the Police Chiefs Council meeting yesterday,' he said, 'and I've stayed on for the counter-terrorism sub-committee this morning.'

Liz nodded. 'There's plenty to talk about on that front at the moment,' she said. Chief Constables from all over the UK convened regularly to exchange information and receive briefings from external agencies about new laws, new methods, new threats. In the past, Liz had attended a couple of them.

'So,' said Pearson, 'is work keeping you very busy these days?'

She was grateful for the question. In recent months, so many people thought it appropriate to open a conversation by asking how she was feeling, as if they alone had thought to ask; worst of all was being asked how she was in her 'inner self'. Implicit in these questions was the unspoken query: *Are you any better yet?* As if grief were a disease to recover from.

'Yes, fairly busy,' she acknowledged. 'I've moved back into counter-espionage. It's busier than I expected. I'm sure you've got plenty on yourself.'

He smiled. 'You can say that again. Every time I start to think I've mastered the job, something rears up and bites me hard.'

The waiter came up and they ordered, then chatted casually for a while, leaving work to one side. Pearson was a lot more relaxed than the robust figure she remembered from the operation outside Manchester, and she found she was able to ask him about himself, which was a relief; she was fed up with having to fend off questions about herself. It turned out he liked football and supported Manchester United, all very predictable (Liz tried not to yawn), but also chamber music and the later albums of Pink Floyd, which was not. He spent most weekends when he wasn't on duty walking in the Lake District or helping his brother-in-law, a fisherman who owned a boat in Southport.

'That doesn't sound like much of a break.'

'Oh, it is,' he said. 'I can't get a mobile signal when we're more than a mile offshore. It's the one place no one can get at me.'

Liz laughed. 'I understand completely. Sometimes I wish the mobile phone had never been invented. Yours seems the perfect solution.'

'There's only one problem with it.'

'Oh?'

'I get seasick.' He made a face and Liz laughed. 'I've tried everything – from Dramamine to brandy – but nothing works. Anyway, what do you do when you're not working?'

Liz paused for a minute. In the past few years the answer would have been simple enough – she'd see Martin, sometimes in Paris, sometimes here. She supposed they had done the usual things couples do – go to a gallery, walk through the park, have dinner together at their favourite places. But what they did didn't seem to matter much; it was being together that counted.

She realised Pearson was waiting for an answer and racked her brains, trying to remember what she had done in the years when she'd been on her own. It seemed a millennium ago. She shrugged. 'My mother lives in the country down in Wiltshire; sometimes I go there at the weekend. It's where I grew up.'

Pearson said, 'I sense a "but" coming up.'

'You're right. My father died a long time ago, but now my mother has a nice boyfriend –' she gave a small laugh '– if a seventy-five-year-old man can be called a *boy*friend. It's just that…'

Again she hesitated. 'Three's a crowd?' Pearson suggested.

Liz nodded. 'Exactly. They're very good to me; when they come up to town we often have dinner or see a play, and I know I'm always welcome down there.' She felt almost apologetic for not appreciating this more, but found herself saying exactly what she felt. 'It's just that before, when my mother was on her own, I used to feel I was looking after her. Dutiful daughter et cetera, though since I'm close to her it wasn't a chore. But now I feel sometimes that she and Edward – that's her boyfriend – are looking after *me*.'

'And you don't like that?'

'Not much,' she confessed.

He nodded sympathetically. 'The problem is that the alternative – not seeing them – can get pretty lonely. At least it was for me.'

'Why's that?' Liz asked. There had been no mention of a wife or children in his account of his weekends, which had surprised her – she knew he was in his late forties.

'I was married,' he said, and Liz instinctively guessed: bad divorce, no children, lots of girlfriends. But he said instead, 'My wife died just a few years after we'd got married.'

'I'm so sorry.'

He looked at her with a smile. 'So am I. It was almost twenty years ago – I was just a copper on the beat then, which tells you how young I was. When people learn that my wife died but also *when* she died, they seem to expect me to say, "That's okay – it was a long time ago." It *was* a long time ago, but that doesn't really help. I imagine you're finding that out yourself.'

'Yes. I can almost hear people thinking, Get over it. I would if I could, believe me.'

'It does get better,' said Pearson, his voice brightening a little. 'It's not that you start to forget the person, or don't think about them every day. It's just that other things happen to you, you meet other people, your life gets full of things that have nothing to do with the person you've lost. And that does help.'

They had ordered coffee and now, when the waiter brought their cups, Pearson shifted a little uneasily in his seat. Liz could sense he didn't often talk about himself; but then neither did she. She changed the subject. 'So how did your meetings go?'

He gave a small half-smile to acknowledge her diplomatic shift. 'They were good,' he declared. 'Funnily enough, something came up in one of them that made me think of you. We had a summary that must have come from your people – they weren't precise about the source, but I assume it's your end of things. It was about increased Russian activity here in the UK, just as you said earlier.'

'Yes, that would be right. It's definitely something we're concerned about. The Russians always had a large espionage component here, and it never exactly went away, but after the end of the Cold War we had a decade of decreased activity. Frankly I think we all became slightly complacent; we were so focused on terrorism. Anyway the Russians are back with a vengeance now, and we're having to catch up fast.'

Pearson was listening carefully. He put his coffee cup down when Liz had finished speaking, and looked thoughtful. 'The thing is, ordinarily this wouldn't have much to do with my patch. You know far more about it than I do, but as far as I understand it, most of the Russian espionage going on in this country is focused on London.'

'It depends where their targets are. But it's true that the key centres of British power – in politics and finance in particular – are inevitably in London, along with the Russian Embassy.'

· Pearson said, 'The reason I ask is that about nine months ago we learned of a Russian who had purchased an estate in Altrincham. That's the Millionaires' Row for footballers in the north – David Beckham and Co. Not perhaps the most tasteful set of mansions, but very large and very expensive.'

'What's his name?'

'Patricov. Sergei Patricov.'

'I've heard of him. I thought he lived in Switzerland.'

Pearson seemed impressed. 'He did. And much as I like my neck of the woods, I can understand that people would wonder why he'd want to switch Geneva for Manchester.'

'Do you know why he did?'

'Two reasons – one obvious, one less so. The first is that he'd like to buy Man United. The Glazers own it now, and they've never given any sign they want to sell. But I suppose everybody's got a price, and I think Patricov is hoping they'll like his. He's moved nearby to stir up the fans – it would be crucial to have their support. It's not exactly police business, but we happen to know that he's funding every dissenting fan club that emerges.'

'And the second reason?'

'This is pure speculation.' Pearson looked a little abashed. '*My* speculation, to be honest. We believe that Patricov is actively involved in the anti-Putin movement, and that he's trying to organise dissidents living outside Russia. That makes him an obvious target for the Russian secret service. I think he believes that the North of England is a safer place to be than Switzerland, or the South of England, even if he hadn't got his football club ambitions. London is full of émigrés from Russia; in Altrincham he sticks out like a sore thumb. In some ways, that makes it easier for him to protect himself.'

Liz said, 'Well…yes. That may be true. You could argue that any other Russians showing up would be noticed. Alternatively, you might think as the *only* Russian living there, that makes him an easy target. If security is his reason for moving North, he must really feel threatened. Have you met him?'

'No, I haven't, but I know his head of security. He's British – ex-SAS. I gather Patricov has all the oligarch's usual accoutrements – a helipad in the garden, private jet on call at the airport, bullet-proof windows in his Jaguar XK-E, and of course a blonde wife twenty years his junior.'

Liz laughed. 'What about security?'

'He has security guards galore. But they aren't armed – we've made it clear they can't carry weapons and I don't think they'd dare risk it. What a way to live,' he added, shaking his head.

'If Patricov's careful about who he sees, that will help keep him alive. Litvinenko might still be breathing if he hadn't taken tea with his killers.'

'I know. And I was thinking, it might be useful if I went and had a little chat with Mr Patricov.'

'Good idea. Give him some advice. We don't want another dead Russian on our hands.' It was said jokingly but Liz could see that Pearson was weighing something in his mind. After a short pause he added, 'It would help if I had some back-up when I went to call. He might not pay too much attention to the local policeman. The English equivalent of Inspector Boris Plod from Novgorod.' He paused as the waiter put down the bill in front of him. 'I don't suppose you could send somebody to come with me? Lend a bit of serious weight.'

Liz looked at him, surprised by Pearson's request. In her experience Chief Constables rarely admitted they might need help. She thought for a moment, wondering if she should send Peggy Kinsolving, or perhaps a protective security specialist. Then she thought again. He was asking for someone with seniority. 'I could probably come myself if you think it would help,' she said.

Pearson smiled broadly. 'That would be splendid, if you could spare the time. It wouldn't be for a while; Patricov's away in Switzerland apparently.'

'There's just one condition,' Liz said with mock sternness.

'What is it?' He looked worried.

'That I don't have to go to a football match while I'm there.'

15

J ASMINDER WAS AT HER desk in one corner of her flat's living room, writing an article for the magazine, when the phone rang. She thought it might be Laurenz, who was away in Paris on bank business for a couple of days, but it was her friend Emma.

'Hello, stranger,' said Emma. 'Long time no see. Or hear for that matter.'

'Actually I was about to ring you,' said Jasminder, telling herself she really had intended to tell Emma about putting her name on the job application form. 'How are you?'

'Fine, thanks. Though not as busy you, it seems...'

Jasminder replied cautiously, 'What do you mean?' As she spoke she drew the curtains across the window with one hand; the streetlight outside had just come on and was casting a rather nasty yellow glow into the room.

'I've had two visitors this evening. But they weren't interested in me: they wanted to know all about you,' announced Emma.

'Really?'

'Yes. They were very polite. They showed me identification right away – both were from the MOD. They said they carry out background checks on job applicants who will have access to classified material. Apparently you're one of them. Talk about a dark horse! Honestly, Jasminder, you might have warned me they'd show up.'

'I'm sorry. I should have done, but I never thought it would come to anything. I had an interview with a head-hunter for a job, but they told me not to tell anyone about it. I put you down as a personal referee, and I should have asked you first. I'm very sorry. I hope it wasn't too embarrassing.'

'What kind of a job is it?' Emma asked. 'It must be very important, judging by all the stuff they wanted to know about you.'

'I'm sorry but I can't tell you anything at the moment. It's probably not going to amount to anything anyway.'

But Emma wasn't so easily to put off. 'You're the last person I'd expect to work for some hush-hush part of the Government. What's got into you? I thought you disap-proved of all that spooky stuff.'

Jasminder didn't know how to respond. It was true that on the face of it the job was unlikely to interest her – she was a most improbable candidate for it. She looked across the room at her bookshelves. The books were all about liberty and civil rights, and the abuses of both by govern-ment. There was nothing there to suggest that she might one day end up working for the people she had spent so much of her life criticising. Instead of trying to explain she asked, 'Did they ask you lots of questions?'

'Tons,' said Emma dramatically. 'Where did we meet, how well did I know you – that sort of thing. Then it got more personal.'

'What did they want to know?' asked Jasminder, suddenly feeling invaded.

'I suppose it's standard stuff, but it still caught me by surprise. They wanted to know all about your boyfriends.

Don't worry,' added Emma with a laugh, 'I didn't tell them about Oscar.'

He had been an ill-advised fling during a holiday Jasminder and Emma had taken to the Greek islands. He lived in London, but had turned out on their return to be a clingy drip rather than the exotic character encountered in the Paxos sunshine. On the wall Jasminder could see the small watercolour of Gaios harbour, all pinks and blues, that she'd bought on that very holiday.

'Then they wanted to know if you had debts, or drank to excess. So I said no, of course. Did you take recreational drugs? Any petty theft or shoplifting habits? Any "extreme behaviour"? That's when I was glad they weren't asking about me! Then they wanted to know your views on civil liberties and whether I thought that made you a revolutionary and likely to be disloyal to the state. Honestly, Jas, it was like the Inquisition. I got a bit cross at that point and told them you had always been perfectly open about your views and they were shared by lots of very loyal citizens, including myself. That shut them up.'

Jasminder laughed. Emma said, 'Actually, by the end they almost seemed disappointed by how pure you've been. I wanted to invent some peccadillos for you, but other than stealing my chips in restaurants, I couldn't think of any. Aren't you going to tell me what this is about?'

'I will soon enough. I didn't think they'd want to talk to you. I thought they'd decide I was completely unsuitable.'

'Well, all I can say is that I have my suspicions. I think you've applied for that MI6 job I read about in the *Guardian*. They were advertising for a Director of Communications. I wouldn't have thought it was your scene, but good on you if that's what you want. Maybe you'll be able to make them think a bit more like the rest of us. When will you be allowed to spill the beans?'

'Soon probably; when they tell me I haven't got the job. But I just don't know exactly.' And a few minutes later, after Jasminder had promised to fill her in at the earliest possible opportunity, Emma rang off.

Jasminder got up and went into the kitchen, feeling unsettled. She'd left the radio on, but for once she didn't find the sound of classical music soothing and switched it off in irritation. She hadn't until now faced the possibility that they might actually offer her the job and didn't know what she would do if they did. She was pondering this when the phone rang again. This time it was Laurenz calling from Paris.

'Hello, my sweet,' he said. 'I tried you earlier but your phone was engaged.'

'Yes. I was talking to Emma. You know that job I said I might apply for? Well, I filled in a form and sent it in and now they've been to see her to ask questions about me.'

'That's good. It shows they're taking your application seriously. I hope she said nice things about you. What did they ask?'

'All sorts of personal stuff. They wanted to know about boyfriends.'

'Did she tell them about me?'

'No. I haven't told her about you. I've hardly seen her since we met.'

'So they won't be coming to call on me then?'

'No chance. I didn't put your name on the form. You didn't come into the category of co-habitant.'

'Oh, good, because I'd rather you didn't. What with my wife and all this legal stuff, I don't want to get some sort of record with the authorities.'

'Well, we'd better not start co-habiting then.'

He laughed. 'Not officially, anyway.'

16

THEY EXPECTED A LOT for £9.27 an hour, Kevin Burgess thought as he looked at his watch. When he'd left school it would have seemed like loads of money, but now that he was twenty-five with his own place to pay for, it didn't seem much at all. It was time for his break, all of twenty minutes – he barely had time to swallow his tea. It usually took him five minutes to get up to the hut where he and the gardeners gathered, and then there was a wait for the kettle to boil, the tea to brew and the mugs to be filled. By the time he'd taken a few sips he'd be watching the clock, knowing that his boss, Reilly, the head of security, would be out soon, making sure no one was skiving when they should be back at work. Reilly was ex-Army (some said ex-SAS), and though he certainly seemed to know his stuff, the man had clearly never readjusted to civilian life.

Of course it all sounded very glamorous – Kevin's friends and his girlfriend Linda had oohed and aahed when he'd told them about his new assignment from the agency. There were plenty of mansions in the neighbourhood, occupied by football stars and businessmen, but even by the standards of Altrincham's Golden Triangle, The Gloamings was something special. The job came with its own uniform – today, as always, he wore a blue jacket with *Gloaming Security* printed on the back. His was a bit tight and he was thinking of asking for a new one. Kevin was a big lad – over six foot tall and more than fifteen stone, though he knew that at least a stone or two of this was excess padding.

It was galling to think that with the money that was being spent just on the grounds – there were four full-time gardeners working there – Kevin and Linda could have bought a mini-mansion for themselves. And inside, with its eleven bedrooms, each with its own bathroom, and eight reception rooms, The Gloamings was just as lavishly staffed: there was a housekeeper, two maids to assist her, a cook, two cleaners and a full-time chauffeur.

Not to mention the security staff. Kevin Burgess patrolled the grounds, and there were two others in the team so that the gardens were guarded twenty-four hours a day. Inside there was an office full of CCTV monitors that showed the view from over a dozen cameras, both inside and out. Under Reilly's command, there were three men on duty in the house – one for the front door, the other a roving presence (though not allowed upstairs) and the third to sit and watch the monitors. Add a Russian goon or two – they seemed to change every few weeks – and you'd find Fort Knox less well protected.

Which made it downright weird that the object of all this protection – Sergei Patricov, number fourteen in the *Sunday Times* Rich List – was so rarely there. People said his private jet did a million miles a year, which didn't surprise Kevin. The man certainly travelled in style. One of the gardeners swore Patricov had hired an entire carriage of the train on one occasion when fog meant he couldn't fly to London. And as for cars, the antique-looking barn (built the year before) was full of them – including a Rolls, a Bentley, a Jag, a Mercedes limo, two Range Rovers, and in case anyone felt like slumming it, a four-door Peugeot saloon.

But mostly the cars sat idle, save for the odd expedition by Patricov's lady – Nina. Was she his wife? They called her Mrs Patricov, but she didn't look much like a wife. She was nearly always at the house, though to the likes of Kevin virtually invisible. She spent a lot of her time in the solarium, a sort of conservatory that had been converted into an indoor swimming pool and sun lounge, complete with changing rooms. The staff – including security – were strictly forbidden from intruding on her privacy there.

In fact, though he had been here over two months, Kevin had only seen Nina on a couple of occasions, and then he'd just caught a glimpse of dark sunglasses and blonde hair. By contrast Patricov, despite his many absences, was a big presence when he was at home. He could be found in the orchid house sniffing his exotic flowers, or hitting balls against the backboard of his tennis court, or just sitting on the terrace, drinking a gin and tonic, watching the gardeners weeding the beds and cutting the grass. He was always friendly, happy to say hello to everyone – security guard or important guest – though one of the maids who was going out with a gardener was reported to have said that according to the housekeeper he did have a temper on him.

Everybody was saying that he wanted to buy United, and you could see him in the role – backslapping his favourite players, cheering from the directors' box at Old Trafford, soaking up the attention while showing himself to be a regular bloke. As if! Regular blokes didn't own their own planes and helicopters, or spend more money every week on staff than most people earned in a lifetime.

Still, Kevin thought it would be great if Patricov bought the team. They'd have an owner so rich he could buy all the best talent, and one who not only lived in the same country – unlike the Glazers – but actually nearby.

When Patricov was away, his sidekick was in charge – a Russian called Karpis. He didn't actually live in the house but you wouldn't have known that from the way he popped up at the oddest times. He was a nasty piece of work, thought Kevin; where the boss was outgoing and jolly, Karpis was dour and aloof. He was a tall well-built man who wore dark suits and sometimes a black leather jacket; the effect was oddly menacing. His deep voice fitted the film villain of Kevin's imagination, though his English was excellent and only slightly accented. Even Reilly, despite his tough-guy air, showed Karpis respect, and it was interesting that when Patricov spoke to the Russian he seemed to do so as to an equal rather than a subordinate.

It looked as if it was going to rain soon, so Kevin headed quickly for the shelter of the gardeners' hut. He had just taken a first sip of tea when his intercom went off. Damn! He put down his mug and looked at the little device. It was flashing, showing the number *11* over and over again. He sighed. This meant the small back gate at the far end of the grounds, where a sensor covered the entrance, along with a monitor and entry phone and a CCTV camera secreted in the branches of a beech tree. Lately the sensor had taken to going off unpredictably. The first time Kevin had raced down there, certain he would find an intruder. But after a dozen repetitions he had learned to take his time, knowing he would find the gate – which could be opened only by a numeric keypad – undisturbed, sitting there virtually smirking at him as he confirmed yet again it had not been touched.

Still, he had no choice but to take this seriously. Orders were orders, and it would be his job on the line if he ignored the signal; Reilly had more than once made that clear. So Kevin put down his mug and went outside, where he cursed again; it had started to rain, not hard but steadily. By the time he had made his way to the gate, he could feel the downpour soaking through his clothes.

He came round the slight bend in the walk, ready to re-set the sensor and enter the code on his pager that would tell the security man inside the house – sitting warm and dry in front of a bank of monitors – that it was just another false alarm. But Kevin saw to his surprise that the gate was open. Ajar rather than wide open, but enough to trigger the sensor and set off the alarm that had in turn sent a signal to his pager.

He was still not suspicious; someone had probably failed to close the gate properly. But who would that be? Patricov was away, Nina never ventured anywhere this far from the house, and the iceman Karpis would never pick a chilly, wet day for a stroll outside. That left the gardeners, who were all working in the rose garden today, and security – which meant Kevin and his colleagues on the earlier shifts. Yet they were the one group certain not to open or close the gate, since their job was to stay inside it, making sure no one else came in.

He was puzzled, but not yet alarmed. Then in the mud on the inner side of the gate he saw some odd holes. They looked like the plugs of earth extracted from golf greens to aerate them. He closed the gate and looked at the plug holes again – they went up the path towards the house and he followed them, occasionally losing the trail where the grass was still firmly in place, then finding it again in the odd patch of exposed mud.

As he was getting closer to the house itself, the trail of odd marks suddenly veered off, heading towards the solarium. Now they were easy to follow and took him to the door at one end of the long low structure. Unusually it was open; he had never seen it anything but shut.

Kevin paused, wondering what to do. Entry into the solarium was strictly forbidden; he had never seen even a maid enter the sanctum. But it looked as if this intruder had gone in – why else was the door open? He should probably raise the alarm and call for back-up from the house, but if he paged the security office or rang Reilly on his mobile phone and it turned out no one was there (except for privacy-loving Nina), Kevin would be in deep trouble. On the one occasion he had alerted the house it had been a false alarm and Reilly had exploded, accusing him of panicking and scaring the wits out of everyone for no reason.

So he wouldn't alert anyone, but should he go inside? Kevin wanted to do a proper job. It was what he was paid to do, and what he was good at. What if right now somebody was attacking Nina, or stealing her bag, or vandalising the swimming pool?

He went on into the building, leaving the door open, thinking that would provide some excuse for his actions. He found himself in a little atrium. There was a glass door on one side and he could see the pool through it: about twenty metres long, four lanes wide, with water the colour of aquamarine. There was no sign of Nina. There were a couple of other doors leading from the atrium – changing rooms, one marked with a shadowed silhouette of a man, the other of a woman.

He was about to enter the men's room when he heard noises coming from behind the other door. It sounded like a woman's voice. He hesitated, wondering if he should go in there. What if Nina was being assaulted? What if the intruder was robbing her, or even worse? Kevin unhooked the little cosh from his belt, and felt for the can of Mace he had been given by Reilly on his first day. But then he realised that the woman didn't sound scared and a moment later heard the low bass tones of a man. With a start he recognised the voice – it was Karpis's. Kevin immediately wanted to get out of there. But it couldn't have been Karpis who had come up from the gate. So where was the intruder? Whatever Nina and Karpis were up to wasn't Kevin's business but he couldn't leave without making sure that no one else was here.

And then he heard a different kind of noise, coming from the men's room this time. It was a sort of shuffling and clicking as if someone was walking around in hard-soled shoes. He took a deep breath, tensed, and pushed open the door. He had the Mace out and his cosh in his hand, and the first thing he saw was a holster hanging from a hook next to a black leather jacket. In the holster was a snub-nosed .38, an automatic.

There was another scuffing noise and Kevin swung round. It was then he saw the intruder, a good foot or so below his eye line. It was a young boy, maybe ten years old, and five feet tall at most, wearing jeans and a hooded fleece. On his feet were football boots – they had made the strange plug-like marks. The boy turned to face Kevin, with a look on his face that was at once curious and frightened.

'What are you doing here?' Kevin whispered. He was putting the cosh back in his belt, and feeling very stupid.

'Are you Mr Cough?'

'What?'

'You know… Mr Patrick Cough.'

Patricov. Kevin sighed with relief. 'Come with me,' he said in a whisper, and led the boy out of the room then back through the atrium until they were by the entrance to the building. 'I'm not Mr Patricov,' he told the boy. 'What did you want with him anyway?'

The boy reached inside his fleece and for a moment Kevin tensed again. But it was harmless – just a shirt. A football jersey, in fact, in the colours of Man United: red and white.

The boy said, 'My dad said he was going to buy United. I want him to sign the shirt for me.'

Kevin nodded, but he was mystified. 'How did you get into the grounds?' he asked.

The boy shrugged. 'I came through the gate at the back.'

'But you need a code for that. You know, numbers you punch to get in.'

'I didn't. The gate was open.'

Kevin thought for a moment. He couldn't see any point in reporting this, or worse still taking the boy to the house. Reilly would have a fit; the boy would get in trouble, and Kevin would probably get the sack.

'You'd better come with me,' he said, and the boy's eyes widened. But gradually he relaxed as they walked down past the tennis court and along by the lime trees. He told Kevin that his name was Brian, he supported Man United (surprise, surprise) and his dad had pointed out the house of 'Patrick Cough'. The kid added that his bike was hidden in some bushes down the path and that he lived on an estate less than a mile away.

As soon as Kevin opened the gate, the boy shot off. Kevin watched him disappear into the woods, feeling perplexed. It was bad enough that the kid had got in so easily, though that seemed innocent enough. Karpis's presence in the pool house, however, didn't seem innocent at all – Kevin remembered the clothes in the men's changing room and the sound of talking coming from the women's. And he also remembered the holster and gun, slung on a hook next to the clothes. Did Karpis have a special licence from the Home Office to carry it? Kevin thought it improbable. Possessing a handgun in the UK would get him arrested. What was he so frightened of that he would take the risk?

17

H E HADN'T EXACTLY LIED to Peggy Kinsolving, Miles Brookhaven reflected; he just hadn't told her the whole truth. He had gone to the Middle East, as he'd said he would, though only as far as Dubai International airport. There he'd spent three hours wandering round the terminal looking at bling in the vast array of shops. He could have bought a different watch for every minute of the year without making a dent in the stock on display. Not that he was at all interested in watches. He was using the mirrors and reflective glass counters to try and see if anyone was taking a particular interest in him. It was practically impossible – in the constantly moving crowd of assorted races, dressed in everything from jeans and tee-shirts to khandoura and keffiyeh; from mini-skirts and stilettos to abayas, saris, and burqas – to detect a pattern or to remember a face. But after an hour or so of watching, he'd felt reasonably sure he was on his own.

From Dubai he'd caught a flight on Thai AirAsia, and now he was looking out of the window as the plane began its descent over the unprepossessing approach to the Ukrainian capital of Kiev. The city itself sprawled in all directions, and over the tip of one wing he could see the Dnieper River as it flowed south towards the Caspian Sea.

He had brought with him only a small carry-on bag and after landing went quickly through passport control, where he received a stony look but was asked no questions. Passing through Customs with no delays, he entered the arrivals hall and soon spotted a little moustached man in a shiny grey suit, holding a sign that read *M. Laperriere*. This was Vasyl, sent by Miles's colleagues in the Kiev Station.

Vasyl led the way outside to an open-air car park and indicated his car, an old Impala saloon that was missing a hubcap. Shivering from the cold, Miles got in the back and waited while Vasyl tried unsuccessfully to get the engine to turn over. After several tries he got out and, lifting the bonnet, fiddled around with something. Then he got back in, the engine caught and they set off. Miles wasn't at all taken in by the pantomime with the engine. He recognised classic Agency training. Vasyl was checking for any other cars hanging back and waiting for them to leave.

Miles sat sideways in the back seat keeping an eye out of the back window as Vasyl took the E40 heading east, away from the city. After several miles they turned off at the signpost for Voloshynivka, and proceeded down its one commercial street until they came to a municipal park. It looked badly run-down, with muddy paths that must once have been gravelled. In the playground, the solitary swing had lost a rope and its seat dangled upside down, swaying around wildly in the harsh wind.

Vasyl stopped the car halfway down one side of the park. He pointed ahead with a grunt towards another parked car, a silver Volkswagen Golf. When Miles got out, Vasyl made a sweeping U-turn and parked facing back the way they had come.

Miles walked to the parked Golf and got in the back where he sat at an angle to a tall man, roughly his own age, who was sitting in the driver's seat with the engine running.

'Hello, Mac. Fancy meeting you here.'

'Hi, pal. How's it going? Sorry to fetch you out to this hole but I think it's important.' Mac had a pinched, pock-marked face and a throaty voice that always reminded Miles of a tough-guy detective in a Dashiell Hammett novel. There was nothing Bond-like or smooth about Mac. He continued speaking. 'I'm pretty certain our guy is for real, and he wants to tell his story to someone who knows England.' Mac gave a shiver, and fiddled with the dashboard control to increase the flow of warm air. 'Godawful winters they have here. We watched your arrival and you're clean. Vasyl would have noticed anything on the road.'

Then he handed a bundle over the seat to Miles in the back. It was a man's jacket, of thick grey tweed with soft brown leather buttons. 'It may be a bit big – it's a size forty-six. I couldn't find a forty-four. There's a passport in the inner pocket,' added Mac. 'It's Irish, and you're Sean Flynn.'

'How imaginative. Next time let's use Murphy.'

Mac laughed. 'Hopefully you won't be needing it. There's a wallet, too, with Flynn's international driver's licence. Langley had it made up, so the mugshot's real enough even if the name isn't. There's money as well – about four hundred bucks' worth in the local currency. They're called *hryvnia* – you get a little over twenty to the dollar.'

'What about his money?'

'It's in the usual place.'

Miles nodded. He took off his own jacket, checking first that it still held his wallet and passport, then he emptied his trouser pockets of loose change and his keys and put them into his jacket pocket. He handed this bundle back to Mac, saying, 'Look after it. I don't want to get stuck here.'

Mac replied, 'The garage checked out the car yesterday, and it's good to go. You've got a full tank of gas, oil's fine and the tyres are nearly new. It's a stick, five-gear. It'll be dark soon and there's snow in the east, so take it easy – they don't plough for shit in this country. Mind your speed: the local cops can be a nuisance, though near the front speeding is taken for granted. I've put a map on the passenger seat here and marked the route. It's a straight shot and your stopover's exactly halfway there.' He turned to look at Miles. 'I think that's it, unless you've got some special requests.'

'Flashlight?'

'In the glove pocket.'

'Thermal underwear?'

Mac just laughed.

They both got out of the car. 'Good luck,' said Mac, but it was understood they wouldn't shake hands.

Miles said, 'Let's make it the Caribbean next time.' Then he sat down in the driver's seat of the Golf. He turned the heater up high and watched as Mac got into the back of the Impala and it drove off, heading for the Embassy in Kiev. Miles gave it five minutes, studying the map, which had the route annotated with a marker pen, then set off himself, heading east and south towards the war zone.

He drove for five hours, stopping only to eat some fried eggs at a roadside café just before it got dark. The road wasn't bad, and though it snowed at one point for a little while, the surface had been gritted and the Golf handled well. After the next town he turned on to a side road and followed a winding path, more track than road, until he saw a Cyrillic sign for the farmhouse he was looking for.

There was a closed gate at the front of the property, with a long chain wrapped around its top bar but no padlock; when he had opened it and driven through, he stopped and closed the gate again, putting the chain back as before. He drove another hundred yards until the track ended in a small farmyard, with a house on the far side. He parked as instructed in its adjacent wooden barn, closing the doors carefully when he left so that his car was not visible from outside.

The farmhouse front door had a modern keypad and he punched in the numbers: 07/04/76 – Mac's small homage to America's Independence Day. Inside the ground floor was unfurnished, except for a kitchen with fridge-freezer, table and a pair of pine chairs. Up the bare wooden staircase he found a bedroom in which a small heater was blowing out hot air. Before turning on the light he pulled the thick curtains tightly across the windows. Then he went downstairs again to explore the kitchen. In the fridge he found beer, wine and vodka as well as some ready-made sandwiches wrapped in cling film, and assorted snacks. He was too tired to eat the sandwiches but he poured himself a generous slug of vodka and took the glass and a plastic carton of stuffed olives upstairs to the warm bedroom. 'Cheers, Mac,' he said out loud as he downed the vodka quickly and munched the olives. Then still in his clothes he lay down, huddling under two feather duvets, and fell asleep. He dreamed that he was still in Dubai, looking at watches.

Miles woke early, while it was still pitch black outside, and got up straight away. He stayed just long enough to eat one of the cling-filmed sandwiches and drink a large mug of instant coffee, into which he poured the cream off the top of a glass bottle of milk. He put the other sandwich in his pocket; he had no idea where his next meal was coming from. Then he made the bed and washed and dried his mug, leaving the sparsest evidence that anyone had stayed the night.

He drove through sparkling snow-covered fields into the rising sun, heading further east across the vast rolling steppes. There was little traffic at first, but as the morning progressed people were out and about in the small towns he travelled through. When he stopped for petrol (he'd been told to fill up as and when he could) the attendant was friendly but spoke no English. He mentioned his destination, checking he was on the right road, but the man only shook his head. 'Boom!' he said, almost wearily. 'Boom, boom.'

Soon Miles saw signs of the conflict; a motley mix of army vehicles drove past him, heading away from the fighting. Then he came to a roadblock manned by Ukrainian regulars, who looked at his Irish passport with curiosity then waved him through without asking his business, so he had no need to deploy his cover story that he was a freelance journalist writing human-interest stories about war zones.

His rendezvous with the source was in a second farmhouse within a dozen miles of the fighting and less than twenty from Donetsk, where the Malaysian airliner had come down. This was a grander affair than his previous night's lodging. It was not really a farmhouse at all, more an old-fashioned hunting lodge built out of rough stone, with a roof of handmade mocha-coloured tiles. He banged the heavy iron knocker on the wooden door and waited. He felt the familiar stirring of anxiety that always preceded a meeting with a new source. The door was opened by a short, dumpy middle-aged woman dressed in what appeared to be a homespun woollen dress with an apron tied around her waist. She looked so much like the apple-cheeked farmer's wife from a fairy story that Miles wondered if she could be one of Mac's colleagues got up as a peasant for the occasion. He found the thought rather comforting.

She showed him into a long living room, which was warm from a blazing fire at one end. The woman disappeared and returned a moment later with a tray that held cold meats and two large rolls, as well as a glass of steaming tea. She pointed upstairs and put her folded hands against her cheek to indicate that was where he would be sleeping, then she gave a little bob and left the room. A few minutes later he saw her from the window, walking down a path towards another, smaller building a few hundred yards away. He hoped she was going to report his safe arrival to Mac.

Miles looked around the ground floor and went into the kitchen, which was so spotlessly clean that it was obvious no one had cooked in it for a long time. He searched through the drawers and found a steak knife. It had lost its edge but had a sharp point, so it would do.

When he went upstairs he discovered that the only bed had been made up, presumably by the woman who had just left. Putting his bag down, he took off his jacket and laid it on the bedspread, pushing back both lapels until its inner lining was fully exposed. He found the central seam and carefully inserted the steak knife's point into one of the tiny knots, then twisted until it came loose. He repeated the process until the entire line of thread was visible and he could pull the two sides apart with his fingers. The left half of the lining flapped free and he reached behind it, extracting an envelope that was sealed on the back with tape. Ripping it open, he counted the hundred-dollar bills inside; it was all there. He rolled the bills up and put them in his trouser pocket, then went downstairs and back to the living room.

A man stood by the fireplace. He was holding an automatic pistol. As Miles entered the room, the man turned and pointed the gun at his head.

18

'Y ou must be Mischa,' said Miles Brookhaven, standing still in the doorway with his hands held loosely at his sides. It seemed the safest thing to do and he had nothing to defend himself with anyway. If he were wrong about the identity of this man, Miles was probably going to get shot. 'I'm Sean Flynn. My colleagues in Kiev said you had requested a meeting. It sounded urgent, so here I am.'

The man stared at him, then lowered the gun. He was dressed in black-and-olive combat fatigues, and was tall and powerfully built, with a rough beard and dark eyes that seemed too small for his face. He jammed his sidearm into the holster at his waist, leaving the butt sticking out. Miles stepped forward and held his hand out. The man shook it with a hard grasp. Miles noticed that the Russian had been eating the rolls and drinking the tea from the tray the woman had brought. 'I bet that's cold by now,' he said. 'Would you like some more?'

Again the man stared. Then his face broke into a grin. 'I have a better idea,' he said. He went to a knapsack he'd put down on a chair. Retrieving a bottle of vodka from it, he said, 'You got glasses?'

Brookhaven laughed. 'Sure to be some in the kitchen. Wait a second.'

Thank goodness Mischa spoke decent English – with about twelve words of Russian to his credit, Miles had been worried about how he would communicate with the informant. His request for a translator had been turned down – sending one man close to the war zone was danger-ous enough without doubling the risk, and in any case, they'd said, it was not necessary.

In the kitchen as he searched for glasses he wondered what Mischa had to tell him that could be so important. He had been told that the Russian had been an accidental find, a 'walk in', who'd approached the Agency via an American journalist who was one of the first to get to the site of the Malaysian aeroplane crash. Mischa had been there 'advising', or more accurately directing the Ukrainian rebels who were guarding the site and disguising what had happened. Miles's colleagues in Kiev had picked him up and had been meeting him since then in conditions of the utmost secrecy, and at high risk to Mischa himself. He was an officer in a special unit who'd been sent undercover with some of his men to train the rebels. His information about the extent of Russian involvement and the type of advanced weaponry they had supplied to the rebels was proving unerringly accurate, and crucial to the West's understand-ing of the situation. His motivation hadn't been explained to Miles, though money obviously played a large part in it, but the Kiev Station was apparently satisfied that he was genuine and clearly knew a lot more about him than they had thought necessary to tell Miles.

He returned to the living room with a couple of glasses, to find Mischa staring gloomily out of the window. He nodded as Miles lifted the vodka bottle, then watched as the American poured out two hefty shots of the liquor. '*Skål*,' said Miles, lifting his glass and trying to lighten the mood.

Mischa smiled wryly. 'Cheers,' he said. He drained his glass in one go.

Miles followed suit, and almost choked as the fiery liquid went down his throat. He managed to say, 'You speak excellent English.'

'I was a postgraduate at Birmingham University – in computer sciences.'

'And then the army?' It seemed an improbable switch, but had to be voluntary. Mischa was a good ten years past draft age.

The Russian looked at him with amusement. 'You are wondering how an educated man can end up like this?' He pointed to his fatigues. 'I am a technical specialist in advanced weapons,' he said. 'Not one of the ranks.'

Miles nodded as he refilled their glasses, and they both sat down in the armchairs by the fireplace. The Russian said shortly, 'I asked them to send me a British expert and they have sent me another American. I have not much time. I need to get back before dark or questions will be asked. So are you a British expert? Can you get information to them quickly and secretly?'

'Yes,' Miles replied. 'I live in London and I am the Agency's chief liaison with the British agencies. I can get your information directly to them as soon as I get back.'

'Good,' said Mischa. He put his glass down on the side table next to his chair. 'I hope you are aware of the conditions I set.'

'I am.' Miles stood up and took the roll of bills from his pocket. He handed it over to the Russian, who had remained sitting. 'It's dollars, as you requested. I think you'll find it's all there.'

The Russian riffled the bills with his hands, and seemed satisfied. Then he said warily, 'You do understand this is a down payment. I will expect the rest in due course.'

'Provided your information proves correct,' Miles felt obliged to add. The sum agreed was $10,000 – and he had just handed over half of it. The amount was less important than the principle of part-payment – it was believed that paid sources should always be left hanging slightly, to incentivise the further flow of information.

'It will,' Mischa said sharply. 'If you listen carefully, there will be no chance of any disagreement.'

I'll be the judge of that, Miles thought. Yet soon he found himself gripped by the story the Russian told him.

Very briefly Mischa sketched the origins of his over- tures to Western intelligence, seeming to assume that Miles would be familiar with this part of the story. He'd been sickened by the atrocities he'd witnessed in Ukraine, committed by the fighters he was supposed to help. After they'd shot down the Malaysian airliner, firing a missile system they were not trained to use, he was made respon- sible for helping disguise what had happened in an attempt to shift the blame on to the Ukrainian government forces, and now his conscience could bear it no longer. When he came across the American journalist on the site, he decided to try to use him to get in touch with American intelli- gence. It was an enormous risk; the journalist could have publicised his story, or he might not have made the contact on Mischa's behalf, or Mischa himself might have been ordered back home to Russia. But the contact was made and since then he had been crossing the lines at great risk to himself to pass information.

But it was not simply the downing of the passenger plane, or the fact that his own Russian colleagues had urged the Ukrainian rebels on to ever-more brutal tactics, that had persuaded Mischa to consort with the enemy; it was also a growing conviction that Russia was reverting to the despotic totalitarianism his generation thought had been overthrown forever. Democracy had not come to his country, despite the promise of those first post-Cold War days, and Mischa was becoming more and more convinced that it never would.

Miles had heard this sort of talk before from informers from Russia and it was credible as far as it went, but the fact that it was almost always accompanied by requests for large sums of money rather took the shine off the idealism.

Having got his justification off his chest, Mischa turned to the story Miles had travelled all this way to hear. It had come through his elder brother Sasha, who was a middle-ranking officer in the FSB in Moscow. Sasha, unlike his younger brother, was not an idealist. Rather, he, like many of his colleagues in the FSB, was a cynic – cynical about the way the country was governed, cynical about the way the FSB behaved and the things he was required to do. And, like many cynics, Sasha – when suitably fuelled by late-night vodka during Mischa's visits from the front – liked to talk.

On Mischa's last visit home Sasha had started describing how the FSB had worked to prepare the ground for the Russian takeover of the Crimea. How they had covertly influenced the Russian-speaking population, stirring up and spreading dissension and separatism until the annexation became the desired outcome for the majority of people. Now they were doing the same in East Ukraine.

Sasha had said that he was working in the department responsible for that type of covert action, but not in Ukraine – in Western Europe. There were two types of target in the West. The first, said Mischa, was Russians themselves, émigrés who were thought to pose a threat to the homeland.

Miles was growing slightly impatient. 'That's nothing new. We've seen it already, with Litvinenko.'

Mischa shook his head. 'Litvinenko was ex-KGB. He was betraying his former colleagues. His murder was vengeance rather than the removal of a threat. I'm talking about something different. Since all the activity here,' and he waved an arm towards the window, 'Putin's position is increasingly unstable. Sanctions are having an effect, and the people most affected by them are those who have got rich by corruption. Those who have been his supporters. They can't move their money around as they could, and their stakes in oil and gas are worth half what they were. Until now, they needed Putin, but not any more. Putin is terrified they will fund a coup against him, and he may be right.'

The result, according to Mischa, was that the FSB were initiating a new campaign to undermine and destabilise the leading opponents of Putin living abroad. Action of various kinds would be mounted to destroy their position; it might be by damaging them financially or by destroying their reputation by scandal of some sort or even assassination. It would take place wherever they were living – in Switzerland, Hong Kong, the United States, but particularly Britain. The methods would vary, but all these plots would be organised and initiated by FSB agents working undercover.

'Do you have any details of these plots?' asked Miles. The news was concerning, but in the absence of specifics there wasn't much the Western authorities could do: increase security, issue warnings, threaten further sanctions if Russian state involvement could be proved. ·

'Not yet,' said Mischa. 'I will need to speak to my brother again but that's not possible until I go home.'

Miles nodded, but he was disappointed. Was it just for this nebulous warning that he'd come all the way to the eastern edge of Ukraine? His colleagues in Kiev had been taken in by this man, who now seemed to have nothing worthwhile to impart.

Mischa said, 'I will of course do my best to find out more, but I hope this is of value.' When Miles said nothing the Russian seemed to sense his disappointment, for he added quickly, 'There is something else I also learned from my brother.'

'Yes?' Miles's voice was flat. This was when agents liked to lie. Seeing their handlers unimpressed, they began to invent.

'You know the term "Illegals"?'

'I do.'

'Then you will know the Russian security service's interest in using them.'

He did, very well. All intelligence services put agents into target countries with false identities – using third-country nationalities. The KGB had had particular success with this technique during the Cold War – famously with the Portland spy ring, run by a KGB officer under cover as a Canadian businessman.

Mischa continued, 'My brother is involved in this area.'

'Oh.' Miles was careful to sound neutral.

'Yes. But the programme has changed.'

'In what way?'

'In the past they were used for collecting intelligence. Now they are part of the destabilisation programme. The programme is in two parts. As I said, the first is to destabilise the opponents of Putin; the second is to destabilise the target countries themselves by undermining leading politicians, encouraging separatist parties, reinforcing minor parties to create unstable coalitions, giving covert support to religious extremism or whatever will be effective in the different countries. It is an ambitious and long-term programme.'

'Do you know if any of these Illegals are in place? And where?' asked Miles, desperately trying to get something concrete to make this trip worthwhile.

'Very few are in place yet. It takes time to build up the cover and to train them. Sasha told me that one is in America, but he is no use to them as he is ill – lymphoma is the term, yes?' When Miles nodded, he said, 'There are two in France, living as a married couple, and there is another at work in England. Sasha is proud because that is the country he works on and that case is turning out to be the most satisfactory.'

'Why?' asked Miles, suddenly leaning forward in his chair, then as suddenly relaxing as he told himself not to show such obvious interest. 'Has this Illegal managed to achieve something?'

'Not yet, I think. But Sasha said that he is well on the way to a major destabilisation. Sasha's bosses are very pleased with him.'

'Do you know what nationality he has or what his target area is?'

'No. All I know is that he is a man and at the time when I was talking to Sasha his success was quite recent.'

'And you say this is different from the oligarch programme.'

'Yes – but both are part of the larger destabilisation programme.' Suddenly Mischa looked at his watch. 'I must go. It will be dark in an hour or so. I hope I have been able to help.'

And with a quick handshake he was gone. Watching him from the window, cycling off down the track to the road, Miles didn't know whether he had been told something of great importance or a fairy story. If it was true, it was alarming. The Russians would not be mounting Illegal operations, with all the preparation, back-up and risk they involved, unless they had some very serious intent, and whatever that was it was not benign.

19

JASMINDER EMERGED FROM GREEN Park Underground
station into a bright, warm spring day. She was early so she
decided to walk to the interview even though, unusually for
her, she was wearing a smart suit with a rather tight skirt, and
shoes with heels. Carlton Gardens, the letter had said, and
she'd had to look it up on Google Maps. Pall Mall, she knew,
was lined with grand clubs but she had never even noticed the
anonymous street running between it and The Mall, leading
to Buckingham Palace. This was not a part of London she
frequented.

When she had woken up that morning she had almost
decided not to go to the interview. She would ring and
tell them she had changed her mind, she thought. The job
was not for her and she couldn't understand how she had
got herself into the position of applying for it and then
agreeing to attend an interview. But after a cup of coffee
and a bowl of porridge curiosity had begun to get the
better of caution. She still wasn't entirely sure which
agency she was involved with, though the advertisement
in the *Guardian* had made it fairly obvious it was MI6,
and she found it totally bizarre that they should even be
considering her.

The rather severe grey-haired lady in a raincoat who had called at the flat one evening to do what she described as Jasminder's 'security interview' had not been at all forthcoming. 'It's an agency of Government,' she had said. 'If you are called for interview, you will learn more about the post then.'

As Jasminder headed away from Piccadilly and down Queen's Walk she saw a few people sitting in deckchairs in St James's Park, chatting and enjoying the first real sun of the year. She was jealous; the nearer she got to her assignation at Carlton Gardens, the more anxious she felt. What's the matter with you? she asked herself. You don't want this job so why are you worrying about it? But she knew the answer. She wasn't used to failing and she didn't want to fail at this. Even though she was mentally reserving the right to turn them down, she didn't want them to reject her. She walked on, along The Mall and up the Duke of York's Steps, where she turned left along the line of grand, anonymous buildings until at the end of the road she saw the number she was looking for, and the front door of the house.

The bell was answered by a middle-aged woman in a dark jacket and skirt, which looked like some sort of uniform. To Jasminder she appeared to be a carbon copy of the security-interview woman who had come to her flat, except that rather unexpectedly this one smiled warmly and invited her to sit down in a kind of waiting room, furnished with brown furniture and chairs with leather seats and button backs. The windows were obscured by heavy net curtains, making the whole room dark and gloomy after the bright sunshine outside. Jasminder's spirits sank further; now she definitely wished she hadn't come.

'Help yourself to coffee,' said the smiley woman, waving at a thermos jug on a table. But Jasminder didn't feel like coffee; she sat down uneasily on one of the leather chairs.

She didn't have to wait long. After no more than three or four minutes, the door opened and Catherine, the woman who had been with the head-hunter when Jasminder had first discussed the job, stood in the doorway. 'Good morning, Jasminder. They're ready for you now.'

The room they went into was very different from the waiting room. Jasminder's first impression was that she had walked into the drawing room of a small stately home. Facing the door, set in a curved wall at the end, tall windows looked out over The Mall to St James's Park. A blind was partly drawn down over one window where the sun was trying to glance in. To her left, as Jasminder followed Catherine into the room, chintz-covered armchairs were arranged round a marble fireplace, but in front of them were three men in dark suits, sitting in upright chairs on the far side of a polished mahogany table. Catherine indicated an empty chair facing them and sat down herself on a chair next to it.

'Good morning, Miss Kapoor,' said the man in the centre of the group. 'It's good of you to come and see us.' He was thin-faced with a prominent nose. Even in her own nervous state, Jasminder could see that he looked anxious.

'I'm Henry Pennington of the Foreign and Common-wealth Office,' he continued, 'and chairman of this selection board. Before we proceed further I should say, as I'm sure you are aware, that this post involves a high level of security clearance. We are not asking you to sign the Official Secrets Act at this stage as you may not be selected for the post. However, I must ask you to observe confidentiality about anything you may learn as a result of this interview. Do you agree to those terms?' As he spoke, he was gently rubbing his hands together in a washing motion. The dry sandpapery sound was very audible in the quiet room.

'Well, yes,' replied Jasminder cautiously. 'But what does that mean? That I can't tell anyone I have been to this interview?'

Henry Pennington looked even more anxious and uncomfortable and his hand-washing intensified. There was a short silence then the man sitting to his left said, 'No. Of course not. It means that if we reveal any of the nation's secrets, you must keep them to yourself. If we do that, we'll warn you.' He smiled reassuringly at her and said, 'Back to you, Henry.'

Pennington cleared his throat. 'Before I introduce my colleagues on the board,' he said, frowning, 'I should tell you that we are interviewing a shortlist of people both from inside and outside the public service for the new post of Director of Communications in the Secret Intelligence Service. You have seen the outline description of the post and Sir Peter – ' he nodded to his left ' – will tell you some more about how he sees it. But let me introduce the members of the selection board. This,' indicating the man who had spoken to her, 'is Sir Peter Treadwell, Chief of the Secret Intelligence Service. He is referred to as C.'

'That's MI6,' said Sir Peter cheerfully. 'Good morning, Miss Kapoor.'

'And this,' went on Pennington, indicating the man on his right, 'is Mr Fane, also of the Secret Intelligence Service. Miss Catherine Palmer you have already met, I think.'

Jasminder nodded in response to the introductions and waited. She could feel the tension in the room and had an almost irresistible urge to laugh. This was clearly going to be like no other selection board she'd ever attended.

'I will ask C to start by telling you some more about the post, which will be on his staff.' Pennington leaned back in his chair, clearly relieved to be passing the baton.

'Thank you, Henry.' Sir Peter sat forward and smiled at her. 'You must be wondering why you are being interviewed for a post in SIS, Miss Kapoor. Well, I envisage the role as serving as the day-to-day interface between SIS and the public and media. That's why we are describing it as Director of Communications.

'From time to time I make public speeches with input from various parts of the Service; the Director of Communications will be responsible for pulling this material together and drafting what I say. But more important, and arguably more influential, will be contact with the media and through them the public. I want that to be a lot more open than it has been in the past and I want it to be done by a person who is not seen as a faceless spook or anonymous propagandist. I'd like someone already known outside the covert intelligence world, someone seen as open-minded and honest. They need as well to grasp the complex balance that has to be struck today between civil liberties and security.'

He paused briefly, then said, 'I should add that not everyone in the Government, the Foreign Office or SIS itself agrees with me that this should be the way we do it.' A little snort, just audible, came from the direction of the man called Fane.

Jasminder said, 'Thank you for the explanation. It does sound an interesting position but I don't understand why you think I might be suitable. I feel sure that you and I would differ very much on the balance you talk about – and where the line should be drawn. I think both of us might be accused of hypocrisy if I were to join you. People would say I'd sold out to the establishment, and that you were just trying to curry favour with your critics.'

'Thank you for being so frank, but that's not how I see it.' Sir Peter was no longer smiling; his elbows were on the table and his expression was intense. 'I know your reputation is for supporting civil liberties of all kinds against what you see as incursion by the state. You're also concerned that, using the excuse of terrorist threats, governments will intrude unnecessarily on private lives.' Jasminder was about to reply, but he went on: 'Believe it or not, so am I. But what impresses me about your position is that you also acknowledge there is a real threat from extremism, and that the Government does have a duty to protect its citizens – even if that involves some surrender of civil liberties. Have I got that right?'

Jasminder nodded and began to relax a little. The chairman, Pennington, had made her want to laugh with his mix of pomposity and nerves, but she liked Sir Peter, who seemed straightforward. As they continued their discussion, she sensed she might enjoy working with (and for) this man, and could feel a growing fascination at the prospect of being involved in this mysterious world.

It was only when it was the turn of the third member of the panel, Mr Fane, to ask the questions that she again began to feel that she was in the wrong place. This languid-seeming gentleman in pinstripes, lounging comfortably in his chair in this elegant room, was exactly what she'd been expecting from the interview and just the sort of person guaranteed to make her feel uncomfortable. His questions took a completely different line from Sir Peter's and were aggressively posed. How could she possibly move from the untrammelled freedoms of academe to the restrictions of a closely controlled environment? Was she used to knowing secrets? More important, was she good at *keeping* them? Did she realise how intrusive the media could be? Could she work with colleagues who didn't share her political views? Could she get along with people who thought her naïve, and despised her brand of liberalism?

As each question was posed, with elaborate old-school courtesy, Jasminder felt her temper rising, but she managed to control herself and reply politely, if increasingly curtly, until he prefaced a question with 'My dear Miss Kapoor', when she finally snapped. 'I'm not your "dear", Mr Fane. And if that's how you address women you barely know, then I hope you're not typical of the men in MI6. If you are, I would feel quite uncomfortable about being closely associated with them, let alone representing them to the public.'

There was a short silence. Fane looked slightly stunned, and then Sir Peter intervened. 'Thank you, Geoffrey,' he said firmly. To Jasminder he said, 'As I mentioned, there are different views in the Service about how our interface with the public should be managed, and you have just heard one of them from Geoffrey. However, you have also heard the route I intend to pursue and I hope you think it's the right one.'

Geoffrey Fane said nothing. He leaned back in his chair, long legs stretched out in front of him, a look of supercilious distaste on his face. Henry Pennington suddenly roused himself as though he had just remembered that he was the chairman of the selection board. Looking (and sounding) more anxious than ever, he turned to Sir Peter.

'Have you any more questions for Miss Kapoor, C?'

'No further questions, thank you. Is there anything more you would like to ask us, Miss Kapoor?'

Jasminder, who had been more shaken by Geoffrey Fane's attitude than she was prepared to show, asked whether there was a great deal of opposition within the Service to the creation of the post. 'I would not wish to find myself caught between a hostile media and hostile colleagues, attacked from both front and rear as it were.'

'I can assure you, Miss Kapoor,' replied Sir Peter, 'that I attach a great deal of importance to the creation and success of this post. There will be no attacks from the rear, as you put it. I will be responsible for ensuring that.'

Jasminder nodded. 'Thank you. That's my only question.'

After this, Henry Pennington wound up the interview and Catherine stood up and escorted Jasminder out of the room to the front door.

'Don't be put off by Geoffrey Fane,' she said. 'He's a traditionalist and suspicious of any change. But he's not a bad old stick really, and he's very good at his job. If something new seems to be working, he'll get behind it. And anyway it's Sir Peter who will be calling the shots, as you saw for yourself. Do ring me if you have any queries, and I hope we meet again.' With that, she shut the door, leaving Jasminder to walk back down Carlton Gardens, her head in a whirl.

20

'YOU READY?' IT WAS Peggy, knocking on Liz's open
door and walking into her office.

'Ready for what?' asked Liz, looking up from what she
was reading. 'Oh, yes, of course. I forgot Miles brought the
meeting forward. I was thinking he was coming this
afternoon.'

'Reception's just rung to say he's in the waiting room.
Shall I go and get him?'

'Perhaps I'd better go down. It seems only polite, as I
haven't seen him for a few years.'

'I thought you didn't want to encourage him?' said Peggy
with a grin.

'I don't. But we've both grown up a bit since those days
and he is the senior Agency man here now. Have you
booked a meeting room? It's a bit of a squash in here.'

On first catching sight of Miles Brookhaven through
the glass door of the waiting room, Liz was quite surprised
by the change in the man. When she'd first encountered
him – it was at a meeting in Whitehall when he was the
junior officer at the CIA London Station – he had been
like a large puppy. An Ivy League puppy, she thought with
a private smile. He'd sported light-coloured suits and

striped ties and she remembered an absurdly new-looking Burberry raincoat that he always wore, whether it was raining or not. In those days he had admired everything English. She wondered if time and experience had changed that.

As she walked into the room he leaped to his feet. He still towered above Liz, though he seemed thinner than she remembered and his face had lost its boyish openness. He was wearing a well-cut dark grey flannel suit and a plain tie, and looked distinguished and serious.

'It's wonderful to see you again, Liz,' he said, shaking her hand.

'You too. You look fit.'

'Never fitter,' he said, and smiled at her; Liz knew that his return to work had involved a long climb back to health.

They took the lift upstairs, standing for a moment side by side in silence. Then Miles said, 'I heard about your friend, Liz. I just wanted to say how very sorry I am.'

'Thanks, Miles,' she said, feeling relieved when the lift doors opened. She didn't want to talk to him about Martin and risk showing her feelings. As they walked down the corridor, she changed the subject by mentioning that Peggy would be joining them.

'Good,' said Miles emphatically. 'I was very impressed with her when I met her the other day.'

They settled around the table in a small meeting room where Peggy was waiting. A window looked east down the Thames, giving a fine view of the flurry of buildings being erected along the South Bank. 'How was your trip?' Peggy asked Miles. 'I was expecting a suntan.'

'You were?' he replied, puzzled.

'Yes. But I suppose you didn't spend a lot of time outside.'

Miles continued to look puzzled, then his face cleared. 'Oh, yes. I told you I was going to the Middle East to meet a new source.'

Peggy nodded. 'I've been looking forward to hearing what he had to say. That is, if you can tell us.'

'I certainly can. In fact, that's what I've come to talk to you about. I should first admit that I misled you slightly when I said I was meeting him in the Middle East. In fact I only passed through Dubai on my way to Ukraine.'

'Goodness,' said Peggy. 'I can see why you haven't got a suntan.'

Miles grinned broadly. 'More like frostbite,' he said.

Liz and Peggy listened while he described his journey and the meeting with Mischa. 'He's a source of our Kiev Station's. They don't know his name, though his story seems to check out. The stuff he's been giving them has been very useful, they say.

'Anyway, when he suddenly announced that he had information about activity in Western Europe and the States, they brought me in. I found him pretty impressive.'

Miles went on to relate what Mischa had said about the two-pronged operations in the West. 'Destabilising or killing the anti-Putin oligarchs is no surprise, of course,' he said. 'We've seen it already.'

'Yes,' replied Peggy. 'But if we can get advance information on targets and methods, that will be very helpful. We were completely taken by surprise with Litvinenko. And we still don't know if any of the others who've died over here were murdered.'

'It's the other part of this programme that interests me most,' said Liz. 'The use of Illegals to destabilise societies in the West. Put like that, it's ludicrously ambitious. They were very successful in Ukraine but how on earth could they hope to make any impact here? Ukraine must have gone to their heads.'

'It sounds to me like something from the Cold War,' said Peggy. 'You remember how the KGB tried to infiltrate peace movements, and anti-nuclear movements in Europe, to try to weaken the West's ability to defend itself if the Cold War ever turned hot?'

'Yes. But they had a large British Communist Party to work with in those days and plenty of members who were happy to help them make trouble,' said Liz. 'They poured money into it, but at the end of the day I don't think they got much benefit from it at all.'

'But our two countries never went to war. It might have been very different if we had.'

'True. But what could the Russians do here nowadays that would have any real weakening effect?' Liz looked sceptical.

'Ruin the economy,' suggested Miles. 'Though I imagine they'd try to do that remotely by cyber-attack.'

Liz said, 'Maybe it's nothing as fundamental as that. I think they'd save financial attack until we really were at war.'

'Perhaps,' said Peggy slowly, 'it's just an effort to disturb and confuse. To damage morale and confidence; encourage separatism; try to magnify our problems, in some way, so we don't have the resources or the will to intervene in Ukraine, say, or the Baltic States if Putin decides to go for them – that sort of thing,' she ended uncertainly.

'That's a pretty big programme for one Illegal,' said Liz with a smile.

'Let's just think about that,' said Miles, coming to Peggy's defence. 'Remember, he said that one Illegal was just the start. What are the current troublesome issues? Non-economic, I mean. One is young people being recruited to fundamentalist groups. Then there's the possible break-up of the UK through separatist movements. And the possibility that you might leave the European Community – that might please Russia, as they'd hope it would weaken Europe. And what about the non-renewing of Trident? I'm sure they'd like that. There's quite a lot when you come to think about it.'

'Oh, yes.' Liz was getting into the spirit now. 'And what about the anti-snoopers who nearly knocked me out the other day? I'm not sure they need much encouraging, but they could do our intelligence effort quite a lot of harm if they got the law changed on interception, for example, so GCHQ's powers were restricted. I bet the FSB would love that. But,' she added, coming down to earth, 'this all sounds terribly far-fetched. I can't believe the Russians would spend resources on it.'

'Well, if we are to believe Mischa, they are doing just that. And not only here. He said there were two Illegals already placed in France and another in the US. Langley and the FBI are working on that. But... and this seems to me to add urgency to the situation... he said that in Britain their Illegal has had some recent success. His brother was crowing about it. I took him to mean success in getting access to information or being alongside people with access. Mischa implied they'd got something they wouldn't normally expect to secure so soon.'

There was silence in the room while they all considered the problem. 'So,' said Liz, 'we are looking for a person, could be a man, could be a woman, who has fairly recently appeared in some milieu or other, we don't know what. All we do know is that he or she won't be Russian and they won't be English. That's right, isn't it?' She turned to Miles.

He said, 'Yes, I'd say the one here is almost certainly not English. The country's just too small for him to masquerade as a native very easily.'

Peggy put her head in her hands. 'How are we going to get anywhere with this? I wouldn't know where to begin. It really is looking for a needle in a haystack.'

'I'm sorry to be giving you such a headache,' said Miles with a smile. 'I wish I had more information. But I'm hoping to get something else out of the source before too long. My Kiev colleagues have set up a communication link with him, but they have to be very careful.'

'Let's not forget about their campaign against the oligarchs,' said Liz.

'That may be just as hard to pin down,' Miles acknowledged. 'I'm not sure how much my source's brother has to do with it. The anti-Putin ones will be the ones most at risk, of course, but they don't always make that obvious to outsiders.'

'Mmm,' said Liz. She was thinking of her lunch with Pearson, and his story about the new arrival in Altrincham. 'At least we can track down those who live here and make sure they are aware of the risks.'

'Yes,' said Peggy, 'and I've just remembered what Charlie Simmons said at our meeting. He'd analysed some traffic that reminded him of the pattern that occurred before the Litvinenko murder. It suggests this might all be connected. It could be coincidence, of course, but I wouldn't want to count on that.'

21

A s Jasminder woke up she became aware of noise in the street outside. It was normally fairly quiet in the mornings, with just an occasional car going past, but she could hear raised voices and what sounded like people talking on telephones. She got out of bed and peeped out from behind the curtains to see what was going on.

On the pavement outside her house a group of about twenty people had gathered. Some had cameras, one man was standing on top of a small stepladder, some were holding microphones. Most were clutching cardboard coffee cups from the shop round the corner in Upper Street. She peered at them in astonishment, wondering what it was all about. She wished Laurenz were here with her, but he had gone off for almost a week to see clients.

Then the phone rang and Jasminder flinched. But it was Catherine Palmer calling her.

'Good morning, Jasminder,' she said. 'Sorry to ring you early but I've just been told that there's a lot of media interest in your first day with us.'

'I was wondering why there was a posse of cameramen and reporters outside the house. I've just seen them from the window.'

'Are they there already? It's going to be on the *Today* programme too. There'll be a discussion just after eight o'clock about whether we've done the right thing in appointing you. C is going to take part, arguing against some MP who thinks the heavens have fallen in. It should be worth hearing.'

'I'll catch it on Listen Again when I get to the office. I was thinking of setting off before eight.'

'That's what I was ringing about. I think you should stay put for the moment. We'll send a car for you at about nine. We're going to try and get the media called off on the grounds that they pose a threat to your security. Some of them will have got bored by then anyway as they'll have missed the morning news deadline but I expect others will hang around. Our advice is that you should just walk straight out of the house and into the car. Look pleasant, smile at them and say 'Good morning', but don't answer any questions. We don't want this to be more of a news story than we can help – not until you've got your feet under the desk and can plan how you are going to deal with media attention in future.'

Jasminder moved well away from the window. 'OK. Will the driver call me from the car when he gets here? I wouldn't be surprised if some of the journalists don't ring the bell before long. They'll start getting impatient if nothing happens and I don't want to answer the door to them.'

'Yes, I'll tell him to do that. And we'll have to send a security team round to survey your house now it's become public knowledge where you live.' Catherine's voice was sympathetic. 'I'm sorry about all this, Jasminder. It'll die down before too long.'

'I hope so.' Jasminder sat down heavily on a kitchen chair, near to tears. 'I don't know what my neighbours will think of all this. It's always been a rather quiet street.'

'I'm sorry – it would have been better if it could have stayed like that. But the cat's out of the bag now so we'll have to cope with it.'

As she sat in her kitchen, drinking coffee and listening to C justify her appointment by making a case for greater openness, Jasminder wondered if she had made a dreadful mistake in accepting the job. She had been very happy in her old life, establishing what she knew was a growing reputation. Though she had frequently found her students irritating, she had loved her work at the immigration charity and felt that she was really making a difference to people's lives.

After her clash with Geoffrey Fane she had resolved not to take the MI6 job, even if it were offered to her. But she had been invited in to Vauxhall Cross for further discussions with Peter Treadwell, and had been more and more impressed by him and his clear views on where the Service should be heading. She had also met several of the senior people and had liked them. She had even re-encountered Geoffrey Fane on one of her visits and had found him rather polite in a formal, courteous sort of way – she remembered what Catherine Palmer had said about how good he was at the job and how he would get behind change once it had happened. So when a letter came offering her the job, Jasminder had decided to accept. Now she had to live with the consequences.

22

JASMINDER HAD A GOOD deal of experience of the British media. Not only did she edit a monthly magazine, she'd written articles for the broadsheets, she'd been doorstepped by the *Daily Mail*, she'd done *Start The Week* on Radio 4 as well as joining panels in discussion programmes. She'd even done *Question Time*, the television programme that had made her mother so proud. So she thought she understood the methods and madness of the British press.

What she hadn't experienced before was being at the heart of a media frenzy. She hadn't realised how explosive a story combining a spy agency with a young, attractive, ethnic-minority woman would be, or how long the excitement would last.

It was bad enough finding the same gaggle of photographers and reporters outside her front door on the second morning that she went to work, but many of them were also there when she came home, and some were still around on her third day in the new job. Someone had even tweeted her presence at the local bistro when she'd had supper there with Emma.

Jasminder hated the intrusion. But it got worse when a decision was taken by MI6 (C himself apparently) that her private residence had to be made more secure. Since she had become such a celebrity editors had been warned not to identify her house, but some of the photographs they had published made it pretty clear where she lived.

So Jasminder came home one evening to find a small team of technicians installing new locks on her front and back doors. The carpet was rolled up and wires had been laid for panic buttons. Her front door sported a shiny new video entry system and the lady who lived in the upstairs flat was standing on the stairs complaining about the effect all this was going to have on her. Was she safe? she wanted to know. Were they going to be murdered in their beds? Jasminder's once cosy place no longer felt like home; she was living in Fort Knox.

At MI6 her first week was filled with a relentless series of induction briefings. She understood the need for these, but it was still frustrating not to be able to get on with the work she'd been appointed to do – though even that presented a complication: Jasminder's job was to represent the Service to the world outside, yet the media enquiries pouring into MI6 at the moment were all about her, not the Service.

As she hastily drank a cup of tea during a short snatched break and looked at the stack of phone messages on her desk, she found herself dreading a return to her newly fortified house, and yet another media scrum outside the front door in the morning.

Then Laurenz once again came to the rescue. Since her first night with him she had seen him several times, but then suddenly he'd gone away – seeing clients in Copenhagen. On her way home after the third day at work her mobile rang, she looked at the number and answered it at once. Her voice must have given her mood away for Laurenz said, 'Hi, darling, I'm back.'

'Thank God.'

'You sound terrible. What's the matter?'

She explained, and he said at once: 'The bank owns a flat and I'm using it. Come and stay with me for a few days until the fuss dies down. Don't worry, it will. Nothing lasts for more than five days in the popular press. Get some things and take the tube to Moorgate. Text me when you're at Angel station ready to get on the train and I'll meet you at Moorgate where you come up from the Northern Line.'

So seven-thirty saw her clutching a small overnight bag, on the up escalator at Moorgate station. She waved when she saw Laurenz standing at the top, waiting for her. As they walked along Moorgate he explained that the bank's flat was normally reserved for colleagues visiting from abroad; Laurenz had been loaned it temporarily while his divorce worked its messy way to a conclusion because his own flat was let.

The apartment, in a tall glass-faced block, was small: one reasonable-sized living room with a galley kitchen screened off by a granite counter with bar stools, and one bedroom. It was modern, impersonal and soulless, but also blissfully private. Laurenz said he didn't have a clue who else lived in the building. He rarely saw or heard anyone. The most he noticed was the hum of the lift going up and down. 'I thought we'd eat in,' he announced, handing Jasminder a large glass of Sancerre. 'That way you can stop looking over your shoulder every thirty seconds.'

He cooked garlic prawns and pasta, and they ate at the counter, sitting on the bar stools. When she asked him where he'd learned to cook, he shrugged. 'My mother wasn't often around, and my father thought being in the kitchen was unmanly. I didn't have much choice: if I didn't cook, I didn't eat.'

'This was in Norway?' she asked, eager to learn more about his background.

'Of course,' he said simply. 'But I want to hear all about you. How's the new job going? Have you learned loads of secrets? Tell me everything.'

She smiled. 'No, I haven't learned any secrets yet. I've spent my time learning who does what and where everything is and trying not to get lost in that complicated building. And fending off the media, who all want to interview me about my background and my thoughts on working women and careers and all sorts of other stuff that I'm not going to talk about.'

Laurenz grinned. 'You're the perfect role model. But hang in there! They'll get used to you.' They fell silent until Jasminder asked about his work at the bank.

'I work exclusively with private clients. Wealthy individuals, unsurprisingly. Some of them are quite interesting – especially the ones who've made their money themselves. You don't have to be an intellectual to make a fortune, but you can't be stupid either. And there are some real eccentrics.' Jasminder laughed as he described the software inventor who put gloves on to shake hands; the oil mogul who installed solar panels on his house on the Norwegian island of Jan Mayen, only to discover it received less sunshine than any other place in the world; and the hedge-fund founder who had amassed the world's largest collection of ten-pin bowling balls.

'How bizarre,' she said. 'I'm not sure I've ever met anyone really rich.'

'These are people who have so much money that they can do anything they want, indulge absolutely any interest they have. However weird it seems to the rest of the world, they don't care – they can afford not to. But when it comes to money, they are deadly serious, and they can get very worried. The world seems increasingly unstable to the very rich. For these people globalisation is a two-edged sword: it's easy now to make investments all over the world in countless different ways; it's hard, though, to find places where you feel your money is safe.'

'Is that what you do for them then?'

Laurenz nodded. 'For the most part, yes. There's a lot of hand-holding involved. They often invite me to meals or to stay in their places. They like the pretence that I'm a friend. But the bottom line is that they have hired me to protect their most important interest – which is their assets.'

'It must make for a strange relationship.'

'It does. There's no real friendship in it, in spite of superficial appearances. They expect a high level of fiscal performance, and you don't get any applause for doing well – it just means they keep employing you. But if their cocoa futures dip for six hours, I'll get a phone call right away, no matter what time it is, and it won't be very friendly.'

They had moved to the sofa, and he was pouring Jasminder some coffee now. She asked, 'How can you cover such a range of investments, and in so many places?'

'It's not easy. I travel a lot, as you know, and I talk to people who travel even more than I do. But I'm heavily reliant on data banks. They're not always very good, and the private sector will always lag behind governments in collecting the best information. That's what I envy about your job.'

'What do you mean?'

'Simply that you have access to unparalleled collections of data. Your new employers have the money to buy all the private ones, but they also have their own sources – and the CIA's. And probably the French, German, Spanish and Scandinavian intelligence services' as well if they need them. It's a pity people like me can't have access to them – I mean, to the unclassified parts of course. I bet ninety-nine per cent of the information is perfectly harmless, in terms of security, but it's all completely locked up, and the security services hold the key.'

He paused for a moment, then seemed to think of something. He said, 'If you really want to change the image of the organisation, a first step would be to let people with legitimate purposes have access to some of your research data. Then you wouldn't have Snowden-types stealing millions of documents without any regard for what should be secret and what not. There wouldn't be any point in exposing stuff that was already available.'

Jasminder nodded; it seemed sensible enough, provided that what needed to be secret was kept separate from what didn't. That should be easy enough to do, she thought.

'Sounds a good idea,' she said. 'But I'm very new to all this. It may be more difficult than it sounds. I like knowing more about your work, though. My friend Emma was asking me about what you do and I realised I couldn't actually tell her.'

'Why did she want to know?' The question was sharp.

'She's one of my closest friends, so naturally I told her I was seeing you.' Jasminder felt his eyes fix on her. 'Is there anything wrong with that?'

He smiled suddenly. 'Of course not.'

'Emma's hoping to meet you. I thought we might have dinner one night.'

His smile turned briefly back to a frown, and Jasminder wondered if she'd offended him again. She usually felt so relaxed with Laurenz; she didn't like this sudden feeling of walking on eggshells. Then he smiled again, and she was pleased until she realised how her own mood was becoming dependent on his. I must be really falling for him, she thought, if I'm acting like such an impressionable schoolgirl.

'I'd love to meet Emma,' he said, and Jasminder was about to suggest some dates when she saw his hand was held up, like a traffic policeman stopping a lorry. 'But not just yet. Let me get this wretched divorce out of the way, and then you and I can go public. I can meet your friends, and you can meet mine, and perhaps some of my clients too. That is,' and he said this shyly, endearingly, 'if you'd like to do that?'

'That would be wonderful,' said Jasminder, her doubts melting away.

'But I almost forgot,' he said, getting up from the sofa. 'I bought you a present. To celebrate your new job.'

'Oh,' said Jasminder, surprised and delighted. 'That's really kind of you.'

As she was speaking he got up from the sofa and went to open a drawer in the kitchen. He took out a box.

'Here you are,' he said, handing it to her. 'It's a new phone – the latest iPhone. I hope you like the colour.'

'It's beautiful,' she said, taking the phone out of the box. 'But that's a terribly expensive present.'

'I wanted to be sure you kept in touch. You can keep it on your desk in the office and I'll know I can always get through to you.'

'Oh, dear. I'm afraid that won't work,' she laughed. 'We're not allowed to take private mobiles into the office. We have to keep them at the door and collect them when we leave the building. But you can always leave messages on it and I'll pick them up as soon as I go out.'

He looked disappointed. 'Put it in your pocket. They'll never know.'

'I think they might,' she replied, smiling. 'And you shouldn't be encouraging me to break the rules. You'll get me sacked.'

'Well, okay then. Leave it at the door.' He paused and looked at her, grave-faced. 'I certainly wouldn't want you to get the sack.'

23

THE FOG WAS JUST lifting at Heathrow airport, allowing the early-morning long-distance flights that had been stacked overhead to land, filling the Immigration Hall with weary arrivals. In the Departure Hall Miles Brookhaven, along with thousands of other frustrated travellers, was scanning the departure boards for information about when his flight to Washington was likely to take off.

He hadn't wanted to make this journey. He didn't think it was necessary and, if it hadn't been for Andy Bokus's insistence on a face-to-face meeting, was sure it could all have been sorted out in a video conference. Andy Bokus, Miles's predecessor as CIA Head of Station in London, had left Britain under a bit of a cloud. A gruff, son-of-the-soil sort of man, he had never liked the place. He hated the weather, he didn't like London, and above all he didn't like the Brits, particularly Geoffrey Fane of MI6, who he thought, rightly, patronised him.

Andy was nonetheless rather good at his job, and the London Station had done well under him. Yet after he'd spent years asking for a new posting, Bokus had finally got his wish − though only after he had made a misjudgement and lost a potentially useful counter-terrorism source to Russia. Now, after six months' rest and recuperation leave, he was back in Langley as Head of Counter-Intelligence Operations in Northern Europe, which meant that he was still involved in some of the London Station's activities.

What had triggered Miles's flying visit to Langley was a message that had come in the day before from the Kiev Station. Mischa, the Russian military source Miles had met, had resurfaced. Shortly after that he had left Ukraine but no one knew where he'd gone and nothing had been heard from him. The Kiev Station was under instructions not to try and contact him as he was seen as a potentially valuable long-term source; nothing was to be done that might put him at risk. But a message had come from him. He was in Estonia for a month and wanted to see the 'British expert' again; he had more information. He would provide contact arrangements when a meeting was confirmed, the message had said.

The communication, which Kiev had sent to London and Langley simultaneously, had triggered a rapid response from Bokus. No one was to contact Mischa in Estonia, and Miles was to come to Langley for a meeting. So here he was, hanging around at Heathrow, expecting to spend more time in the air in the next twenty-four hours than he would on the ground – that is, if he ever got off the ground at all.

Heathrow eventually got itself back to something approaching normal and Miles's plane landed at Dulles airport in the early evening, several hours late. He stayed the night at the guest house near the HQ building at Langley and turned up early and grumpy for the eight-thirty meeting. Rather to his surprise he found that it had been moved from Andy Bokus's office to the grander suite of the Director of Counter-Intelligence.

This post was now held by someone Miles had not met, a new man called Sandy Gunderson. His predecessor, the legendary Tyrus Oakes, known as 'The Bird', was a small thoughtful man with outlandishly big ears and an obsessive habit of taking voluminous notes by hand on yellow legal pads, even in the most sensitive meetings. People speculated about what happened to the notes afterwards. Some said it was just a nervous habit and that they were immediately destroyed, others thought that he was saving them up for his memoirs, but only his secretary knew for sure. And she wasn't saying.

Gunderson, Oakes's successor, was too new to have acquired a nickname, and from the look of his office was almost fetishistically tidy – his desk and the table in the windowless conference room attached to it were bare. The walls held only framed photographs of the Agency headquarters, and the chrome-and-leather chairs looked more functional than comfortable. There was not a legal pad in sight or any person except Gunderson's secretary. Miles was early.

'Mr Gunderson will be along in a moment,' she said, placing a plate of pastries and a jug of coffee on the table. 'Help yourself.'

Ten minutes later the meeting that Miles had come so far to attend got under way. Round the table were Andy Bokus, looking slimmer and fitter than when Miles had last seen him, and a tall, square-jawed man in a dark blue suit and gleaming black shoes, who was introduced as Bud McCarthy from the FBI.

At the head of the table sat Gunderson: early fifties, thin-faced, rimless glasses, intense pale blue eyes. Reminds me of photographs of Himmler, thought Miles, who had studied the Second World War at college. But Gunderson began in friendly enough style.

'I've called this meeting to discuss our response to the message from your friend Mischa asking for a meeting in Estonia, Miles. And thank you for coming over at such short notice, and to you too, Bud, for coming across. We have no one here from our Kiev Station, but Miles, you've met their source so maybe you'd begin by reminding us of the background and the intelligence he provided.'

Miles outlined the circumstances of his meeting in Ukraine and reminded them of Mischa's information about Illegals and Russian efforts at subversion and disruption in the West. 'His information came from his brother who is an FSB officer working on the programme,' he added. 'He specifically mentioned the US and France – and Britain, where he said the Illegal was having success. I was described to him as a British expert, so as he's asked to see me again, I assume he has more information about the British operation.'

'Thanks. That's useful background. Now, Andy, you have concerns about a meeting in Estonia, so would you tell us your angle?'

'Yes, I certainly have,' replied Andy Bokus. 'Estonia is a hotbed of Russian activity at the moment. The FSB has a large station there and the GRU too. Our station is covert. We're watching what's going on and keep pretty close tabs on the situation. We're as sure as we can be that they haven't sussed us out. We have some excellent sources and are working ourselves into a position to pre-empt the Russians, if and when they start the sort of disruption operations that have been so successful in Crimea and Eastern Ukraine. Estonia's population is roughly one-third

Russian, and as in Ukraine there's tension building between them and the indigenous people, which the Russians are stirring up.

'I'm fairly sure we've identified your Mischa. He is officially part of a military delegation holding consultative meetings with their Estonian counterparts on cross-border security. But his real mission, we've learned, is to assess what kinds of weaponry and manpower Russia would need if the decision were made to do another Crimea and send in covert forces. We think it's unlikely, because of the NATO umbrella there, but you never know what our friend Vladimir is going to decide to do. Now that we think we've identified Mischa, we've got the Moscow Station working on identifying his brother, the source of your stuff, Miles.'

'OK. Thanks for that, Andy. Miles, I think that explains the background and indicates why Andy is so concerned about a meeting with Mischa in Estonia.'

Before Miles had a chance to reply, Andy Bokus broke in again. 'I sure am,' he said. 'The Station has put in a mighty effort to get where they are and they don't want someone like you – and let's face it, Miles, you are not exactly unknown to the Russians – coming in and blowing it up.'

Gunderson broke in, looking at Miles. 'You would of course do a completely professional job, but I can see his point, Miles. In the little fish bowl of Tallinn, you might well be identified. Even if you kept clear of the Station, you might alert the opposition and conceivably blow Mischa's cover into the bargain.'

Miles was annoyed. He resented Andy's tone and the implication that he was going to go barging in, but he decided to suppress his irritation. He didn't want to get into an undignified slanging match in front of Gunderson and the FBI man, who so far had said nothing. So he replied, as calmly as he could, 'What are you suggesting we do, Andy? I don't feel we can ignore Mischa's request for a meeting. If he has more information about the FSB's operation in Britain then we must try and get it. We can't ignore an Illegal's operation against our main ally. After all, it may well affect our own interests if it is successful. And what about the Illegal in the States?' He turned to the FBI man. 'Bud, what do you feel about it? Would you be happy for us to turn down Mischa's request?'

Bud looked embarrassed – as though interfering in a family squabble. 'We're working hard to find the Illegal they've put in over here. Your source said he was suffering from lymphoma, so we're searching for foreign nationals being treated for the disease. We've narrowed it down a bit – we're not looking in remote rural areas – but the pool of possibles is still pretty large. Obviously we'd value anything more that might help us find him.'

Gunderson said, 'Miles, your report said there was a couple operating in France.'

'That's right.' He looked at Bokus. 'Any news on them?'

Bokus shrugged. 'Maybe, maybe not. We spoke to the DGSI and they got pretty excited. They claim they have their own informant, who said the Russians have planted someone in the National Front Party, close to Marine le Pen. It's not clear if this "someone" could be the same person your friend Mischa is referring to. The French, in their usual way, aren't telling us much.' His irritation was obvious. 'Until we know more, there's no way of saying.' He was looking almost accusingly at Miles, as if he were responsible for the French service's intransigence.

Gunderson cut in now. 'Okay, that's the state of things from our end. What's your take on this, Miles?'

'If Mischa has more information on Britain and wants a meeting right away while he's in Tallinn, I think we should meet him.'

He paused while Bokus made huffing noises.

'But if Andy is uneasy about me going in, and I admit I'm not unknown to the Russians, then perhaps we should send someone else.' Miles paused for a beat. 'One of the Brits maybe.'

Gunderson looked at Bokus, who was turning red in the face. '*MI6?*' he spluttered. 'I'm not having one of Geoffrey Fane's golden boys trampling around Tallinn. They'll be just as well known to the Russians as you are. They'll stand out like a sore thumb.'

'Actually I wasn't thinking of MI6,' responded Miles calmly.

'Who then?' Bokus said sarcastically. 'Scotland Yard? Or is Sherlock Holmes on your books these days?'

'No, MI5. If there's an Illegal working in the UK it's primarily their business. They don't have any presence at all in Tallinn, and there's far less chance of one of their people being detected. I was going to talk to Liz Carlyle. I've worked with her before; she's very good.' This time he looked at Gunderson. For all his bluster, Bokus wasn't going to make the final call on this one.

But he also wasn't going to go down without a fight. Bokus clasped both hands on the table, squeezing them together as if he was trying to crack a nut between them – or perhaps Miles's head. 'Sandy,' he said to Gunderson, 'this is crazy. Carlyle's okay,' he said grudgingly, 'but it's not Five's kind of work. I know the Brits – Geoffrey Fane at Six will take over Mischa as quick as you can whistle. In six months' time Mischa will be sitting in a British safe house, spilling his guts out with fabricated stories, when he and his brother could have stayed in place, working for us. It doesn't make sense.'

'I don't agree.' Miles knew he had a fight on his hands. He didn't know Gunderson well enough to say whether he was a man to cave in to the sheer force of Bokus's bluster. 'There's no danger of losing Mischa as our source. MI5 would see him in Tallinn, get whatever he has to say about the British operation, but that's it – once he's back in Moscow all his dealings would be with us again. But unless you can tell me how we can a) safely meet the guy in Tallinn ourselves, or b) get his information about the British operation without someone meeting him, then I think we've got no option but to ask the Brits to do it. And if it's going to be the Brits, then my firm recommendation is that it should be Liz Carlyle.

'Look, we're not talking about a meet in a hostile country. Estonia's a NATO ally, for God's sake. It gets swarms of tourists from Britain all year round. They arrive on cruise ships and low-cost flights every day. I'm quite sure Liz Carlyle can slip in, do the job and slip out undetected.

'I don't see that we have anything to lose. If we go ahead alone, we could compromise the source, and screw up Andy's operations; equally I think it would be a great mistake simply to refuse to meet him. If we did that we'd lose whatever intelligence he has access to now, and we'd almost certainly lose him as a source in future, not to mention screw up any chance of recruiting his brother.'

'Bud?' asked Gunderson softly. 'Have a view?'

The FBI man thought for a moment, then shook his head. 'Not really. Outside our bailiwick. Just to say we'd welcome anything more this Mischa has to give on the guy with lymphoma. Could save us a lot of trouble. But anything else I said would be pure opinion.' Miles suppressed a smile; Bud obviously dealt in facts and hadn't grasped that what they were asking for *was* his opinion.

'Okay,' said Gunderson, planting his elbows firmly on the table. 'Thanks, everyone, for your advice. There's strength in both sides of the argument but I don't see any possibility of compromise. Miles, you're the only one of us who's actually met Mischa, so it's your judgement I'm going to back on this one. Let's go with the Brits, assuming they're willing to play ball. I just hope this Carlyle woman's as good as you say.'

24

IT WAS SATURDAY MORNING and Peggy had just had another row with Tim. It seemed that nowadays whenever they had a conversation it ended in a row. And sometimes, as had just happened, the entire conversation was a row. What's more, she was seeing less of him these days than when they had lived in separate flats. He was here as a physical presence, but they usually spoke only at meals; the rest of the time he spent closeted in the little room he used as his study, with only his computer for company. Though that seemed enough for Tim.

He had always been a hard worker, studious and immersed in his books to the point of obsession, but lately he seemed consumed by something altogether different – something he didn't want to share with her. Time was, he would tell her about his latest interpretation of some Metaphysical poetry or the interesting discoveries he had made about seventeenth-century London. But now the only discoveries he brought up were accusations – against MI5, which he knew she worked for, against GCHQ and MI6, or in his wilder moments, against 'The Establishment'. As far as Peggy could tell, Tim was working as hard as ever, but not on John Donne.

At first, she had thought it would pass, telling herself that he'd lose this new infatuation with cyberspace and go back to his true love – English literature. But there didn't seem to be any sign of it, and she'd noticed that the manuscript of his book seemed to be stuck on the same page as weeks before – months actually. So what was he doing instead? She knew he was constantly on the internet – he'd exceeded their monthly BT allowance by twenty gigabytes when the last bill came. He must be busy doing something.

In desperation, Peggy decided to find out. She tried not to think of it as snooping, though she knew it was. But she was deeply worried about Tim and, if she was to help him, she had to find out what was going on.

She waited for ten minutes after she'd heard the door bang when he'd marched out after their latest argument then went into the study. She stood with her back to the door and looked around. The usual neat piles of scholarly tomes, reference books and student essays were no longer on the desk. They had been replaced by a mess of press cuttings, computer magazines, political journals, and among all this, a copy of the unauthorised biography of Julian Assange. The laptop lying on top of the muddle was switched on. After hesitating momentarily, Peggy sat down at his desk and picked up the mouse. She knew his password and he knew hers; it was no big thing, they'd always shared everything. She typed it in and the machine sprang into life.

Opening his internet browser, she started by examining his online History; what she found was both bewildering and alarming. A mixed bag of blogs, chat rooms, *samizdat*-like publications – all patently disaffected, all addressing the same topics: the danger posed by the security services in the West. Some of the talk was philosophical and abstract; some of it was about making sure adequate safeguards were in place when Government surveilled its own citizens, and some of it was much more worrying – technical discussions of how to hack into Government sites and divulge classified information. Peggy wasn't sure how much of this was illegal, but to her mind it was entirely wrong.

The more she looked at these sites, the more Peggy realised that there was a whole subterranean world that shared these views. Julian Assange and Edward Snowden were the two most famous public faces of this movement – if you could call such a hodgepodge of hackers, 'libertarians' and anarchists a 'movement' – and the chat room Tim frequented most often, according to his History, was called The Snow Den.

Her bafflement growing, she wondered where on earth this new preoccupation of Tim's had originated. He had never been a political soul, didn't usually play much of a part in dinner-party discussions when controversial topics came up – like immigration or cutting the size of the Welfare State. He was happiest talking about a play he had seen at the National, or the poetry of Philip Larkin, or Hawksmoor churches in the City of London.

Peggy couldn't for the life of her see the catalyst for this transformation in him. He hadn't seemed unhappy before: he'd never complained about his job, he liked to teach, and didn't even grumble when buried in exam papers to mark. His research had been going well, and she remembered how excited he had been when the encouraging letter had come in from OUP.

Something must have happened some time ago, and more recently perhaps, *someone*. But who could that be?

They had a wide circle of friends, who like Peggy and Tim were in their early thirties, and in the early stages of careers. A few had had children; most were waiting until they were established enough, and well off enough, to start families. None, as far as she knew, were remotely interested in this underground world where Tim now seemed to be spending his waking hours.

She opened his Mail and looked at his Inbox. There was very little there. He must have cleared it quite recently. Then she turned to his Sent box – an email to a student who'd been ill, arranging an extra tutorial; a jokey one sent to his cousin, who lived south of the river and collected bad puns. Next she glanced through his Delete folder; it hadn't been emptied for several days. Most of it was spam he'd deleted without opening – insurance offers, retail sites of all kinds, phony bank alerts. But then one caught her eye – it was an email Tim had sent to Marina*382@gmail.com a few days ago. Opening it, she read: *New account all set up and ready to recieve mail. T.*

She sat there, stunned. What did it mean? But she could guess – Tim had set up another email account, one he hadn't told her about. Why did he need that? Unless it was to hide something from her. Like... Marina. Whoever she might be.

25

Liz enjoyed driving. She liked to be alone, listening to the radio and thinking things over without having to talk to anyone. But this journey had been a bit more than she'd bargained for. She'd set off from her mother's house in Wiltshire at eight o'clock in the morning, thinking she'd arrive in Manchester at lunchtime – the AA route finder had told her it would take four hours. But heavy traffic on the M4 and lane closures on the M62, which had her stuck behind a long line of lorries, meant it was three o'clock before she finally reached her hotel.

Manchester was foreign territory to her, brought up as she had been in the South. Recently work had brought her here several times but those had certainly not been relaxed or happy visits; she was hoping for better with this one. She had found a good online deal at a rather trendy hotel in a converted warehouse near the railway station. It seemed to be staffed entirely by beautiful young people in black – PIBs as Peggy Kinsolving called them – and Liz amused herself by watching them floating elegantly about as she waited to check in, behind a man who complained loudly to the receptionist that he hadn't been able to rent a Mercedes from Avis when he'd landed at the airport. This was not a milieu Liz was accustomed to; it certainly didn't match the traditional idea of Manchester, she thought, as a few minutes later she took her electronic room key and ascended in an all-glass lift to her room.

Pearson, who'd said he'd pick her up, laughed when she gave him the name of the hotel. He warned her that the restaurant he'd chosen for dinner had none of the urban chic of her hotel and was in a rather run-down part of town. 'But the food's very good,' he'd promised. 'I've known the chef since he was a schoolboy.' So she left the smart suit and heels that she had been intending to wear in her wardrobe and put on trousers and a blouse and jacket instead. But she kept on the gold strand necklace and earrings that Martin had given her two years before.

Pearson turned up in a jacket and jeans and an open-necked shirt, so she thought she'd got the sartorial tone about right. Instead of the police car with driver she had expected, he was in a BMW estate that had seen better days. As he drove them out of the centre of town conversation was somewhat stilted, but by the time they came to the restaurant in an old industrial part of the city they were chatting away companionably.

'This area will be developed quite soon and all these old factories and cottages will be turned into desirable flats and houses. This is the place to invest your money,' he told her.

'Sadly I haven't got any to invest,' she replied. 'I spent more than I have on my flat in Kentish Town.'

'Nor me,' he replied with a grin. 'Policemen don't get paid enough to become property investors. Never mind. Let's go in and drown our sorrows.'

The restaurant was in an old two-storey factory building that looked as though it could have been a pottery; a bulbous chimney that might once have served as a kiln poked upwards on one side. It seemed to be the only occupied building on the street. As he parked the car and went and held the door for Liz, Pearson explained that the chef was also the owner of the restaurant. 'Mike has a short lease on the building until the restoration of the area starts. But he's hoping to be able to establish a reputation. He has big ambitions and sees himself here as Manchester's Jamie Oliver when it's all become trendy and upmarket. But he's pretty good already, as you'll see.'

It was clear that the staff in the restaurant knew the Chief Constable well. A smiling woman came straight across as they went in and held out her hand. 'Good evening, Mr Pearson,' she said. 'Welcome back.' Pearson introduced Liz and she too received a warm handshake. They were shown to a quiet table in a corner of the room and as soon as they'd sat down the barman came across with a glass of white wine for Liz and a half-pint glass of something for Pearson. More smiles and 'good evenings' and Pearson said to Liz, 'I hope that's all right for you. They've seen I'm driving myself so this will be non-alcoholic. It's not bad actually,' he said, taking a sip.

When the food had been ordered, with advice from Mike in the kitchen relayed by the waitress, they settled down to talk.

Pearson said, 'We're due at Patricov's place tomorrow at ten. I'll pick you up at the hotel at nine-thirty if that's okay.'

'That's fine, thank you. Who will be there, do you think?'

'Patricov obviously, and possibly his wife. Also there's a character called Karpis – he seems to be a kind of sidekick, possibly a secretary or something – who's joined Patricov fairly recently.'

Liz said, 'I checked our files on Patricov last week, but frankly there isn't much there. He made a lot of money during Yeltsin's time. When they were setting up a government computer service, he bought one of the divisions, then made a fortune leasing those services back to the government.'

Pearson said dryly, 'Sounds like a licence to print money.'

'In his case it was. He was one of the early billionaires, and continued to thrive under Putin at first. Then for some reason he left Russia; we don't know why. Since then, he's become a major investor in some high-tech companies, mainly in America.'

Pearson nodded. 'All that fits in with what we know. But I've had one of my staff do a bit of digging – I wanted to know if Patricov might pose any sort of threat to the Putin regime. The chap helping me is doing an Open University degree in politics so he was especially keen on the project.'

'And?'

'Patricov has gone to great efforts to keep away from any dissident movements among Russians living in the West. He makes a point of keeping his distance: now he's moved up here that's probably easier. To all appearances he's like any other international businessman, uninvolved in politics, no ideology; just your average multinational plutocrat, with the private jet, younger wife, and multiple residences.'

Liz said, 'I sense a "but" coming.'

'That's where Jenkins – he's the chap who's helping me – came into his own. It seems that about a year ago there was a meeting in Surrey of a group of exiled Russian oligarchs. Jenkins went through the internet with a fine-tooth comb, finding a reference here, a reference there. And the picture he managed to put together suggested the oligarchs discussed their security – what they should be doing to protect themselves from Putin's henchmen if they came after them. Also – this is the interesting bit – ways in which they could try to destabilise the Russian regime. In particular, they resolved to use their influence to persuade Western governments to keep the pressure up by intensifying sanctions.

'There's a bit of guesswork here but it looks as though they realised they needed to use lobbyists and went on to hire some of the best. In the States they used a private company, founded by a former senator. Very discreet, and very influential. Lobbyists have to be registered, but since the company was privately held, very little was known about its activities, or its clients.'

'Okay...' said Liz uncertainly, not sure where all this was going.

'But then suddenly the ex-senator decided to cash in his chips. He sold his lobbying firm to a larger company – one that was publicly held. At which point all sorts of things had to be declared to the shareholders, which in a private company could be kept secret. Like the names of their clients, including the oligarchs paying for the anti-Putin lobbying.'

'Don't tell me: Patricov's name was on the list of clients.'

'Actually, the name was Nina Todyeva.'

'Who is?'

'*Mrs* Patricov. Todyeva was her maiden name.'

'Golly,' said Liz appreciatively. 'Full marks to your Mr Jenkins.' He sounded in the same league as Peggy Kinsolving, whose expertise at extracting information online was in Liz's experience second to none. She said, 'So much for Patricov's lack of interest in politics.'

'Exactly. If he goes to such lengths to hide it, then he really must be afraid of the Putin regime.'

'What about this man Karpis you mentioned?'

'He worked for one of Patricov's competitors in the Russian IT business. Then he fell out with his boss, and Patricov wooed him to come here. As far as we know, he doesn't have any political affiliations – declared or not. My understanding is he joined Patricov for the money, pure and simple. I doubt he has the faintest idea that his boss is bankrolling an anti-Putin campaign.'

'Do you know all this just from Jenkins's combing the internet?'

Pearson smiled. 'Sometimes you get lucky,' he said. 'Patricov hired a local head of security when he moved here. A man called Reilly, ex-SAS. He also happened to stand in as my driver for three months when my regular man was ill. Reilly's a very solid kind of guy, more than willing to help. And our interests align: we don't want anything to happen to Patricov and neither does he – it's what he's paid for.'

'That's a lucky break.' Liz paused, thinking. Then she said, 'I wonder if Patricov has stuff on Putin that makes him a particular threat.'

Pearson shrugged. 'I don't know. It's possible. Hopefully we'll get a better sense of that tomorrow.'

They both turned down the waiter's offer of dessert, and Liz found herself stifling a yawn. Pearson laughed. 'You've had a long drive today. We'd better skip coffee,' he said. 'I'll run you back to the hotel. But first I must just say thanks to Mike. It was a pretty good meal, I think.'

'It was delicious. I'd like to say thanks too.'

As they were getting up from the table Mike appeared in his chef's hat and striped apron. After much handshaking and the injunction to Liz that she must come again next time she was in Manchester, they managed to escape.

Back in her room at the hotel Liz thought what a pleasant evening it had been. She liked Richard Pearson; she
could relax with him and she'd like to get to know him
better, but it was hard to see how they could ever see much
of each other when they were living two hundred miles
apart.

26

KEVIN BURGESS HAD BEEN keeping his head down since discovering Karpis with his employer's wife in the changing rooms. He hadn't mentioned what he'd seen to his boss, Reilly, nor did he tell him about the trespassing boy in case it led to questions about how the kid had got in and how Kevin had discovered him in the changing rooms as well.

There had been no other incidents since then. As spring began to take hold and the daffodils opened in the garden, the big wooden table and a few chairs were brought out of the gardeners' shed; on fine days the tea break took place outside under a twisted old apple tree, its buds just showing the first signs of bursting open. There were still plenty of days, however, when rain and a solid wind forced everyone back into the shed, and this was one of them. Kevin had found a place by the stove and was standing sipping his tea, his clothes gently steaming in the warmth, when the mobile in his pocket sprang into life.

Reilly was calling from his office in the big house. 'Kevin, I need to see you in my office, straightaway. Where are you now?'

'Just on tea break, Mr Reilly. I'll come now.' Taking a final gulp, Kevin plonked his mug on the table and hurried out into the rain. Reilly's office was at the back of the house and the way in was through the kitchen. Kevin wiped his feet carefully on the mat, nodded through the passage window at the cook, a heavy-set Polish woman who had never been heard to speak a word of English, and went through a pair of swing doors into Reilly's office, a small square room, formerly the butler's pantry. It felt warm and cosy to Kevin, coming in from the damp garden.

Reilly looked up from his scrutiny of the security team's duty rosters. 'Oh, God. I hadn't noticed it was raining. Hang your coat up over there. Bloody spring. The sun was shining when I got here. Have a seat.'

Kevin found Reilly rather daunting. He was always friendly enough and he wasn't a big man, but there was an air of suppressed energy about him – like a spring that might uncoil at any moment. Kevin was envious. He felt sure that Reilly could incapacitate an enemy in seconds, and what's more, probably had, on many occasions.

Reilly said, 'I see you're on your own this morning.'

'That's right, boss.'

'We're expecting a visitation. The Chief Constable, in fact.'

Burgess raised an eyebrow, and Reilly smiled. 'He's not coming to arrest anyone, Kev. It's a courtesy call, but I expect he'll want to check our security set-up while he's here. Someone from the Home Office is coming with him, but you don't have to worry about them.'

'Okay. Is there anything special you want me to do?'

'Not really. But make a recce outside before they arrive, just to be sure everything's in working order. We don't want to look silly because we've got a duff camera or an unlocked gate.'

Kevin nodded. 'Okay, boss. Will do. What time are they coming?'

'About eleven.'

He went first to check the outbuildings, making sure they were locked, then he called into the control room to see that the CCTV cameras dotted around the grounds were all showing a clear picture, and after that walked down to inspect the outer perimeter. He had just rattled the gate in the back wall, glad to find it locked, when he heard someone approaching along the path. It was Karpis, wearing his black leather jacket. He seemed startled to find Kevin there.

Karpis was a tall man, with an aggressive manner. Kevin found him quite intimidating.

'What are you doing?' the Russian demanded now.

'Just checking the gate, sir.'

'You're meant to be guarding the house,' said Karpis suspiciously.

'Yes, sir. But Mr Reilly asked me to check the grounds as well because Mr Patricov has visitors coming.'

'Oh. I haven't been told. What sort of visitors?'

Why didn't he know? Kevin wondered. He said nervously, 'I was told it's the police.'

'Christ,' said Karpis wearily. 'Another local bobby.' He pronounced it 'booby'. 'The last one who came here was a fool.'

Burgess didn't reply to this. He said instead, 'And someone's coming from the Home Office too.'

'What? Why didn't you say so?'

Perplexed, Kevin was going to explain that he had only just learned about it, but Karpis was already striding back towards the house.

Kevin was surprised that Karpis hadn't known of the impending visit. He was in charge of the household even more than Patricov, due to the owner's many absences; it was hard to believe anything of importance could take place without Karpis's approval or knowledge. And if Patricov hadn't told him, then wouldn't Mrs Patricov have done so? Kevin remembered the voices he had heard in the changing room.

He finished checking the perimeter of the grounds, then walked slowly back towards the house. He'd nip into the camera-monitor room for a minute, he decided, and warm his hands, then stand outside conspicuously on the terrace for the duration of the police visit.

He had just passed the tennis courts and was angling towards the kitchen door when he heard the sound of gravel being disturbed on the apron by the garages. Looking up, he saw one of the Mercedes with Karpis at the wheel, speeding towards the front gates. Where the hell is he going? Kevin wondered, surprised he wasn't waiting for the policeman to arrive. Karpis wasn't scared of the police; that much was clear from the dismissive way he'd spoken. So what was the problem? Why would someone from the Home Office send him scurrying off like a scared rat? Kevin shrugged. Maybe the Russian had passport problems.

27

L IZ HAD MET RUSSIAN oligarchs before and been to their houses. She thought she knew what to expect, as she told Richard Pearson as they were driven to Altrincham. A vastly expensive and probably famous painting by an Impressionist hanging above a hideous pink velvet sofa; eighteenth-century French furniture with curly gold arms and legs; heavy brocade curtains with lots of gold braid and tassels; not to mention a kitchen full of gleaming fridges stuffed with caviar bulging from Lalique bowls the size of a Labrador's head, and enough *foie gras* to fill a dustbin bag.

Pearson laughed. 'I think you've had a bad experience. Sergei Patricov is supposed to be quite sophisticated.'

'Let's see,' said Liz. 'I bet I'm right – though I'll admit to a bit of exaggeration.'

But Patricov turned out to be very different. He might have a private jet and a willowy blonde wife (neither was in evidence), but the man himself was dressed like an English country gentleman – a real one, not one off the pages of a lifestyle magazine – in a slightly saggy tweed jacket, Viyella shirt, and polished brown brogues. His living room was tasteful rather than grandiose – the paintings on the wall were good watercolours but not recognisable, the furniture was solid antique brown, and the Persian rugs pleasingly worn.

Patricov did not seem at all surprised by Liz's presence. To him, she supposed, all foreign authorities were much the same: officials to be tolerated and placated. He was charming from the outset, leading them into the long drawing room of the house, offering coffee or tea, waiting patiently for them to explain their business, so he could respond civilly and wait for them to go away.

Which all made Pearson's task that much harder, thought Liz, as she watched while Manchester's most senior policeman discreetly moved their polite small talk towards pithier subjects. 'As you know by now, there are a fair number of celebrities living in this area.'

Patricov nodded. 'Of course. It is remarkable what a man is paid these days to kick a ball around.' There was a twinkle in his eye. 'I have studied the economics of football in your country. It appeals to me both as a game and as a business proposition.'

'We're used to advising our more affluent citizens on their security arrangements. They usually find it useful and I like it because it helps to keep the crime figures down,' Pearson said with a smile.

'I would be happy for you to look at the arrangements here. I have hired a man who seems to be excellent – a former member of your Special Forces.'

'Good choice,' said Pearson.

Patricov turned to Liz. 'And you, Madam, are from the Home Office?'

'I am,' Liz replied. This was a cover she had used many times. If necessary she could discuss the minutiae of the department's policies and even its internal structures.

'You are London-based, yes? You have come a long way to see me.' It was a question really – why was she here?

'Yes, I have. Recently, I have been visiting prominent émigrés from your country.' She smiled. 'Most of them live much closer to London.'

'Yes. I believe Weybridge is now known as Moscow West.' Patricov gave a short laugh. 'What is it you wanted to talk to me about? My papers are all in order, I hope.'

'I'm sure they are, but that's not my area. The Chief Constable mentioned security, and he was primarily thinking of your protection from home-grown criminals. But I have another concern: your security from a different and more dangerous type of criminal – those sent here by aspects of the Russian Government. Specifically, we know that some of your compatriots who have come to live here have been pressurised in various ways by agents from Moscow. And, as you know, some have been killed.'

Patricov's eyes were narrowing now and a slight frown had replaced his smile. 'So… you must be from your security services. You are talking about dissidents – those who have loudly proclaimed their dislike of our President.'

'Not only such people. It depends – Moscow seems to define the term "dissident" quite broadly.'

'Not in my case, I promise you. I am on very good terms with President Putin.'

'Some of the Russians living here are not on such good terms.'

He looked at her sharply, and spent a moment measuring his response. 'I know. Inevitably, I have encountered some of them. There are social events, though I usually avoid that sort of thing. We do things for charity, and then we might talk about the things we miss in Russia. We drink a little,' he said, adding with a little laugh, 'perhaps not always a little. And sometimes we sing. But that's all. No politics, at least not when I have been present.'

'Do you ever go back to Russia?' asked Liz casually, though it was a key question – anyone under threat wouldn't dare.

Patricov paused, then said, 'I have not in fact been back for some time. But you should not attach any importance to that; my business interests are no longer there. I can go back any time I like. Officials may not put a *lei* around my neck, like they do in Hawaii, but they will be perfectly happy to see me, I assure you.'

Patricov looked at his watch, then pressed a buzzer that hung discreetly on the inner side of his chair arm. Within seconds there was a tap on the door and a man came in. He didn't look Russian, and Liz guessed this must be Reilly, head of security and acquaintance of Pearson's.

Patricov introduced them, and Pearson and Reilly acted as if they didn't know each other. The Russian said, 'Where is Karpis? I wanted him to escort Mr Pearson around with you.'

Reilly said, 'He's gone out, Mr Patricov. One of the guards saw him drive off about half an hour ago.'

'Really?' Patricov looked annoyed. He was about to say something but thought better of it. 'Never mind, I will come too then.'

For the next half hour they had a guided tour of the grounds. Reilly described the regular patrols his staff made; Liz saw one of them standing on the rear terrace looking vigilant – it seemed rather posed. After inspecting the elaborate CCTV system, they watched as Reilly triggered one of the sensors fixed to the rear gate. Pearson and Liz adopted expressions of interest throughout. When they got back to the house Patricov dismissed Reilly, then turned to them. 'Adequate?' he asked, with a hint of challenge in his voice.

'Most impressive,' said Pearson solemnly.

'You would like to see the monitor-room?'

'That's not necessary,' said Pearson. 'I know it's linked to the local police station.' He looked ostentatiously at his watch. 'We've taken up enough of your time, so unless you have any questions for us, we'll leave you in peace.'

Patricov nodded and shook hands with them both. 'A pleasure to meet you,' he said pointedly to Liz. 'You may reassure your colleagues in London that this is not a hotbed of political activity.' He laughed at the patent absurdity of this. 'Now football is a different matter. There I do have designs,' he said jovially.

As they drove away, Pearson asked Liz, 'What do you make of that?'

'Well, we certainly got the charm offensive.'

Pearson smiled and she went on: 'But I think there's something fishy about our Mr Patricov. I don't buy his protestations of love for the Putin regime. It didn't ring true, especially with what we know from your chap Jenkins.'

'I agree. He protested too much. And where was Mrs P? Don't oligarchs like to show off their wives?'

'Not this one. He's a bit smoother than the rest. What I wondered was where his henchman Karpis went, and why. Patricov was as surprised as we were to hear he'd pushed off.'

'It was almost as if Karpis knew we were coming and didn't want to meet us.'

Liz said, 'We must be scarier than we look. Either that or he has something to hide.'

Pearson laughed. 'Maybe it's both.'

28

'And so Langley would be very grateful if Liz ... would go to Tallinn to meet him.'

They sat in a spacious room on the second floor of Thames House, since Liz's usual meeting room on her own floor had already been booked. The view here faced away from the river – in the distance, you could see the chimney pots of a brick block of flats, leased mainly to MPs, and the crown of a large plane tree.

Miles Brookhaven was reporting on his meeting at CIA HQ, at which the request from Mischa for a meeting had been discussed. He had explained the concern in Langley that nothing should be done to risk exposing their covert Station in Estonia.

He said, 'I gather that the Russians are there in force and they're keeping a close eye on what's going on in the country. My face is well known to them from various encounters over the years; even if I kept clear of our Station and used a completely new cover, Langley thinks it possible I might be noticed. It's too much of a risk. Which is why they are asking Liz to go.'

Geoffrey Fane had been invited to the meeting by Liz, who had thought it better to involve him when decisions were being taken, rather than let him find out afterwards and make objections. Fane had brought Bruno Mackay, who was still looking, to Liz's eye, paler and thinner than when she had first worked with him. Foreseeing difficulty, Miles had briefed Liz and Peggy in advance of the meeting, and they were all prepared for Fane's objections.

Fane said, 'So, now Andy Bokus thinks it's his job to dictate to us who should go where.' Fane had never got on with Bokus during the years when he was Head of the CIA Station in London. 'I suppose he doesn't think it important that Europe is being threatened by Illegals. Now he's left London, we've become far less important than his precious Station in the Baltics. And what about the Illegal in the US? What has the Bureau to say about that?'

Miles replied levelly, 'Of course it's of major importance. We all accept that. There is no suggestion that we should ignore Mischa's request for a meeting, only that someone other than myself should go. It seemed to me, and I suggested it, that the ideal person – the person who was least likely to arouse any suspicion in Tallinn – was Liz.'

'I would be happy to go,' she said, judging that the time had come to stick her oar in. 'That's if you agree, Geoffrey.'

'I should add,' said Miles, 'that our new Director of Counter-Intelligence, Sandy Gunderson, chaired the meeting. He asked me to say that he would be very grateful if Liz would do this. I don't think you have met Sandy yet, Geoffrey. He particularly asked me to send his regards and say that he was looking forward to meeting you.'

'Hmm,' replied Fane. 'Well, I have no objection in principle to Elizabeth going. I have every confidence in her good sense. But I continue to feel it's rather high-handed of Langley to choose between our case officers. But please give the Director my regards. I would like to host him in London when he has time to pay us a visit.'

'Of course. But I know he's hoping to see you in Washington soon. He particularly asked me to extend an invitation.'

'Thank you,' replied Fane, slightly mollified by this flattery, obvious though it was. 'But now, as to the matter of who should go to Tallinn, what is your opinion, Bruno?'

'Well,' he replied, 'I think Liz would do an excellent job and she is probably the best person to go.'

Liz could hardly believe her ears. This was not the Bruno she had known several years ago. Whatever it was that had happened to him in Libya, it seemed to have made him a changed man. Bruno went on, 'I am as well known to the Russians as Miles is, and offhand I can't suggest anyone with the appropriate background knowledge whom the Russians wouldn't recognise. And after all, we have to remember that Mischa is offering information on a security threat to the UK – that's right up Liz's street.' He turned to her. 'Of course we'll be ready to provide assistance with cover identity and any other back-up that you may need. We'll let our Station in Riga know you're coming and they'll be ready to help if you get into any difficulty.'

'Thanks, Bruno,' said Liz. 'I really appreciate that. It should be pretty straightforward – unless Mischa is under suspicion by his own side. But I take it there's no reason to think that?' She turned to Miles.

'No. I think it's fairly clear that he isn't – and obviously we want to keep it that way. He will be making the contact arrangement and he's probably the best one to judge what's safe for him in Tallinn. He's been there for several weeks already and must have a pretty good idea of the lie of the land.'

'Miles mentioned to me a couple of days ago the possibility that I might go,' began Liz.

'I see,' broke in Fane. 'It's all been squared between you.'

'Not at all, Geoffrey,' said Liz. 'It depends on your agreement, as I've made clear.'

Fane was scowling. He said grudgingly, 'Very well. Let's hear what you propose.'

'Peggy has been doing some research into possible covers. Peggy, why don't you tell us what you think?'

She leaned forward, looking pleased to have a chance to speak at last. 'It seems to me that it would be best for Liz to go as part of a group. I've found a cultural tour leaving next week that still has a couple of vacancies. It's run by a company based in Cambridge that organises study tours to different parts of the world, led by experts of various kinds. This one is led by a professor who's an expert on the Baltic States. It's called "Historic Estonia" and it's just three days based in Tallinn.'

'That sounds ideal.' It was Miles speaking. 'But what would your cover be, Liz? And what's your reason for signing up so late?'

Peggy said, 'I thought Liz could be a single woman, who gave up work a year or so ago, as a schoolteacher or a librarian or something, to look after her widowed mother, who has just now died. So she's taking a break to recover from that before looking for a new job.'

'You mean she's a dotty spinster,' said Bruno with a grin, suddenly reverting to his old form. 'I like that.'

Fane seemed to like this too, and the meeting broke up with a general agreement to go ahead along these lines. Peggy stayed behind with Liz after the others left. She said, 'I'd like to go with you. I could be your niece or cousin or something. I'm sure it would be helpful to have someone else there.'

Liz thought for a moment. 'I don't think that's a good idea. I think I'd feel more comfortable knowing you were here looking after this end.'

Peggy's face fell but she said nothing.

Liz said, 'What's up? You don't look too good. Is something the matter?'

Peggy's lips tightened, and for a moment Liz feared that she'd said the wrong thing. But then Peggy gave a big sigh and said, 'It's Tim.'

'What's happened to him?' asked Liz. Tim wouldn't have been her type, with his pale, languid air and attachment to vegetarian food, but he'd seemed to make Peggy happy, which had been enough for Liz.

'Oh, nothing substantial,' said Peggy. 'He's just acting so... *weirdly.*'

'What's he doing?' The likeable thing about Tim, as far as Liz was concerned, was his mild eccentricity – lover of John Donne and also the Grateful Dead; never seen in anything smarter than jeans and an anorak.

'He spends more time on the internet than with me. I wouldn't mind – at least he isn't texting all the time – but I happened to see what he is looking at, and it scares me.'

Porn, was Liz's first thought – it seemed to be the bane of males using the Net. But Peggy said, 'He spends his time in chat rooms, discussing Government surveillance, the need for full disclosure, and the iniquities of the Western intelligence services.'

'You mentioned that before. I'm surprised; I didn't realise he was interested in politics,' said Liz mildly.

'He didn't used to be. He's changed, Liz.' Peggy looked baffled, and very upset. 'He used to admire Dante. Now Edward Snowden is his hero.' She added bitterly, 'A bit rich, considering the job of the woman he lives with.'

'Oh, dear,' was all Liz could think of to say.

Peggy hesitated, and Liz waited patiently. She didn't want to push her friend into confidences she might regret, but she could see something more was preying on Peggy's mind. Finally Peggy said, 'The thing is, I opened up his laptop.' She looked embarrassed. 'It was very peculiar. He'd sent an email that suggested he's set up *another* email account – or is about to. It was almost as if someone had told him what to do. He hasn't mentioned it to me, but that's definitely what it looks like.'

'You mean, it's so he can communicate with someone else?' asked Liz. It did sound odd; if Tim wanted privacy why would he need someone else to help him arrange it?

'The email was from someone signing herself Marina. We don't have any friends called Marina.'

'It could be entirely innocent,' said Liz, though it didn't sound it. Tim seemed an improbable philanderer, but one never knew. No wonder Peggy was so upset.

'I suppose so,' said Peggy wistfully. 'But then why keep it secret?'

'People do things for all sorts of reasons. You mustn't jump to conclusions.'

'I know. And I feel terrible for snooping.'

'It's completely understandable. You must be worried sick about him. It's not as if you were prying for the sake of it.'

'I think he's got another girlfriend. I could bear that – it happens – but why hasn't he told me?'

Peggy looked anguished, and Liz wanted to comfort her. But she wasn't convinced it was that simple. 'It doesn't explain everything, does it? I mean, you said he'd joined these political chat rooms. That's not about cheating on you.'

'Who knows? Maybe his new girlfriend likes politics. And maybe she has a poster of Edward Snowden in her flat.' Peggy sounded deeply hurt rather than angry.

'Can you talk to him?'

Peggy shook her head. 'He'd only get angry. And want to know how I knew any of this. If he thought I'd been going through his laptop, he'd go spare. And probably move out.'

Let him, thought Liz, but one look at the misery on Peggy's face meant she couldn't possibly say it. Part of Liz thought Peggy would be better off without Tim, now that he was acting like a creep. But part of her was curious about what was going on – she wondered whether it was worth having a closer look at what he was doing. After all, he was living with a member of the intelligence service. Was he a security risk? Surely not mild-mannered Tim.

29

IT WAS HER THIRD week at Vauxhall Cross, and at lunchtime Jasminder left the building after collecting her phone at reception. She found a message on it from Laurenz asking her to ring him. He answered at once. 'Ah, good,' he said, 'your new guardians are letting you use your phone.'

'No, it's just I've left the building for lunch. It's such a nice day I thought I'd take a walk along the river. Do you want me to pick anything up for supper while I'm out?'

'No. I thought we'd go out tonight. I have a surprise for you.'

'Really, what is it?'

'That would be telling, and then it wouldn't be a surprise. I'll see you at the flat first, okay?'

'Yes, I'll make sure not to stay late tonight.' She was intrigued.

As she passed Vauxhall Bridge, heading upstream on the bright spring day, Jasminder decided she had never been busier – or happier. Work was demanding; she was expected to learn all the background to her job and do it simultaneously. Already she'd spent whole days visiting GCHQ at Cheltenham and MI5 across the river, only to find a new stack of paper had accumulated on her desk in her absence, which made no allowance for the fact she'd been away.

But the job was fascinating, and she didn't mind burning the midnight oil, especially now that she had Laurenz for company. Though they would occasionally meet after work in a wine bar or a restaurant for supper, most nights they stayed in, and he cooked – something he said he enjoyed, which was a good thing, since Jasminder's cooking skills stopped at scrambled eggs. He seemed to have an uncanny sense of when she wanted to talk about her day, and when work was the last thing she felt like discussing.

The only odd thing about their relationship, something that seemed odder still as time passed, was that they never saw anyone else as a couple. He'd already rebuffed her suggestion that they meet up with Emma so firmly that she didn't dare propose it again. But what about his friends? Laurenz did talk sometimes about his work, and the geopolitical risk assessments he made for his clients. When Jasminder and he watched the ten o'clock news together, inevitably there would be a report of something going on somewhere that would have an impact on one of Laurenz's clients' holdings. But he didn't seem to have friends among his colleagues, and sometimes she wondered if he even had any. There was a man called Karl at the bank, who would come up in conversation from time to time, but according to Laurenz, Karl was a pain, rather than a pal. To be fair, Laurenz had told Jasminder that he worked largely on his own. She wondered if he preferred it that way. No one would have called him a social animal.

But this evening he surprised her all right. They went to a local bistro, where he insisted on ordering a bottle of wine. When their starters came he leaned forward and clinked glasses with her.

'Are we celebrating something?' she asked curiously. He seemed in exuberant spirits.

'I hope so,' he said. 'You know how you have been complaining that you never meet any of my colleagues?'

'Well, not complaining, just wondering really.'

'Perfectly understandable. But as I have tried to explain, I haven't lived in the UK very long, so it's true I don't really have friends here. However, I'm not a hermit and I do have colleagues and some of them are friends. It's just that they're spread all over the place. Banking is so international these days.'

She nodded slowly. He went on, 'A couple of years ago one of my pals at the bank got married, and the whole group of colleagues who knew him realised that we only ever got to see each other socially at special occasions – like a wedding. But you can't plan on those happening very often. More importantly, we realised that months could go by without our getting together and we needed to meet periodically to exchange views and keep in touch.'

'And?'

'So now our bank has an annual conference, usually held somewhere exotic. The problem is it only last two or three days, and it's quite intense – lots of meetings and presentations; outside speakers come in and clients. It's not an excuse for a party; we all work very hard.'

'It certainly doesn't sound like a jolly to me.'

'Far from it. But we always go to a good place. This year we're meeting in Bermuda. Have you ever been?'

Jasminder shook her head. He said, 'It's where the bank has its headquarters, though that doesn't mean we have a great big building – more of a house with offices in it, really. But Bermuda is lovely – even nicer than the photographs. White sand beaches, blue skies, friendly people, good food. I worked there for a while a few years ago, and didn't want to leave.

'Anyway, some of us usually stay on after the conference to relax and have a bit of a holiday, and occasionally clients and speakers join us. We'll have wonderful meals, play some golf perhaps or just lie by the pool. It's a brilliant way to decompress, and best of all, it lets us see each other for more than a few snatched minutes between conference sessions.'

'Are partners invited?' she asked hesitantly.

'Absolutely. That's the whole point.' He paused. 'If you'd come this year, you'd meet my colleagues and I could introduce you to some of our clients as well.' He put down his glass and reached over for her hand, gazing at her with a smile. 'It would mean a lot to me for them to meet the person who is making my life so happy. My close friends know what I've been going through with this wretched divorce. I want them to see how much better things are.'

'I'd love to,' Jasminder said, but her face gave away the fact that there was a problem.

'But…?' he said.

'I've only just started this job, and I don't see how I can ask for time off so soon.'

'I have thought of that, don't worry. You could join us at the weekend. One of my clients is also a good friend – he's absolutely stinking rich.' Laurenz held a hand to his face in mock apology. 'Or should I say, highly affluent?' Jasminder laughed. Laurenz continued, 'If you could take just one day off, then it would work out perfectly. Discover a great-aunt whose funeral you have to attend. It's only a day, after all. You could fly out on the Friday, and be with us in time for supper. We'd have all day Saturday, most of Sunday, and then that night this client of mine will be flying back to London – on his private jet. We could get a lift with him, and you'd be at your desk first thing on Monday morning. Everything would be paid for.'

'By the bank?'

'By me.'

And before she could object, he squeezed her hand again across the table. 'Don't say no, please; it would give me such pleasure, and I promise you'd enjoy yourself.'

They walked back in the slowly gathering dusk to Laurenz's flat. He put his arm through Jasminder's and said, 'See? I'm not the mystery man you thought I was.'

She laughed, partly in relief that he understood how strange she'd been starting to find his behaviour. She said, 'Does this mean you'll finally agree to meet Emma?'

She felt his arm stiffen, almost imperceptibly. 'Of course,' he said carefully, 'but that might take a little longer. I'm still quite wary of my wife, and our negotiations have reached a critical point. I don't want to do anything to jeopardise things there. I hope you understand.'

Jasminder told herself she did, though she still couldn't see why having lunch – or even dinner – with Emma was going to make any difference to his divorce settlement. But she sensed it would spoil the evening to push the point. She said instead, 'I meant to tell you, I'm going to be away for a couple of nights next week.'

'Where?'

'I'm going to Berlin. With C and the senior management team,' she added; she had only been told that afternoon. 'He's giving a speech to a meeting of European intelligence heads.' She paused. 'Please forget I mentioned it. I shouldn't have said anything.'

'Don't be silly. Anyone would realise that intelligence agencies need to meet regularly – especially these days. You can trust me, and besides, who would I tell? Karl at the office?' he added sarcastically.

'I know,' she said with a little laugh. 'It's just that I'm finding it hard to get used to the fact so many things are confidential where I'm working now.'

'I can imagine. You're used to openness. You used to believe in it so strongly.'

'I still do. And C's speech is going to be about the need for greater openness with the public. That's why he wants me there. I'm having sessions with the press, both about my own role and about the speech.'

'Have you seen it yet?'

'I've seen a version. I don't think it's the final text.'

'Any good?'

'Yes, actually it is. I helped draft part of it but he's made a lot of amendments and additions. He writes very clearly.' Like most of his staff, she thought. She had learned very quickly to respect the acuity of her new colleagues at MI6. Contrary to her preconceptions, there were no duds among them as far as she could tell. She said now, 'He says he wants me to help him with all his speeches in future.'

'That's great. You know, I used to write speeches,' Laurenz said.

'When was that?' asked Jasminder, impressed by the addition of yet another string to his bow.

'A few years ago. I did it for the president of the bank when he had to address outside organisations. I'm not sure I was very good at it; I bet you're much better than I ever was.'

'I don't know about that.' She was struck as always by his modesty. Laurenz was clearly good at almost everything he turned his hand to, but you would never know it from his diffident manner. She said, 'I've given a lot of talks in my time, but to be honest, I usually just take a fistful of notes I've scribbled and wing it. But C's speech is a proper text. The intention is to release it after the event.'

'I'd love to see it, and your suggestions too. May I?'

At first, Jasminder was taken aback. She actually had the speech in her briefcase, along with her comments and several offered by senior officers whom C had asked to read his early draft. Geoffrey Fane had made clear his own disagreement with its call for greater openness and pointedly corrected a few minor grammatical errors; Wheatcroft, another old hand, had tried to tone down its frank account of the Service's past penchant for secrecy.

The text of the speech she had in her bag was 'Confidential', which was practically the lowest level of document classification, and that was only because C didn't want it to become public until after he had given it. It was hard to see what harm there could possibly be in letting Laurenz have an advance look. There was nothing secret about it, really; part of the purpose of giving it was to have it covered in the media.

'Why not?' she said. They were waiting for the lift in Laurenz's building. 'I'd be interested in what you think. Just don't tell anyone you've seen it.'

She said this lightly but with a touch of concern Laurenz must have picked up. He put an arm around her and said soothingly, 'You don't have to worry about that.'

30

I N BERLIN, C's SPEECH went down well with the conference audience comprised of senior members of European intelligence services and some European politicians. While he was speaking, a text of the speech was released to invited members of the media and afterwards Jasminder conducted a Q&A session with them.

That had proved very challenging: many of the reporters seemed sceptical about the new ideas for greater openness just outlined. BBC's *Newsnight* wanted to know why the press had been excluded from the event. In fact, how did they even know that the text they had been given was what he'd actually said?

Jasminder replied that many of the intelligence officers attending did not wish their identities to be known publicly, for obvious reasons. And she could assure the *Newsnight* team that they had the actual text. Next a reporter from the *Guardian* pressed Jasminder on what he described as her volte face on civil liberties.

Was she not colluding with a secretive intelligence service in helping it to pretend that it was being more open? Would they now tell us, for example, what actual harm had been done to

Western countries by whistle-blowers revealing the massive intrusion into the privacy of innocent people?

Not without jeopardising the safety of employees and sources and thus compounding the damage that had been done, was how she'd fielded this.

Yes, but damage to the intelligence services was one thing; what damage had been done to ordinary Western citizens?

Well, most people felt the intelligence services were working on behalf of the public, not to oppress them but to try and keep them safe, so damage to the former meant damage to the latter.

Didn't this contradict Jasminder's own concerns, expressed often enough in the past, about the need to oversee security activities, to make sure ordinary people's rights were not abused?

On the contrary, the new openness was intended to address just that issue. And so it went on.

Jasminder was used to being the interrogator on such matters and it had been an extraordinary feeling to be the target of these questions, but afterwards a reporter from the *New York Times* had come up and told her she'd been a breath of fresh air in the clandestine world of intelligence. Better still, C had said he'd heard she'd done very well, and even Geoffrey Fane, who no doubt had a source in the press conference, gave a clipped 'Alpha work, my dear, alpha work' as he passed her in a corridor on her return.

She'd gone home on a high, and for a change Laurenz came over to her place. He brought with him a bottle of champagne with a bright red ribbon tied around its neck. He seemed almost as excited as she was, which was very flattering. 'I want to hear all about it,' he said.

'Read tomorrow's *Guardian,* and then you can decide how I did in the Q&A. As for C's speech, you've already read it!'

'I know, but what about the sessions – were they good?'

'I wasn't at any of them. They were discussing high-level intelligence. That's not my area.'

'Really? Do you see the papers for them?'

'I saw the agendas, so I know what areas they were discussing, but not the papers – they're Top Secret.'

'Still, what you do see must be fascinating. I'd love to see the agendas.'

She nodded vaguely, feeling uneasy. When Laurenz added, 'Could I?' she wished she hadn't said there was anything at all she was allowed to see – other than C's speech.

'Laurenz, I'm really not supposed to show you anything. I'm not even meant to talk about my work.'

He waved his hand dismissively. 'Bah! Everybody talks about their work with their partners. Do you really think your C doesn't tell his wife why he's had a bad day at the office? Or when something's gone terribly wrong and he's worried sick?'

Actually, from what she'd seen of C, Jasminder was pretty confident he didn't. Throughout MI6, there seemed to be very little casual chat about work of the kind you'd find in any other workplace. People at Vauxhall seemed, without making any kind of an issue of it, to operate under a code of 'need to know' that everyone understood. It was an ethos that made life simpler, Jasminder had come to realise, because it avoided your having to decide all the time who you could talk to about what. When in doubt, you simply didn't open your mouth.

Sensing she couldn't adequately explain this to Laurenz, she said simply, 'I know what I say to you will never be repeated. But that's not the point.'

'Well, what is the point then? What's the problem?' His voice was distinctly less gentle. 'Don't you trust me?'

'Of course I do.'

'It's not as if I'm asking you to reveal your nation's secrets, is it? It's just an agenda for meetings that have already happened. For God's sake, lots of people must know the agenda now and it's all over anyway. Don't you understand – it could assist me a great deal. If I know the "hot spots" for intelligence services, then it will help me know where I have to protect my clients. They won't know why; no one will.'

'But I'm not supposed to—'

'Can't you help me with this little thing? If you had a memory stick, it won't take much more than a nanosecond to download the agenda, and maybe some of the papers too. No one would know.'

'On the contrary. If I did that, I happen to know that a signal would flash across half the screens in the IT security room, saying an unauthorised download was taking place. Memory sticks are *forbidden*. Even having one in your bag or your pocket can get you suspended.'

'All right,' Laurenz said, but he wasn't through yet. 'What about a photocopy? The agenda must have been photocopied for the meetings and it can't be more than a page or two.'

'That would be just as bad,' said Jasminder, wishing he would understand.

'But it wouldn't trigger an alarm if you brought one home. And I can't imagine they look through your bag every time you leave. You had C's speech at home after all.'

She didn't reply to this and waited a second before she said, 'Anyway, should we go out to eat tonight? I haven't got much in the house.'

Laurenz was standing by the window, his back to her. He gave a deep sigh. 'I think it might be best if I just went home.'

'Why?' she asked in surprise.

He turned to face her, a gloomy expression on his face. 'I can't live with distrust again. I had that with my wife all the time – *where are you going? Where have you been?*'

'But I'm not like that,' Jasminder protested. It seemed terribly unfair, comparing her reluctance to violate state security with his wife's jealousy and possessiveness.

'It amounts to the same thing. No one in the world would know you'd helped me except us. And, believe me, it would help me a lot. My business is always competitive, but lately it's got even worse.' Laurenz added dolefully, 'I hate to admit it but I think I'm falling a bit behind. Last week one of my major clients threatened to leave me. He said he wasn't sure I was "cutting edge" enough.'

'That's terrible. Why didn't you tell me?'

'I didn't want to trouble you with my worries – you have enough on your plate. And,' he said, then hesitated, 'I was worried you might think less of me.'

'But you know I respect you. Everybody has setbacks sometimes; you must never think I don't understand that.' She felt it was critical to reassure him; there was something so awful about his apparent distress. She couldn't bear the thought of his walking out now. 'Listen, I will get you the agenda. But you must promise me that even if it helps you with your clients, no one will ever know.'

He came over to her with arms extended. 'No one will know,' he whispered into her ear, and as he enveloped her in a reassuring hug Jasminder hoped he wouldn't ask her to do anything like this again.

31

L IZ HAD NO DIFFICULTY in recognising her tour group
at Stansted airport. The fluorescent orange baggage
tags bearing a logo and the words 'Uni Tours' could clearly
be seen even across the crowded concourse. The group
looked much as she expected – mainly middle-aged, middle-
class, more women than men. She was the youngest by far,
except for the leader, Professor Anthony Curtis, who was
standing in the centre of the group, holding a clipboard.

'Ah, Miss Ryder,' he said when Liz introduced herself
under her cover name. 'Welcome.' He ticked the list on his
clipboard. 'You're our last member so we can all check in
now.' He herded the group towards the desk for the Easy
Jet flight to Tallinn.

Professor Curtis, who held the Chair of Baltic History
and Politics at Cambridge, looked to be not much older
than Liz – in his early forties perhaps. He was a short man
with cropped blond hair and a small pointed goatee beard.
His teeth gleamed white in his tanned face and when he
smiled he looked startlingly like the smaller, younger
brother of Richard Branson.

He shepherded his flock through check-in, and assisted
a couple of elderly Scottish ladies, the Misses Finlaison, to

lift their hand baggage onto the X-ray machine. One of them had put her sponge bag in her hand baggage and was unwilling to abandon some of the larger items. It wasn't until Liz, who was next to her in the queue, promised to go with her to the chemist's in the departure lounge to replace them that she could be persuaded to move on, by which time a queue of grumbling passengers had built up behind them.

As the only single traveller, Liz found herself sitting next to Curtis on the plane. 'Thanks for your help with Miss Finlaison,' he said, with a flash of his gleaming teeth. 'I thought we were in for trouble there.'

'Happy to help. They're both very sweet,' said Liz.

'I noticed you only booked to come last week. Was it a sudden impulse?'

'Well, yes. It was really,' replied Liz, moving into cover mode. 'My mother died three weeks ago.'

'Oh, I'm sorry,' murmured Curtis.

'It wasn't unexpected. In fact it was something of a relief. She'd been ill for over a year. I've been looking after her and, when it finally happened, I felt utterly exhausted. The doctor said that after everything was sorted, I should take a holiday. But I don't like sitting on the beach, so I looked for something more interesting and I came across this tour. It still had a vacancy and I decided to come. I've never been to any of the Baltic states before and I thought Tallinn looked lovely. And obviously it has a fascinating history too.' She paused, waiting to see how this went down with the Professor.

'I'm so glad you were able to join us. It is nice to have someone more my own age,' he replied with a grin. 'These tours can tend towards the geriatric. I have to be careful not to overdo the walking, but there will be time for wandering around. I don't pack too much in or people start to flag.'

That's good, thought Liz. I should be able to get away without being noticed.

They chatted on and off for the rest of the flight. Liz found out that his father, now dead, had been a banker in Gothenburg, and his mother was from Sweden. He'd spent a lot of his childhood there. When his father retired the family had moved to Cambridge and he now lived with his mother in the old family home. He was unmarried.

In return for all this information, she fed in a bit more of her cover story: she had been a primary school teacher in Norfolk until her mother had fallen ill, and had given up work to look after her mother at home in Wiltshire. Norfolk turned out to be a bit of a cover mistake as Curtis knew the county well and wanted to know where she had lived and which school she had taught at.

'I lived in Swaffham,' she said, mentally thanking Peggy for her thorough brief, 'and I taught at a school in a nearby village, but it's closed now.' Thankfully he turned out not to know Swaffham, so she was spared deploying her detailed knowledge of the Market Place and surrounding pubs.

By the time they'd arrived in Tallinn and checked into the hotel, it was five in the afternoon local time. Nothing was in the programme until a pre-dinner orientation talk by the Professor at seven, so Liz took the opportunity to go off by herself and reconnoitre the town – and locate where she was due to meet Mischa in two days' time.

The hotel was in the centre of the old town in what had formerly been a merchant's house. Liz stood in the street outside for a moment, looking at it and thinking how charming it was with its white-painted walls, gables and steeply sloping red-tiled roofs. Like an illustration in a copy of *Grimms' Fairy Tales*, she thought.

The town was busy, full of tourists of various nationalities. As she strolled around she was alert for surveillance but could discern no sign of anyone taking a particular interest in her. She returned to the hotel in time for the talk, confident that her real purpose for being there remained undetected – or as confident, she thought, as you could be in an ex-Soviet republic.

She listened with interest to what Anthony Curtis had to say about the troubled recent history of Estonia – how it had been often overrun, first by the Danes and the Swedes and, more recently, in turn by the Russians, the Germans, and the Russians again. Since the break-up of the Soviet Union and the withdrawal of Soviet troops, Estonia had flourished commercially. It had become known for its entrepreneurial ventures in IT, with dozens of start-up companies forming a Baltic version of Silicon Valley. But it was a precarious prosperity. The ethnic mix of the country made it vulnerable to the sort of destabilisation that had taken place in Ukraine.

Liz thought of Mischa who, if the Americans were right, was there to assess what weapons would be needed if the Russians did decide to act; she thought too of the covert CIA Station that Andy Bokus was so anxious to protect. It was clear to her that meddling was already going on here in a big way.

By dinnertime the whole party seemed to know that Liz Ryder had just lost her mother, and everyone was being so sympathetic that she began to feel rather guilty about killing off her remaining parent. The Misses Finlaison showed signs of wanting to mother her themselves, enquiring solicitously where she was going to live and what she would do next. She managed to avoid sitting next to them at dinner and chose a seat next to Major Sanderson, whose wife had temporarily deserted him to join a group of ladies. Anthony Curtis sat on Liz's other side.

She soon discovered why the Major's wife had chosen to sit somewhere else. Like most of his generation of middle-class Englishmen, the Major had superficially good manners but a penchant for talking exclusively about himself. Liz relaxed and let her mind wander as, for the better part of two courses, the Major described in detail his long career, which stretched from Aden to Antrim. It was only as he paused to spear his last piece of pork, cooked with potatoes in a briny sour cream sauce, that Anthony Curtis was able to weigh in from Liz's other side.

By this time she had let her guard drop to the point that when he suggested they go to the bar to try one of the Estonian liqueurs, she agreed. This turned out to be a mistake: by the second glass of something fiery with an unpronounceable name, Professor Curtis was showing unmistakably amorous intentions. 'It is so good to have someone young here for a change,' he said dreamily, moving closer to her on the sofa.

'It's lovely to be here,' said Liz, with a mournful smile. 'But I feel sad about my poor mother. She suffered a lot, you know. It was cancer of the pancreas. Very nasty and painful and nothing could be done for her. They say it's the silent killer; you can have it and not know until it's too late.'

When Professor Curtis recoiled slightly, Liz stood up and said tearfully, 'I think I had better go to bed now. Thank you for such an interesting day.' And with that she walked mournfully out of the bar, leaving Curtis to finish his drink alone.

32

THE FOLLOWING DAY HAD a full programme of visits to the sights of Tallinn, led by Professor Curtis. Liz went with the party, not wanting to appear anything other than a normal, interested tourist, and spent the day keeping in the centre of the group, trying not to be left alone with Curtis. He had suggested the previous evening that on the third day, which was a free day for tour members to do what they liked, he might give her a private tour of the city. As that was the day fixed for her rendezvous with Mischa, the last thing she wanted was Curtis hanging around. She needed to prevent him from getting any opportunity to renew his offer.

She was also trying to spot any surveillance, though it was impossible to know where it might be coming from. Both Andy Bokus's covert Station in Tallinn and MI6's in Riga knew that she was here, and they also knew her alias and the programme of her tour party. She had agreed this was a sensible precaution in case she got into any difficulties, and she had also been given a method of contacting them. But Liz had insisted that they keep well out of the way, since she didn't want either Mischa or any of his colleagues who might be watching him to become aware of interest from the other side.

As her party went from church to church, she saw nothing to concern her. The churches were full of tourists grouped round their respective leaders, each no doubt explaining in their own language, as Professor Curtis was in his, how much the styles of architecture here varied, ranging from the elaborate onion domes of the Russian Orthodox churches to the stark simplicity of the Scandinavian Lutheran buildings, with their needle spires pointing to the sky. It was a reminder, said Curtis somewhat portentously, of how occupying regimes may come and go, but religious faith endures. Liz wondered how much of this would survive if Tallinn became the front line of a trial of strength between NATO and a newly aggressive Russia.

In the afternoon the focus changed from religion to politics with a visit to the Hotel Viru, the Cold War tourist hotel, where the rooms were bugged by the KGB. On the twenty-second floor there was a control room for the wiretapping operations, and the party marvelled at the antiquated technology – the enormous tape recorders and the little room at the back with the notice on the door saying *Zdes Nichevo Nyet*, where listeners had sat with headphones on, eavesdropping on the tourists in their bedrooms.

'What does that mean?' asked one of the Finlaison sisters, pointing to the Russian sign.

'It means "There is nothing here",' replied the curator to general laughter.

Liz wondered how much of the same thing was still going on, conducted nowadays from an FSB listening station or from the CIA's covert surveillance, rather than the top floor of a hotel. What was certain was that the technology would be a lot less noticeable than these old monsters, and today's targets were likely to be politicians and visiting NATO or EC delegations, not tourists.

The following morning Liz had breakfast in her room. She wanted to avoid getting swept up with any of the group and then having to lose them in time for her meeting with Mischa. So she was annoyed to hear a cheerful cry behind her just as she was leaving the hotel.

'Liz! Good morning, my dear. How are you today?' It was the Finlaison sisters. Liz stood still, holding the door open for them. She didn't want to arouse their interest by being rude. One of the sisters said, 'We're going along to the market square. They tell us there's an ethnic market and folk singing there today. We thought we might get some souvenirs and a present for our niece. It's her birthday next week. Would you like to walk along with us – unless you've got other plans?'

'That would be lovely,' said Liz. 'I was just going to wander around but I'd like to see the market.'

It was a bright, windless but cool morning with a clear, pale blue sky overhead. 'We are so enjoying this trip,' said the younger Miss Finlaison, enthusiastically. 'Tallinn is such a beautiful city. I do hope it's doing you good, my dear,' she added, taking Liz's arm.

'Thank you,' Liz replied, feeling a terrible fraud for playing on their sympathy. 'It is a lovely place and I'm feeling a lot better.'

In the cobbled square in the heart of the old town, stalls with striped awnings were trading briskly. Most of the selling was being done by women in embroidered skirts and blouses, and head dresses decorated with lace and strings of tiny silver coins which rested on their foreheads. They were selling handicrafts and all kinds of food and drink – from bread and cakes to honey and strange-shaped bottles of brownish liqueurs that looked, thought Liz, likely to blow your head off.

The square was crowded, and after five minutes she had successfully lost the Finlaisons and drifted off discreetly, pretty confident that the two women would still be inspecting the native wares of Estonia when she returned from her meeting.

It took her twenty minutes to reach St Olaf's Church. There was no need for a map; its spire was clearly visible from the market square and it was only a short distance away. But she needed to be sure no one was following her, so she proceeded with caution. She wandered, apparently aimlessly, through the small alleys and lanes of the Old Town, doubling back twice as if returning to the square. She remembered that Peggy's briefing note for this trip had described how the white stone tower of St Olaf's, the tallest in the city, had an observation platform high up, which had been used for almost fifty years by the Soviets as a radio tower and surveillance point. As she wandered, Liz kept track of her position simply by looking for the stiletto-sharp spire.

When she eventually reached the entrance to the church, exactly five minutes before the scheduled meeting time, she was confident she hadn't been followed.

There was a tour group of Chinese visitors inside, crowding the centre of the nave, so Liz went down a side aisle and took a seat. She stared upwards at the windows and the ceiling like an interested tourist. At the same time she kept an eye on the door, but no likely-looking person came in. She wondered for a moment about a couple, obviously American from their clothes, but they soon left. Then four women in what looked like locally bought winter coats arrived. They genuflected to the altar before sitting down in one of the back pews.

After a few minutes the Chinese left and Liz made her way towards the Sanctuary, crossing in front of the altar. Though the church was Baptist now, much of the original Catholic finery of its interior had been retained. Slowly she headed through an open doorway to a little hallway, which she knew led to an annexe – a chapel that had been built early in the sixteenth century and had survived the lightning strikes and fires that had several times destroyed the main church. Normally open to the public, the chapel was closed today, signalled by a thick red cord strung between two brass stands barring entry to the double doors at the end of the hall. Looking around, Liz saw no one paying her any attention, so she quickly skirted around the red cord, climbed four steps and opened the door to the chapel.

She blinked as her eyes adjusted to the thin, tawny light thrown out by the only illumination in the room – two tall candles by the small altar. There was just enough light for Liz to make out the little room's four rows of pews. As instructed, she went and sat in the third-row pew at its farthest right-hand end, next to the side aisle. She sat quietly, her eyes fixed on the altar with its gold cross ornately studded with gems, a hangover from Catholic times.

She was a little early, but within a few minutes heard the door open and then footsteps that stopped by the last row of pews. She didn't turn round, but waited for Mischa to say, 'The altar is very old.' She would then reply, 'How old?' And he would say, 'Old enough,' then sit down directly behind her. If they were interrupted, they would look like two people seeking solace or praying quietly, away from the tourists filling the main body of the church.

But instead a familiar voice said, 'Hello, Liz. How on earth did you find this place? I'd been coming for years before I discovered it.'

Liz's heart sank. It was Curtis, and he moved around the pews now and stood by the end of hers, smiling. Glancing back, Liz saw the door to the chapel stood wide open – anyone coming past could look inside and see them, especially Mischa.

She had to get rid of Curtis fast, but she mustn't be rude or seem angry at being disturbed – that might simply make him even more curious about her.

'I needed a few minutes alone,' she said, hoping he would take the hint.

He didn't, and sat down at the end of the pew in front, half turned round so he could talk to her.

'Yes. It is a lovely quiet place,' he said. 'I always come here when I'm in Tallinn, but I never bring the tourists. I don't want to spoil it. But I'm glad you found it.'

Liz's heart sank. She could see that he was settling down for a pleasant afternoon with her. She had to get rid of him somehow or this trip would have been a waste of time.

Then all of a sudden the quiet was shattered by a mobile phone ringing. Liz jumped. Surely it wasn't hers. She'd turned it off.

It was then she saw out of the corner of her eye a figure pass by the open door. She couldn't make out the face, but it was clearly a man: well-built, and wearing an olive-coloured top. The figure hesitated in the doorway, looked in then quickly moved past.

It must be Mischa. He would be spooked to see two people in the chapel and to hear the phone ringing. He'd be thinking that the meeting had been blown. She must stop him leaving somehow.

Curtis had his phone to his ear. 'Yes. Why? What's happened?' He listened for a moment then said, 'OK. I'll come straight away.' He rang off and looked at Liz regretfully. 'I'm sorry. It was the hotel. Something's happened to one of the party but they wouldn't say what over the phone. I'm afraid I'll have to leave you, but have a good afternoon and I'll see you later.' He got up and hurried out, closing the chapel door behind him with a bang.

Liz had to get to Mischa fast.

33

L IZ WENT BACK TO the main church and stood by the rood screen, searching frantically for the man she'd glimpsed. There was no one in the nave's pews remotely like the figure she'd seen in the doorway. Then in a side aisle she saw a man standing by one of the church's massive columns, examining a stained-glass window. He wore an olive-coloured military-style sweater and dark canvas trousers.

Without glancing around him, the man lowered his head and started walking slowly towards the church's entrance. It was as if he were in two minds about leaving. Liz strode rapidly down the centre aisle, fast enough to reach the door first. Then she turned down the side aisle and walked straight towards the man in the olive sweater. Looking straight at him, she caught his eye as she stopped several feet in front of him. 'The chapel is free now,' she said, then walked past him and down the far aisle of the nave.

Alone again in the private chapel, she sat down feeling confident that at least Curtis would not reappear – whatever the phone call had been about, it had got rid of him. She was less certain that Mischa would come to the chapel again, and groaned inwardly at the thought that she had come all this way only to miss her meet by sheer bad luck.

She sat alone for what seemed an eternity. She wondered if she should go looking for Mischa, though his failure to show up suggested that even were she to find him, it might merely spook him for good.

Then the door creaked slowly behind her. Someone took a step, then one more, then stood stock still. Liz waited tensely, not daring to look behind her.

'They say the altar is very old.' The words came out easily, only slightly accented.

Like a clergyman intoning a response, Liz said, 'How old?'

There was a long pause. 'Old enough.' Then he walked forward and sat down in the pew directly behind her.

'Hello, Mischa,' said Liz.

'Who was that man with you before?' he demanded.

'He's the leader of the tour group I am with.'

'Why was he here?'

'It was just bad luck. He was looking round the church. He knows this chapel and recognised me and wanted to chat. He's got nothing to do with this and he doesn't know why I'm here.'

'Who was the phone call from? What was it about?'

Good question, thought Liz. She had been wondering herself whether that phone call had been divine intervention or whether one of her minders was looking after her. But she said, 'It was the hotel. Something has happened to one of our party and he had to go back to sort it out.'

'What has happened?'

'I don't know but I'm sure it doesn't affect us. It's probably a small accident. The other members of my group are fairly old.'

She couldn't see Mischa's face as he was sitting behind her but she sensed he was reassured. Then he said, 'I did not expect to be meeting a woman today.'

'Is that a problem?'

'Of course it's a problem. Especially when the woman is young and attractive. If a man had been here this tour leader would not have been following him.'

'I don't know about that. He might have found him attractive too.'

She heard a small sigh that suggested Mischa was amused.

Liz said, 'Anyway, here I am, for better or worse. Shall we get down to business? You said you had some urgent information.'

'I do. And it's very valuable. What can I expect in return?'

Miles Brookhaven had warned her to expect this. She said firmly, 'I am not going to pay you now. I've come to hear what you have to tell us. Your contract is with the Americans and if I tell them that your information is of value, they will pay you.'

'You must think it will be of value. You've come a long way to hear it.'

'Of course I am interested to hear anything you have to say about Russian activity in my country. But so far what we've learned is too vague to help us. I need something we can act on.'

She could sense that Mischa didn't like her tone. But she needed to get the whole story, whatever he knew, not just a few snippets at a time, doled out, confident that in return he would receive a nice fat packet of dollars.

He said quietly, 'You understand where my information comes from?'

Liz nodded.

'Then you know it is not always consistent. My source,' and he paused, unwilling still to say it was his brother in the FSB, 'is not aware of our discussions.'

'He doesn't share your view of the regime?'

There was a pause. 'No,' said Mischa at last. 'But then he did not see the bodies from the airliner shot down in Ukraine. I did.'

Liz could hear the emotion in his voice but sensed a conflict between his loathing of a regime that could kill so many harmless people and his unwillingness to criticise his own brother. She said nothing. Mischa went on, 'My point is that what I learn from him is not always thorough or complete. He is not aware that I tell anyone else what he tells me, and it is not a report he is giving me. I am not in a position to ask him too many questions because that might seem suspicious. And there are no documents – that is simply not possible. You understand?'

She did. Mischa could raise topics, ask general questions, and at the end of a vodka-fuelled evening try to get his brother to boast and tell him what was really going on, unaware of course that Mischa would promptly take what he told him and sell it to Western intelligence. She said, 'Yes. I do understand. And just as you must take on faith that you will be rewarded for your help, so we take on faith that what you tell us is exactly what you have learned from your source.'

'Very well,' he replied. 'We have an understanding.' And he started to talk, quickly but clearly, while Liz listened carefully.

When he returned to Russia from Ukraine, Mischa saw his brother at a family reunion, but there had been little chance to talk to him. It hadn't seemed to matter, since there would be plenty of time for them to meet now that

Mischa was back home. But then out of the blue Mischa was told he was being sent to Estonia. He wanted the chance for a good talk with his brother before he went so suggested they rent a small dacha for a few days and do some fishing.

On the first night they had a drinking session. 'I did not try to match my brother,' Mischa said, as if acknowledging a handicap. 'He drinks more than me on any given day, and I needed to be able to report back with a clear memory of what he said.'

'Good thinking,' said Liz mildly, wishing there could be a little less partying and a little more hard information.

Mischa may have sensed her impatience. He explained that before his brother became too incapacitated, he'd asked him how things were going at work. Splendidly, his brother had replied, which could normally be discounted as his standard response (he never admitted to difficulties, either at work or at home), but then he'd added that he had recently scored something of a coup. Oh, said Mischa, what was that? And his brother said, you remember how I told you we had placed someone in the UK – an Illegal? Well, they have targeted someone who is now very important in their intelligence services.

Mischa pointed out that his brother had told him more or less the same thing the last time they had met. For a second he thought his brother would get cross, but instead he broke into a grin and said, Yes, but I didn't tell you we had *two* Illegals there.

Surprised by this, Liz asked, 'Two Illegals, are you sure?'

'Absolutely. My brother repeated it because I must have looked surprised.'

'Are the two Illegals aware of each other?'

'Absolutely,' Mischa said again. 'They could not help but know of each other's presence in your country. You see, they are partners.'

'Do you mean, they're married?' Liz was astonished. 'Or do you mean they're working partners?'

'It is hard to say. I think they have worked together somewhere else, perhaps as a married couple. But whether they are in fact married, I do not know. I doubt even my brother knows. Remember, they have no "real" identities any more.'

Yes, thought Liz, their lives are all bound up in the roles they are playing.

'Okay,' she said, her mind starting to race with possibilities. Somehow she felt confident it would be easier to find a couple than it would a lone wolf. Then again, two needles in a haystack weren't that much easier to find than one. 'Did he say anything else about this couple?'

'Yes. He told me that their purpose originally was subversive – trying to weaken the country by encouraging disruptive activities. It was left to them initially to find the best way of doing that. At first they had focused their attention on the intelligence agencies and trying to weaken them by helping and encouraging their opponents.'

'And?' said Liz. This was more precise than anything he'd told them before. But she could hear a note of triumph in Mischa's voice. 'Something's changed though, hasn't it?'

'Yes. My brother said the first Illegal was working on a woman, who had become tied in to the intelligence services in some way. I told him that was a stroke of luck, and he said that luck is what failures call the success of their betters. He was annoyed with me, and that was when he told me the second Illegal had also managed something extraordinary.'

'Did he say what that was?'

Mischa nodded. 'I must go soon. They will open this chapel shortly.'

'Tell me first. What was extraordinary?'

Mischa hesitated, and Liz could sense him weighing the benefits of telling her against the rewards he might reap by leaving this disclosure for a later meet. She said, 'There will be something for you if you tell me now. If you don't, I cannot promise to meet you again. That is not meant as a threat, but as a fact.'

This seemed to tip the balance for Mischa. He stood up. 'My brother said the operation has changed. It has been renamed. It is now called Pincer.'

'As in a trap?'

'Something of the sort. He said the other Illegal is targeting a man, and that through him a second of your secret services might be infiltrated.'

Liz saw that he was preparing to leave and said quickly, 'So they're mounting a dual attack?'

'Not yet, I think,' he said. 'But I do know for sure that they are getting close to it.'

Liz was stunned by this revelation that not one, but two of the UK's intelligence services were under attack. Operation Pincer seemed the right name for such an ambitious plot. But before she could ask anything else, Mischa was gone.

34

THE BBC WEATHER WEBSITE said that Tallinn was fine: 21 degrees and clear skies. Peggy looked glumly out of one of the windows of the fourth-floor open-plan office, and wished again that Liz had taken her too. In London a westerly wind had swept in from the Atlantic, bringing rain and a cold wind. It felt more like autumn than spring, thought Peggy grumpily.

Until recently she'd always looked forward to the end of the day and to going back to the flat and seeing Tim. But things had changed. Now she found herself dawdling at her desk, almost looking for extra things to do, anything to reduce the hours she spent in his company.

So when the phone on her desk rang just as she was thinking of packing up for the day, she was pleased rather than annoyed – and delighted when it turned out to be Jasminder, suggesting they meet for a drink. It gave Peggy just what she wanted: a good excuse for being late home. She'd text Tim to warn him, and with any luck he'd find his own supper and retreat to the study and she wouldn't have to cope with his inevitable surliness.

She met Jasminder in a wine bar near Embankment station, in one of the vaults below the railway bridge.

Jasminder was looking stunning. She'd had her hair cut into a chic bob, and wore a smart raincoat, tightly belted. She was sitting in a corner nursing a glass of white wine.

Conversation flowed easily now that Jasminder knew where her friend worked. By coincidence, when she'd come round Thames House on an introductory tour, one of the people she'd been introduced to was none other than Peggy, who had laughed at her amazement.

'How's it all going?' asked Peggy now. 'Are you sorry you took the job? The press have been giving you a bit of a hard time.'

'Not at all. I'm really enjoying it – in spite of all that,' said Jasminder, sipping her wine. 'I had my doubts at the beginning, as you know. But I was wrong – the job is fascinating. C has been very supportive and I think he really is committed to greater openness. So I don't feel at all as if I've sacrificed my principles – which as you know was what I was most worried about.'

'And Geoffrey Fane? How's that old brute been behaving?'

Jasminder laughed. 'I think he still thinks my arrival signals the end of the world as he knows it – and it probably does. But to be fair to him, he's been very friendly.'

'Yes, he would be,' said Peggy. 'One thing about Geoffrey is that he's a gent. But that doesn't mean he'll take it all lying down. Just watch your back for when he sticks the knife in.'

'I hear you, but honestly, I don't think he will.'

'Hmm.' Peggy sounded sceptical. Then something buzzed, and Jasminder reached into her bag. She brought out a shiny green iPhone.

'Ooh, nice,' said Peggy admiringly.

'I know. It was a gift. I'd never spend that much myself.'

'Is it something urgent?' Peggy asked as Jasminder looked at the message.

'No. It's my friend Laurenz. I'm meeting him in a bit – in front of the National Gallery.'

'Is he the guy you mentioned before? You know, when we were filling out your application form?' From which, Peggy also remembered, any mention of a boyfriend or partner had been omitted.

'That's the one.' Jasminder seemed too pleased to be embarrassed. 'We met when I got mugged,' she added. 'Do you remember, it was just before that lecture where we first met? He was the one who chased the men off.'

'I remember. Are you seeing a lot of him then?'

Jasminder nodded. She suddenly looked shy. 'I usually stay at his place now. When there were all those reporters round my house, he rescued me.'

'Isn't that dying down? The press is known for its short attention span.'

'Yes. They've gone now. But Laurenz is still a bit nervy about them.'

'Why does he care? It's you they're interested in.'

'I know. But he's a very private person and very protective of me.'

'What does Laurenz do?'

'Don't laugh: he's a private banker.' Peggy couldn't help but smile, and Jasminder said ruefully, 'I know, it seems unlikely – Miss Civil Liberties going out with a representative of capitalism. But at least he's not a hedge-fund manager. And, surprisingly, he shares my view on a lot of things. He's remarkably liberal on many issues.'

'But presumably his clients aren't. Is that why he doesn't want them to see him in the newspapers?'

'Probably.' Jasminder hesitated. 'There's something else too. He's going through a divorce and it's been very unpleasant. He says he doesn't want his wife to know about me until everything's settled. He said it would only make things worse if she knew he was seeing someone else. I think they're arguing over money. He says she's trying to bleed him dry.'

'Sounds nasty. But I wouldn't have thought the fact that he was seeing someone else would make any difference. I don't think the courts expect any man to be a monk these days.'

Jasminder shrugged, then glanced at her phone again. Peggy said, 'Did he give you that?'

'Yes, when I got the job at MI6. He's very generous. If I let him, he'd pamper me the whole time.'

Peggy smiled, trying not to think about how long it had been since Tim had given her a present. It wasn't that she expected them; on his lecturer's salary he wasn't in a position to flood her with gifts. Actually, the nicest thing she'd ever had from him was a bunch of wildflowers he'd presented her with on her birthday. It just would have been good to know sometimes that he still wanted to please her.

Jasminder said, 'I'd better be going. Laurenz is one of those irritatingly punctual types.'

'Did you say you're meeting him by the National Gallery?'

'That's right.'

'I'll walk up with you, if you don't mind. It's on my way.'

'Great. I can introduce you. That will be a first. He's never met any of my friends.'

'I'll just get the bill,' said Peggy. She was curious to see this man who seemed to have Jasminder wrapped around his finger. Odd, how this impressive young woman – a role model to others, known for her ability to take strong positions and argue the toss with anybody from aggressive television interviewers to senior government ministers – was acting like a besotted teenager.

Outside it was still light as they walked up to the Strand, then cut across Trafalgar Square towards the steps in front of the National Gallery. The tourist season was just beginning, and by the fountains young visitors were posing for each other in front of Nelson's Column. As they walked by it, Jasminder suddenly waved and Peggy saw a tall man in a dark blue suit, standing on the steps at the north end of the square, lift his hand in response.

As they approached, Peggy hung back a bit and waited while Jasminder and the man embraced. Peggy felt slightly awkward, especially when he didn't even look at her; she wished now she had simply made her own way home. But Jasminder turned, holding the man's hand, and said, 'Laurenz, I want you to meet a friend of mine. This is Peggy Kinsolving.'

Peggy put on her warmest smile. 'Hello,' she said, trying to sound as friendly as she could.

Laurenz nodded at her, but didn't say hello. He was a handsome man, almost dauntingly so – with a strong jaw, deep-set eyes, and dark hair that he brushed straight back.

'I'm just on my way home,' Peggy explained, in case Laurenz thought she was hoping to horn in on them. 'But it's very nice to meet you. Jasminder's been telling me about you.'

'Has she?' he said, and Peggy could see that Jasminder was sharing her own discomfort. 'Do you work with her?'

'No,' said Peggy emphatically.

'How do you know her then?' he asked rather abruptly. He seemed suspicious.

'We met after a talk I gave,' Jasminder said, and Peggy added, 'I'm a big admirer of Jasminder's – like a lot of people.'

Though this was intended to please Laurenz it had the opposite effect. He scowled slightly, then put his arm through Jasminder's until she'd turned and faced him. 'We're running late,' he said, and started to lead her away.

Jasminder looked back at Peggy, with a helpless expression that seemed almost beseeching, as if asking her to understand.

'Nice to meet you,' Peggy called out to Laurenz with a cheerfulness she didn't feel. 'I'll ring you,' she said more quietly to Jasminder, but her friend had already turned around and Peggy doubted she'd been heard.

35

'SO THE MYSTERY DEEPENS,' said Bruno Mackay.
He was obviously in better spirits and recovering
from whatever it was that had happened to him in Libya.
His yellow spotted tie demanded to be noticed and his
pinstripe Savile Row suit disguised his thinness – or perhaps
he's regaining a bit of weight, thought Liz. Somehow she
would feel more comfortable with the old self-satisfied,
patronising Bruno than she had with the rather grey shadow
of himself of a few weeks ago.

'Yes. Now we seem to be looking for two people,' she
said. Liz had just finished describing her meeting with
Mischa. They were gathered in the same conference room
in which they had first heard from Charlie Simmons that
something was stirring and might be heading their way.
They had moved on a lot since then but it was still impossible to know whether what they were now learning had
any connection to what Charlie had reported.

This was the frustration of counter-espionage, thought
Liz: too many vague leads, too little hard intelligence. She
wanted to see the threat – like she could see the terrorist –
and to understand what she was trying to prevent. But this
was more like walking into a dark room, knowing someone

else was in there too, reaching out to try and touch them while at the same time dreading making contact for fear of what they might do.

'If I've got it right,' said Peggy, ever practical, 'what he's saying is that there are two foreigners in the country – and we don't know what nationality they are pretending to be – who are manipulating people in a position to do damage to the intelligence services. I don't see what we can possibly do with information that vague.'

Liz said, 'Hang on a minute. Mischa was more precise than that. What he was saying was that they came here with the broad brief of finding ways of damaging and weakening the country. They first focused on the intelligence services and on getting alongside our critics and encouraging and helping them. That sounds like a classic subversion operation. But then he said that recently the operation has changed its aim because they have got close to two people, a woman and a man, who are actually in or very close to the intelligence services – that means us and you, Bruno, or else possibly GCHQ. It's less likely to be Defence Intelligence.

'Mischa said that the two Illegals are working in partnership, as they have done before, though whether here or somewhere else, I don't know. Since they each have a different intelligence service in their sights, they've renamed the initiative, which is now called Operation Pincer.

'Make of that what you like,' Liz concluded with a shrug. 'But,' she added, 'you can be sure that if the FSB are congratulating themselves on a success, then it's serious. If they've penetrated us and you, Bruno, we're right back to the Cold War. Heaven knows what damage will be done.'

'Well, it certainly sounds terrible,' said Peggy. 'And so clever as to be almost incredible. Are you sure Mischa is kosher, Miles, and not just spinning us a story to get lots of your lovely dollars?'

Miles Brookhaven shrugged. Like Bruno he wore a suit, but his tie was striped and his shirt a white Brooks Brother button-down at its most conservative. He said, 'Our Kiev Station thinks he's reliable. He's given them some good stuff about Russian activity in Ukraine.'

'From what he said to me,' Liz responded, 'it wasn't brilliant work on the Illegals' part. They got lucky. Something happened that they weren't expecting, and they took advantage of it. Though I don't think Mischa's brother put it that way to his bosses. It sounds as though he's taking credit for a brilliant coup.'

There was silence in the room for a moment.

'This doesn't make sense,' said Bruno. 'How could someone who looked at first as though they would help undermine the intelligence services, suddenly get inside one? None of us is going to start employing Wikileakers or Snowdenistas. Not nowadays.'

Peggy said, 'They might not be one of us. Think back to the Cold War. We used to try to recruit the window cleaner at the Soviet Embassy or the gardener at the flats where the Bulgarians lived. They often turned out to be very useful.'

'True,' said Bruno, with a grin. 'But even MI5 wouldn't have regarded a window cleaner as a coup, so I don't suppose the FSB does.'

Peggy groaned, Miles smiled and Liz said, 'I don't think it's the window cleaner at all. I don't know how this has happened but I think the female they've targeted has recently joined either one of the intelligence services or perhaps the Home Office or the police or even the Foreign Office. Anyway they've got themselves inside and that's why Mischa's brother is so excited. The male target's either not in play yet, or their position isn't as helpful.'

'I would guess romance is involved somewhere in all this.' It was Miles speaking.

'Romance?' said Liz.

'He means sex, Liz,' said Bruno. 'He's just too well brought up to say so. You know, the old-fashioned honey trap. In that case we're looking for a lover boy pursuing the female target.'

'Don't be so sexist,' said Peggy. 'It could be a seductress.'

'It could be same sex in both cases,' agreed Liz. 'We just don't know as yet.'

Peggy worked late, feeling buoyed by the meeting. She'd met Miles a couple of times while Liz was away, and far from the slightly naive American she remembered from the past, she now thought him relaxed, friendly and clever. After months of Tim's bad-tempered outbursts, many directed at her, she found spending time with a courteous but quick-thinking man a welcome change. She knew Miles didn't have a wife, and found herself wondering if he had anyone in his life. Peggy thought not: he'd made a passing reference one afternoon to the 'bachelor supper' awaiting him, which he confessed was going to be a takeaway. If there hadn't been Tim to think about, Peggy would have offered to make him supper.

She was feeling more confident of finding the Illegals. If they'd somehow infiltrated MI5 or MI6, then they were operating on turf she knew well. She liked this kind of pursuit, and was good at it. Hadn't Liz told her the best antidote to personal troubles was immersion in the job? It looked as though that was how it was going to be now, and Peggy left work feeling much better than she had when the day began.

The Underground was packed, and she just managed to squeeze herself and her briefcase into a carriage. As the train moved on out of the centre towards North London, the crowd gradually thinned and she was able to get a seat. She wondered if she would find Tim at home. They were partners in name only nowadays, she realised sadly. They still shared a bed, though there might as well have been a wall of steel dividing the mattress for all the intimacy there was between them.

She had not looked at Tim's computer again, or even gone into the room he used as his study. But the memory of 'Marina' rankled, and Peggy couldn't help imagining – or fantasising, since she had nothing to go on – about what this Marina did and who she was. A *femme fatale* no doubt, mature, exotic, good-looking – all the things Peggy worried she wasn't. Marina would have been attracted by Tim's intelligence, his intensity, and – not that Peggy saw much of it these days – his gentle kindness. They probably shared the same political views; she could hear Marina's withering take on Peggy's choice of career.

That is, if Tim had told her what his partner did for a living. He had promised never to do that – even his parents thought she worked at the MOD in HR. Yet Tim had always been so open by nature that Peggy couldn't help but believe that the man who had once shared everything with her was now sharing it with someone else.

When she left the Underground it was dusk and the streetlights were coming on as she turned on to her street. The road on both sides was lined with cars – parking was at a premium out here, since so many of the houses had been divided into flats, with multiple cars per building. She watched as a hundred yards ahead of her a maroon Vauxhall saloon was trying to back into a rare but rather small space.

Parking aside, Peggy liked her neighbourhood; it was quiet, unpretentious, and the only celebrity living within a mile of it was a second-division footballer. She reckoned it was only a matter of time before Tim moved out. She liked the flat, but wasn't sure she could afford to stay there on her own. She supposed she'd either have to find a flatmate, which she didn't really want to do, or move to a smaller place. She tried to cheer herself up by deciding it would be good to find somewhere closer to work. It would feel odd to live on her own, but at least there would be no tension each evening when she turned the key in the door.

She noticed that the Vauxhall had given up trying to squeeze into the space and was driving slowly along the road towards her, its driver looking for somewhere else to park. It was then she heard footsteps behind her. She glanced back and saw a slim male figure in a hoodie walking fast towards her. She couldn't see his face properly but there was something alarming about him, especially when she remembered how Jasminder had been attacked.

Peggy decided to cross the street, where a man in a dark suit and tie, wearing a hat with a brim that shadowed his face, was standing doing something with his phone. As she crossed, the Vauxhall saloon was about fifty feet in front of her, moving very slowly. Peggy could see the driver, a woman in her forties, still searching for a parking space.

When Peggy reached the far pavement, the man was standing there staring at his phone, his free hand in his jacket pocket. She had started to walk round him when he said, 'Excuse me.'

She looked up just in time to see him raise his arm. He was holding a short truncheon, and as his arm came down Peggy flinched and turned away. The truncheon missed her head but hit her hard on the shoulder, and the pain was excruciating. The man looked ready to hit her again so she ran into the road just as the Vauxhall drew level with them. The car braked sharply and Peggy staggered into the side of it then fell hands first onto the bonnet. She rolled instinctively, just in time to avoid the truncheon, which missed her head and slammed down with such force that it dented the steel of the bonnet.

Peggy was now standing in front of the car. To her surprise, the female driver was staring at her – as if nothing were wrong. Peggy opened her mouth and screamed. The man in the suit, still holding the truncheon, seemed to be deciding whether to come at her again, then suddenly he flung open the passenger door and jumped in. The woman at the wheel seemed entirely unsurprised, and Peggy realised she was working with the man.

Peggy managed to take two steps towards the pavement as the car accelerated sharply, narrowly missing her, and sped away. Looking around, stunned and rubbing her shoulder with one hand, Peggy could see no sign of the hooded figure anywhere.

She felt dizzy and knew she was going into shock. A door slammed nearby and she heard a man shouting as he ran towards her. 'Are you all right? What's happened?'

Peggy's dizziness was worse now. 'I need to sit down,' she said, and the man led her to the low wall separating his front garden from the pavement. Someone else appeared as she tried to catch her breath; it took a moment for her to realise that it was Tim.

'Peggy, are you all right?'

'I'll be fine,' she said. She looked up and was relieved to see that his face was filled with concern. 'Someone hit me,' she said, close to tears. 'They hit me with a stick.'

'Who was it?' asked Tim, bewildered.

Peggy's head was starting to spin, and she grabbed the edge of the brick wall to steady herself. 'It was a set-up. There was a car... A woman... She drove him away.'

'Who? What do you mean? Did he take anything?'

But Peggy didn't answer. She was starting to feel very sick indeed. She heard Tim say, 'Don't worry, I've called the police, and they're sending an ambulance as well.' She looked up and saw him holding his phone in the air. It must be new, she thought dimly. But she'd seen it before... Then she realised it was the same kind of phone as Jasminder's. When did he get that? Peggy wondered vaguely. She closed her eyes, and could hear Tim talking to their neighbour. She was straining to hear what he was saying when gradually his voice faded clean away. Peggy had passed out.

36

'I'M SO SORRY. Is the funeral in London?' said C's Private Secretary, Mrs Dwyer.

Jasminder was startled. She was prepared to answer all sorts of questions about her non-existent aunt, but it had not occurred to her that anyone would want to know where the poor lady was being buried. She hesitated, then said, 'Leicester.'

'Ah,' said Mrs Dwyer, who had worked for five Controllers before taking on the new C; it was said she knew more about the Service than its official historian. C himself was not in his office – he was at meetings in Whitehall all morning, so Jasminder didn't have to offer him her bogus excuse for the planned absence on Friday.

'I grew up in Leicester,' she explained, regaining her composure. 'Most of my family still lives there.'

'Well, I'm very sorry,' said Mrs Dwyer. Her voice was sympathetic, and Jasminder felt bad for lying to her. She wished she'd simply decided to call in sick on Friday instead, or even take a day's leave. But Laurenz had pointed out that one of the MI6 technical boffins who'd spent so much time rewiring her house might show up to check on some aspect of her new security system. Since she'd be halfway to Bermuda by then, it didn't seem a good idea to pretend she was at home.

'Thank you,' said Jasminder. 'Please tell C I'll be back in on Monday.'

She went away feeling slightly troubled, but cheered by the prospect of her trip to Bermuda at the end of the week. And tonight Laurenz would be back, after spending the weekend with a client in Spain. In his absence she'd tried to see Emma, but she had been busy – there'd been a certain coolness in her voice on the phone, and Jasminder realised it had been several weeks since she'd been in touch with her closest friend. That would have to change, she decided, taking heart from Laurenz's recent declaration that his divorce was finally coming through and soon he would be happy to meet all her friends, including Emma.

That evening when Jasminder went to his flat, she found Laurenz already back from Madrid. He was leaving before her for Bermuda, since he had the two conference days to sit through, and seemed preoccupied, almost harried, as if on some deadline she didn't know about. For once Jasminder felt that she was more relaxed than he was. At dinner he ate quickly, and was unusually quiet. Finally, she asked him if something was wrong.

'Wrong?' He stared at her blankly, as though looking through her. 'No, not at all. But these are important meetings in Bermuda, and I feel a bit exposed.'

'Why's that?'

'I told you,' he said impatiently, 'I'm not having the best of years.' He sighed. 'One of the less fun things about these annual conferences is that we're all expected to bring something special to the table.'

Jasminder wasn't sure she understood. But Laurenz was staring at her intently now, and she felt uncomfortable.

She was obviously missing something, and the easy connection she had always felt with him was for some reason absent tonight. She said, 'What sort of special thing do they want?'

'Information of course,' he snapped.

'What are you going to bring them then?'

'That's the problem. I haven't got anything special at all. Thanks to this wretched divorce, I haven't kept my eye on the ball. At least, that's what some of my clients seem to think. That's why I asked you for help, if you remember. Now my own colleagues may reach the same conclusion.' He leaned back, eyes fixed on the wall behind Jasminder's head. 'To tell you the truth, I'm seriously worried.'

'I'm sure it will be all right,' she said soothingly. 'It's been a hard year for you; surely they can all understand that.'

He made a small scoffing noise that left Jasminder feeling foolish. 'Sympathy is not much in evidence in the banking world. It's strictly dog eat dog.'

He said this so cynically that Jasminder was taken aback. This wasn't the easy-going, confident man she'd come to know. She wanted to do something for him but could only say feebly, 'I wish I could help.'

'Do you?' said Laurenz, lowering his eyes until they were level with hers. She felt as if he were looking at her for the first time.

'Of course,' she said, wishing he would smile, or at the very least not sound quite so bitter and low. 'You know I want to support you, Laurenz.'

He ignored this and said, 'You could help me, you know. Help me quite a lot.'

'Really?' She said this innocently, but part of her sensed what was coming – and dreaded it.

'You have access to all sorts of information. Even a few snippets would let me make a mark at the meetings.' He seemed to notice she was stiffening. 'There you go,' he said. 'You act as if I'm committing a capital offence when I haven't even asked you for anything.'

'You know I'm not allowed to share information with people outside the Service.'

'But you already have.' He was staring at her, without any of the sympathy he usually showed. She wanted to explain that her help that time had been a one-off, and he shouldn't be asking her again. But she knew he would just get angry if she said that. Jasminder felt cornered by his unblinking gaze, and found herself growing upset. She wished it were the weekend already, with the bankers' meetings over and Laurenz back to his usual self. She tried to buy time while she thought of the best way to steer him off this topic. 'What were you wanting in particular?'

He leaned forward across the kitchen counter, resting on his elbows with both hands under his chin. 'I'll tell you what would really knock their socks off... Russian strategy.'

'What do you mean – Russian strategy?'

'Everyone wants to know whether Russia is planning on moving into another border country – say Latvia or Azerbaijan. Think about it: nobody pays much attention to those countries normally, but if the Russians were to go into either of them, it would have a global impact. People would run for safety – buy dollars, buy gold, get out of the stock market.'

'You seem to know a lot about it already. Can't you just talk about that?'

'Bah!' he said, and his voice was even more scathing. 'What I think about what Putin might do doesn't matter.

What my "sources" think about it, and what they think NATO would do in response, would grip everyone's attention.'

'What sources?' asked Jasminder, and as soon as she'd said it, realised that she was the source.

He waited for the penny to drop, then said, 'You've got access to JIC reports, I bet. They have to have assessed Putin's strategy and considered NATO's possible responses – if there's a Russian move into the Baltic States, for example. If I could get up and say: "Here is the Western governmental view of what might happen, and how the West would respond," then I bet even the Chairman would forget about his golf game for a minute.' Laurenz laughed, but he didn't sound amused.

Jasminder was rocked back by this speech and stared at him in shock. How did he know about the JIC? The average man in the street was highly unlikely to have the abbreviation for the Joint Intelligence Committee on the tip of his tongue, but then she supposed no one would ever confuse Laurenz with the man in the street.

After a moment she said, 'I don't see JIC reports.'

'Maybe you don't, normally, but I'm sure you could if you wanted to.'

'No, honestly, I couldn't,' she said, frustrated by the sceptical expression that spread across Laurenz's face. 'It's all done on a need-to-know basis. And I don't have any need to know.' She realised she was sounding plaintive now, but couldn't help it. She had been completely knocked off balance by his demand. 'I can't exactly say, "Hello, I need to see the JIC assessments on Putin's strategy, to help my boyfriend."'

'You're high-profile, Jasminder. You can ask for anything you want. They wouldn't dare say no. If you were to leave now, MI6 would look very foolish. Your boss C in particular.'

He spoke with such assurance that she wondered momentarily if he was right. Did she really have that kind of power? Could she simply crook a finger and have all the innermost secrets of the British intelligence services laid out for her scrutiny? For a moment she found the prospect exciting, then she realised its fundamental absurdity. What she'd told Laurenz was correct: information in MI6 was handled on the strict basis of need to know – even the closest of colleagues didn't discuss their cases with each other unless they were actually working together. If she started asking for highly classified material – like the minutes of JIC meetings, or copies of the papers sent to the Cabinet – alarm bells would go off and she would be questioned right away about why she had made the request. She couldn't think of any plausible reason at all.

She said now, 'I'm sorry. There just isn't any way I can get that kind of information. Not for you, not even for myself. No way at all.'

She wanted to look away from Laurenz's relentless gaze; she knew that what she was saying was true and wanted him to understand it too. But she forced herself to lock eyes with him until finally he shrugged. 'I thought you wanted to help,' he said.

'I do,' she protested earnestly. 'Just not that way – I can't do it. You must understand that.' When he didn't reply, she added, 'I would if I could.'

'So you say, but the thing is, I'm *sure* you could. It just takes a little imagination.' He saw her mouth tighten, and he sighed again. 'Let's leave it for now. We can talk some more about it when we're in Bermuda.'

Jasminder wondered how that would help, since she thought he wanted the information in time for his meetings. But she said nothing, just hoping the tension between them would pass. Laurenz said, 'You'll meet my colleagues then. They can explain the kind of pressure we're under.'

'Oh,' said Jasminder, a little disappointed. The last thing she wanted to talk about in Bermuda was the pressure of work. She had thought she was going there to be with Laurenz and to relax.

'Yes,' he said, nodding at her, 'my friends are very keen to meet you. You'll find you have lots to talk about with them.'

37

TIM CAME TO SEE Peggy the day after she was admitted to the Royal Free. She had a private room – not because she was being given special treatment, but because she'd hit her head when she'd fainted, and the doctors at the hospital were concerned about concussion and didn't want her in a noisy ward.

Her collarbone had been fractured by the blow she'd received, and her left arm was in a sling, which the doctors said she was going to have to wear for six weeks. They'd been concerned too about nerve damage to her shoulder, and had put her through the claustrophobia of an MRI scan. She'd been terrified but had closed her eyes and gritted her teeth for the twenty minutes she'd lain enclosed in the doughnut-shaped machine.

The pain was constant but not acute – and the morphine helped, though the drawback was the dreams it seemed to spawn. She woke sweating and in a panic after one particularly horrible one – this time the man with the phone hadn't jumped into the car but was chasing her around it. She was trying to run away from him but her legs moved in jelly-like slow motion – only to find Tim standing at the foot of her bed.

'Hi there,' he said, a little awkwardly, 'they don't let you bring flowers so I bought you some grapes.' And he plonked a plastic box of green grapes on the bed. They looked rather dry, as if they had seen better days. Tim had always been hopeless at giving her presents and she'd once seen it as a rather charming aspect of his unworldliness, but now she wondered if it simply meant he didn't care.

A nurse came in behind him and, seeing the grapes, offered to find a dish for them. When she'd left the room Tim sat down. 'So how are you feeling?' he asked, perching uneasily on the edge of the high-backed vinyl chair, his hands dangling loosely between his knees.

'Not too bad,' she said. 'They're giving me something for the pain. The doctor says I probably won't need an operation.'

'That's good news. How long will you be in?'

'Another night or two. I'd come home now if I didn't feel so woozy.'

'Have the police been to see you?'

'Yes – twice, in fact.' There had been a bright woman constable who'd been sufficiently struck by Peggy's description of the attack – and by her elliptical description of her job – that she'd asked for a Special Branch detective to come in a few hours later and question Peggy further about her assailants.

'I bet that's more than they usually do,' said Tim cynically. 'Especially for an ordinary mugging.'

'They don't think it was an ordinary mugging.'

'Really? Why not? The guy was after your handbag, I bet.'

'Dressed in a suit? With a woman waiting in a car to help him make his getaway? That's not how most muggers operate.'

'You'd be surprised. Lots of people are desperate these days. Not just young delinquents either. Besides, if it wasn't a mugging, what else could it be? Don't tell me it was terrorists – or Edward Snowden!'

Peggy didn't have an answer, and if one occurred to her, it wouldn't be something she would want to discuss with Tim. She was certain the attack on her had been planned, and she assumed it would have something to do with her job; there was nothing in her personal life – no spurned lovers, no stalkers, no arch-enemies – that could make someone want to bash her brains in.

But there was no obvious answer to be found. Working with Liz, Peggy spent most of her time behind the scenes, analysing intelligence, doing research, investigating leads. Occasionally of late she had been operational – almost always interviewing people and always under cover. The last time had been the year before, when she had gone to question an old lady who lived next door to a house in Manchester suspected of sheltering terrorists. For that Peggy had posed as an electoral registration officer; before that she'd played other roles, a pollster, a student looking for a room and once a District Nurse. She'd never disclosed her real name, or where she lived or her real job, so it was hard to see how she could have been identified by someone or why they would want to kill her.

For that, she felt quite sure, was what this attack had been about – there was no mistaking the lethal intentions of the man with the cosh. She shuddered as she remembered the force of the blow that had missed her, but dented the bonnet of the car.

She pulled herself together and looked at Tim. Remembering what had happened to her brought to mind a question.

'I noticed you've got a new phone,' she said.

Tim shifted suddenly on his seat. 'Yes. Why?'

'I was just wondering when you got it.'

He shrugged his shoulders, but looked uncomfortable. 'A couple of weeks ago.'

'Did you buy it? It's very smart. It must have cost the earth.' She knew he didn't have the £500 or so that iPhones like his went for. Some months he didn't even have his share of the rent.

'Not really,' Tim said reluctantly.

'Well, have you signed a new contract or something?'

'No. But what does it matter?'

'Well, of course it matters. If you've taken out an expensive phone contract, how are you going to pay your share of the household bills?'

'Well, I haven't.'

'So where did you come by such a fancy phone?'

'From someone I met.' He spoke jerkily. 'Through a group.'

'A group?'

'Online,' he snapped. 'An online group. People who think like me about civil liberties. But they think of their own free will, unlike the clones you work with.'

'So you made a friend online and they gave you an iPhone?'

'It wasn't like that.' He looked embarrassed, but said angrily, 'I met the person actually, since you ask. And we share the same views.'

'About what?'

'The internet. The need for freedom of speech. Thanks to your lot, no one can be sure that communications are confidential. Snowden showed that governments can look at anything – and they do.'

'It would take at least a couple of million people to look at everybody's email. Frankly, we have better things to do.'

'That's not the point. You can't feel safe on the internet. You never know for sure that Big Brother isn't snooping on everything you do. Phones are much safer.' He looked at her defiantly. 'I'm not doing anything wrong. The state is. I don't want them poking about in my business.'

Peggy shook her head, partly to clear the cobwebs induced by the sedative, partly in disbelief. She had heard most of this before from Tim, but it was still utter codswallop. How on earth could an intelligent man think that accessing the internet on a phone was any different from doing so on a computer, or safer if it came to that? Someone had been filling his head with rubbish. She said, 'This "friend" of yours, is female?'

'As a matter of fact, she is. But that's nothing to do with it.'

'Oh, really? She admires your ideas, I suppose; so much that she gives you expensive unsolicited gifts. I wasn't born yesterday, you know.' Peggy found herself growing angry, if only because Tim was being so unforthcoming. If he were having an affair, if he had found someone else, it would hurt, yes, and it would mean their relationship was over. But then why couldn't he say so?

'I promise you, it's not like that. Marina – that's the woman's name – isn't interested in me that way.'

So maybe this woman was taking him for a mug. Though that didn't explain why she'd given him an expensive phone. Peggy said angrily, 'And what about you? Is your interest purely intellectual?'

'I barely know what the woman looks like. I only met her for the first time at that talk we went to. You know, the one Jasminder gave before she joined the Spooks.'

'Spooks? Is that what you call us now?'

'It's just a name, Peggy,' said Tim, but he looked ashamed of himself.

She frowned. 'I still don't understand – especially if this Marina woman is only interested in your mind – why she gave you a phone. It doesn't make any sense. It would be like my giving some casual friend a laptop for Christmas. Over the top, inappropriate, and actually downright weird.'

'I explained – it's to keep our exchanges confidential. And anyway, it's not what you think. Marina has a friend who beta-tests phones for Apple and had a few spare. She asked if I would like one. I said, of course. So she gave me one. It may look weird,' he acknowledged, sounding defensive, 'but that's the truth.'

Peggy didn't know what to say. Fortunately the nurse came in just then, to take her temperature and blood pressure, while another woman brought supper on a tray. By the time she'd set it down and filled the water jug, Tim had left. Peggy didn't mind that he hadn't even said goodbye.

38

IT HAD BEEN A long day, and Liz had got back to her flat wanting nothing but a hot bath, a large glass of white wine and perhaps a chunk of Cheddar and a biscuit, when the phone rang. All thoughts of these creature comforts disappeared when the desk officer at Thames House informed her that Peggy Kinsolving had been attacked, and was now in the Royal Free in Hampstead, receiving treatment. She would be all right, the desk officer assured Liz, but had been quite badly hurt.

It was another twenty-four hours before Liz saw Peggy in the flesh, though by then she had already made two trips to Hampstead. Peggy was being scanned on the first occasion; the next time, she was in a drug-induced sleep, which the nurses said would not wear off for several hours. There was no sign of Tim at the hospital, though apparently he knew all about the incident and had visited; a nurse told Liz he'd actually been on the scene just moments after the assault. There didn't seem to be anyone else to notify: Peggy's father had died many years before and Liz knew that her mother was in a home, suffering from advanced dementia.

This time she found Peggy wide awake – and looking grumpy. 'So,' said Liz, handing her a box of After Eights and a paperback edition of *Cold Comfort Farm*, 'what's the prognosis?'

Peggy explained she'd be in for another day or two. 'The doctors tell me I can come back to work next week.'

'Take your time. I'd rather you were fully fit before you return.' Liz paused, then said, 'By the way, I've spoken to Special Branch. We're trying to work out who did this to you, and why, but I can't say we've got very far.'

Peggy shook her head wearily. 'I am sure there's something behind it but I've thought and thought and I can't work out what it is.'

'Well, try and leave it for now or you won't get better. Anyway, have you got everything you need?'

'Yes, thanks. And thank you for the chocs – and the book. I've never read it.'

'It's very funny. I hope it won't hurt you to laugh.'

Peggy grinned, and for a moment looked her old perky self. Then the slight melancholy Liz had noticed recently in her young friend re-emerged, settling on her face like a gloomy mask. Liz said gently, 'Has Tim been to see you?'

'Yes. You must have just missed him. He brought me those,' and she pointed to the grapes that were beginning to shrivel on their plate. Liz couldn't help smiling at the unattractive-looking specimens, and was relieved to find Peggy smiling too.

Then she said, 'Liz, if someone you knew and liked – a friend, let's say, but nothing more – suddenly offered you an iPhone, would you think it odd?'

'You mean, as a present?'

Peggy nodded.

'Well, I'd say it was pretty unusual. Why? What's happened?'

'Tim was given a phone by… someone called Marina.' A tear start to roll down Peggy's cheek. 'He said they talk in an online chat room. A bunch of kindred spirits apparently. Snowdenistas one and all.'

'I remember you telling me he was getting involved with those people.'

Peggy nodded, her expression grim. 'He says it's purely a sharing of interests, but it sounds pretty fishy to me.' She sighed, then winced as she moved her shoulder.

Liz said sympathetically, 'You mentioned things had been difficult lately.'

'That's putting it mildly. But I thought it was his politics that had changed. I didn't think—' Peggy stopped talking and looked away. Liz noticed another tear fall. She felt for Peggy, but something in this story didn't seem as obvious as her friend thought. If Tim were seeing someone else, wouldn't he have just come out and said so? He had always struck Liz as slightly weak, even nerdish, but duplicity seemed out of character for him – if anything, he was painfully ingenuous.

'You know, Peggy, what he's saying is probably true. These kinds of internet friendships can be pretty intense, but without becoming – well, intimate in that sense.'

'I wish you were right. But somehow I don't think so.'

They talked for a few minutes more, until Liz could see Peggy was growing tired. 'Listen, I'll be back tomorrow, and bring you another book.'

'I don't want to spoil your weekend, Liz. I'll be fine here; they're looking after me very well.'

'I know, but I want to make sure you're getting better. Call it selfish but I need you back at Thames House ASAP.'

'Okay. Thanks so much for coming. It's cheered me up.'

'Good. See you tomorrow.' Liz left, glad she had come, but not just because Peggy had brightened up. There was something odd going on and she wanted to know more about it – and about this Marina woman who had befriended Tim and doubtless egged on his paranoid fantasies. Who was she and what was she up to? Liz wondered whether Jasminder knew her. If she was a hardline civil libertarian maybe she wrote articles for Jasminder's magazine. She must get Peggy to ask her. It was certainly worth finding out more, if only to reassure Liz herself that nothing dangerous was going on.

There was only one thing to do, she decided. With Peggy still in hospital for another day or two, this was the perfect time to tackle Tim.

39

T HE PLANE LANDED TWENTY minutes early, and with very little delay at passport control and customs Jasminder was soon in the baggage hall. She had brought rather a lot of clothes for a weekend, uncertain what the dress code would be. Thinking that in a place like Bermuda she would need something fairly glamorous for the evenings, she'd been shopping in her lunch breaks and had equipped herself with a choice to meet all situations. The airport confirmed her view that this would be a pretty glitzy weekend – the shops were expensive designer-label-only outlets, and the passengers in the terminal were dressed in the casually smart outfits of the rich.

A tall man in a chauffeur's hat was standing by the barrier with a sign bearing her name. He gave a curt nod when she approached him, took her bag and led her to a black limousine parked directly outside. They drove across the causeway from the airport, and after a few questions from Jasminder about Bermuda had received only mono-syllabic replies, they travelled on in silence.

They continued for a few miles more, past colonial-style houses set back from the road. Jasminder felt she could have been in Surrey, except for the occasional palm tree and the hints of sand beneath the manicured lawns. The sun shone in an unbroken blue sky, but it was cooler here than she'd expected – just 70 degrees Fahrenheit according to the thermometer on the car's dashboard – and she reminded herself that she was in the North Atlantic, not the tropics. They had just passed the umpteenth golf course when the driver turned off through open gates towards a spacious bungalow that sat a good hundred yards from the road. A large and beautiful Cedar of Lebanon tree stood on the front lawn, but the grass was six inches high, as if the gardener had been ill or the mower didn't work. When the chauffeur pulled up in front of the house, Jasminder could see that its pale ochre paint needed refreshing, and that at one end of its low slanting roof a few tiles were missing.

The chauffeur took her bag and escorted her to the front door, then shook his head when she asked how much she owed him. She rang the bell, but when the door swung open from her inadvertent push, she stepped inside, into the hallway. Open arched doors led to rooms on either side, but when she peeped in, there was no one about.

'Hello,' she called out cautiously, then repeated it more loudly. There was no response at first, but then she heard a door close at the back of the house. A moment later, a woman came towards her down the narrow hallway.

'Jasminder?' she asked. She was blonde and expensively packaged – as if on show rather than holiday. She wore a skin-tight dress of rainbow stripes, and white high heels that looked uncomfortable. Her arms and bare legs were the colour of caramel, and her skin had the leathery look that comes from too much exposure to the sun.

'That's me,' said Jasminder with a smile. The woman did not smile back.

'Let me show you where you're staying,' she said. She led Jasminder to the back of the house, down a corridor with closed doors on either side. The last door turned out to lead to Jasminder's bedroom.

'Is Laurenz here?' she asked. There was no sign in the room of his things.

The woman shook her head. Pointing to a connecting door, she said, 'His room's through there. They're all in a meeting, but you'll see him at dinner. It's at seven at the club.'

'The club?'

The woman looked at her expressionlessly. 'The golf club. It's just over there.' She pointed through the wide window of the bedroom. Turning to look, Jasminder could see a few holes of a golf course. Did anyone do anything else in Bermuda?

The woman said, 'You can walk there in a few minutes. If you want, I'll go with you so you don't get lost. There's a pool at the back,' she added – pointing behind the house. 'Feel free to use it. And help yourself to anything in the fridge.'

'Thank you,' said Jasminder.

'See you just before seven then,' the woman said, and left the room.

The bedroom was small and stuffy – the air conditioning seemed woefully underpowered. Jasminder opened the connecting door and walked through to Laurenz's room. It was the same size as hers, and though one of his suits was hanging in the cupboard and his shaving things were in the bathroom, it seemed equally soulless. It was certainly not the luxurious accommodation he had implied there would be. Still, Jasminder decided, she mustn't grumble; not many people got a free holiday to Bermuda.

Going back to her own room, she decided to have a swim, and changed into a new bikini she had bought for the trip. Taking a bath towel with her, she went out of the back door of the house and found the pool set behind a group of squat palmettos. The pool was small, kidney-shaped, and didn't look very inviting; clusters of flying beetles were flitting on and off the surface of the water and some were floating on it, apparently dead.

Two recliners were positioned in the shade at the far end and Jasminder went and lay down on one of them. She should have brought her book, she thought, then realised how tired she was.

When she opened her eyes again she was cold and, looking at her watch, discovered she had slept for an hour and a half. It was almost six-thirty. She went into the house, where no one else seemed to be about, including the woman she was starting to think of as Miss Glamour Girl. In her bedroom Jasminder considered what to wear for dinner – would it be smart or casual? She compromised, and put on smart trousers and a pretty, flowery top, with silver sandals. She applied a little makeup, brushed her hair, and went back to the front of the house. There she found Glamour Girl waiting in the sitting room, turning the pages of an old copy of *Vogue*.

'Hi, Jacintha, all set?' The other woman stood up. She was wearing a low-cut black evening dress, with a heavy gold necklace, dangly earrings and a pair of gold bracelets that jingled when she moved her arm.

'It's Jasminder. And yes, I'm ready. But what's your name?'

'My real one is long and unpronounceable. But you can call me Sam. Everyone else does.'

They went outside and Sam closed the door firmly behind them. Jasminder followed as the woman went through a gate in the back garden that led on to the golf course. As they walked along one of the fairways, Sam asked, 'Have you known Laurenz long?'

'Not really. It's been a couple of months since we started seeing each other. How about you? Have you known him long?'

'I suppose so,' Sam said vaguely.

'Do you work at the bank?'

Sam looked startled. 'The bank – me? Lord, no.' She gave a little artificial-sounding laugh and went on, 'I know these boys socially. I help arrange their little get-togethers, and make sure they have a good time.'

Jasminder nodded. It sounded as if Sam was some sort of hostess, and a well-paid one from the looks of her. She wondered where the other women were. Surely Jasminder wasn't the only partner there.

As they approached the clubhouse, she saw a group of men having drinks on the veranda. Laurenz was there, standing among them, and when he looked up she waved cheerily. He gave a little salute back, but he didn't come over to her, just kept on talking to the other men. Jasminder told herself to be more restrained. She didn't know many bankers in London – perhaps they were a stuffy bunch.

With Sam, Jasminder walked up the steps of the veranda. The men turned as one and examined them both, with an assessing stare that was plain rude. The two women joined the group and a few introductions were made, but Jasminder found it hard to catch anybody's name. Though they were all speaking in English, the men all looked more East European than British or American, except for one African who said he was from Zimbabwe.

The men were drinking cocktails, big measures of spirits served in oversized whisky glasses, but when the waiter came to her Jasminder asked for a spritzer. She had never been a big drinker and this looked as if it would be a heavy evening. From time to time, Laurenz looked over at her, but he didn't join her, and Jasminder felt both awkward and a little upset that he hadn't come over to welcome her. None of the other men seemed particularly anxious to talk to her and so she stayed standing next to Sam, who was prattling on about the comparative merits of shopping on Bond Street and the Rue de Rivoli. It looked as though the two of them were going to be the only women at the dinner.

Eventually they all went inside to a small private dining room. There didn't seem to be anyone else at all in the clubhouse apart from a couple of waiters. Jasminder found herself seated next to Sam, despite there being no other women present. On her other side was a giant bear of a man, with rough black hair and sideburns that came halfway down the sides of his face.

'I am Kozlov,' he said in a thick Russian accent. He held a bottle of red wine in one hand and, without asking her, filled her large goblet and then his own to the brim. He took a big gulp then said, 'And you are Laurenz's special friend. The one he often speaks of.'

'That's nice to hear,' said Jasminder, as a waiter put a plate of dressed crab down in front of her.

'And with a very special job,' said Kozlov, with a grin.

'I don't know about that.' Had Laurenz really talked about her job with this man? She hoped not.

'You are being modest,' said Kozlov, digging into his crab. He chewed nosily while looking at her. 'You are what Westerners call "deep waters", no?'

'Deep waters?' asked Jasminder, puzzled.

'You know what I mean. There is much information in that head of yours, but you do not act the part. You sit like a modest schoolgirl, when you know more than everyone in this room combined. I congratulate you on your cleverness.'

Jasminder felt embarrassed and alarmed. What on earth had Laurenz told this man about her? It sounded as though he'd described her as being a mixture of C and James Bond. It was absurd.

Fortunately Kozlov changed the subject, and began to regale her with stories of his own business prowess and his travels around the world. Las Vegas was his favourite city, he explained, partly for the gaming tables and partly for its culture.

'Culture?' asked Jasminder, unable to hide her amazement.

'Yes. You see, in Las Vegas they have many hotels now that are replicas of the world's most beautiful places. There is one with a canal as beautiful as the Grand Canal in Venice; another is based on the Parthenon. Et cetera, et cetera. You no longer have to go to all these places to see the sights. Now you can see the beauties of the world just by visiting Las Vegas.'

A waiter came and took their plates and then put new ones down, each with a large steak on it. Jasminder sighed inwardly. She didn't like beef and wished there had been an alternative available. She took some salad and moved the meat around on her plate to make a show of eating it, while hiding bits under the salad. Kozlov cut away at his, chomping away with gusto.

He was on his third goblet of wine when dessert came, and by then Jasminder had heard even more about Las Vegas, and far more than she wanted to know about the racy nightlife of Hamburg and Cologne. She had tried once or twice to catch Laurenz's eye, but he never looked over. It was almost as if he were intentionally ignoring her, and that just added to Jasminder's growing discomfort. This event was nothing like she had imagined, and these people were very far from the sophisticated group of international bankers and their elegant wives and partners that she had expected to meet. In fact, she reluctantly admitted to herself, the gathering was vulgar and tawdry, and Laurenz must know it and that was why he wasn't talking to her.

After dinner they all went back in a group to the bungalow. Sam walked with Jasminder. She was clearly slightly tipsy now, and seemed friendlier. She said in a loud whisper, 'I'm sorry you got stuck with Kozlov at dinner. He can be a bore.'

'He did seem a bit of a rough diamond.'

Sam laughed. 'That's putting it mildly. But these are good guys, even if they lack a certain polish. The only thing is, Jacintha...' And she paused, coming to a halt until the others were out of earshot. 'These men mean well but they can be a bit rough. If for some reason they wanted a person to do something, they would expect the person to do it.'

'What do you mean?' Jasminder suddenly felt cold. 'Do what?'

'Whatever it was they wanted. And my advice would always be to do whatever they ask. The alternative can be very unpleasant, in my experience.'

Sam walked on, and Jasminder, now thoroughly scared, followed her. In a moment they had caught up with the men – before Jasminder could press Sam on what she'd been saying. Was this a warning? It certainly sounded like it. Why was she here – apparently the only woman invited to join this group? What did these men expect from her? She thought back to her last conversation with Laurenz when he'd pressed her for information. She'd told him she couldn't provide it but why did Koslov know about her job? What had Laurenz been telling them? Surely some-one as subtle and kind and intelligent as he was didn't really count these people as his closest friends.

With a growing sense of panic she joined the men in the sitting room, where Kozlov was standing by a tray full of liquor bottles, dispensing large measures into brandy balloons. Jasminder judged it best not to show her alarm, so she smiled and asked for a Crème de Menthe. She managed to drink some of it but found it difficult to swal-low the sweet, cloying stuff and eventually abandoned her glass on an empty bookshelf.

She would have liked to quiz Sam further, but the woman was in full flow with one of the men about where he could buy some underwear for his girlfriend, so Jasminder decided to go back to her bedroom and try to work out what was going on. She would have liked to talk to Laurenz but he was in a huddle with his cronies, though he did look over and smile at her for the first time that evening, and when she motioned that she was going, he lifted his index finger to indicate he would join her in a minute or two.

When she got back to her bedroom she felt suddenly very tired. She could hardly keep her eyes open and her fear seemed to have floated away on waves of fatigue. These men seem awfully crass, she thought hazily, more like overgrown boys than mature citizens. Was this really what the world of finance was like? Jasminder had thought bankers were all educated at public schools, wore hand-made suits and belonged to gentlemen's clubs on

Pall Mall. These men tonight could have been supplied by central casting for a film about spivs.

She sighed and got into bed, thinking what she would wear the next day. She vaguely heard Laurenz come into his room and was aware that he looked in through the connecting door, but before she could say anything, she'd fallen asleep.

40

IT WAS RAINING BY the time Liz arrived at Peggy Kinsolving's flat. She had decided to risk going there without giving Tim advance warning, but when no one answered the bell it looked as if her gamble hadn't paid off. She was standing on the doorstep, more to shelter from the rain than in any hope that he was in, when a thin voice came through the intercom.

'Hello?' It was Tim's voice, sounding uncertain.

'Hi, Tim, it's Liz Carlyle, Peggy's colleague.' They had only met in the flesh a handful of times.

'Oh, hi. Peggy's not here. There're not letting her come home till tomorrow.'

'Actually, it's you I've come to see.'

'Me?' He sounded alarmed. 'What about? They said Peggy was fine when I rang a few minutes ago.'

'I'll explain if you buzz me in.'

There was a pause. 'The thing is, I was about to go out. I'm running late, in fact.'

'It won't take long. But do let me in, please. I'm getting soaked standing out here.'

After a moment, the buzzer sounded and Liz opened the door. She went up two flights and found Tim standing in the doorway to the flat. He was barefoot, in jeans and a tee-shirt, and looked as if he hadn't shaved for a couple of days. It certainly didn't look as though he was going out but he didn't seem eager to let her into the flat either. 'What's this about?' he asked, his voice both anxious and defensive.

'I had a couple of questions I wanted to ask you,' said Liz.

'About the attack? I only got there after they had driven off.'

'No, it's not about the attack. May I come in?'

Tim hesitated. 'Is this official?'

'It can be if you want it to be,' said Liz firmly. 'I'd rather keep it an informal chat, but it's up to you.'

'Okay,' he said. 'You'd better come in.'

The living room was surprisingly tidy, but then Liz remembered Peggy saying that nowadays Tim spent most of his time online in his study. Liz could see through the open door of the little kitchen that there were dirty dishes and a frying pan stacked in the sink, and there was a faint aroma of fried onions.

'Why don't we sit down?' she said, and before he could object sat herself in the armchair. Tim slowly took a place at the far end of the sofa.

'Would you like some tea?' he asked. 'Or coffee maybe?'

'No, thanks.' She didn't want to delay things any further. The more time Tim had to think, the more likely he would be to obfuscate or even tell outright lies. 'Peggy said you're spending a lot of time online these days. I gather you've got very interested in civil rights issues, especially as they affect the online world. Is that right?'

'Yes. There's nothing wrong with that. Or are you suggesting there is?'

Liz sensed he was stoking himself up for a fight that wasn't going to happen – she'd debate the pros and cons of it on another occasion. She said, 'I'm not suggesting anything; I'm here to ask questions.'

'I don't have to answer them,' he replied aggressively.

'No. Though if you don't cooperate now, I'll be forced to call in Special Branch and we'll reconvene in an interview room at a police station. As I said before, it's up to you.'

'You're not charging me with anything, are you?' Concern now outweighed defiance, which Liz took as a good sign.

'I'm not, at present, but I don't know what the police will do if you refuse to answer questions.' This was pure bluff, since she had nothing against him at all and was merely trying to gather some information. But it worked – Tim's eyes widened in surprise. 'I'm not refusing,' he protested. 'You haven't asked me anything yet.'

'Well,' said Liz. 'I believe you've recently been given an iPhone by someone you met online.'

'No, I met her in the real world. She was at a talk I went to – Peggy was there too.'

'Jasminder Kapoor's talk at King's College?' When he nodded again, Liz said, 'Tell me more about this woman. What's she called?'

'Marina.'

'Marina what?'

'Just Marina. She's never told me her last name.' He seemed worried that Liz would doubt this, for he said again, 'It's true, I swear: I don't know her last name.'

'I believe you,' said Liz calmly. 'But tell me about your exchanges with her. Were they by email?'

'At first. She asked me to set up a new email account; she said my existing one wouldn't be safe.'

'Safe from whom?'

He looked at Liz and for the first time smiled a little. 'You lot, of course.'

'You mean, the intelligence services.'

'Yes. Marina said they would probably be checking my normal email account, because of my membership of some online groups.'

'Really?' This sounded paranoid even by Snowdenista standards. Unless Marina was asking Tim to do something illegal for her. 'So you opened a new account.'

'Yes.'

'What did she want to talk to you about?'

'At first it was just about the issues we were discussing in the group. Frankly, I couldn't see why she was being so furtive. People have a right to think about these things.' A hint of defiance had resurfaced, but just as quickly subsided again. 'I thought she was a bit paranoid if that was the whole purpose of the new account. I've never tried to hide my views, and none of them have been illegal. I'm *not* a terrorist and I don't support what terrorists do.'

'All right, but you said "at first" you thought that's all she wanted. What else was there?'

He stared at Liz for a moment as if she'd just sprung a trap, which in a sense she had. Finally he said, 'She started asking me questions – about Peggy.'

'What kind of questions?'

'About her job.'

'Had you told her where Peggy worked?'

He was looking more and more like a rabbit caught in a pair of very bright headlights. He said jerkily, 'Not in… not in so many words. I might have told her that my girl-friend… well, hinted at it. But that's all.' He paused, then said quietly, 'I'm sorry.'

You ought to be, thought Liz, picturing the exchanges. Tim probably wanted to impress his mysterious new friend; he would have suggested an inside knowledge of intelligence, supplied courtesy of his partner. She said, 'What exactly did Marina want to know about Peggy?'

'What her job was. Did she work in a special section? Was she out and about, or was she a desk person? That sort of thing.'

'And?'

'And what?' he asked, sounding mystified.

'What did you tell her?' Liz asked, readying herself for the worst. She just hoped Peggy hadn't trusted him with anything important.

But Tim looked surprised again. 'I didn't tell her anything. I didn't have anything to tell.' He seemed to take Liz's expression for scepticism, for he started talking very fast, as if desperate to persuade her. 'Look, I know where Peggy works – the building, its name, and what goes on there. I know you work there too. But I don't know anything about what she actually *does* there. Peggy never talks about the details of her work. Never. Oh, once in a while she might say she's had a bad day, and sometimes she might say it's been a good day. But she never tells me why.' He looked agitated. 'You have to believe me. Even if I'd wanted to pass on important information to Marina, I couldn't have, because I didn't know any.'

And Liz could tell that what he was saying was true. Forget about Tim and his crackpot views; the fact was, the only information he could have that would be of any value to an enemy would have to come from Peggy. And Peggy was a real professional, which meant Tim didn't know anything of substance at all. Liz felt a deep sense of relief. But she still needed to know who this Marina was, and what she was really up to.

'I've got that,' she said. 'And thanks for explaining. But there's one thing I still want to ask you about. This phone the woman gave you – if you couldn't tell her what she wanted to know, why did she give it to you?'

'I suppose she was hoping I might change my mind. When I'd told her I didn't know anything about Peggy's work, she was very disappointed. I didn't hear from her for a while. But I also had the feeling she didn't entirely believe me. Anyway, she turned up one day, in the street outside. She was waiting when I came out of the house, in a car. She called me over and I got in to talk to her. She told me even my second email account wasn't safe any longer, and that she wanted to keep in touch about internet snooping and civil liberties – all the stuff we'd talked about before. But in future, she said, we'd have to do it by phone. She said a friend of hers did contract work for Apple and had a spare iPhone going. Would I like it? I wanted to say, "Do I like Christmas?" I mean, who would turn down a free iPhone?'

Yes, thought Liz, and who would think it rained silver dollars in Peru? There was something so naïve about Tim that she'd have laughed had it not been so serious. This Marina woman would have realised early on that he was so gormless she could persuade him of anything. But why give him a phone? It seemed peculiar – unless there was something rum about the device itself.

'Did she give you an email address? How are you supposed to contact her?'

'She's put a special app on the phone. She said it was super-secure – the snoopers couldn't get in. I have to use that. She tested it and it worked. It wipes off messages when you've read them.'

'Wow. That sounds clever. Can I have a look at it?'

He looked flustered. 'Why? It's just a phone. Expensive, but anyone could go out and buy one.'

'I'd like to see it. Please.'

She waited. After a moment, he shrugged. 'Okay.' He got up and went into his study, and came back with it. 'Here you go. One iPhone.'

Liz held it in her hand and thought for a moment. There was something wrong here, but she couldn't put her finger on it. 'How were things left with Marina?'

'Left? They weren't really. I hadn't heard from her for a few weeks, and suddenly there she was in the street, in a car. I don't know how she had my address. Anyway, there she was and she offered me the phone and said if I ever wanted to talk in future, I should use the app to contact her.'

'Did she give you her number?'

'No. I don't need a number. I'm just supposed to use the app – but I never have, except when she tested it in the car.'

'I see.' Liz wanted to ask if it hadn't occurred to him that the whole thing was very strange and perhaps he should have told Peggy about it, but she didn't think it would help just then. There would be opportunity later to quiz Tim in more detail. So she said calmly, 'I want to take this phone away. I need to get some people to look at it.' When she saw him starting to protest, she added, 'I'd be really grateful if you'd cooperate with me on this. You've been very helpful today, and I'd appreciate it if you'd help with this one further step. In the meantime, if you hear at all from this woman via email – or in any other way – I'd like you to contact me right away.'

He considered this, and finally nodded. 'All right. But it's not very likely to happen, you know. I felt Marina pretty much gave up on my knowing anything she wanted. That's why her giving me the phone was such a surprise. I didn't think I'd hear from her again.'

41

I N THE MORNING JASMINDER woke early. Bright sunlight was finding its way through the slats of the Venetian blinds at the windows of her room. To her disappointment, she realised she was alone in the bed; Laurenz must have stayed in the room next door. She told herself he hadn't wanted to disturb her after her long flight, though part of her also felt a little resentful that she had come a long way in order to sleep alone.

She lay in bed dozily for a few minutes, wondering what the day would bring. She hoped it would be more fun than the evening before, and that she and Laurenz could get away from his boorish colleagues. She got up, stretched for a moment, then walked to the connecting door. It was only seven o'clock, but Laurenz was an early riser, and she was sure he wouldn't mind her coming in. She tapped lightly on the door with her knuckles, but there was no reply. Poor thing must be tired; he'd been working so hard for the last few days, she thought, so quietly turned the door knob to peep into his room.

There was no one there. The bed was made, and there were no clothes on the chair; he must have got up extra early, and let her sleep on. She decided to get dressed and go and look for him; perhaps he was having breakfast, or sitting out by the pool. Then she saw the note on his dresser.

J

Have emergency meeting in Hamilton. Back after lunch. Relax and enjoy yourself. Everyone else will be around.

Lx

So much for spending most of the day together. The thought of sitting around in this shabby bungalow with these awful people, waiting for Laurenz to come back, was suddenly too much. She was tired of being second-best to his wretched bank.

She showered and dressed in some light cotton trousers and a blouse, then went out to the front of the house. There was no one in the kitchen, and the dining room was empty but breakfast had been laid out on a side table – a variety of breads, heavy-looking and dark, slices of cheese and chafing dishes with scrambled eggs, sausages and bacon. She poured herself a cup of coffee from a tall urn, and made do with a piece of chewy pumpernickel, wishing there were some fruit or yoghurt. As she finished she heard the front door open, and when she went out into the hall saw Kozlov in an armchair in the sitting room. He was wearing a jacket and open-necked shirt, with pressed dark trousers. It did not look like the costume of a man intent on relaxing.

In the far corner she saw the African man from the night before, staring intently at an open laptop. Near him a large television was on, but there was no sound and it was showing a street scene with people walking along the pavement in front of a row of shops. The camera didn't move – it must have been some sort of CCTV, perhaps a security camera, she thought, set up to monitor the same place throughout the day. Jasminder couldn't see it very well, but the scene did not look like Bermuda and it struck her as vaguely familiar.

As she went into the room, the African turned off his computer and the TV screen went blank. He got up and walked out without a greeting or even a glance in her direction. But Kozlov stayed put and boomed, 'Good morning. I see you have had a good English lie-in.'

Jasminder looked at her watch; it was just eight o'clock. What time did these people get up on holiday? She said, 'Thank you. Laurenz has a meeting this morning, and I wondered if anyone was going into town.'

'There is a car and driver – he picked you up when you arrived.'

'That's right. Is he available?' She hadn't realised the driver was on call.

Kozlov shook his head. 'Sadly, no. He is with Laurenz in Hamilton.'

'Right. Well, perhaps I can call a taxi.'

'Unfortunately, there is no telephone here, and it is impossible to get a signal for a mobile phone.' Kozlov grinned.

This seemed curious. Her experience of the business world was limited, but it was odd that they would stay somewhere without any communications. Especially bankers. She wondered if there were buses nearby. Or maybe she could just stroll around the neighbourhood. Anything must be better than sitting by the pool, counting beetles. 'There wouldn't be a bicycle, would there?'

Kozlov looked at her as if she'd asked for the use of a horse. Then he laughed. 'You seem very keen to get away. And this after I so enjoyed our conversation last night. Let us continue it. Sit down,' he said, pointing to a matching armchair opposite his.

Reluctantly, Jasminder found herself doing what he asked. 'It's just that it would be nice to see something of Bermuda,' she said.

'Of course. I am sure that can be arranged. Later.'

She didn't like Kozlov's tone. He was acting as if he were somehow in charge of all of them. He continued, 'I want to ask you some things.'

'What sort of things?'

'Laurenz has told me about the work you do. It must be fascinating. To have access to information other people would give their right arms to see.'

'I think you have the wrong idea about my job. I am in Communications – like PR work. I just deal with the press and the media on behalf of my employers. I am not involved in secret work and I doubt if I know much more than you do, or any member of the public.'

'That seems to me most unlikely.' Kozlov's expression was no longer as friendly. 'From what Laurenz has told me, you have access to information that has been very useful to him. And that's without your even trying very hard. He was grateful to you, and so will I be.'

'I don't know what you're talking about.' She didn't know how to deal with this man; inwardly she was furious. This was all Laurenz's fault; he must have been boasting about her and her position in MI6. Some of her anger came out now. 'This is not something I want to talk about. I am afraid you've been misled.'

Kozlov had got up from his chair now and was standing between Jasminder and the door. When he looked down at her it was from an intimidating height. He said, 'Let's not play Miss Innocent, all right? You passed on confidential information to your lover – that's fact number one. You have access to information he and I and other colleagues would benefit from – that is fact number two. Fact three, in case you are wondering, we will be happy to reward you for your services. Cash is possible, or if that would be difficult, payment in kind – holidays, "gifts" (you may want a car some day), travel. None of these are out of the question. But they require delivery from you.'

'Delivery? What are you talking about? What do you mean – delivery?' She wished Laurenz would come back and sort this out. Whatever he'd said, this man had got the wrong end of the stick. How could Laurenz have put her in this position?

Kozlov seemed to read her thoughts. 'No, I am not misled, and if you are right now thinking that your Laurenz has no idea that we are having this conversation, then you are sorely mistaken. I know everything that has passed between you, and all that you have so far supplied. Do you understand?'

She didn't understand at all. She felt completely bewildered. Who was this Russian man and what did he want from her?

She didn't have to wait long – he suddenly thrust a piece of paper at her, perhaps confusing her silence with acquiescence. Despite her better instincts, Jasminder scanned the page. It listed items of information: JIC meeting agendas; JIC papers on Russia and former Soviet satellites; internal MI6 strategic analysis papers on Russia and former Soviet satellites; field reports from MI6 officers in Russia and former Soviet satellites, especially the Baltic States of Estonia, Latvia, and Lithuania.

Kozlov was still looming over her. 'I want you to memorise this list, and then I will destroy it. When you return to the UK, I want you to begin collecting these materials immediately. Laurenz will brief you on the best ways to transport this information out of the Vauxhall building.'

She was frightened yet also outraged by what she was being asked. It was the stuff of spy novels and films – bribing an intelligence officer to provide classified information. She had never in a million years imagined something like this happening to her.

She had to put this man straight. 'I think you've taken leave of your senses. And your attempt at bribery is insulting. I don't know who you are working for, though I'm starting to have a pretty good idea, and I don't think it's a bank. But you can tell them I won't do any of this – I wouldn't dream of it.' And she threw the paper on the floor.

She would have stood up but Kozlov was now only a foot or so away from her chair, looming over it threateningly. It suddenly struck her that their conversation was being recorded. She wanted to dissociate herself as much as possible from what he was claiming. 'I have never given Laurenz any confidential information,' she said loudly, knowing that, strictly speaking, this was not true. How she wished she had refused his request back then. 'And if Laurenz knows we are having this conversation, then why isn't he here?'

'He'll be back,' Kozlov said flatly. 'Though I think you may find him slightly different from the Laurenz you think you know. But that's not the issue right now. You had better consider this: the help you gave Laurenz is documented – you took out papers from your workplace, which you are expressly forbidden to do. How do you think your famous C would react if he knew about that? You'd be out on your ear as the Americans say – and that's if you're lucky. Please don't think I'm bluffing. If you refuse to help, you won't get past Passport Control at Heathrow without your Special Branch asking you to speak to them in a small room. Your career will be over, your reputation in shreds.

'But if, on the other hand, you act like a mature citizen of the world and help us with our modest requests, then you will continue to enjoy the prestige and benefits of your new position, continue to have a high reputation in your country, and if you like, enjoy some extra benefits as well of the kind I mentioned.' He paused to let her take this in, then added in a softer, more reasonable voice, 'Look, nothing we want you to do would endanger your country or its interests, I assure you. You would in fact be working for the peace we all want to have – nobody in Russia wants a return to the Cold War. So, will you help us?'

Jasminder suddenly went cold; her hands and legs were shaking. She had to get out of this room, out of this bungalow, into the air, but first she had to make it absolutely clear to this man what she was thinking.

'I won't do it,' she said, firmly. 'I would rather resign than betray the Service.'

'You would rather go to prison?'

Jasminder had never been bullied successfully, and she wasn't going to let that change now. What this man was asking her to do was inconceivable, whatever the consequences – she knew full well that if C or anyone at Vauxhall learned about what she had done for Laurenz, then her days at MI6 would be over. But she didn't hesitate. She said, 'Tell your people they have picked the wrong person to approach, both because I don't know anything of value, and because I wouldn't ever tell you if I did.' Kozlov had taken a step back, so she stood up. 'Now if you'll excuse me, I think I'll take a walk.'

She didn't see it coming, not until his open palm hit her with immense force on one cheek. The noise was like a firecracker going off, and the pain was excruciating. Jasminder stumbled and then fell back into her chair. Tears were running out of one eye and her nose was beginning to bleed; the skin on her face was alternately burning and numb. Kozlov was standing over her, his open palm poised to hit her again, his face a picture of barely controlled fury. He said harshly, 'All right, you stupid little English bitch. We'll see what you will and won't do.' He called out, 'Siyamba.'

Within seconds the African man had come back into the room, and Kozlov motioned at the television set. 'Turn it this way, so she can see,' he ordered.

The African went over and twisted the screen so it faced the chair. It was the same picture, but this time Jasminder saw it clearly and knew why it was familiar. The row of shops it showed ended in a larger store on the corner, with a sign above its windows: *Kapoor & Sons*. It was early after-noon in Leicester, and the pavement was crowded with Saturday shoppers. People were going in and out of the Kapoors' mini-market, and she could imagine the scene inside – one of her brothers would be there, supervising the tills, occasionally going back to the meat counter where the butchers would be working flat out to serve the custom-ers buying their Sunday roasts.

'You recognise this place, don't you?' Kozlov said.

She nodded, confused. Why were these people filming one of her brothers' shops? What did it mean?

Kozlov went on, his voice low and menacing: 'We know quite a bit about your family. They've done very well, haven't they? Hard graft, I think the English call it. But they're proud of their little sister, too, I think. You were the clever one, but you've stayed close. It helps, your not having children, I suppose; it keeps you interested in them, and their families.'

There was something ominous in his tone now, though the words were innocuous enough. He said to Siyamba, 'Switch cameras now.'

The man held a remote in one hand and he clicked it. Immediately the screen shifted, and it took Jasminder a moment to make sense of it. The view now was from a pavement across a leafy, tree-shaded street. On the opposite side there was a gate and what looked to be a playground, with buildings behind it. A group of people, mainly women, waited by the gate; in the background a door opened in the largest building and dozens of small children poured out, then rushed towards the gate.

'This was yesterday. It's a school as you can see. Full of lovely little children. All sorts – some white, some black, some Asian. You have a niece called Ali, don't you?'

The apple of Jasminder's eye; she liked all her nieces and nephews, but Ali was her favourite. 'You dote on that child,' her brother had once said, laughing. 'But I won't let you spoil her.'

Kozlov said now, with chilling cheerfulness, 'I think you may see your niece in a minute.'

Sure enough, from out of the helter-skelter mob of little kids, the camera focused on one who was running ahead, already halfway to the gate. It was Ali, tiny in her little grey blazer and skirt, with a smile of such high-spirited innocence that it touched Jasminder's heart. The girl suddenly jumped into the waiting arms of her mother – Jasminder's sister-in-law, Laxme. Then the screen went blank.

'You see,' Kozlov said, in a sinister whisper. 'We know exactly where she is. It would be a terrible thing if Ali had an accident… so I want to give you another chance, just to make sure that little girl can go on running out of school each day to her mother. Shall we have another look at my list?' He bent down and picked the paper off the floor.

And now Jasminder saw that she would have to say yes after all. She wasn't going to be doing it for money, or for love – she thought bitterly of how Laurenz had betrayed her. She wasn't doing it, in fact, for any shameful reasons. She was doing it for Ali – to keep the little girl from harm. She didn't have any choice.

42

L AURENZ WAS ACTING LIKE a marriage guidance counsellor, trying to help a client understand that her marriage was over. He said, 'Things change, Jasminder, and that includes relationships. Think of it like this: we're entering a new phase. No longer lovers, it's true, but still close. Terribly close.'

They were sitting in the lounge area of a Lear jet. The owner, a Russian Jasminder hadn't seen during her brief stay in Bermuda, was not travelling with them; Laurenz said the jet would return for him the following day. So Jasminder and he had the cabin to themselves, and sat opposite each other in the white leather extra-wide seats by the wings. A steward had placed two glasses of champagne on the table in front of them, then retreated discreetly to the galley behind a curtain up by the cockpit. None of the rules of commercial aviation seemed to apply to private jets, for they had bypassed security checks and watched as their bags were put straight into the Lear jet's hold.

Jasminder hadn't touched her champagne. She watched Laurenz as he talked on. He didn't seem aware that her love for him had turned to contempt. Though she was still struggling to take in what had happened to her, still stunned by the transformation in... everything in her life, one thing was clear in her mind: she despised this man. He had played on her emotions to exploit her and now she would do whatever she could to damage him.

After her traumatic encounter with Kozlov, she had been desperate to see Laurenz, hoping against hope that this nightmare would turn out to be just that – a bad dream – and that what Kozlov had said about Laurenz knowing everything that was happening to her would turn out to be a monstrous lie.

But when Laurenz had returned from Hamilton, she knew at once that Kozlov had been telling the truth. The man who came back to the bungalow was not the charming, loving figure she had fallen for, but a new Laurenz – one who greeted her with a distant, perfunctory smile and an air of calculated detachment.

The rest of the weekend had gone by in a blur. There had been another awful dinner at the club, with Sam pretending to be her friend – Jasminder knew better – and Laurenz placed yet again far down the table. She had been unable to eat a thing, sitting there nauseated by the smell of the heaped plates of food and the great goblets of drink that the men were liberally swilling down, thinking of the threat to little Ali. She had tried to stay awake that night, determined to question Laurenz about what had happened, but he had remained behind at the club and she had fallen asleep out of sheer exhaustion, feeling utterly miserable and deeply scared, before he returned.

'We'll still be seeing a lot of each other,' Laurenz told her, as the plane taxied down the runway. 'In fact, it's crucial that we do.'

She spoke at last. 'I don't know how you think I'm going to get all this information you want. I've already told you that I don't have that kind of access.'

'But you're well placed to get it.' He spoke loudly, to be heard over the noise of the engines as the jet accelerated forward.

'How can you be so sure?' Shock was turning to anger now. 'You know nothing about my work. You've completely misled that hideous Koslov, just to boost your own position with whoever it is you really work for. How dare you tell me what I can do when I tell you I can't?'

'Of course you can. You just need to use your imagination a bit… and I'm going to help you with that.' He sighed as though confronted with a stubborn child. 'Jasminder, you are highly intelligent and *very* attractive. You must know that.'

'Don't you patronise me! I thought you were something different, someone to be admired, and I fell for you, I'll admit that. But now I know better – you are a ruthless, dishonest bastard and your friend Koslov is worse. If I do anything it will be for Ali – certainly not for you.'

Laurenz shrugged his shoulders as the plane lifted off. It shuddered briefly as it hit a patch of low-lying cloud, then stabilised as they climbed steeply into the clearer sky above. He said, 'Have it your own way.'

She went on, 'But I don't know how you expect me to get hold of all this stuff. What I said to Koslov was true. I don't see all the things he thinks I do. His list is ridiculous.'

'Beautiful and intelligent women wield great power. There can't be many men who wouldn't be attracted to you.'

'So what do you expect me to do – seduce C? I happen to know he's happily married.'

270

To her great irritation, Laurenz laughed. 'That's more like it! This is all a bit of a game, you know. The sooner you see that, the easier it will be for all of us.'

'Okay,' said Jasminder, not meaning this at all. 'What's the plan? How do you want me to proceed?' She hated saying the words, but reminded herself that the only reason she was doing this was to keep Ali safe. She was going to look for every chance she could to get back at this man.

'I need to know everything that comes across your desk. Understood? Everything. And you need to start making friends at work – if necessary, intimate friends.' His meaning was clear.

She said, 'It's not that easy.'

'Of course it is. I'm sure MI6 people socialise with each other all the time. They have to – all people in intelligence work do. It's so much easier that way: it means they don't have to lie about their job, or stay quiet while other people talk about theirs. You'll soon make lots of friends at Vauxhall; you just need to be more outgoing – and obviously single.'

She was single now, thought Jasminder bitterly. She had gone to Bermuda for a weekend with her boyfriend, and was coming home with a spy.

Laurenz said, 'I need to know who you have told about us – that you've been seeing me.'

When Jasminder hesitated, he said impatiently, 'Come on. Cooperate. Remember your niece.'

'I told my mother I had met someone – that was when I Skyped her last. She's in India. She doesn't know your name; I was waiting to tell her.' Her mother was always hoping Jasminder would settle down with a nice Indian boy, and pretending someone called 'Laurenz Hansen' was an Indian wasn't going to work.

'Who else?'

'I told my friend Emma.'

'Ah, yes, the worthy Emma. I don't think we have to worry about her. I never met her. You must just tell her it didn't work out with us. What about that friend in Trafalgar Square?' He was watching her intently.

'That was Peggy Kinsolving. I told you about her.'

'Yes, you did. She works for the other mob across the river. Does she know my name?'

Jasminder felt his eyes on her. 'I can't remember, but I suppose so.'

'Have you spoken to her recently?'

'No. I rang her last week and left a message, but she didn't reply. I was a bit surprised; I thought I'd try again when I got back. I like her.'

'Good. I want you to ring her. But I also want you to tell her how upset you are. You and I have split up. We're still good friends; we'll still see each other occasionally; but the sex wasn't working. Have you got that? And don't think of telling her anything else – like the truth – or I'll know.'

'Yes, but she'll probably be surprised. I told her it was getting serious. And what do you mean, you'll know?'

He smiled. 'Don't think you're our only source in Britain,' he said. 'We have many eyes and ears. So just blame me for the break up – with my divorce pending, I realised I shouldn't rush into things. I needed time on my own. She'll understand, I'm sure.'

'Do you want me to say the same thing to Emma?'

'Yes, and to anyone else you might have told about me. We're just friends now… mates as the English like to say… and that will be good enough cover for our meetings.'

'Some friend!' She gently stroked the side of her face where Koslov had hit her. It was very tender to the touch, though so far there was no visible bruising. 'I wish you'd never saved me from the men in that park in Islington. But I suppose that was all a set-up.' In her mind, Jasminder had been going over the whole of her relationship with Laurenz. 'I didn't even work for MI6 in those days. Why did you choose me?'

'We saw your potential,' he replied with a grin. 'But don't try to work it out. Just focus on how you are going to get the material we want. I'll be helping you work out your plan at our meetings.'

'Meetings?'

'Yes. I'll want to see you regularly – sometimes at my flat, sometimes in other places. The only difference now is that I'll be your mentor, not your lover – though we could have sex sometimes if you liked.'

Jasminder shuddered but didn't reply. She felt sick at the thought of his touching her. The sex, like everything else, had been an act. He had never cared about her at all. He had been reporting everything they'd done to that dreadful Koslov. Between them they'd been manipulating her into a position where she had no choice but to cooperate. Looking at the cool and unemotional expression on his face now, she resolved again to do her very best to destroy him.

Laurenz turned to her and said, 'Now I think you should try and get some sleep. These chairs are quite comfortable, and you can recline them almost back into a bed. You've got a big day tomorrow, and I want you to hit the ground running.'

43

T IM MEANT WELL, BUT he wasn't much of a house-keeper. By her third day at home, Peggy was back in charge of the washing machine and the dishwasher. Tim was still cooking his vegetarian meals, though they were no longer the gloopy stews of the past. He'd bought himself a new cookery book and they were now eating rather tasty nut roasts and rissoles which Peggy consumed without complaint, knowing that until she had two working arms again, it was safer for her to keep out of the kitchen.

She stayed at home for a week after she came out of hospital. She was still on painkillers and feeling very tired – shock, the doctor told her. She saw more of Tim than usual, as he worked from home for at least a part of most days. She soon realised that something about him had changed. The pre-accident version of Tim – sulky, snappy, secretive and often aggressive – had been supplanted by a quieter, sadder, man who seemed, frankly, rather *embarrassed*. He wasn't the same lovable man she'd lived with for several years, before he'd got involved with the internet chat rooms – the scholar, who'd been full of enthusiasm for his university work, full of ideas but endearingly hopeless at anything practical. This was a third version of Tim – easier to live with than the Snowdenista but sad, even depressed, and if anything too keen to follow Peggy's lead. She was mystified by the sudden disappearance of the stroppy cynic she'd been living with in the past few months.

Then she learned the cause of this sea change. On the evening before she went back to work, they were sitting over supper when Tim said, 'I had a visitor when you were in hospital.'

'Really. Who was it?'

'Liz Carlyle.'

Peggy was surprised; Liz had come to see her in hospital. Why had she also come to the flat? She said as much now.

Tim stirred his supper with his fork uneasily. 'She wanted a word with me.'

'Oh?' She could see he was feeling awkward.

'It was about my phone. The iPhone I was given.'

Peggy merely nodded, bracing herself for what was coming next. Doubtless Tim would blame her for mentioning the phone to Liz. There would be the usual rant about the security services, the usual cry that 1984 was here.

But instead he said, very mildly, 'She seemed to think I'd been very naïve about this woman Marina – exchanging emails then accepting the phone.'

'Oh,' said Peggy, startled.

'Perhaps I have,' said Tim, looking away. For a terrible moment, Peggy thought he was about to cry. But he pulled himself together and said, 'Liz took the phone away to have it looked at. She asked me to tell her if I had any more emails from Marina.'

'I see. Have you?'

'No, and I don't expect to. But I'd like you to tell Liz when you see her tomorrow—' And he stopped, his cheeks flushed.

'Tell her what?'

'That I'm sorry and I'll let you both know if I hear anything.' He suddenly gulped, and his eyes were misty. 'I've been such a fool.'

'I don't know about that,' said Peggy softly. 'I admit this woman Marina has behaved pretty strangely, but it might be quite innocent. Who knows? She might just be a bit of a nut.'

'I don't think so,' said Tim sadly, and she could tell from his tone that he didn't believe Peggy thought so either.

Peggy went back to work early on Monday – she was in the office well before eight o'clock – but Liz was already there. 'I couldn't let you beat me in,' she said with a smile. 'How are you?'

'I'm fine,' said Peggy, though one arm was still in a sling. 'Eager and raring to go.'

'Let's have a coffee and I'll fill you in on what's been happening,' said Liz, and they took the lift to the ground-floor café.

'So how's Tim?' asked Liz as they sat down at a corner table.

'Well, it's all a bit peculiar. He's being very nice at the moment – almost weirdly nice. I gather you came to see him while I was in hospital.'

'I did. I hope you don't mind, but that phone business alarmed me.'

'I understand. I thought it seemed very odd too. And I think Tim gets it, now he's thought about it. Whatever you said, it shook him up. In a good way. It's as though he's seen sense.'

'I'm glad.'

'He asked me to tell you that if Marina contacts him, we'll be the first to know.'

'Excellent.' Liz seemed a little abstracted.

'One more thing about that phone,' said Peggy. 'It came to me in the hospital, then I forgot about it and I've just remembered again. I've seen another one just like it.'

'I'm not surprised,' Liz replied with a smile. 'Those iPhones are very popular.'

'No, that's not what I mean. Another one that's the same model, the same colour, and which someone had recently been given as a present. It may just be a coincidence – I expect it is – but I thought I should mention it.'

She had Liz's full attention now. 'Who had this phone? And who gave it to them?'

'Jasminder Kapoor. You know, the new Communications Director at Six. I admired it when she put it down on the table the other day while we were having a drink. She told me her boyfriend gave it to her to celebrate her new job. He didn't seem to realise she couldn't take it in to work with her.'

'Who is this boyfriend? Have you met him?'

'I just saw him fleetingly the other day. He was waiting for her outside the National Gallery and I was walking with her on my way home. His name is Laurenz Hansen. Apparently he's Norwegian, works for a private bank. He didn't seem very friendly. She said he's shy of meeting her friends at present because he's going through a sticky divorce. Sounded a bit odd, I thought, but maybe it's different in Norway. She seems devoted to him. She met him when he saved her from some muggers.'

'I can't see how meeting her friends could affect his divorce in any country.'

'That's what I thought, but maybe he's afraid they might tell his wife he's having an affair.'

'It all sounds rather unlikely.'

'Yes, it does. But Jasminder seemed to buy it. I only met him by accident. Why, what are you thinking?'

Liz paused for a minute, then she said, 'I'm thinking this phone business seems quite a coincidence – maybe too much of one. One phone comes from a woman making what looks like a classic approach to Tim, who happens to live with a member of MI5. Then a man gives exactly the same phone to a newly appointed member of MI6.'

'I know – it's weird. What have you done with Tim's phone by the way? Was there anything odd about it?'

'Well, there was something a bit strange, but I don't know whether it was sinister or not. The phone had an app on it that Tim was supposed to use to contact Marina. In fact, he said he'd never used it, so presumably the app had never been opened. I sent the phone to Technical Ted upstairs but he couldn't work out what it was. It was an app he'd never seen before and he couldn't open it. He said there was nothing else on the phone, which seemed a bit rum since Tim himself told me he had been using it. So the phone has gone to Charlie Simmons in GCHQ and I'm waiting for his report.'

Peggy thought about this for a moment. 'The only thing is, there's no connection between Tim and Jasminder. Tim doesn't even like her; he thought her speech at the university, that evening when I first met her, was wet. And when she came to the flat once so I could help her fill in her application form for the job in Six, he blanked her out.'

Liz leaned across the little table. 'That's not the connection I had in mind. I was thinking more about the people who gave them the phones – Marina and this man Laurenz.'

'Do you think they're connected?'

'I'm not sure. But when I saw him in Tallinn, Mischa talked about a pincer movement – that requires two claws. I don't think we should jump to conclusions yet, but this looks to me horribly like a pincer movement. Two claws closing in on MI6 and MI5. Just what he said.'

'But Tim's not in MI5,' said Peggy, her face suddenly very pale.

'No, but you are. And they were not to know how close you and Tim were, or whether you took papers home or talked to him about work.'

'But I never take papers home,' said Peggy, on the verge of tears, 'or talk about work to Tim.'

'I know that, but they must have seen it as a golden opportunity. When they found out what sort of person Tim is, they probably realised they weren't going to get any further.'

Peggy looked shocked.

'It's all right,' said Liz firmly. 'Stop thinking about what might have happened. It didn't. But now we've got to make sure we stop this Laurenz character doing whatever he's up to with Jasminder. Did you see her application form? What did she say about him?'

'She didn't mention him, actually. She asked me what I thought and said that she'd only known him a very short time and he'd only stayed at her flat once, so we agreed it didn't seem to qualify as a co-habiting relationship. But I know that they're much closer now and she stays with him at his flat, so she should have declared him. Shall I find out?'

'Yes. Get in touch with Personnel over there and ask them to look at her file. Don't alarm them, but say they shouldn't mention it to Jasminder at the moment. We don't want to set the cat among the pigeons.'

I have a strong feeling that the cat may be alarmingly near the pigeons already, thought Peggy as she got up to go to her office in the open plan. But I haven't a clue how it got there.

44

PEGGY HAD THE BIT between her teeth now. She had learned from the Personnel department at MI6 that Jasminder had not declared Laurenz Hansen as her cohabitee. Peggy guessed why – it was part of Laurenz's exaggerated desire for secrecy. She suspected that he had put pressure on Jasminder to keep their relationship secret, and felt annoyed for her friend. Peggy was increasingly convinced that there was something wrong about Laurenz, and she was determined to find out what it was.

It took her just two days to put together a comprehensive dossier, but to her intense disappointment she found that she couldn't fault the man. His credentials were all in order. His Norwegian passport was legit, and its details of date and place of birth (12 February 1974 in a village outside Bergen) had been officially confirmed by the Oslo Home Ministry, then (less officially) by the Lutheran Synod of Bergen, holder of the local parish records.

So far, so clear. Entering the UK, Hansen had supplied a local London address, in a street off the City Road in Islington. It was a new flat in a small modern block, let on a short-term lease signed by Laurenz Hansen. A credit-card check had found his rating unimpeachable: he used a

Visa card in the UK, and an American Express Diamond card when he travelled. He banked in London with Lloyds, where he had a little over £26,000 sitting in a variety of accounts.

All of which was perfectly fine and untroubling, compared to the mystery Peggy uncovered when exploring Hansen's employment record. He was a private banker – Jasminder had been clear about this when talking to Peggy about him – but it was proving awfully hard to find the bank. Each month £11,000 was deposited in his Lloyds current account from one in Zurich held by something called M. Q. Hayter & Co., but Peggy had found no record anywhere of any kind of financial institution, much less bank, operating under that name. Tellingly, too, Hansen's lease agreement with the flat's owner had asked for the name of his employer, but the line had been left blank.

Peggy liked to do a thorough job and was disappointed with her failure. 'Why wouldn't he put his employer's name on the form?' She and Liz were discussing the dossier in Liz's office. Outside a brisk wind stirred the trees along the Embankment, and on the Thames a heavy swell made progress slow for a rusty barge, which was chugging upstream.

'Who knows? Bankers are very secretive sometimes. No doubt for their own protection.'

'You'd think the landlord would want to know. I gather the flat's in a nice building; the owner would want to feel confident Hansen was good for the rent.'

'You're right, but if Hansen gave him six months' cash as a down payment, his qualms would have gone away pretty fast.'

'But why bother doing that unless he was covering his tracks?'

'Hard to say. Could be a dozen reasons. I don't want to jump to conclusions.'

'That means you've got one in your head.'

Liz laughed. 'You're right! But I'm going to keep it to myself until we've dug around some more.'

'I'm not sure where else to dig. I've checked every possible financial registry, but there's no Laurenz Hansen listed in any of them. The Revenue haven't anything on him either. He hasn't filed for Non-Dom status here.'

'Jasminder did tell you he had been moving around a lot.'

Peggy nodded. 'Yes, she did, though she also made it sound as if he was always on top of things. The last thing a banker would want is trouble with the Revenue.'

'I'm going to make a call or two,' said Liz. 'I'll let you know if I find anything out.'

Liz had a little more experience of banks than she'd let on. Almost ten years ago – well before Martin Seurat had entered her life – she had had a relationship for almost a year with a Dutch banker called Piet. Her time with him had been fun, but never very serious – he had been in London less than in Amsterdam, and they had never spent enough continuous time together to grow close. The affair had ended when Piet met someone else in Holland, but Liz had never held that against him, and the two of them had remained friends even after Piet married his new girl-friend, Sylvia. On the rare occasions Piet came to London, he and Liz usually met up for a meal; once he had even brought Sylvia along, and Liz was pleased to find that she was extremely friendly and they all got on very well.

Then two years ago Piet had moved to London, with Sylvia and their new baby, to take up a post with one of the UK's leading private banks. Since then, he and Liz chatted on the phone every few months, and twice she'd gone for Sunday lunch to their roomy house in Putney.

During their relationship, Liz had never told him what she did for a living, but Piet was intelligent and well informed and Liz could tell from their recent meetings that he had a pretty good idea. When she rang him now from her office, he was his usual cheerful, friendly self. 'Sylvia and I were just talking about you,' he said. 'We want you to come to lunch soon.'

'I'd love that. But I was ringing to ask a favour – a professional one. I'm trying to locate someone who's a private banker in London, but I'm not having any luck. I'd rather not say why I want to know, except I wouldn't want the man to learn that I was looking for him.'

'Understood. What's the name of the bank he works for?'

'That's the problem. All I know is that he's paid from an account in Zurich held by something called M. Q. Hayter & Co. I know he works at the London office of an international bank, but if it's this Hayter company, I can't find any trace of it. So maybe it has another name and that's just a salary account or something. The guy I'm looking for is apparently quite senior. He's a Norwegian but based here. I think he may be the head of their office in London. Yet I can't seem to find him.'

'Give me a day, and give me his name. If he is a banker in London, I'll find him for you.'

But when Piet came back to her, he too was empty-handed. 'I can't find him either, Liz. There's no bank registered here called Hayter and no sign of your man. If he's working in London then he's working solo. He's not employed by any bank.'

'If you don't mind my asking, how can you be so sure?'

'When I was at Lehman, before they went bust – thank God I'd got out by then – we used to keep a register of bankers. We called it the "C Book", and C stood for the Competition. The person in charge of the C Book changed every three months, because nobody wanted to do the job for longer than that – if it turned out you failed to list a new arrival to the banking game, you had to buy champagne for all the partners that Friday. Mind you, this was pre-2008.'

Liz laughed, remembering the mad excesses of those boom years. Bankers lighting cigars with £100 notes, or spending more than the average person's annual wage on a single night out at a club.

'Anyway,' said Piet, 'the C Book survived all the ructions and it's still being kept up, and the penalty's the same for missing a name. I called a friend of mine who has access to it and asked him to check. No Laurenz Hansen. No Hansen at all, in fact. As I said, Liz, if he's working at a bank, I would have found him. I'll let you draw your own conclusion.'

When Liz sat down with Peggy to review the Hansen findings, she said, 'This man has covered all the bases very neatly. Except one. It seems he's no more a banker than I am.'

'Then why's he pretending to be one?'

'Probably because it's quite difficult for the ordinary person to check, and it sounds impressive... I don't know. Both perhaps. Jasminder swallowed it anyway. It's quite a good cover – if you're not expecting to come in contact with professionals like us. The banking world is impenetrable to most people. The City could be in Mongolia for all your average person understands it.'

'But why not have a real job if it's a cover?'

'I don't know. Possibly because it might get in the way of what he's really doing – for whatever organisation or country.'

Liz and Peggy looked at each other. They were both absorbing the implications of what they had discovered. Then Liz said, 'We're going to put Mr Hansen under the microscope. We need to have a look at him and what he's up to when he's supposed to be working in his bank. And that includes surveillance. Would you give Wally Woods a ring and warn him that we will be putting in a request for a blanket surveillance operation?' Wally Woods was the chief controller of A4, the surveillance section. 'Tell him I think it's extremely important and he's not to downgrade it just because it's not from counter-terrorism.' They both knew that Wally Woods was a great admirer of Liz's and, if she said it was important, it would get priority.

'OK. But what about Jasminder?' enquired Peggy. 'What do you think she knows about Hansen's background?'

'That's what we'll have to find out. I can't believe she's working with him. Not unless her whole life for the last few years has been some sort of myth. She's been the face of civil liberties, Miss Freedom of Information. It can't all have been a blind.'

'Maybe there's nothing sinister in it at all. Maybe what-ever he's doing has nothing to do with Jasminder.'

'Come on, Peggy. You don't believe that. But we'll find out. You keep in touch with her, just as a friend – like before – and A4 surveillance will find out what Laurenz is up to. But we've got to alert Six. Someone needs to keep an eye on her over there, get alongside her, just in case she is up to something. We need to know if there's anything odd about her behaviour, what she has access to, whether she's asking questions that seem outside her normal sphere of work. She's working very closely with C himself and that must give her enormous scope.'

'I know you're right, Liz, but I just can't believe it. Jasminder is so principled. Why would she be working undercover?'

'I don't know,' said Liz, 'but I hope we'll find out soon. Don't forget what Mischa told me in Tallinn. If this is the pincer operation, we need to know how it's being worked.'

45

E VEN IN HER MOST radical left-wing phase, Jasminder
had felt a strong loyalty to Britain, the country she
was now trying to betray. Guilt had become her constant,
nagging companion. She could not find any excuse for
what she was about to do, except the threat to little Ali if
she refused. That was enough, but it did not diminish the
guilt. She was constantly asking herself if she shouldn't tell
someone what had happened. She could tell Peggy or she
could even tell C himself. Surely they would be discreet
and clever enough to solve the problem. Surely they could
rescue Ali before Koslov and his friends got to her. But
something held her back. She knew how close Koslov's
men must be to the school and to her brothers' shop. They
must be monitoring her family all the time. It would only
take one false move on the part of the police and Ali would
be dead or injured for life.

A couple of weeks ago she had looked for the photograph of Ali standing proudly beside a sandcastle on the
beach where the family had gone for their last summer
holiday. It had been in the back pocket of her purse for
months, but suddenly it wasn't there. She'd realised then
that someone had been through her purse and taken it.

Had it been done just to frighten her, or to help Koslov's men recognise the little girl? She didn't know, but its disappearance chilled Jasminder to the bone.

Then there was the painful personal side of things. She had totally misread Laurenz Hansen; the man she had fallen in love with didn't exist – Laurenz was a different man altogether and he had never loved her. She was just a tool for him to use. It was utterly humiliating, as well as heart-breaking. To add to all that, she couldn't work out how she was going to do what her new masters wanted. At their most recent meeting Laurenz had said that the list Koslov had shown her was just a pointer to the sort of information they wanted. Her personal top target was to find out what sources MI6 had in Moscow. She had told him that that sort of information was the most closely guarded of any and there was no way she was going to be told about individual sources. He'd said she was not using her imagination; she could certainly find out which of her colleagues ran secret sources in Russia and get alongside them. She could observe who travelled to Russia and when and how often. Then she could set about cultivating someone in the right area.

He'd tried to encourage her. No one, he'd said, was expecting instant results, but she needed to show she was cooperating. Her repeated protests that she had been recruited to liaise with the media and to present the outward face of Six to the world, not as an operational officer, were ignored by Laurenz. She'd told him that she was only briefed on operations when they became public, or when it was necessary for her to know about them for drafting C's speeches or for other public presentations. As the face of a new, more open MI6, there was no need for her to have the most secret operational information, and if she tried to get it, it would seem odd and arouse suspicion. So how was she going to satisfy the unrealistic expectations of Laurenz and his employers?

She tried nonetheless. She suggested to C that part of the new 'openness' campaign should be internal, and not just directed at the media and general public. Employees of the Service should understand what Jasminder was there for, she argued, and proposed a series of briefings to the various departments at Vauxhall Cross. C readily agreed, so she gave a programme of talks, and was gratified that so many people came and seemed to listen – they asked her lots of questions at the end. But she soon realised that though talking about her mission raised her own work's profile, it didn't tell her anything about the work of her colleagues.

Then she tried the social side of things. She started eating in the canteen at lunchtime, hoping to meet people, though she felt awkward, even intrusive, joining tables where everyone already seemed to know each other. Lunch was in any case a rushed affair for most people. The public might picture James Bond feasting on lobster and chilled Chablis in a gentlemen's club in St James's, but the reality was that people in the Service worked too hard to waste time lunching – many just ate sandwiches at their desks.

A sense of futility threatened to overwhelm her. Though she was trying very hard, Laurenz gave her no points for that. There was no longer even a pretence of affection in the way he talked to her, and she dreaded their meetings since she had nothing to offer him to keep him from repeating his threats.

She felt utterly alone, and wished there were someone she could confide in. Not her brothers, who would not have understood the sort of people she was dealing with and might well rush off to the police demanding protection. Nor Emma, who wouldn't be able to offer useful advice and might talk to colleagues about the situation. Perhaps after all she should speak to Peggy Kinsolving. Jasminder didn't know her very well, but she liked her – she seemed level-headed and sympathetic. Unlike Emma, Peggy would understand the dangerous position Jasminder was in. Maybe she would ring her the next day and arrange to meet for a drink.

That evening she saw Laurenz at his flat. When she'd first gone there it had seemed smart in its minimalism, a hip bachelor pad that suited the lifestyle of a high-powered international banker. Now it seemed ghastly in its lack of human touches, soulless and grim.

To her consternation Laurenz seemed to sense quite uncannily what she had been thinking. As she sat down on the sofa, he took a seat in a straight-backed metal chair in front of her. 'Keep your nerve, Jasminder,' he said. 'You're at a stage I recognise all too well. You're having difficulties procuring the information we need, and you're starting to despair. You feel trapped, and very sorry for yourself. You're even contemplating confiding in someone, to try and share the burden. But don't worry – it's just a phase, I promise. You all go through it.'

'Who is "you all"?' Jasminder demanded to know.

Laurenz looked at her coolly. 'Our agents, of course.'

She stared at him dumbly. Was that what she was then, an agent of Laurenz and his pals? It seemed inconceivable but she had to face facts. She was employed by MI6, but she'd been recruited by the enemy.

Then, the following day, out of the blue, her luck changed.

She had gone, as she did most days now, to the canteen for lunch, but she was rather later than usual and found no one to eat with. In a way this was a relief, and she was actually enjoying her solitary salad when a man's voice, speaking from behind her shoulder, announced, 'Lady Thatcher said a man my age sitting alone on a bus represented failure, but I reckon having lunch on one's own is just as bad. Would you mind if I joined you?'

By now he had come into sight. Tallish, lean, with sandy-coloured hair and blue eyes surrounded by a network of fine lines, he looked as if he had seen more than his share of trouble. He didn't wait for Jasminder's reply but sat down across the table from her, offering his hand. 'I'm Bruno.'

She shook it and said, 'Jasminder.'

'Yes, I know. I went to one of your talks,' he said, reaching for the jug of water on the table between them. 'Will you have a little more?' he asked. 'It's an excellent vintage.'

Jasminder laughed, something she hadn't done for days.

'I enjoyed your talk very much,' Bruno went on. 'I don't know if you realise it but you're something of a sensation around here. First we publish our history and now we have a PR person – and a very charming one at that, if I may say so without being accused of sexism. Tell me your story. Were you a Fane find?' he asked, his eyes smiling.

'Hardly,' said Jasminder.

'Ah, I get it. He tried to blackball you? The bastard,' added Bruno, but he was grinning and his tone was light-hearted.

'Well, he didn't actually blackball me. I got the impression that he didn't approve of the job at all. It was C who was pushing it. Geoffrey Fane didn't want anyone to be appointed – it wasn't just me.'

'Take heart. Fane's reaction to anything new is invariably hostile, but it never lasts. You should view his opposition to your appointment as a merit badge.' Bruno added in a stage whisper, 'Between you and me, the last C before this one was opposed by Geoffrey Fane when he first applied to join the Service years ago. But when he became C, Geoffrey thought he was fantastic.'

'Really?' asked Jasminder, not sure which surprised her more – Fane's negative reaction to a future C, or Bruno himself. She wasn't at all sure how to take him. He seemed a bit of a clown, and rather indiscreet, which was definitely not a type she'd encountered in the Service before.

'Absolutely. But as I say, Geoffrey always comes round in the end – if the person's any good. And from what I hear, you've made a splendid start.'

'Really? Do people think so?'

'Yes, they do. Even Fane says so. And word of your arrival has reached all the Stations. I was in Moscow last week, and then went to some of those ghastly ex-Soviet republics. You were mentioned several times – and very approvingly. You ought to do a tour out there. They'd love to see you.'

Bruno glanced at his watch and gave an exaggerated look of horror. 'Golly, I know time flies when you're having fun, but this is ridiculous. Jasminder, it's been a pleasure meeting you in the flesh but I must dash or I'll have my head chopped off by You Know Who.'

'Who is You Know Who?'

'Geoffrey Fane, of course. But let's meet up some time. Perhaps some evening after work – and we could find somewhere even nicer than this luxurious canteen.'

Jasminder laughed. 'That would be great,' she said.

Bruno stood and picked up his tray. 'Good,' he said. 'Speak to you soon.'

Jasminder suddenly realised she didn't know his surname, but he was halfway across the room before she could ask. Damn. It would be the first thing Laurenz would want to know. Still, at least she had met someone who seemed senior and well placed; he had even been in Moscow recently. Best of all, it was someone who seemed wildly indiscreet.

46

NOTHING SURPRISED STAFF SERGEANT Wilkinson. He'd served in Iraq and Afghanistan and he'd seen it all – the bad and the good and everything in between. Now he had a comfortable job as resident porter at Georgian Apartments on the borders of Islington and Hackney. It was a smart new building, not Georgian in any sense in spite of its name. Most of the flats had been bought off plan with cash by people who intended to let them, not live in them. He'd settled down in the pleasant porter's flat on the ground floor with his cat and didn't hope for or expect any more excitement in his life. So when a young woman from the Ministry of Defence turned up one morning and told him that as a matter of national security she wanted to ask him most confidentially about Mr Hansen, the occupant of flat three on the second floor, he was neither surprised, alarmed nor even more than casually interested. He rather took it for granted that in a building like this someone might turn out to be of interest to MI5, because he assumed that was where she came from.

He told the young lady, Pamela she called herself, that he saw very little of Mr Hansen. He was often away from town and when he was in residence he was out a good deal, sometimes all night. Sergeant Wilkinson presumed he had a lady friend whom he visited but he had never seen her or any other visitor to flat 2/3. Mr Hansen kept a BMW320 in the basement car park and when he drove it out it was usually a signal that he was going to be away for several days. In fact he had taken the car out yesterday morning and was still away. He got very little mail at the flat and did not use the services of Mrs Hollins, the cleaning lady who did for most of the occupants. Yes, as porter Wilkinson had a pass key to all the flats in case of fire or other emergencies but if he used it, a record would show on the keypad in the flat, so the resident would know and Wilkinson would need a good explanation.

Sergeant Wilkinson readily agreed to phone Pamela's office when Mr Hansen returned. He tucked her card away safely in the inside pocket of his uniform jacket and 'Pamela', alias Peggy Kinsolving, walked off with Mr Wilkinson's mobile number and the registration number of the BMW320 written in her notebook.

Twenty-four hours later an A4 surveillance team had set up a temporary observation post in a half-built block of flats across the road from Georgian Apartments. The camera was attached to a scaffolding pole and hidden by the tarpaulins that stretched across the construction site. A discreet gap gave the lens a clear view of the front entrance of Hansen's apartment block and the ramp to the underground garage.

At ten o'clock the morning after the camera was installed, the monitors in the A4 Control Room picked up the BMW going down into the car park exactly eight minutes before Staff Sergeant Wilkinson telephoned to report its arrival. At about the same time, a few people lounging in parks and cafés and dawdling in shops near Georgian Apartments suddenly began to move purposefully towards various parked cars.

In the A4 control room in Thames House, Wally Woods phoned Peggy. 'Your man's back. We've seen his car but we didn't get a clear picture of him. We've got your description but you're the only one who's actually seen him in the flesh. Would you come up and help us identify him in case he leaves on foot?'

So Peggy spent the next five hours up in the control room, sitting at one of the desks ranged in a line along one wall, gazing at a large TV screen suspended from the ceiling in front of her. The room was busy; several different operations were going on and all the other desks and screens were manned. Peggy found it quite difficult to concentrate on her task, her attention wandering between watching the entrance to the Georgian Apartments and trying to identify the assortment of residents and van drivers coming and going, in and out of the building. Occasionally Sergeant Wilkinson came out, chatting to a van driver or directing someone, but she saw no one who looked anything like Laurenz Hansen. Cups of coffee appeared at her elbow and, at lunchtime, a ham sandwich in its wrapper. Wally Woods liked to make sure guests to the control room were properly looked after – at least those he approved of, and that included Peggy, as a close colleague of Liz's.

Out in the streets, cars were moved, the occupants changed, coffee was drunk, takeaways bought and eaten, until suddenly at three-thirty Peggy said 'That's him!' as a tall dark-haired man, dressed in a smart suit and carrying a briefcase, came out of the door of Georgian Apartments, turned right and walked off down the street in the direction of City Road.

'On the move, on foot, heading to City Road,' said Wally over the microphone as he pressed a button to send the picture from the remote camera to the teams waiting in the cars. Back came pictures from the street as Laurenz headed towards one of them. He walked on, down the City Road in the direction of Old Street tube station. 'He doesn't know we're there,' said Wally to Peggy. 'He's completely relaxed. I thought you said he was a pro.'

'We're pretty sure he is. But he's been getting away with it for quite a bit and he probably feels secure.'

'OK. It's our job to make sure he goes on feeling that way.'

The little procession went on, sometimes with Laurenz leading, sometimes one of the A4 team out in front, until at Old Street Station, Laurenz took the escalator down to the southbound Northern line with just two observers behind him. The others climbed into the cars that had been following and headed off fast to Moorgate station, the next one down the line, as well as stations further on. And it was at Moorgate that Laurenz got off, walked a short distance to a tall block of flats, let himself in with an electronic key fob and disappeared from sight.

'Couldn't see the flat number,' came the report from the team, 'and it looks like an unstaffed block – no porter.'

Wally looked at Peggy, eyebrows raised. 'What next?'

'Could we hang around to see what he does next? And photograph everyone else who goes in.'

'OK.'

'I'm going back downstairs to see what we can find out about those flats. Ring Liz if you need us.'

This meant another long wait for the A4 teams, though the area was ideal for hanging around in – well supplied with cafés and coffee shops, with one right next to the apartment block's entrance. For an hour and a half no one went in or came out. Then from about five-thirty there was a steady stream of residents letting themselves in, mostly young people in office clothes, and some couples. A few came out, went across the road to a convenience store and went back in again. At half-past six came the first visitor. A young woman, brown-skinned, Indian origin probably, thought Wally, still on duty in the control room, receiving all the pictures. She pressed a bell and was let in.

Wally contacted Liz Carlyle, who had rung several times during the afternoon to see what was happening.

'There's a visitor to the block of flats. It may be the one you're interested in. Indian-looking young woman, early thirties I'd say. Do you want to come and look at the picture?'

'Yes. That's the one,' said Liz when she went to Wally's room and saw the photograph of Jasminder, standing at the door.

'She doesn't look too happy,' remarked Wally, who had not been briefed on who this was or the full background to the case.

'No. She looks miserable,' agreed Liz. 'Please will you hang on there and house her if she leaves? And him too if they leave separately.'

Liz went back to her own floor and found Peggy hovering outside the office. 'Any news?' she asked anxiously.

'Jasminder has gone to meet Laurenz at what appears to be a cover flat. She has got herself well and truly in the net. We need to get Geoffrey Fane and Bruno over here to put them in the picture and it's time to brief Miles Brookhaven too. Have we heard from Charlie Simmons what he's made of that phone of Tim's?'

'Just that he's finding it difficult but I'll ring him again tomorrow. Perhaps we should ask him to come down to brief us all. Shall I set up a meeting for the afternoon?'

'Yes. Do that. Perhaps we'll have a bit more on Laurenz by then.'

Jasminder left the flat in Moorgate by herself at ten-thirty and took the tube to Angel then walked home to her flat. She was accompanied all the way by a team of A4, who commented on how very sad and depressed she looked. Laurenz remained in the Moorgate flat until Liz had Wally stand down the teams at eleven-thirty. She thought it unlikely anything more of interest was going to happen that night.

47

THE CAMERA OUTSIDE GEORGIAN Apartments saw Laurenz return at ten the following morning. Then everything went quiet until suddenly at four-thirty that afternoon the feed from the camera came to life. 'It's go,' said Wally Woods into his microphone, as the TVs at one end of the control room flashed, showing the BMW driving up the ramp and turning towards City Road. Minutes later the line from Sergeant Wilkinson buzzed. 'He's left in the car and he's got his overnight bag... told me he'd be away for three days.'

Wally Woods phoned Liz. 'He's off and we're with him.'

By now the registration number of the BMW had been fed into the Automatic Number Plate Recognition system and police forces across the country were looking out for it.

'May I come up?' asked Liz. The control room was Wally's domain and it was strictly by invitation only for desk officers when an operation was on. He did not like anyone looking over the shoulders of his team and making suggestions, unless he'd asked for input. Liz was always scrupulous in seeking his permission and, as a result, always welcome.

When she arrived the chase was well under way. The BMW was making its way north, up Holloway Road and Archway Road, possibly heading for either the A1 or the M1. When they knew which it was, the cars would be able to hang back as the cameras would monitor its progress. 'It's the M1,' said Wally, after a short time. 'Any clues as to where he's heading?'

'I'm afraid not.'

'Well, Maureen's in charge out there so we should be fine, even if he gets up to any funny business.'

Liz knew Maureen Hayes of old. She was an experienced team leader, who'd successfully carried out many operations for Liz, so she sat back comfortably on the old leather sofa that was kept for visiting case officers in the corner of the control room, well away from the operational desks, ready to enjoy the chase.

The BMW drove fast up the M1 with Maureen and her team in pursuit in three cars. Regular reports were coming in as they passed through successive police areas. Leicestershire had just reported when Maureen spoke. 'He's gone up the slip road, junction twenty-one, no indicators. He's doing anti-surveillance. We've overshot. Can you take him, Denis?'

'Roger,' he replied from a car behind. 'We'll take him.'

'Good luck,' said Maureen. 'See you later.'

Denis and the third car, driven by Marcus Washington, turned off at junction twenty-one and took up the pursuit as the BMW headed west, twisting and turning along a series of B-roads. They were driving straight into the low sun, dazzling in the flat countryside of Leicestershire. Denis and Marcus were hanging back so as not to be noticed in the quiet roads.

There was silence for five minutes while the screens showed pictures from the dashboard cameras of shadowy hedges and trees.

'Report, please,' said Wally.

'Contact lost,' announced Denis. 'We're looking for him but these roads are hell.'

Liz groaned to herself. She knew it was difficult and in these circumstances you needed a lot of luck. Then suddenly their luck turned. Maureen and her team partner Sally, who had gone off the motorway at the next junction, had found their way back south through the narrow roads and their camera came to life, relaying a picture of the BMW stationary, with the driver standing beside it, stretching and yawning. 'We have him,' shouted Maureen triumphantly, and the sighs of relief from the other cars were echoed in the control room.

The BMW was parked outside a pub in the centre of the small town of Market Bosworth. Pictures were coming in now of the old whitewashed coaching inn with window boxes and hanging baskets full of flowers. Laurenz was standing beside his vehicle and then, as Maureen watched, he got back in and drove down a narrow lane to one side of the building, on which 'Car Park' was signposted. By now Denis and Marcus had both reached the town and had stopped a little distance from the inn. It was just after eight.

'I'm wondering if he's going to stay the night,' said Maureen. 'It looks very cosy,' she added rather longingly.

'Give it a few minutes, then park in the car park and go in and have a look-see.'

'Roger,' said Maureen, and five minutes later she drove down the narrow lane into what turned out to be a small, walled yard at the back of the building. She tucked her car into a space in the corner and she and Sally got out and strolled towards the back door of the inn, looking for the BMW. It wasn't there.

'Sorry to tell you this, but the target car isn't here. I can't understand it. There's no way out except the way we came in.'

In the stunned silence Sally said, 'Wait a minute… look. There's a row of lock-up garages. They're sort of old lean-to barns, against the back wall of the building.' In the twilight it was easy to miss them. 'He must have put it in one of those. It's the only possible explanation.'

After a glance at Wally, Liz broke in, 'That means he must use this place a lot if he has the key to a garage. It probably also means he's staying the night but we'd better not count on it.'

'Go in,' instructed Wally, 'and see what's going on.'

It was busy inside. A small crowd was standing at the bar, some drinking, others waiting to be served. A number of people were sitting at tables eating supper. Sally went off to the Ladies while Maureen stood at the bar. Out of the corner of her eye she could see Laurenz sitting at a small table in the corner, scanning a menu. Sally's route back from the cloakroom passed directly beside his table. She took Maureen's place at the bar and ordered two Diet Cokes while Maureen went off to the Ladies on the same route, passing the small table where Laurenz was now ordering food from a waitress. The resulting photographs of him sitting at the table came back clearly to the Control Room.

After they had finished their drinks the two women went back to their car and were replaced at the bar by Denis and his partner.

'We're going to park in the street,' said Maureen. 'If we stay here any longer we might get blocked in. This place is very busy. He hasn't got his overnight bag with him and he hasn't had time to go up to a room. I don't think he's staying.'

'Roger that,' said Wally.

From Marcus came, 'I'm moving up closer. It's getting dark and this place is not very well lit.'

Denis came out, having finished his drink, and reported that Laurenz was getting his bill. Cars were beginning to leave the car park now as the diners and drinkers started to drift home. The A4 cars got into position to head off whichever way the BMW turned when it came out of the car park. It was not going to be an easy follow on these unlit roads in the dark. They watched as more cars left the car park but there was no sign of the BMW.

In the control room pizzas had arrived and been eaten at the big central table and Liz was becoming anxious. She knew perfectly well that if anything had happened they'd have heard about it but she couldn't resist asking Wally, 'Could you find out what's going on?'

As she spoke, Maureen's voice came through from Market Bosworth. 'We can't sit here much longer. The pub will be closing soon and this place will be quiet as the grave in another half hour.'

'OK,' replied Wally. 'I think it's time to find out what's going on in that place. Liz, are you OK for Maureen to go in and enquire if he's staying the night?'

'Yes. It's the only option. Let's hope there's someone sensible in there.'

Maureen disappeared inside the inn and in Market Bosworth and London the tension was crackling. After twenty minutes she came out, got into her car and said, 'We've been had. He left at ten; he must have snuck out the back. And we're looking for a black Mercedes saloon.' And she read out the digits of a number plate. Immediately, without waiting for any further explanation, the control room flashed the number to Number Plate Recognition and all police forces.

Maureen went on, 'Mr Hansen rents two garages. He keeps the Mercedes in one and leaves the BMW in the other. His explanation is that he has to drive long distances up to Scotland with passengers and he needs the bigger car. But he uses the smaller one while in London. He's in the oil business apparently. He wanted two garages because it's too difficult to shuffle the cars about when the car park is full. The manager thought it was OK. He paid six months' rent, cash in advance. He showed them his driver's licence and gave them a mobile number, which I have.' And she read out the number. 'I left the manager a card and told him to ring us when Mr Hansen comes back for the BMW or if he hears from him.'

'Sorry, Liz,' said Wally, swinging his chair round to face the sofa. But she had already gone to get Peggy, to set in train tracing the details of the mobile phone.

By ten-thirty reports were coming in of the Mercedes's progress. It had been sighted driving north on the M1, travelling very fast. South of Leeds, cameras at the junction spotted it joining the M62. It must have turned back southwards because it was next reported on the Manchester ring road. But before any action could be taken it had disappeared, presumably having left the motorway, somewhere near Sale.

Wally turned to Liz, who by this time was back sitting on the sofa. 'What would you like us to do next? It sounds like the car could be anywhere in the Greater Manchester area.'

'Could you get a team out from there to scout around, just to see if they can spot the car? It might be parked up somewhere for the night. There's not much else we can do unless there's a further camera sighting.'

48

'I T'S McKAY HERE,' SAID a voice on the phone. It sounded cheerful, and vaguely familiar.

It had been a long day for Jasminder. C was appearing on TV the following day, with the Heads of MI5 and GCHQ, at the first public meeting of the Security and Intelligence Committee, and she needed to get up to speed with the whys and wherefores of the occasion. She was responsible for briefing the media after it was over and C was anxious that the event should receive a good response. She also had yet another talk to give to a department in Vauxhall Cross – this time it was Finance – and though she had given the same talk a number of times already, she still felt the need to familiarise herself with it beforehand. Always at the back of her mind was the growing anxiety that she still had nothing of substance to give Laurenz and it seemed unlikely she'd get anything in the next week either.

The voice on the phone went on, 'McKay... Bruno McKay – you know, the amusing chap you met at lunch the other day? We shared a table, you remember.'

And she did remember, of course. Bruno. She'd looked him up in the Staff Directory after lunch and found there was only one Bruno in Head Office. He worked with Geoffrey Fane, though his precise job wasn't clear from the directory and nor did it give his surname, just the initial 'M'. Now her heart lifted at the mere discovery of this mysterious Bruno's full name. Laurenz had been scathing when she'd reported back to him about her conversation with the man: 'It's no use telling me you've made a great new contact if you haven't even managed to find out his name or what he does. I don't believe you're trying. You'd better be careful,' he'd added threateningly.

'Yes. How could I forget?' she replied, trying to match Bruno's light-hearted tone. 'What can I do for you?'

'Well, Ms Kapoor, I was hoping to see you again.'

'That would be nice,' she said hesitantly, thinking of all the work she had to get through. On the other hand, she was desperate to find something to satisfy Laurenz. 'When were you thinking of?'

'Well, it's almost seven o'clock in Paris, which calls for an aperitif, *oui*? Why don't I meet you in half an hour just outside the building, on Vauxhall Bridge Road?'

Jasminder thought for a moment, comparing the contrasting prospects of a late night spent working in the office then a solitary takeaway curry at her flat, or finding out more about this intriguing-sounding colleague. In the end, there was no contest. 'That sounds good,' she said.

'See you there then,' said Bruno McKay, and rang off.

Fifteen minutes after the agreed time, Jasminder was still waiting on the corner of Vauxhall Bridge Road, wondering where this man McKay had got to. Lots of people were leaving work but there was no sign of him. How long was she supposed to wait?

She'd just decided to give it another five minutes when she heard the toot of a horn, and saw across the street a white Audi cabriolet drawn up by the pavement. It was a warm evening, the car's top was down and she recognised the man at the wheel from their lunchtime conversation. He waved and smiled, and she waved back as she waited for a gap in the traffic to allow her to cross the street.

'Hop in,' said Bruno, leaning across to open the door for her.

They drove off, Bruno talking nineteen to the dozen – most of it proving entirely inaudible, drowned by the sound of the traffic. Crossing the river, he steered through a bewildering maze of side streets until they came to Hyde Park Corner, where he zoomed east on Piccadilly, turned at Fortnum's, then wiggled his way up a side street and came to a halt before a small but smart-looking hotel. The doorman seemed to recognise the car; he came out quickly, opened Jasminder's door, then caught the keys that Bruno tossed to him and got into the driving seat as Bruno shepherded Jasminder into the hotel.

Was he staying here? she wondered. More disturbing, had he brought her here hoping for what the French called a *cinq à sept* in his room? But no, he escorted her up the steps and turned straight into the hotel's small, discreet bar.

'Now,' said Bruno, as the barman came over, 'what'll it be? A glass of champagne? Whisky? Gin?'

'Sparkling water?' asked Jasminder weakly.

'You can have that as a chaser on the side,' he said, and promptly ordered two glasses of champagne.

After a short time spent listening to Bruno's flow of light conversation, Jasminder leaned back against the soft cushions of the armchair, sipping her champagne and starting to relax. Bruno was saying that he had only recently been posted back to London, having been Head of Station in Paris for the last four years.

'That must have been a very busy Station,' said Jasminder, trying to remember what sort of things Laurenz wanted her to find out.

'Of course. Though nothing like as busy as it is back here. Geoffrey Fane is a hard taskmaster. How are you finding it working for C? I'm very flattered you said yes to coming out tonight. I had assumed you'd be rushed off your feet and your social schedule would be chock-a-block.'

'Lots of work,' said Jasminder. 'Not much time for a social schedule.'

'But I imagine there's a partner in your life. Where is he tonight?' said Bruno.

She stiffened slightly, wondering why he thought she was attached. She was all too aware that she had never declared Laurenz to MI6. 'That's where your sources have let you down,' she said, hoping that Peggy Kinsolving was not one of them. 'I'm unattached.'

'Ah. No sources. I was just guessing, actually. Not many women as attractive as you are unattached.'

The flattery was so outrageous that Jasminder couldn't help but laugh. 'I bet you say that to all the girls.'

'Only the attractive ones,' said Bruno with a grin.

Though this light-hearted banter in this comfortable bar with this self-assured man was very pleasant, it was getting her nowhere. She must not allow herself to relax. Jasminder sat up straight in her chair and changed the subject. 'So are you back in London for good now?'

Bruno shrugged. 'Who knows? Things move pretty fast in the Service as I'm sure you've found out. And even now I'm back here, I still travel a lot.'

'Exotic places?' she enquired, hoping not to sound too inquisitive.

'Sadly not. Mostly all the Stations in places Geoffrey Fane doesn't want to go to himself.'

'Didn't you say you were in Russia last week?'

'Yes, and Estonia and Latvia – I'm saving the joys of Lithuania for next year.'

'I suppose the Moscow Station has a busy time at present?' asked Jasminder. This seemed a safe enough question. He'd just think it was natural curiosity.

'It's chaotic,' he replied with a laugh. 'But that's true of most Stations. Except Paris,' he added with a grin. 'I left it absolutely shipshape.'

By now Bruno was on his second glass of champagne. 'I have to say, the main drawback to the Russian Revolution – other than the small matter of the forty or fifty million people Stalin had killed – was that it severed the traditional ties between Russia and France. Ever since then, the Russians have been almost defiantly *nekulturny*. I know there's the Bolshoi and all that, but the veneer is very thin.'

'Even now?' He'd sheared off at a tangent. None of this was going to be of much value to Laurenz, but she wanted to keep Bruno talking about Russia. Something might come out, she told herself, especially if he kept drinking champagne.

Bruno smiled. 'I'd be delighted to give you a sermon on conditions in present-day Russia, but there's a caveat attached.' When Jasminder raised an eyebrow, he said, 'That you be my guest for dinner here. Hotels rarely stand out for their cuisine, but this place is a remarkable exception.'

They moved on to the dining room, which was small and elegant, with crisp linen tablecloths, silver cutlery and beautiful china. Candles on the tables were reflected in mirrors and small chandeliers sparkled. The food was excellent and Bruno was entertaining company, though he seemed incapable of sticking to any one topic of conversation for more than a *bon mot*. Each time Jasminder tried to steer him back towards the topic of Russia, and in particular the workings of the Moscow Station, he made a half-serious, half-facetious remark and promptly talked about something else. She tried the Baltic States but the same thing happened. She didn't manage to find out where the Station there was – or even if there was one.

He seemed much more interested in Jasminder's background, and got her to tell him about her previous life as a civil libertarian lawyer and the dilemma she'd felt about taking the MI6 job. He asked lots of questions and actually seemed to be listening to the answers, and she began to realise there was a deeper, more thoughtful side to this man, though he seemed at pains to hide it behind his flippant front. At any other time she would have liked to get to know this deeper Bruno better, but right now she wanted him indiscreet. And he had started to be just that, describing the personal peccadillos of the Athens Station head and the expenses scandal from several years before that had seen an accountant prosecuted, but it was infuriating the way he wriggled lizard-like away from any attempt to pin him down.

Finally, as they were having coffee (with a small cognac for Bruno), she managed to get the subject back to Russia. 'If Putin's the savage everybody is saying, then there must be plenty of disenchanted people in the government. He can't have turned the clock back completely, can he?'

'No, though he's trying.'

'I mean, there must be plenty of opportunities for us with dissidents or perhaps inside the political establishment. Even in high places.'

'Especially in high places,' Bruno said emphatically. 'Putin has to be a little careful. Live by the sword, die by the sword – that kind of thing.'

'But I suppose it would be very dangerous for anyone to be in touch with the Embassy – let alone the Station – though some of them must want to talk.'

'Talk? What do you mean?'

Jasminder realised that Bruno was not as tipsy as she'd thought. She shrugged, trying to sound casual. 'I just mean we must be able to find good sources of information – other than official ones. Someone was telling me last week that we have more informants in Russia and the Baltic States than we know what to do with. And without all the cloak-and-dagger business of the past.'

'Oh, there's still plenty of that,' Bruno declared. 'Lots of hair-raising escapades I could tell you about.'

I wish you would, thought Jasminder, but he was looking at his watch. 'Golly, time does fly when you're having fun. I suggest we move on.' And he waved to the waiter for the bill.

Outside, the doorman had already driven the Audi into place and was rewarded by something slipped into his hand. Bruno sat at the wheel for a moment. 'Now, where am I taking you?' He paused and Jasminder wondered whether one option might be his place. She was willing enough, hoping he might expand on these exploits he'd referred to. But he added, 'I don't know where you live.'

'Islington,' she said. When he didn't react she added, 'Is that too far out of your way? I can always get a taxi.'

'Not at all,' he said. 'We'll be there in a jiffy.'

And three jumped amber lights and a succession of deft manoeuvres later, Bruno pulled up in front of Jasminder's flat.

She took a deep breath and said, 'Would you like to come in for coffee?' The implication was as clear as she could make it. Her only worry was that her cleaner might not have shown up that day. The state of Jasminder's bedroom as of that morning would have put off any man.

But to her surprise Bruno shook his head. 'Very sweet of you, especially after a long evening listening to me waffle on. But I've got a big day tomorrow so I hope you won't mind if I take a rain check.'

'Oh,' said Jasminder, with a disappointment she could not disguise. Already she could envisage Laurenz's reaction. 'I'll hold you to it,' she added.

Bruno leaned over and kissed her lightly on the cheek. 'We'll tackle the Russians next time then.' It sounded light-hearted but it struck her as an odd thing for him to say. As she said goodnight and got out of the car, she felt as if, for all her questioning, Bruno had been the one who'd got most out of the evening.

49

Peggy came in very early the next day and joined Liz in her office. 'I hope you weren't here all night,' she said.

'Not quite. I did go home.' Liz didn't say that it had been at two in the morning. She'd managed to nap for a couple of hours but was up again at five and here at Thames House by six. 'How's that feeling?' she asked, pointing at the sling on Peggy's left arm.

'Not bad. It's only when I forget about it and knock something that it hurts.'

'Did you get anything on the Mercedes?' Liz asked.

'Yes, it's registered to a private company. I've sent an enquiry to Companies House, but they haven't come back to me yet. They're probably still in bed. I've also got some news on the phone number Hansen gave to the pub – it's a pay-as-you-go, bought three months ago in Manchester. I should have the list of calls from and to it later this morning. And of course, if he's used it since last night we should be able to get a fix on him, but I don't suppose he's stupid enough for that.'

'No. So far he's been very professional. That car swap at the pub was clever.'

'Do you think he saw A4 yesterday? Do you think he knows we're on to him?'

'Not sure,' replied Liz. 'Wally Woods doesn't think so. Let's hope he's right.'

Peggy stifled a small yawn, and blushed slightly when Liz smiled. 'What's going on up there now?' Peggy asked.

'I've just had a report from Wally. Yesterday's teams are holed up in a Travelodge south of Manchester, getting some rest; a new team was sent out from the city as soon as we got the Number Plate Recognition information and they've been scouring around the area near Sale, where he disappeared, all night, but no sign of the car so far. They've passed the number to Greater Manchester Police, but no reaction from them either.'

'Let's have a look at a map,' said Peggy. 'I'm not sure where Sale is.' She tapped a screen. 'Just off the Manchester ring road, apparently. On the south side.'

'Gosh,' she added, as a satellite photo of the area came up on her screen. She turned the computer sideways so they could both study it more easily. 'It looks a rather unpromising place to drive to late at night. Especially with all that complicated counter-surveillance. What on earth can he be doing up there?'

'Well, if he is a Russian Illegal and not a Norwegian banker at all – and given his behaviour that seems increasingly likely – and if we are looking at this pincer operation, then we need to think what connection the Russians have with that part of the North of England.'

Peggy pointed at the screen. 'There's the airport not far away. Maybe he was going there.'

'Or...' said Liz slowly, now peering at the screen as well. 'Look, there... Altrincham. That's where that oligarch

Patricov has his mansion. I went to see it with the Chief Constable.'

'You don't think he could have anything to do with it, do you? I thought he was anti-Putin.'

'That's what I was told. But you never know. It's the only Russian connection I've heard of in that area. I'm sure if there was anyone else Russian in the neighbourhood, the Chief Constable would have mentioned it. I'm going to ring him.'

Liz reached the police switchboard in Manchester, and was put through straightaway. She was impressed; not many Chief Constables answered their own phone, especially this early in the day.

'Pearson,' he said quietly.

'Hello, it's Liz Carlyle in Thames House.'

'Ha! I was thinking about you just the other day. How are things?'

'I'm fine, but something's come up. It's to do with Patricov.'

'I hope you've found out more about him than we have. He's a careful bird, our Mr P.'

'It's not him I want to ask about. We have someone under surveillance here in London – a banker by the name of Hansen. He's Norwegian, or at least his papers all say he's Norwegian.

'Anyway, we followed him yesterday when he drove out of London. I don't think he spotted our teams, but he went through pretty complicated counter-surveillance. Either he's a pro, or he's leading two lives that he's determined to keep separate.' She explained about the car switch that A4 had discovered. 'We've checked the Mercedes he drove off in; it's registered to something called Asimov Holdings. We're trying to run down details on the company right now, but it's private and it's taking us a while.'

'Sounds Russian.'

'I know. Here's the other thing: when we last spotted the car it was on the Manchester Ring Road near Sale. Then we lost it. It must have turned off. Looking at the map, we've noticed that Sale is very near Altrincham and I remembered that that's where Patricov's place is. It's a long shot but I just wondered whether there could possibly be a connection. We've still got A4 teams up there scouting around but they've found no sign of him, and your traffic people have seen nothing of the car, so the trail's gone a bit cold by now. I just wondered if your contact there… Reilly, I think it was… could check to see if by any chance the car went in to the grounds at Patricov's mansion. Could you help?'

'Of course. I'll get straight on to Reilly. Just give me the number plate. He'll know if the car's there and if it belongs to Patricov.'

'If it is there, could he let us know who drove it in last night? That would be a big help.'

As soon as Liz had put the receiver down, the phone rang. It was Wally Woods. There had been no sightings of the Mercedes and he wanted to pull the teams off as they had a counter-terrorist job up there that needed all available resources. The police were still on the alert for the Mercedes but he didn't think there was much more the A4 teams could usefully do on Liz's job unless anything new came up. With a sinking feeling Liz agreed they could stand down. If nothing came from the Patricov lead, they were back to square one and would have to start again from scratch in London.

Liz found it difficult to settle to anything else while she waited for Pearson to come back. She noticed too that Peggy was not her usual bright self. In fact, she looked rather depressed. 'You all right?' she asked.

Peggy nodded unconvincingly and Liz said, 'Sit down. Is it Tim?'

After a moment Peggy replied, 'Somehow it seemed to be easier to cope when he was being aggressive and hostile than now when he's being all contrite and miserable.'

Liz smiled. 'Yes, but you must feel relieved. At least Tim hasn't done anything illegal. He's just been a bit naïve.'

'I'll say,' said Peggy crossly. 'Of course I'm pleased he's not in trouble. But he doesn't come out of this very well. It's not as if he rebuffed this Marina creature; she just seems to have realised he didn't know anything of value and dropped him. He's been a complete ass.'

Just then the phone rang. It was Pearson, calling back. Liz put him on loudspeaker so Peggy could hear. He sounded puzzled. 'Hello, Liz, I've talked to Reilly; he was on duty yesterday. He says the Mercedes did arrive, late in the evening, and it's still there. It belongs to the estate. But your Hansen wasn't the driver. No one new has entered the compound.'

'Are you sure?'

'Reilly is. The only people who've come in are the guards, changing shifts – the same ones as usual; the housekeeper; and Patricov's sidekick, the Russian called Karpis. If you remember, you and I didn't meet him when we visited. He was out.'

Liz tried to make sense of this. Could A4 have goofed about the car? It didn't seem likely; they were always extremely careful. Perhaps after it had last been spotted, near Sale, there had been another switch, and for some reason Karpis had taken the car back to Patricov's compound.

She looked at Peggy, who shrugged, equally mystified. Liz didn't believe this could be a simple mistake. 'Is there CCTV coverage of the entrance to the estate?'

'Absolutely. Reilly's looked at it, just to make sure some-body hadn't somehow slipped in. Nobody has.'

'Could you send me a photograph of anybody who's driven the Mercedes in the last twenty-four hours?'

'I'm sure that's possible, though Reilly's already said he only has film of Karpis with the Mercedes. But I'll ring him again and see what he can do. Oh, and by the way, that company you mentioned is the holding company for the Patricov business.' He rang off and Peggy and Liz looked at each other, completely bemused.

For fifteen minutes they discussed possible solutions to the mystery. Then Liz's desktop pinged with the arrival of a new email. Liz glanced at the screen and sat up. 'It's from Pearson.'

She clicked on the email then opened its attachment – a video clip, labelled 'Karpis' at the bottom, showing a tall man dressed in a blazer and slacks, standing up as he got out of the Mercedes's driving seat. His back was to the camera. Liz swung the screen towards Peggy and they both watched as the man approached the mansion's front door. As he began to climb the stone steps he was picked up by a camera looking down from above the front door. It showed his face clearly. Liz and Peggy spoke together.

'But…' said Liz.

'Isn't that Laurenz?' said Peggy.

'Yes, that's Hansen,' said Liz.

'But why are they calling him Karpis?' said Peggy.

'Don't you see?' said Liz, her voice shaking with excitement as she pointed at the screen. 'Laurenz Hansen is Karpis.'

50

'GOOD AFTERNOON, EVERYONE.' IT was four o'clock and in the corner meeting room in Thames House the sun was just glancing in between two buildings. Peggy, looking harassed, was fiddling with the blinds to try to keep the glare out of Liz's eyes.

'Thank you all for coming at such short notice,' Liz continued. 'I thought it was time to take a view of where this case has got to and reach agreement on what we should do next.' She looked around the table. Geoffrey Fane was there, lounging back in his chair in his usual detached manner, one long, elegantly clad leg crossed over the other, a slight sneer on his face. But Liz knew him well enough by now to be sure that he would be listening closely to everything that was said, ready to intervene forcefully if he didn't agree. In spite of his air of ineffable superiority, she found it a comfort to have him here. He had long experience and she had benefitted from his advice in the past.

Beside Fane sat Bruno McKay. It was twelve years or so since Liz had first worked with him and it had taken him that long to show a more thoughtful, less patronising, and even helpful side to his character. When she thought about it, Liz reflected that she too had probably grown up; she

321

was less chippy, less quick to take offence than she had been twelve years ago. Life, grief in her case and perhaps his too, had changed them both.

Sitting next to Bruno was Miles Brookhaven, looking unmistakably transatlantic with his black polished tasselled slip-on shoes and yet another button-down shirt. Liz was relieved that he no longer seemed to fancy her; his gaze now strayed more often in Peggy's direction. Liz rather hoped any affection on his part might be reciprocated by her assistant, since it seemed clear that Tim was far too weak and feeble for her now.

The final member of the group, apart from Peggy, was Charlie Simmons from GCHQ. Even he was looking somewhat more grown-up than usual. His hair was still standing on end as though he had just got out of bed but he had swapped his pullover for a jacket and his usual tee-shirt for a white shirt with an open neck. And, unusually for him, he wasn't late. He had come down by car with a colleague for an earlier meeting so had not been reliant on the notoriously unreliable trains from Cheltenham.

Liz began, 'I think it will be helpful if I just summarise where we have got to in this case. All of you know some of it but I want to be sure we are all au fait with the latest developments because we need to decide whether we should take action now or wait to see what happens next.'

There was a general shuffling in the room as people sat up in their chairs ready to join in. 'You will all remember,' she went on, 'that the first lead in this investigation came from Miles. His colleagues had a Russian military source in Ukraine who asked to meet a British expert as he had important information to pass on. Miles, you went to Ukraine to meet him and he said, correct me if I get this wrong, that the Russians were planting Illegals in Europe and the US with the aim of weakening or destabilising those countries. That in the UK the operation was proving very promising and the Illegal was getting close to a target.' She paused and looked at Miles.

'That's correct,' he said. 'The source, Mischa, claimed to be disaffected after the Malaysian aircraft was shot down over Ukraine. The other important point is that Mischa's source for this is his brother, an FSB officer, who talks more than he should, when he's drunk. So in other words, our source has direct access to the information. I should just add that he is being paid quite generously by my colleagues in Ukraine.'

'Thanks, Miles. So it was all very vague and there didn't seem to be much we could do about it, except keep our ears to the ground. Then Mischa resurfaced saying he had more specific information. By that time he had been posted to Tallinn and I met him there.

'What he told me was that the Russians are operating two Illegals in this country, and suggested they were a couple. Their original brief was to infiltrate protest movements in the UK and subtly influence them to cause as much trouble and disturbance as possible, with the aim of weakening both government and society. But then the nature of that operation changed. The man managed to get close to a woman who was in some way connected with one of the intelligence services and his partner was targeting a man who might be able to provide information about another of our services. They were now calling the operation "Pincer". I suppose they were imagining a pair of jaws snapping up two of our services.

'That was the background. Now we get on to the current situation, which as you will all appreciate is highly sensitive as it involves a member of one of our services and a close contact of another. It appears that our two Illegals got lucky. We assume that they were targeting the anti-surveillance lobby, probably trawling through internet chat rooms, looking for people to approach, when they must have come across a notice for a lecture that Jasminder Kapoor was giving at King's College, London, where she worked at the time.

'It seems certain that the female attended the lecture. Who knows how many people present were potential targets, but we are aware of one in particular – a lecturer at the college called Tim Simpson – who asked a fairly aggressive question and made it clear that he didn't think Jasminder's lecture was radical enough. Tim was active on the internet, on various anti-snooping blogs. He was approached at the talk by a woman calling herself Marina, and they chatted for a while, then continued their conversation by email.'

There seemed no good reason not to mention that Tim was also Peggy's partner so Liz continued, 'Unsurprisingly, Marina's interest in Tim increased dramatically when she learned he lived with a member of MI5. It was then that she gave him a special phone to use when communicating with her, telling him that it would be more secure from surveillance. Charlie has had a close look at this phone and is ready to tell us what he's found out.' And before anyone could interrupt to ask the identity of the MI5 officer concerned, she turned to Charlie Simmons.

'Yes. Thanks, Liz,' said Charlie, sitting to attention. 'The phone, which is now in bits at Cheltenham, looks like an ordinary iPhone 5c, and it is – but that's not all it is.' Everyone was looking at him now as though he were about to pull a rabbit out of a hat.

'I'm reasonably good at spotting things, but it took me three days to work out what's inside this. They've been very clever. First of all, they fronted it with an app that automatically erases messages and texts that might be lying about. I couldn't find any history of messaging, much less the messages themselves, simply because they'd all been wiped as soon as they were received and read or transmitted.'

Liz said, 'Tim mentioned that to me. He thought it must be for security purposes.'

'He's right, but it also hides a multitude of other sins. Capabilities the person who gave it to Tim didn't want him to know about.'

'What else does it do?' asked Miles Brookhaven.

'The hardware has been rigged. It can be turned on remotely and all the functions can be operated by a third party. The camera's ready to video whatever Tim's looking at; the audio component's set to transmit any conversation on the phone – and *off* the phone too. It's like carrying a microphone around. And the phone can be made to transmit its location. So if Tim had the phone with him, his "friend" would know exactly where he was.'

'The complete works,' said Miles. 'That's got to be state-sponsored. No private individual could do all that.'

'That's the bad news,' said Charlie.

'You mean there's good news?' asked Bruno.

He nodded. 'Yes, and that is… these utilities haven't been used. It's as if someone had decided they'd made a mistake setting Tim up with all this. The links are all fallow; it's like they couldn't be bothered. Very odd.'

'Indeed,' said Fane. He sounded unimpressed.

'Why'd you think that is?' Peggy asked.

'They must have decided Tim was never going to be one of them,' said Charlie.

Fane said, 'So it's a bit of a damp squib, isn't it? This Marina woman doesn't want to play.'

'Oh, I'm sure she does – just not with Tim, when he's so unforthcoming. But she'll keep sniffing around until she finds someone who can be more helpful. In fact for all we know, she may have other people in play right now. So it's important that we find her.'

'How are you going to do that?' Fane still sounded sceptical.

Liz sat further forward in her chair. 'We hope that she will resurface. With Tim or someone else. But that's just one side of their pincer movement. As Geoffrey and Bruno already know, we seem to have uncovered another, even more dangerous, plot that looks set to compromise their service.'

And she explained what they had discovered about Laurenz, detailing how he had met Jasminder, his cover as a Norwegian banker, and how the fact that he had given her the same model of iPhone had spurred them into taking a closer look at the man. She described the recent surveillance operation, and the shock discovery that Laurenz Hansen was actually Karpis, aide-de-camp to a Russian oligarch living near Manchester.

'And this is the same chap who was romancing Jasminder Kapoor, new Communications Director of Six?' said Fane in an incredulous tone. 'How did this interesting personal connection escape the vetters?'

'I'm afraid she failed to declare that she had a boyfriend,' said Liz. 'As soon as we began to suspect there was something wrong about Laurenz Hansen, we checked.'

'Yes. And unfortunately he seemed to find her easier to exploit than Marina did Tim.'

'So this is where Bruno comes in,' went on Liz, 'and why we asked him to get alongside Jasminder. And it seems to me that what we do next partly depends on what he's found out. Over to you, Bruno.'

He had been sitting back in his chair, eyes half closed, but now he came to life. He put his elbows on the table and rested his chin on his hands, pursing his lips contemplatively. 'I haven't any evidence that she's under anyone's control or acting to any brief. But I spent an evening with her, and I have to say it made me more suspicious rather than less. She was clearly under a lot of stress – she looked exhausted for one thing. That may of course be pressure of work, but if that's all it is, I'd be surprised.

'From the outset, she was at pains to let me know she was single and unattached – and if what you say about this Laurenz Hansen is still the case, then that wasn't true. And we all know she has never declared him to the Service, so why is she hiding him? I think, following your investigation and now we know he's actually a Russian and not a Norwegian banker, it's pretty obvious.

'But just to finish on my evening out with her... more tellingly than her claim to be unattached, at least as far as I'm concerned, was that throughout the time we spent together she tried to steer the conversation to the Moscow Station; she especially wanted to know about our informants there. I played along up to a point, but every time I changed the subject, she brought it back to Russia. Then she tried the Baltics. I felt like a trout that won't rise, even when the fly's put right above his nose. I can only give you my impression but I came away thinking something's amiss there; I like Jasminder, but I felt she was asking me things at someone else's behest. I don't believe she personally could give two hoots about the Moscow Station. Someone's put her up to it and she's pretty desperate, would be my conclusion. But I have no proof.' He sat back in his chair.

'We're not trying anyone here,' Fane said sharply. 'The rules of evidence don't apply, or any presumption of innocence. There's already enough here to get her out of the Service, just on her failure in the first place to declare this Laurenz Hansen. And now he's turned out to be a Russian, she may well be looking at a long prison sentence.'

Liz could see that Peggy was about to jump to Jasminder's defence so she broke in with, 'Hold your horses, Geoffrey. We don't know whether Jasminder knows Laurenz is Russian. What do you suggest we do about her?'

'There's only one thing to do. We need to sit down with Ms Kapoor and wring the whole story out of her. Plus,' he added, 'get Charlie here to take her phone to bits and see what that tells us.'

'I'd want to inform C before we called her in.'

'Of course. And actually, I wasn't suggesting *you* interview her,' said Fane. 'This is a Six matter so we'll look after it.'

'That's fine,' said Liz, 'but we need to coordinate the timing with our investigation in Manchester. It's important not to alert Laurenz Hansen, or Karpis or whoever he is, before we move up there. If you tell Jasminder you want to talk to her, she may warn him and he'll skip.'

'What are you proposing then?'

'Hansen is in Altrincham now, at Patricov's estate. I think it would be best if you could interview Jasminder, with no advance warning, at just the same time as the police move in on Altrincham. She may tell you something of value to us when we interview him and vice versa.'

'When are the police proposing to go in?'

'Tomorrow afternoon, assuming Hansen stays at the estate. Otherwise they'll arrest him if he moves out.'

'Are you planning to be there?' Fane asked sharply.

'Yes. I want to interview him myself. The police don't know all the background. But I was wondering if you would come up too, Bruno. You have more up-to-date Moscow knowledge than I do.'

Bruno sat up suddenly, looking surprised. Then a broad grin spread over his face. 'I will be delighted to lend you a hand,' he replied. 'It will be quite like old times.'

51

KEVIN BURGESS WAS TIRED, and his brain, which was never very sharp, was duller than usual. He'd worked the overnight shift at the Patricov estate, then, just as he was leaving for home and bed, Reilly had asked him (told him, really) to come back at noon to work the afternoon shift as well. Apparently some people were coming and Reilly needed the whole security team on duty. Kevin hadn't got his head down till nine-thirty in the morning as he'd had to take the dog out first as usual, and today of all days she'd rushed off after a rabbit – it had taken him three-quarters of an hour to get her back. So he'd only had an hour and a half's sleep, and had snatched a cup of tea and a jam sandwich before getting back to work just on noon.

He'd found both the other two security men, Morgan and Webster, already there. Reilly was in his office on the phone, speaking quietly but urgently, and waved the three of them away, out of earshot, indicating they should wait till he was free. When eventually he came out, he allocated a position to each man.

'We're about to have some visitors. They're official – Special Branch and a couple of people from London. Mr Patricov is away, but his wife is here and so is Mr Karpis.

I want you to watch the entrances as usual; there may be police officers posted there with you. You are not to let anyone in or out without the officers' agreement. If anyone tries to rush you, stop them and press the alert on your intercoms. I'll be in the monitor-room, watching. Is that all clear?'

'Yes, sir,' murmured the men, and Kevin asked, 'Does that include Mr Karpis and Mrs Patricov?'

'Yes, everybody. No one is to leave without police say-so.'

Reilly gave each man his post. Kevin Burgess was told to take the back gate leading into the woods that bordered the estate.

Standing at the gate, Kevin reflected that he had never liked Karpis. He was a cold fish, arrogant and rude. Kevin decided that he would be more than happy to stop the Russian leaving the estate if he got the chance. He wasn't quite sure how he'd do it as Karpis was taller than him and looked very fit. Well dressed and polished he might be, but something about him reminded Kevin of the sort of high-class thug you got in some of those TV dramas. He hoped that the arrival of Special Branch had something to do with Karpis rather than Patricov. Kevin liked the oligarch. OK, he was very Russian, but at least he seemed human and always spoke to the outside staff in a friendly way when he came across them, not like Karpis who was always unpleasant.

An hour went by and nothing happened at the back gate. No one tried to come in or leave. Kevin had gone into a sort of standing-up doze when he heard a police siren. He listened to hear if it was approaching the estate but gradually it faded into the distance. He was wide awake now and tensed at the sound of movement outside the gate. Someone was coming along the path through the wood, not trying to hide their approach – he could hear twigs cracking and dead leaves being shuffled underfoot.

He walked up to the gate and saw on the entry-phone camera a large pock-marked face. The gate was rattling as a man tried to open it.

'Who's there?' asked Kevin.

'Special Branch, mate,' came the reply, and a warrant card was shoved up against the camera. Kevin opened the gate and was joined by a large man in dark trousers and a leather jacket.

'Afternoon,' he said, offering his hand. 'I'm Tom Parkinson, Detective Sergeant. I've come to join you.'

'Glad to see you. What's this all about?'

DS Parkinson shrugged. 'Your guess is as good as mine, mate. Some Russian they want to haul in. Do you know the bloke?' He lit a cigarette.

'The owner's a Russian. Do you mean him?'

Parkinson shook his head. 'No. They said he's abroad. It's some geezer works for him.'

'That would be Karpis. Nasty piece of work.'

'Well, I need you to be my eyes then if he tries to scarper. They showed us a photo of the bloke but it wasn't very clear.'

'Don't worry, I know him all right.'

'The big guns are here,' said Parkinson. 'You know, the funnies, from London. And my chief's here as well. Must be important. They should be in the house by now.'

Kevin Burgess stood with Parkinson and waited. The only sound was a pair of blackbirds in the poplar trees and an occasional car on the far side of the woods. Kevin tried to stay alert, telling himself he had to be ready for something dramatic. But all that happened was Parkinson smoked a cigarette and stood scuffing his feet in boredom.

Then he heard something: approaching footsteps. Someone was walking fast towards them from the direction of the house.

Kevin was standing square on the path ready for whoever it might be when Reilly appeared round the bend, looking hot and breathless, with another man – a blond-haired gent in a blazer, presumably one of the funnies from London, though he looked fit and big enough to hold his own in a fight.

Reilly said, 'Have you seen him?'

'Who?'

'Karpis!'

'No one's been this way.'

'What about a woman? Have you seen a woman?' It was the other man. He had a posh-sounding voice – officer type, authoritative, urgent.

'Do you mean Mrs Patricov, sir?' replied Kevin. 'She's not been here.'

'No, I don't mean her. It's someone else. English. Raincoat, navy trousers, brown hair tied back, five foot seven.'

'No, sir. No one's come this way, man or woman, have they, Sergeant?'

'Not a soul while I've been here,' confirmed Parkinson. 'What's the problem?'

Reilly said, 'Karpis has disappeared. The housekeeper says he was in the house half an hour ago and so was Mrs P. Neither of them's there now. I had to answer the bloody door myself when the police arrived. This gentleman's colleague has gone off the map too. She's not answering her phone. Anyway, I want you two to stay put. If anybody comes this way, hold them. Even Mrs P. If it's the lady from London, get her to ring her colleague. Understood?'

'Yes,' said the two men. Kevin hesitated. He'd had a sudden thought about where they might find Karpis and Mrs Patricov. But before he could say anything, Reilly had turned away and was heading back swiftly to the house with the other man in tow.

Kevin turned to Parkinson. 'Listen, watch here for a minute on your own, will you? I've got to go up to the house.'

'What? They told you to stay here. I don't even know what Karpis looks like.'

'Sure you do,' said Kevin, speaking confidently now that he had an idea of what to do. 'He's six two, dark hair, posh clothes. And he's Russian though he speaks English. Anyway, you heard. Whoever comes along, grab them.'

'What if it's a funny?'

'They're not bloody Russian.' And before Parkinson could protest further, Kevin had turned and walked away fast towards the house.

He knew he could face the sack for leaving his post, but could see from Reilly's air of anxiety that something had gone badly wrong. They couldn't find Patricov's wife or Karpis; had they left the estate – but if so, how did they get out and why? And what about this woman the other guy was asking about? She'd gone missing too. But Kevin had a theory and he was going to test it, whatever the penalty for leaving his post.

He ran at a fast jog up through the gardens, past the tennis court then the greenhouses, and along the bottom of the terrace. At one end of the house there was a triple garage and a small coach house where Patricov's mother was supposed to come and live, though apparently she was a stubborn old bird and didn't want to, so she was still in Moscow.

Then Kevin came to the solarium, where he slowed down to catch his breath. He quietly opened the door to the glass-roofed atrium. On one side were the doors to the changing rooms; on the other the glass door to the swimming pool. He looked through this into the pool. It was still and quiet; there was no one in there. He was just turning towards the changing-room doors when into the silence a voice said, 'Don't move. I've got a gun in my hand.'

It was Karpis, Kevin was sure of it. But why was he threatening a security guard? 'Turn round,' said the voice, and Kevin did, to find himself facing Karpis, who was standing in the open doorway of the men's changing room.

'Go inside,' he said, waving the gun and standing back to let Kevin pass.

There was suddenly a lot to take in. A woman was sitting on a long bench set against one wall, underneath a row of coat hooks. She was wearing a raincoat and had her hair tied back. She must be the woman from London that Reilly and the other man were looking for. On the wall opposite the bench a door stood open to a small room Burgess had never noticed before. It looked like the pump room, with all the mechanics for the swimming pool. There was a woman sitting in there at a table in front of a couple of identical laptops, their screens shining brightly. From the back of her head it looked like Mrs Patricov. She was tapping furiously at one of the keyboards.

'Sit down there,' said Karpis, waving his gun at the bench, then poking Kevin in the side. 'And don't speak. Put your phone on the floor.'

Kevin threw his intercom phone down on the tiles where he saw another phone lying – presumably the London woman's.

As he sat down next to her, he glanced at her face and she looked back at him, raised her eyebrows slightly and gave a furtive nod that seemed to him to say 'Yes, we're on the same side'.

Just at that moment Mrs Patricov shouted loudly from the little room next door. She was speaking in Russian but it was clear from her tone that something was going wrong. She sounded panicky and desperate as she started tapping on the keyboard of the other machine.

Karpis snapped back impatiently.

Mrs Patricov took her hands from the keys, looked over her shoulder at him and said something else that Kevin couldn't understand; but in the stream of Russian he picked up the word 'WIFI'. It was quite clear that whatever she was trying to do on the computers wasn't working. Had Reilly or the police disabled the WIFI?

Karpis swore. He had the pistol trained on a point between Kevin and the woman; that was no comfort since less than twelve inches separated them.

There was another loud exchange in Russian between Karpis and Patricov's wife then Karpis took his eyes off the two captives and looked wildly around the room. His eyes fixed on something in the corner – a red glass-fronted box containing the fire emergency kit. Inside was an extinguisher, a fire blanket and a small long-handled axe.

Karpis strode over to it and smashed the glass with his pistol, showering the floor with slivers of glass. Immediately a loud piercing shriek sounded. The fire alarm had gone off. Swinging round, Karpis pointed the gun back at the two figures on the bench. 'Don't move or I'll kill you both,' he shouted.

He reached into the box and grabbed the axe by its handle with one hand, his other still gripping the pistol. He looked back quickly at his two captives and went to the open door of the little room.

He pushed Mrs Patricov out of her seat, then with a last look over his shoulder at Kevin and the woman, took two steps towards the computers, swinging the axe in one hand. Kevin suddenly realised the Russian was about to destroy evidence – of what, he didn't know, but he knew it was important.

So the moment Karpis lifted the axe, Kevin sprang up from his seat and threw himself at the Russian's back with outstretched arms.

He caught Karpis's arm just before it started to swing down on to the computers. The axe dropped to the floor but Karpis twisted his torso enough to stay on his feet, and as he turned towards Burgess his other arm came round and he fired.

By now the woman on the bench had launched herself at the Russian woman and had got her on the floor. Then the door of the changing room burst open and Reilly and the man from London rushed in. Each had a pistol in his hand, and seeing them Karpis let his own drop.

The noise was deafening. The fire alarm was screeching, Mrs Patricov was screaming and Reilly was shouting. In the middle of the chaos the two laptops sat undisturbed on the table. Kevin was lying on the floor in front of them and couldn't see what was going on. He struggled to get up but couldn't get on his feet; he seemed to have no strength. He didn't know who was shouting and who was screaming. He hoped it wasn't the woman on the bench. He heard new voices but couldn't see who had come into the changing room so he missed the sight of Patricov's wife and Karpis being bundled out in handcuffs. He was very cold and could feel the sticky blood oozing down his arm, then he felt the soft touch of something warm being thrown over him and a woman's voice said, 'Just lie there. You are a complete hero but you've been shot and the ambulance is on its way.' And that was when Kevin passed out.

337

52

WHEN JASMINDER CAME IN to work and read the message from Geoffrey Fane's secretary, she felt interested but not particularly concerned. Would she pop in for a word with Geoffrey at three o'clock that afternoon? There was nothing ominous-sounding about it at all.

She didn't have much time to speculate about the reason for the meeting as the morning was particularly busy. That meant too that she didn't have time to worry about Laurenz and his increasingly bullying tone towards her. She hoped now he would be pleased when she told him the full name of her senior colleague – Bruno McKay – and pleased too when she said that it looked as if McKay might turn into an excellent source. He was a Russia expert, she'd say, who knew the Moscow Embassy well, and what's more he drank a lot and talked freely.

But she sensed Laurenz would be angry that she hadn't actually learned much of substance yet. Doubtless he would order her to sleep with McKay as soon as possible, as if that were a guarantee of being told classified information. Laurenz had already told her that she had two weeks to get him something of value. If she failed – and he said this with complete indifference, which made it even more dreadful – he wouldn't be responsible for the safety of the little girl. Most chilling of all, though, had been his parting shot. Laurenz had said that he was under pressure from his boss Kozlov. You remember, he'd said, the charming gentleman you met in Bermuda. He says that if you don't do better, he will come over here and personally give you a few lessons in persuasion.

Jasminder had put all this to the back of her mind when at quarter to three, just as she was thinking about getting ready to go up to Geoffrey Fane's room, she had a call from his secretary to say that the discussion would be in the Personnel department as there was a big meeting going on in Geoffrey's room. That struck Jasminder as a little odd. If Geoffrey had a big meeting, why didn't he postpone his appointment with her? It couldn't be anything so urgent that it couldn't wait. Also she was a bit disappointed as she remembered his room from her first week when she'd had a series of introductory meetings with senior colleagues. It had struck her as quite beautiful, with its tall windows overlooking the river and its oriental rugs and antique furniture. It had completely changed her view of Geoffrey Fane, who until then she had thought of as cold and unapproachable.

She walked down to the second floor, and into the outer office of the Director of Personnel.

'Hello, Jasminder,' said his secretary, 'Geoffrey's on his way. Have a seat.'

A crawling feeling of anxiety was just beginning to spread through Jasminder's mind. She was not sure what was going on but it was something out of the ordinary. Then Geoffrey Fane arrived and, taking her by the elbow, shepherded her along a corridor to one of a row of small meeting rooms. Two armchairs stood facing each other across a low round table, on which sat a box of tissues and a telephone.

Fane waved her to one chair and sat down in the other.

'Well, Jasminder,' he said, 'I thought it was time I had a chat with you. You've been here a few months now, I think, and I hope you are enjoying the work.'

Jasminder nodded enthusiastically. So this was all it was. Just a catch-up conversation.

'We're all agreed that you've made a splendid start.' Fane paused and considered her. 'But recently it's been noticed that you have been looking very tired – rather strained, in fact – and we have been wondering why that is, and whether anything in particular is worrying you.'

Jasminder felt her stomach give a lurch and her heart start to beat faster and louder; for a brief lunatic second she wondered if Fane could hear it thumping in her chest. She said, struggling to keep her voice steady, 'No, I'm fine, thank you. It is hard work, but I enjoy it. I'm very happy here.'

Fane looked at her; his eyes were deep and somehow sad. 'I was wondering,' he went on, 'whether it was your relationship with Laurenz Hansen that was worrying you.'

Silence fell between them. The name hung in the air. A cold sweat crept over Jasminder and her stomach clenched with nausea. She couldn't think. 'Who?' she said.

Fane raised an eyebrow. 'Before you say any more, I should tell you that this conversation is being recorded. Jasminder, it is very important that you tell me the truth. I can help you with many things but I can't help you at all unless you tell the truth. Now please explain to me what your involvement is with this man.'

Jasminder was trying to recover, but she did not know what to do. How much did the Service know already?

How much should she keep back? How had they found out? What had they found out?

'Yes, I know Laurenz Hansen. He's a banker.'

'Is he? And how well do you know him?'

Jasminder tilted her head and looked down, a gesture intended to demonstrate shyness while giving her time to think. Eventually she lifted her chin and looked Fane in the eye. 'For a time he was my boyfriend. But not any longer. Why do you want to know?' she asked, trying to wrest some control from Fane.

But Geoffrey Fane ignored the question and said, 'Tell me how you met him?'

'He saved me from some muggers when I was walking home from the theatre in Islington.'

'Does he live in Islington?'

'No. He has a flat in Moorgate. It belongs to his bank.'

'Did it not strike you as strange that he came along at just the perfect moment to save you?'

Jasminder was silent. It had never occurred to her at the time that there was anything staged about her first encounter with Laurenz in the gardens – he had saved her, after all. But now she knew the whole thing for what it was – a completely fabricated set-up. She had been hoodwinked and made a complete fool of. Laurenz had never cared for her at all. He had used her ruthlessly, and in her initial gratitude for being rescued, she had let him into her life, and then into her heart. How stupid and gullible she had been.

Fane was continuing, 'I'm very much afraid, Jasminder, that you have been completely and utterly *duped*. Laurenz Hansen is not a banker and he is not Norwegian. But I think you may already know this. I think that may be why you have been looking so stressed and worried recently.'

Jasminder was no longer thinking clearly. She did not know how to respond to this gently spoken but persistent man. But she was not yet ready to give up.

'If he's not a Norwegian banker, what is he?' she demanded.

Fane's mouth set in an expression of regret. 'I think you've found out by now. He's Russian and working for their intelligence service.'

'You're joking?' Jasminder was playing for time now. She didn't know where this was going and Geoffrey Fane was in complete control.

'I wish I were,' said Fane, and there was a sadness in his voice that chilled Jasminder. Why wasn't he being more hostile? 'We've learned a fair amount about Mr Hansen, you see. I think we know pretty clearly what his task here is. You are ideally placed to help him carry it out.'

'Is there any evidence for this?'

Fane shrugged. 'Well, enough to deport Mr Hansen, that's for certain. False passport, false papers, false job; those will do to send him packing. But as far as you're concerned, it's not so clear what he managed to accomplish.' He was looking right at her again. 'I was rather hoping you might be able to help on that score.'

'I don't see how. I am happy to admit I know Laurenz Hansen, and happy to admit that for a time we were... intimate. But not any longer. And never did I have any knowledge that he was anything other than what he claimed.'

'But after your relationship stopped, you did continue to see him... We've been watching Mr Hansen for some time.'

'Well, yes, I did see him occasionally after we broke up. I usually stay friends with my ex-boyfriends.'

'Did Hansen take an interest in your work?'

'Of course he did,' Jasminder said. 'There was a lot of publicity about my joining the Service – but no more than any boyfriend would. And he understood that what I did was highly confidential, and most of the time classified.'

'I'd think *all* of the time would be the safest description. So he didn't ask you for information? No documents or emails, that sort of thing?'

'Of course not.'

'Good,' said Fane, and Jasminder started to relax a little. Then Fane added, 'Still, we understand that he gave you a special phone.'

'You have been spying on me!'

Fane drew himself up in his chair. 'Jasminder, I'm trying to explain in the gentlest possible way that the man you are seeing is a foreign intelligence officer – one opposed to everything we stand for here, and whose aim is to undermine this country. I know your views about surveillance; I appreciate your steadfast defence of civil liberties; I yield to no one in my admiration for your ideals and principles. But this man Hansen has been trying to use you as his agent to damage the Service and undermine national security. I and my colleagues would be remiss – more than that, we would be criminally negligent – if we didn't do everything in our power to stop him. With what you know of us and the Service, I am sure you understand that?'

Suddenly, the silence that followed this remark was shattered. The phone on the table rang. Fane stared at it briefly, as if he didn't understand what it signified, then he picked it up. 'Fane,' he said sharply, and listened for several minutes while Jasminder thought through her situation.

She had been taken aback when Fane first spoke Laurenz's name, but this was turning out better than she'd first expected.

Fane seemed to be kind and understanding, and from what he was saying, had no evidence at all of Jasminder's efforts to help Laurenz. If she could hide those from him, he might accept that whatever Laurenz Hansen was, Jasminder didn't know about it and wasn't directly involved in his plans.

Then Fane hung up and turned to face her. He looked even more regretful.

'That was the police in Manchester. They've managed to locate and detain Laurenz Hansen in Altrincham. It seems he spent much of his time there, but under a different name – that of Vladimir Karpis.'

'So he is Russian,' Jasminder murmured.

'Yes. Does his name or that location ring any bells for you?' Fane's manner now was still quiet and calm, but slightly less friendly than before.

'No. Laurenz was often away, but he said he was abroad on business. And I never heard about anyone called Karpis.'

'I see. I understand your mother now lives in India?'

'That's right.' He must have been looking at her personnel file.

'But you still have family in Leicester, I think? Your brothers. They're in business together. Is that correct?'

She nodded, puzzled. 'They own a small chain of grocery shops. Why do you ask?'

'Because for some reason, Hansen or Karpis or whatever we want to call him had a webcam set up that was watching one of your brothers' stores. We know because we can see the shop's name on the screen — Kapoor & Sons.'

Jasminder didn't say anything, but waited tensely. Fane went on, 'Curious, don't you think? But there was something else. Film of a little girl coming out of school – they focused the camera shot right on her. Would she be the daughter of one of your brothers?'

344

Jasminder froze and blanked out Fane's voice, no longer concerned about herself; Ali was all she was worried about. He pressed her: 'I said, is she your niece?' Jasminder nodded. She didn't trust herself to speak. Everything was over now. They would work it all out and know what she'd done – been trying to do.

Fane leaned forward and spoke very gently now, his voice barely above a whisper. 'Jasminder, we don't know each other very well, but everything about you tells me that you would never willingly try to damage the Service or the country. If you had decided that your conscience wouldn't let you keep working here, then you would have done the honourable thing and resigned. You would never have worked for a hostile country, I'm absolutely positive. Unless,' and now he leaned back in his seat again, 'it was under duress. Unless... you'd been threatened. Or worse – your little niece had been.'

Jasminder was looking at Fane now, and he held her gaze. For all his supposed arrogance, his legendary ruthlessness, all she could see was sympathy in his eyes, and an expression on his face that told her that he understood. Then she started to cry.

Fane waited patiently while she crumpled a tissue and began to wipe her eyes. 'Take your time,' he said gently. 'We have all the time in the world. And your niece is safe now, and so are you. We've got Laurenz. So when you're ready, why don't you tell me what really happened?'

And when she'd finished wiping her eyes, Jasminder began to speak. It seemed almost involuntary; she felt she was operating on autopilot. But her overwhelming feeling was one of enormous relief.

She said hesitantly, 'It all started that night when I was attacked on my way home...'

53

SARAH GORDON WAS LEANING on the balcony railing, looking out over the Thames as the sun set. The
sky was a glorious pinkish-red and the colour was tinting
the buildings in Tower Hamlets across the river, making
them look a lot more beautiful than they were in full
daylight. To her right the windows in the towers of Tower
Bridge were glowing as though pink lights were switched
on inside. She was sipping a last glass of champagne while
behind her the caterers were clearing up the remains of a
drinks party.

She loved her riverside apartment with its wonderful
view. As a senior executive and part-owner of a property
development company, she'd been able to buy it off plan
before the other flats were marketed. The building was an
old brick warehouse with beamed ceilings and huge
windows; she knew as soon as her company acquired it
that it was going to be stunning. Once she'd bought her
part, she'd made very sure that the conversion was done
beautifully, with no expense spared.

There was always something to look at from her balcony
whatever the time of day. The river was surprisingly busy,
though there were not many ships nowadays of a size to

need the roadway on the bridge to be raised to let them through. But when it happened, she found it very exciting to watch the great arms lift themselves up into the air as they had been doing ever since the bridge was built at the end of the nineteenth century.

She drained her glass and sighed with contentment. It had been a good party. Clients and prospective clients loved coming to the apartment and the view was the great draw, especially for the foreigners. She decided to ring the restaurant in the basement and get them to send up some supper. Her busy life didn't allow much time for shopping and cooking. Though she had a splendidly equipped kitchen and a dining table that seated twelve, most of her entertaining was done by caterers. She went inside to phone the restaurant and say goodnight to the caterers and when she came out on to the balcony again the colour had faded from the sky. Instead of glowing pink, all the buildings were returning to a dull flat grey. The traffic had died down a bit on Tower Bridge although it was never really quiet, even in the middle of the night. There were not so many pedestrians as there had been earlier. Maybe there was something good on TV – perhaps a football match – and everyone had hurried home to watch it. Sarah didn't have time to watch TV, though she had several large shiny sets in the apartment – and she had no interest in sport.

It was beginning to grow chilly now and she was just thinking of going inside to get a shawl when she noticed a woman lingering on the suspension part of the bridge, just before the tower on the near side. She was slim and rather smartly dressed in a short bright blue jacket over what seemed to be a blue or grey dress – it was difficult to see precisely from this distance, in the fading light. The woman looked as though she might have come straight from her office. She had bobbed dark hair, which obscured the side of her face as she gazed over the railing into the water below. There was something odd about the way she was standing, looking down at the incoming tide that was flowing fast now under the bridge. That stretch of water was quite shallow at low tide but the river was filling up fast and the mud bank had long since disappeared. While Sarah watched, the woman walked on slowly, almost dreamily, as though unaware of her surroundings or of anyone else – she almost collided with a man in a dark suit, walking at a fast march, looking straight ahead, on his way somewhere.

There was a trance-like quality about the woman's movements. She stopped from time to time to stare out upstream, then she'd walk on a few paces only to turn around and retrace her steps.

Sarah was beginning to feel very uneasy about the way the woman was behaving, wandering up and down while everyone else on the bridge was hurrying past, so she went inside to get the binoculars her business partner had given her when she moved into the apartment At the same time, not knowing quite why, she picked up her phone which was lying on a table.

When she came out again the woman was still there but she had stopped wandering up and down and was standing just beside one of the towers. As Sarah watched she put one foot on the bottom of the railing and slowly began to climb up it. Just as Sarah hit the first button on her phone, the woman reached the top of the railing and jumped and all that Sarah could see of her was her head bobbing in the water as she was swept away fast upstream by the tide. While Sarah was shouting at the operator, the head disappeared from her view and she could see no more of the woman.

On the bridge where she had climbed over, a small crowd was gathering and a man with a phone pressed to his ear was gesticulating and pointing down into the water. Sarah turned away feeling sick just as the doorbell rang. 'Restaurant service!' shouted a voice. She opened the door and said to the waiter, 'A woman's just jumped into the river!'

'Oh, dear, madam,' he replied calmly. 'It does happen from time to time. It's always very sad. Shall I set the table and pour a glass of wine?'

'Yes, please,' said Sarah automatically as through the open window came the sound of police sirens.

54

'WHAT I DON'T UNDERSTAND is how you knew they were in the pool house.' Miles Brookhaven was sitting across the desk from Liz in her small office. It was Saturday morning and he was looking more than usually relaxed in a linen jacket and open-necked shirt, though rather like Geoffrey Fane he somehow never lost his well-pressed appearance. Liz had got back from Manchester late the previous night. After the tensions and excitements of the day she'd spent at Patricov's house and grounds, she found Miles's easy manner rather soothing.

She said now, 'It wasn't exactly rocket science, more of a lucky guess, really. Everybody was convinced that Laurenz Hansen – Karpis, I should call him, although I don't suppose that's his real name any more than Hansen is – had somehow left the estate, especially after they'd searched the house and couldn't find him. But I didn't see how he could have got away that easily. I thought he must still be there somewhere. There are plenty of outbuildings, so while Bruno and the security chief checked the perimeter, I started looking in a few other places. The garage, the coach house. And then I came to the swimming-pool block.'

'What happened when you got there?'

'I suppose I was a bit stupid because I barged straight in. Karpis was there, along with Patricov's wife – in a little room where all the equipment for the pool is stored. But they also had all sorts of wiring and computers and phones in there.

'Patricov's wife didn't know who I was when I appeared; she just looked at me in surprise. But Karpis could tell right away that I wasn't some stray person who'd wandered in. I don't know if he knew that the place was being raided, or whether he'd been holed up there when we'd all come to the house. But whatever he thought, he wasn't going to take any risks, so he pulled a gun on me.

'I'm still a bit confused about the order of what happened after that. But I know that Karpis told me to sit on a bench and that shortly after that Kevin Burgess, a security guard, turned up. God knows why, but he did. At that point, I remember that Mrs P and Hansen started yelling at each other in Russian. She was trying to wipe the computers, to get rid of the evidence. You see, they'd been watching Jasminder's family in Leicester, to blackmail her into working for them.'

Liz sighed and looked out of the window. Summer had taken over from spring, but the river was unseasonably grey and choppy. 'Poor girl. It's tragic that she didn't trust any of us enough to tell us what was going on. You'd think she might have told Peggy – she'd got quite friendly with her. But she didn't. I suppose she still felt like a bit of an outsider. Anyway she's told Geoffrey Fane everything now, and I assume she'll have to leave the Service. I expect Six will let her make some excuse to explain why she's going after such a short time; it's sure to be rather embarrassing for C. It was his idea to appoint her.'

Miles nodded. 'It's a shame that she didn't confide in Peggy. I hope Jasminder will be OK. I expect the media will be sniffing around trying to root out the full story.'

'I'm sure Geoffrey and C will work out some line to take, but Jasminder will need a lot of support. She mustn't be left on her own to cope with it. I'm going to suggest to Geoffrey that Peggy takes on a support role.'

'Good idea. But go on with the story. What happened when the security guard arrived?'

'That's when things started taking off. The laptops weren't responding; they seemed to have frozen up. I think Pearson, the local Chief Constable, had ordered all external communications from the house and grounds to be cut off before the raid started. Mrs Patricov was getting hysterical, and Karpis must have decided to destroy the actual computers since they couldn't delete their programs. He broke the fire panel to get out the axe and smash the machines, and it was then the alarm went off.

'That brought Bruno and the Chief Security man running, thank God. But before that, Kevin had jumped on Hansen and I'd grabbed Mrs P. That's how Kevin got shot. Apparently he's OK – or will be. He'll stay in hospital for a bit. Anyway we got the computers, and all their webcam shots are safely on DVD now.'

'So Patricov's wife was in on it with Hansen. Does that mean Patricov himself was part of it, too?'

Liz shook her head. 'I don't know, but it seems unlikely. There'll be a lot of enquiries to be made – with the Swiss in particular, since that's where Patricov lived before he came to England. He married Mrs P in Geneva just a couple of years ago.'

'Do you think he knew she was working for the FSB?'

'We may never know. Both Hansen and Mrs P are in the hands of Greater Manchester Police. Bruno and I are going to question them once they're moved to London, but I don't suppose they'll talk. And I should think it's pretty unlikely that Patricov will ever come back to Altrincham. One thing's certain – he won't be buying Manchester United now.'

Miles grinned. 'It would have been sensational if you'd discovered that a great British sporting icon was being run by the FSB. How Putin would have laughed!'

'That's a thought,' said Liz. 'I wonder if we'd have got more powers to investigate, when the fans found out.'

'We'd have all got the sack as a useless waste of space,' said Miles, laughing. 'Except for you,' he teased her. 'You and your team would have been promoted. Speaking of which, what have you done with Peggy? Have you given her the weekend off?'

'Certainly not,' Liz said with mock-severity. 'She's solving the mystery of Mrs Patricov, I hope. But, Miles, I can't thank you enough for sending Mischa our way. He gave us the lead that kick-started the whole investigation.'

'Glad to help,' he said casually, but Liz knew it wouldn't have been that easy. Miles would have had to persuade his colleagues to give her access to such a valuable source. She knew Andy Bokus was directing CIA counter-intelligence in Europe, and couldn't believe he would have been happy about the Brits seeing Mischa on their own.

'I'm afraid it won't be happening again in future,' said Miles.

'Oh?' Had Bokus won a rearguard action against further Anglo-American cooperation?

'Mischa's gone back to Moscow. He's told us he doesn't want to help any more.'

Liz said, 'Maybe his brother's left the FSB.'

'No, I don't think so. It's more to do with Mischa himself. He's scared, I think. Now that he's living directly under the Putin regime, he's suddenly realised the risks he's been running. I suppose the prospect of a firing squad does concentrate the mind.'

There was a knock on the door and Peggy came in looking cheerful. Miles leaped to his feet and Peggy smiled and blushed slightly.

'Good morning, Miles,' she said. 'You look very relaxed.'

'I can afford to,' he replied. 'You've been doing all the work. Have a seat.' He offered her his chair. 'I'll prop up the desk.'

'This office is ridiculously small,' said Liz, 'but I daren't complain or I might lose it altogether. So what's the news?'

'Exactly what we thought,' said Peggy. 'It's her all right. Mrs Patricov and Tim's email friend Marina are one and the same.'

'Tim recognised the photograph then?'

'Yes. He was quite sure.'

'Just a minute,' Miles broke in. 'Before you two get all carried away, can you explain what you're talking about? Who is Tim again?'

Liz explained. 'Mrs Patricov, or Marina as she also called herself, chatted up someone named Tim at a lecture Jasminder gave at King's College, London.'

'Oh yes, I remember that from our meeting. The woman was called Marina.'

'Right. She gave him that phone, which you heard Charlie Simmons talking about at the meeting. When Mrs Patricov was caught yesterday with Hansen – Karpis – it got us wondering whether she might be the mysterious Marina. And thanks to Tim, we now know she is.'

Miles nodded. 'So you've uncovered the Illegals partnership that Mischa was talking about, right? The pincer operation. Karpis and Mrs Patricov are its two jaws.'

'Yes, I'm confident they are. It seems to have been originally designed to infiltrate the civil liberties movement but then they got an unexpected bonus – Jasminder was recruited by Six and Tim turned out to live with an MI5 officer. So their focus changed, though fairly soon I think they decided to drop Tim since he didn't tell them anything and concentrate on Jasminder, who was both wonderfully positioned and more vulnerable. Hansen seems to have been very clever about the way he manipulated her. No doubt we'll hear all about how it was done when Geoffrey reports back on his interview with her.'

'Poor thing,' said Peggy. 'It must be so dreadful for her. Will it be all right for me to get in touch?'

'You should wait till we hear from Geoffrey. I expect Six have put her somewhere safe until they decide what to do next.'

They sat in silence for a moment, thinking about the full implications of what had happened.

'Will Ms Kapoor have to face charges?' asked Miles.

'I doubt it,' replied Liz. 'I don't suppose she gave them anything of much value. From what Bruno said after he'd taken her out, she seemed to be thrashing around in a very unfocused way. But obviously she'll have to go.'

'I wonder what she'll do next.'

'Hard to say,' said Liz. 'If she wanted to, I'm sure she could go back into a civil liberties job. No one in the outside world will know why she resigned; I imagine the press will blame MI6 – say that C's campaign for openness was just a sham, as evidenced by Jasminder's quick departure. Six may have to put up with that – it's better than having the real story get out, since then the press would take the opposite line, and ask in outraged tones how the Service could hire someone so obviously untrustworthy.' She shook her head wearily. 'But anyway, Jasminder will know why she left, and she'll know that we know. I imagine it's going to be difficult for her – emotionally, if not professionally.'

'Case closed then,' said Miles, getting up from the corner of the desk. He turned to Peggy. 'Congratulations on a job well done. Could we have a drink some time to celebrate?'

'I'd like that,' she said, smiling.

'I'm due back at the Embassy now; the Ambassador's having a do for the staff. But I'll be in touch soon.'

After he'd gone Liz looked at Peggy, and they both smiled. 'He's really sweet,' said Peggy.

'Sweet on you, I think you mean,' teased Liz, pleased to see her blush. It was clear to Liz that Peggy's life with Tim was over. She had already told him she wanted to move out of their flat to be closer to work, and from her account of the conversation it seemed clear that he'd understood this meant moving without him. It was sad in many ways, but he'd done too much damage to make their relationship recoverable. He was contrite, but that did not alter the fact that he'd done it.

Still, there was Miles Brookhaven to take Peggy's mind off Tim. Liz found herself wondering what it would be like to have that kind of prospect in her own life. After Martin's death she had thought she would never want to be close to anyone again – she would concentrate on her work and have her memories and that would be enough. She didn't know if that had changed – or if it ever would. But now that Martin had gone, for the first time for years she had no one to share her relief that the case was over – no one to relax with. There was a cold empty void in her life, one that used to be filled with the warmth of their close mutual attachment. It was a gap that one day – she had no idea when – she would like to fill.

55

M ILES HAD BEEN GONE for ten minutes and Peggy had just come back with much-needed coffee for them both when Liz's phone rang.

She picked it up and a familiar voice said, 'Fane here.'

'Hello, Geoffrey. I was about to ring you. We've just been having a wash-up with Miles. Tim, the lecturer from King's, has definitely identified Marina as Mrs Patricov. I've also heard from Chief Constable Pearson in Manchester. Apparently Hansen–Karpis hasn't said a word, but Pearson thinks Mrs Patricov will sing like a bird when Bruno and I question her. But any news of Jasminder?' She hadn't yet heard the details of Fane's interview with her.

There was a long pause at the other end of the line. Finally he said, 'There is actually. I'm afraid it's bad.'

'What's happened?'

'I'm very sorry to tell you that Jasminder's dead.'

'Dead?' said Liz. Her stomach lurched. She could see Peggy watching her. Her face had gone pale. 'What happened?' Liz asked.

'Drowned,' said Fane. He sounded short of breath. 'Her body was found this morning under the Albert Bridge.

Apparently, she jumped off Tower Bridge last night. A woman in a flat overlooking the bridge saw her and phoned the police. There was a man nearby but she'd gone over before he could stop her. The tide was coming in fast and they've been looking for her all night. It wasn't until low tide that they found her. The only identification was a receipt from a shop where she'd paid by credit card. It's taken this long to confirm it was her.'

'You're saying she jumped into the river?' Liz could see Peggy's enquiring expression, and could do nothing but look back at her grimly.

'Apparently. There's no question of her being pushed. The woman in the riverside flat saw it all quite clearly and was on the phone immediately.' Fane paused for a moment then went on, speaking quickly. 'Jasminder had already resigned from the Service. I made it quite clear that we weren't going to prosecute her and that we'd help her in every way we could. I was very sympathetic; I didn't criticise her or blame her in any way—' His voice faltered; he was obviously upset.

'I'm sure you dealt with it perfectly, Geoffrey. None of this is your fault. It sounds as if you couldn't have been kinder to her.'

Fane waited a moment to reply. 'It's good of you to say so, but I can't help feeling – I mean, I was the one who questioned her. We'd prepared a safe house for her to go to while I finished the questioning; then we were going to discuss how she was to deal with the media. But I agreed she could go home to collect her things. I should have sent someone with her, but I didn't. That was my fault.'

It was clear that all this had deeply shaken Fane – he who had so opposed Jasminder's appointment must have come round to it. He would have been terribly shocked at

359

first to learn of her betrayal. Or was that too strong a word? No, thought Liz. Admittedly Jasminder had been pressurised into doing wrong, which made it explicable – but not, Liz thought, defensible. Jasminder could have asked for help as soon as Laurenz Hansen had turned the screw. That had been her fatal mistake, 'fatal' now being the word.

'There will be a memorial service of course,' Fane said, as he regained his composure. 'In the meantime we'll have the press to deal with.'

'Yes. That will be bad for a time; the media will blame us – that's inevitable. It's more important that you don't blame yourself. You did what you had to do, and you could have been much harder on her than you were.'

'Well, I must have been hard enough,' said Fane bitterly. Liz realised there was nothing more she could say to help him. She muttered a few more words of sympathy, then Fane said goodbye abruptly.

Putting down the phone, Liz looked at an anxious Peggy. 'Jasminder's dead, isn't she?'

'I'm afraid so. She was found drowned in the river this morning. She jumped off Tower Bridge last night.'

Tears welled up in Peggy's eyes. 'That's a horrible way to go. She must have been desperate. What on earth made her do… *that?*' Then she shook her head abruptly. 'What a stupid question.'

Liz said, 'She must have found it impossible to see a way through. She was going to have to leave the Service; she would have had to explain why it hadn't worked out, and what had gone wrong. It would all have been lies, too, because she wouldn't have been allowed to explain what had really happened. And then what could she have done next? I suppose she couldn't see a way forward.'

Peggy slumped in her seat. 'I feel terrible. I think she and I could have become good friends. But instead I helped unearth her secrets.'

'You didn't have a choice,' said Liz. 'You did the right thing. Think of how you'd feel, possibly years from now, if she'd stayed in place and relayed intelligence to the Russians. You'd have been like all those colleagues of Philby, Burgess and Maclean who couldn't believe that their friends could be spies. But instead you did your job, and helped expose a plot that could have done tremendous damage to the country.'

Peggy sighed. 'I'm sure you're right. And thank you for the kind words.' She stood up. 'I think I might go for a walk, if you don't mind. I'd like to clear my head.'

'Of course. Then go home. You've worked hard enough for one week. They're bringing Karpis and Marina down to Paddington Green police station this afternoon and Bruno and I will start the interviews tomorrow. But I'll be in the office early on Monday – something new's come in and I'm going to need your help.'

Peggy nodded and left the room. Liz sat still for a minute, suddenly feeling overwhelmed herself. She knew she'd been right to speak to Peggy that way, but recognised as well that sometimes the professional requirements of their jobs rode roughshod over personal feelings. It had to be like that, of course, but it didn't make life any easier. She had her own guilt to bear; if she hadn't rather mischievously suggested Jasminder to MI6, none of this would have happened.

Her phone rang again, and reluctantly she answered it. 'Liz Carlyle.'

'That's good,' said a cheerful voice. 'I guessed you'd be at your desk even though it's Saturday.'

'Who is that?' said Liz, feeling annoyed at the intrusion.

'I hope it's your favourite policeman. For the moment anyway. Chief Constable Pearson at your service, ma'am.'

Liz smiled. 'Always a pleasure to speak to you.'

'I'm in Tate Britain. They say the restaurant's very good here. I hope you haven't had lunch yet because, on the off chance you'd be free, I've booked a table. If you had time, we could look at a picture or two after lunch. I've never understood Francis Bacon myself and I thought maybe you could provide a brief tutorial.'

'Fat chance of that.' Liz glanced out of the window and saw that the river was calmer now, the swell dying as the tide turned. She shivered as she watched it briefly, thinking she would never see it again without remembering Jasminder. Then she said, 'We might give Francis Bacon a miss this time. But lunch would be lovely, thank you.'

A NOTE ON THE AUTHOR

Dame Stella Rimington joined the Security Service (MI5) in 1968. During her career she worked in all the main fields of the Service: counter-subversion, counter-espionage and counter-terrorism. She was appointed Director General in 1992, the first woman to hold the post. She has written her autobiography and nine Liz Carlyle novels. She lives in London and Norfolk.